CAPTIVE!

Steens hit her with his gun in the middle of the forehead, and again on the crown of the head as she went down.

Each blow made a sound like a mallet striking a gourd. Chi thumped to the floor, and then it was quiet.

Books were scattered all over the room, and pages fluttered in the fireplace's draft. Steens stepped back and stumbled over the remnants of the crushed table. Men stared at Chi, breathing heavily and clutching at themselves, wondering if she was dead.

"Kill her," Majors said shrilly. . . .

CORD

Hunt The Man Down

Owen Rountree

BALLANTINE BOOKS • NEW YORK

Library of Congress Catalog Card Number: 84-90853

ISBN 0-345-31019-5

Manufactured in the United States of America

First Edition: June 1984

Chapter One

CHI ALWAYS SAID SHE COULD TELL A GOOD hotel from across the street. Good hotels had curtains in the upstairs windows and were not located over saloons. Good hotels had signs done with stencils instead of freehand, and town ladies did not cross the street to avoid passing in front of them. What good hotels did not have was some hombre sitting out front in a captain's chair with a rifle across his knees, looking at ease and ready to kill.

So the Rancher's Rest in Twin Falls should have been all right. There were clean lace-edged drapes blowing from the open windows above the veranda. And the collie dog on the plank boardwalk opened one eye and seemed satisfied and went back to sleeping as they tied their horses to the hitching rail. On the way to the center of town they had passed rows of Lombardy poplar in green spring leaf along the irrigation ditches, and white lilac blooming by the dooryards of the homes on the shaded side streets, and clean, sweet-smelling laundry on lines flapping gently in the breeze. The occasional passersby looked occupied with their own legitimate business, and generally well-fed, and the main brick-cobbled street was mostly swept clean of horseshit.

The only trouble was that this was Idaho Territory, and Cord had known all along they should never have crossed its border, no matter how many miles it saved in their travels, the uneasy feeling like a back itch just out of fingertip reach.

But Cord had turned from instinct and Chi's misgivings and years of outlaw experience, and led them into this town anyway. He told himself that something like fate had taken charge over reason, and in fact he felt that he and Chi had been wandering dumb and preoccupied through the last few

1

months. He did not seek trouble, and so he convinced himself it would not seek him, tunneling his vision straight downtrail and denying the past.

Sure as hell would never freeze, he should have kept them clear of Idaho, and this fine safe hotel with its blowing curtains and free, engraved letterhead stationery and gilt-leaf Bible, but even now Cord could not get his mind off the notion of an afternoon nap and then some drinks along with the sunset.

Even now that the trap was sprung, and the small room was filled with guns pointing their way.

Goddamn it, Cord thought almost petulantly, *this isn't right*. They had been suckered, come riding into this modern town of Twin Falls and up to the Rancher's Rest, had paid for two rooms with silver money and settled in like sensible weary travelers. They had taken lunch, and later Chi came down to his room to share a smoke and make medicine with the one called Jaeger. Cord had kicked out of his boots like a man at perfect ease.

And now this shit.

Jaeger sat in a straight-back wooden chair by the curtained window. He was a stocky man, and he wore a freshly brushed derby hat and a dark brown gabardine suit, a stiff collar, and a striped tie. He reached inside his coat and took out a little .45 with a two-inch barrel, the one Colt called the Shopkeeper's Model in the lithographed advertisements. Jaeger showed them the gun and his wide-toothed smile.

Jaeger, the prevaricating, gap-toothed son of a bitch.

Chi sat on the bed, back against the wall, knees drawn up, and hands hidden under her woolen serape, only the bottom half of her high, hand-tooled black leather boots visible. Cord stood between the door and window in stocking feet, feeling planless as a dog stopped in the middle of the street.

A moment before, the place had erupted with men with guns. Two came out of the closet at the same time two more came through the door. These four were holding down on Cord and Chi with revolvers while Jaeger played with his little Colt and a sixth man kept an eye on things from the balcony, sweeping the room through the open window with a Winchester carbine, leaning forward so the curtains wouldn't whip across his face.

Unlike Jaeger's citified duds, these men wore trail clothes, though to Cord's eye they had neither the quiet confidence of lawmen nor the hard-edge cold-bloodedness of true gun handlers off the bandit routes. Their bravado was diluted by the reek of their nervous tension.

Cord raised his hands shoulder high and after that no one moved. The derby-hatted man looked up at Cord, grinning like a spook, and said, "You remember me. Jaeger is the name." This was a little extra smartass bullshit on his part; they'd met him an hour or so earlier.

Chi was looking at Cord too, and he thought he saw an accusation: *Idaho*, her glare said. *This would not have happened in another place.* But then she gazed around the room and found a better target. "Later on, Mister Whoever-You-Are," she said to Jaeger, "when we are beyond this trouble, there will come a time to settle scores. You will be the first. We will come looking for you right off, *cabrón*."

"There won't be no later on," the stocky man said, going on with his grinning while the other men looked as if they wished he'd get on with business. "No later on like that, anyway." Jaeger spun the cylinder on his little Colt and listened to it clack. "You don't want to fool with me, lady. I'm a U.S. Federal Marshal, and it's more trouble than it's ever worth, killing a Federal Marshal. Don't have to tell you that, lady."

A red-faced man near the door said, "Let's get moving."

Jaeger glanced at him and pursed his lips. "Right at this moment," he said to Chi, "I am on detached duty on assignment of William Deane Majors, Governor of this Idaho Territory."

"I know what you are," Chi said darkly.

Jaeger watched her for a moment. "I am the Governor's bodyguard and personal detective, and you know what that means. The Governor runs things in this neck of the woods. There's paper on you hereabouts, lady. If the Governor wants, he can have you gut-shot and dragged naked through the streets. Or I could kill you right now, and sell your hides like you was buffalo."

"But you're not going to," Cord guessed.

"Not just yet. It's probably a mistake." Jaeger rose from his chair. "Put on your boots, Mister Cord. You have some traveling ahead."

Cord felt like a damned fool while he hitched up his gray-white cotton stockings, which could have stood some washing, and got himself into his boots. He was sweating a little when it was done, and for damned sure no longer preoccupied with naps and evening drinking.

"You could use some foot powder," Jaeger said and made a show of pinching his nose. He turned away from Cord's anger to the red-faced man. "They are all yours, Mister Steens. Don't lose them along the way."

Jaeger tipped his hat to Chi as he went toward the door, and nodded to Cord. "Good to see you folk," he said. "People like you are money in the bank." He closed the door softly behind him.

The stink of apprehension in the room thickened in Jaeger's absence. Steens, the leader of this sorry crew, had a lopsided, liver-sprung gut, and the pock-thickened nose in the middle of his florid face betrayed an ongoing hard romance with whiskey and tavern-life indolence. He looked around vacantly for a moment, as if he had lost track of his next move.

"You, lady," he said finally. "Get your hands out in the open."

Chi looked at him and did not move.

Another man sidled up behind Cord and eased the Peacemaker off Cord's right hip. Jaeger had left it there through their confrontation, as if he took some small thrill in playing with the unpredictable. Cord lowered his arms halfway and no one objected. They were all watching Chi anyway.

"Come on, lady." Steens voice was a nasal whine. "Don't screw around."

Cord knew Chi would not risk gunplay in this small room. Two or three shots and the air would be opaque with black-powder smoke, and no doubt these edgy men would go on firing blind. Too much flying lead and no room to dodge, so people would be hit, probably them included.

But Cord still tensed and readied to move with the action. Chi would push hard as she could anyway, because stupid nervous men with guns galled her no end. Trouble was, stupid nervous men tended to react in irrational and irrevocable ways.

Chi's right hand eased out from under her serape. She held her Peacemaker flat on her palm like a gift, not threatening anybody, smiling at these men like they were fools. She extended her arm to one of the men, and he gulped like a schoolboy and reached for the gun. Chi tipped her palm, and the gun dropped to the floor, clunking hollowly.

The man, another gray-faced barroom drifter from the looks of him, bent down for the Colt, and Chi kicked him in the face. Her leg up shot out fast as a bullwhip and the instep of her boot smashed into the man's nose, snapping his head back. Bone cracked and droplets of blood arced through the air. The man howled and fell sideways, dropping his own weapon and clutching at his face. More blood seeped between his fingers as he curled into himself on the floor, gurgling like he was drowning, legs twitching and his body quivering.

Someone laughed.

But after that they were all quiet and no one moved, because it was a way to kill. A kick like that could send nose-bone stabbing deep into a man's brain. So they watched for a silent moment to see if he was dead, but then he cursed and struggled to his knees. There was a long general sigh— of relief or disappointment, Cord couldn't tell which.

Steens shook his head like a man come up from underwater and snapped, "Lady!"

Chi smiled up at him almost sweetly. Steens leveled his gun on her face and took a menacing step, and Cord moved instinctively to intercept him.

A gun barrel slammed down across Cord's temple and he was not surprised, since he was seeing all this a moment before it took place, like some half-remembered dream. He missed the floor with his foot and fell with his hands still at his shoulders. Darkness condensed around a pinpoint of vision and swallowed him headfirst.

Chapter Two

FIRST WAS THE FLASHING PAIN, SYNCHRO-nized to the wagon's progress: the quick sparks of hurt coincident with the creaks and moans of the hard-sprung buckboard as it banged along through the ruts. First there was only the ache, familiar as an old but well-remembered enemy, and then Cord heard the squeaking of harness and the clomp of hooves on hardpan dirt, and nothing else while he tried to come back to himself.

He was bound up like an animal. Leather thongs cut into his wrist and pulled his arms behind his back, and his shoulder joints throbbed. His feet were tethered to the wagon box, and someone's dirty neckerchief was knotted across his mouth. Cord explored his confinement carefully with his eyes still closed, recalling what had happened, what had brought him to this fix.

He opened his eyes to darkness. He twisted around and saw down the tunnel of the hoop-supported canvas tarp over the wagon bed a landscape of sagebrush hills and rimrocks shadowed by the bright moon. Three of the men from the hotel room were following close behind on horseback, talking once in a while in voices that did not reach inside the wagon. A lucifer flared and someone lighted a cigarette, and Cord envied the man his freedom.

Cord used his elbows to pry himself over on his side, feeling out the limit of possibilities. The effort brought renewed flashes of pain in the back of his eyes.

Chi was there beside him, tied and gagged and awake. Her dark eyes were luminous in the reflected light and stared at him without expression, but he knew her; he knew how she felt. At times like this he could usually force himself to

6

find the patience to wait it out, or could at least accept the futility of struggle for the moment. She could not. She hated to give up her freedom, especially at the hands of cowardly bullies like Steens and his gang of trash. She would not tolerate this, and would seethe with her anger and unleash it to take its own head if given the slightest opportunity.

Cord gave her a look that said, "Are you all right?" Chi nodded and turned away. Was some of her anger reserved for him and his foolhardy insistence on riding them into this bad business?

But there was nothing he could do about that either, not right now, except to lie easy and send the pain far away. Breathe deep and catalog the relaxation of each muscle, one by one, until they were all gone slack and the flashing was stopped, or dimmed anyway. They'd need to get well quickly as they could.

This was serious as trouble got, and they had gone down before it like children.

But that was just more history. Cord worked on his pain, concentrating on the rhythm of Chi's breathing to control his own. At least he was coming to himself, for the first time since winter. Maybe pain was the currency of liberation.

Cord delighted in the coming of spring, and had since earliest childhood memories. On the East Texas farm where his father and mother had made their failed lives, there came a time—sometimes nearly a month, other years less than two weeks—when the land turned green and in came spring. It had been springtime when Cord left the farm for good, springtime of his sixteenth year, but not until after the green time when the hot cloudless skies reclaimed the brief moisture and the land went brown once more.

But this year Cord's pleasure had come hard. Every cup of coffee tasted sour, and every new thing looked born to die.

They spent Christmas in Juárez across the Rio from El Paso and West Texas, and for a few weeks he and Chi had been at ease and drifting closer, taking risks with their relationship they had never dared before. Cord knew it was dangerous, but he would not draw back. Who knew where it could have led...?

He didn't get a chance to find out, not then, because of an old debt owed to a broken-down west Kansas prairie wasteland sheriff named John P. Kinsolving. By the time they rode out from that snow-bound carnival of death, things had changed.

There had been a girl named Aggie there, damaged and helpless and orphaned by those who were whole, and Chi had taken her in. Chi had come to the verge of admitting feelings of maternity—or anyway sorority—impossible yearnings within the framework of the life Chi had chosen. But as with her feelings for Cord, they were denied before she had a chance to accept or reject them. The girl Aggie died, and so did something in Chi: She had seen the special value of her woman's impulses, so long suppressed as unsuitable to her outlaw ways, and mourned herself as well as the girl.

Cord understood: He had suffered black melancholia a time or two, and Chi had helped him resurface. So he tried to show her the same casual solicitude, to give her the same easy space, even while wondering where all this was carrying them.

Back there in Juárez, Cord had found himself toying with an extraordinary notion—settling down with Chi. That spring the idea returned, stronger than he'd ever allowed; maybe it would move her from her sadness. Anyway, he told himself, working on courage and ways of saying it, there was nothing more ruinous than running too long outside the law. Banditry was no trade for old men—or old women. Hell, maybe he was coming tight to the end of his own string; maybe they both were. Here was something he could abide: Chi, and a hideout rancher life with her.

All through the breaking of spring such thoughts had invaded his mind, and still he did not voice them. Not just yet, he thought. There was business to see to first.

The break came in Denver, and after that Chi began to get better.

They had drifted north with the mild weather, settling in at the Brown Palace, figuring to stay a week or so, sampling civilized living, until Cord lost patience with the city. He always did in a place where it was half a day of trouble to ride out and gallop your horse for an hour to blow the stink of so many people from your nostrils and your mind. On the second day Cord sat in the hotel's smoking lounge, dressed in clean brushed clothes and smoking a cigar and feeling vaguely foolish. Around him were bankers and lawyers and capitalists in suits and vests and collars and low shoes, shooting Cord sidelong glances. Cord grinned at them and thought, *At least I do my thieving in the open.*

On the side table was a copy of that day's *Rocky Mountain News*. A section entitled "Correspondence from the Territories" on an inside page caught his attention, but even so he almost missed the three-line item nestled in the middle of one of the dense columns of type. It reported, without comment, that the Montana territorial warrant on Cord and Chi, charging them with the robbery of the Equitable Bank in New Willard, west of the divide on the Clark's Fork of the Columbia, had been dissolved, the statute of limitations having run its course.

There was good news. A Federal warrant on them—for a robbery they had nothing to do with—had been quashed six months earlier, and now this. The only trouble still hanging over their heads from the past was an old Pocatello bank job.

Maybe Cord sensed even then that the Pocatello business would draw them back to Idaho. Still he did not come out and tell Chi what he felt, but only watched her get better and worked on guessing if she shared his desires in any way.

They rode north to Cheyenne and west to Laramie, and then over South Pass and up Green River past the old mountain-man rendezvous camps. There was still snow in the mountains north of Big Piney, but not enough to slow them much, and then they dropped down into Jackson Hole. One place and then another, but none perfectly right for both Cord and Chi, and neither sure what the right place would look like if they found it.

At least they had the sense to stop wandering when they reached the afternoon shadows of the sharp-edged spires of the Tetons. They camped for a day and watched the snows go off and the great herds of elk drift across the ranchland meadows, and decided this was a place they could abide for a time.

Always before, they had spent their resting time in hotels, a room for each. This time, without asking Chi, Cord rode into Jackson town and asked in a saloon about places to stay, and the barman mentioned a spare cabin out at old man Pederson's place, on the flat near the meandering path of the Snake, not far south of the river's headwaters at Jackson Lake.

"We'll take a look-see," he said to Chi back at camp, not asking, and turned quickly away. He tried to make it seem a natural bit of business, but when he looked up her face was flushed and he felt his own blood rise. Here was another big and tricky step beyond their simple gun-partner deal.

The cabin was tight-chinked and on the river, two rooms with a real plank wall between them, and the back room further divided by a blanket hung over a wire. It would do, Cord told Pederson, and handed the old rancher some currency. The old man mumbled thanks and luck; he seemed a little abashed by Chi's dark beauty. At that moment so was Cord. Here was a new and more intimate approximation of family than ever they had chanced.

But it did not turn out to be so difficult, this living together. Pederson's main spread was on the shelf above the river, and they traded ranch work, mainly feeding cattle, for fresh eggs and milk, and last year's spuds from Mrs. Pederson's root cellar. In the late afternoons they came in and built a fire, and in the evenings they read or played cribbage. They talked too, not so much or so often by other peoples' lights, but enough so that some of the darkness of that time in Kansas began to lift. Or they sat quiet in the lantern light, digesting a good steak from one of Pederson's beeves, warmed by the tamarack crackling in the stone fireplce, and Cord would play at thoughts of living like a settled country man.

They had been there the better part of a month when Chi said, "If it's ranchwork we want, maybe we ought to look in on your *hermano*."

Cord was a little startled. His brother had settled into a small rancher's life in the Owyhee River country of northern

Nevada; there had been trouble with the big, open-range stockgrowers when he was starting out, and Cord and Chi had given him a hand dealing with it. Cord was also a tad jealous. Brother Jim had been Chi's lover for a night.

But so had other men. That was okay; that was part of the relationship they had invented and made work. Cord and Chi were not lovers, so there was no jealousy, even for a brother.

Her suggestion didn't mean she wanted Jim, Cord told himself. Maybe she thought it would do him good to see kin again. Maybe she was restless, getting like he got.

Maybe you never came to know a woman's secret life, however long you lived in the same house with her, and no point in trying to work one out. Cord had seen the damage such make-believe could sponsor.

"Fine enough," Cord said and set about packing their gear.

The prudent route led south to Salt Lake City and then west across the Great Salt Lake Desert. But that way was dry and hot and never pretty any time of the year, and besides, Mormons in such concentration made Cord uneasy. There had been a time in his youth when he had embraced devoutness until he was sucked into a passionate vortex from which he barely pulled free, and since then the touch of orthodoxy—the religious brand anyway—chilled him.

The quicker and easier trail went dead west over Teton Pass and down to the Snake, following the river through Idaho Falls to Twin Falls, then cutting south across the rolling Nevada highlands to the Owyhee headwaters country. Trouble was, that route passed through Pocatello, where people were apt to have a keen memory of that old bank job.

They took the short road anyway.

They were not blindly reckless; they gave the town a wide berth, riding a full extra day out to the edges of the desert before turning south to the Snake again. Cord had tasted danger all the way, like a faint metallic sharpness in their canteen water, and he ignored it.

Now, lying in the back of the covered buckboard and

listening to his brains rattle, Cord wondered if he had disregarded the risk because a part of him was courting it. There had been times in his past when restlessness had been transmogrified into recklessness, times when he sought trouble as a test of the strength of his destiny.

Anyway, someone had spotted them, and put a name to them, and tracked them down, and this mess had begun.

They had been minding their own business and making their way through a bounty of chicken in white gravy and dumplings when the man in the derby hat came into the side-street cafe. Jaeger came over to their table and told them his name, and stood there looking timid and awed in his citified dress. He held his hat in both hands and worried at the narrow brim, the picture of a man who would rather be entering account-book figures in a small, precise hand than approaching the famous deadly outlaw couple Cord and Chi.

That was Jaeger, a good actor and a bad son of a bitch.

"I've been robbed," he announced after they let him sit. He kept his voice low and darted quick rabbity looks to either side. "They have had the advantage of me, and I cannot go to the law."

He told them a story of twenty years behind the counter of a hardware store, starting when he was a pup, clerking and saving his pennies and nickels and dimes all that time against his boss's promise to sell out to Jaeger upon his retirement. "All those years," Jaeger said, "my ambition was to have my own business and fair profits, in a place where law was on the side of decent folk. I saw myself unlocking the door of my store every morning, sweeping my sidewalk and greeting folks who passed and being called mister." Jaeger looked over their heads, as if his dream were written on the chalkboard menu. "There was a woman," he said.

"Lots of times there is," Chi said.

"She was beautiful," Jaeger said, looking from Cord to Chi through misted eyes. "She had that kind of long blond hair that's straight all the way except where it curls up the back."

Her name was Looney, Jaeger said, and she lived outside of town with her two brothers. They had a little pig-farm place. The golden sister came shopping at the hardware, fingering the fabrics like all the ranch women did, then buying a keg of nails. She took her time, and they talked. Before she left, Jaeger asked permission to court.

Jaeger drank coffee as he told his story, taking long noisy slurps. Within a month they were married, and a week after that the girl had finagled him into putting his savings into a joint account at the Twin Falls Bank and Trust. The rest of the story was simple as it was predictable: the girl took the money and went back to her brothers. Jaeger stared into his coffee as if he would weep.

"So you see how it is," he said. "I want my money back, and I can't go to the authorities. The word would get out sure, and I would be the laughingstock of this town and its environs. People in these parts don't care if you lose a woman. That's only natural. But they never let you forget when you lose your money." Jaeger's embarrassment would not allow him to meet their looks. "One of those men isn't even her brother."

Looking back now, Cord thought, *There was a nice touch*.

In that Twin Falls cafe, Cord went on eating, studying the little man, and listening. They could use the money Jaeger was offering—$1,000—but they weren't desperate for it, and anyway they knew better than to get involved in some family spat. "First thing," Cord said, picking his teeth, "you and her will get back together, and we're out in the cold."

"It's not like that," Jaeger pressed. "They are gone away to see to some business, over to Boise." The Looneys had a safe, an old Rossbach Express Company box; Jaeger saw them fiddling with it once when he went to pay his respects to the so-called brothers. With them gone, there wasn't anyone for two miles in any direction. All Cord and Chi would have to do—Jaeger guaranteed it—was ride out to the pig farm, blow the hell out of the safe, gather up the money, and fetch it back to him.

"You got some grand idea of us," Cord said. "We could ride out with the whole works, and you'd never see your own name above that hardware."

Jaeger shook his head: That wasn't their reputation—once he'd recognized them he sort of asked around about what folk had heard—real discreetly, he added quickly. Anyway, they were his only chance.

"At least think about it," Jaeger pleaded.

"We'll meet up," Cord said, though Chi was frowning. "In a couple hours. Your place."

That was no good, Jaeger told them. He lived in a boardinghouse, and everyone knew how boardinghouse widows loved to snoop.

"Take a room," Jaeger said. "Stay at the Rancher's Rest. Nap up, and I'll come by at two o'clock, like you said." Jaeger stood, smiling. "You been on the trail. Get some sleep."

Some sleep.

Chapter Three

IT WAS PAST MIDNIGHT, BY THE MOON AND Cord's instinct, when the wagon stopped. Two of the guards climbed down from their horses and stretched saddle-cramped muscles, taking their time and ease, now that they were clear of town. One of them lighted a cigarette and said something in a low voice to his partner, who laughed. Light no longer flashed at the back of Cord's retinas, and the pounding in his head was down to a dull ache. He'd had hangovers that were worse. He must have slept for a time, falling off another edge into mild shock, but he was better now. Except for that sense of fatality he could not shake.

"Cowboy!" It was one of the guards, letting down the tailgate at the foot of the wagon. "Lie easy, lady. We are going to get the both of you out of here, and no reason for you to make it hard."

The man crawled into the dimness of the wagon, and past him Cord saw that his partner had his revolver drawn and was covering them. The guard undid the rope tethering Cord's feet to the wagon-box ring, but left his ankles strapped together, even pulling the thong a little tighter. He did the same for Chi, then sat back on his haunches and looked them over, grinning. His breath smelled of salted fish and whiskey.

"A couple of ducks for the plucking." He shook his head, as if to say, "Ain't this a humdinger," and called, "Beano! Leather that gun and give me a hand."

The other man leaned in at the tailgate, and the two of them dragged Cord and Chi from the wagon box like sides of beef. Cord's shirt caught on a snag on the rough flooring and tore, but he concentrated on going with the manhandling and staying relaxed, so his head would not explode again.

When they were propped up against the rear spoked wheel, all five of the men gathered to look them over, the three who had been horseback, the florid-faced Steens, and one more from up front on the wagon seat. Steens pursed his lips judiciously, as if viewing the trophy from a good hunt.

"Too bad she's got her legs tied together," one of the others said.

"Shee-it, Hank boy, that one'd kick your nuts up into the roof of your mouth."

"Not if she was out cold."

"That's about the only way you getcher women anyway, Hank boy. Even then, she'd give you a disease for spite."

"Kiss my ass," the one called Hank said. "Nothing new anyway," he added solemnly.

"Nothing new for damned sure."

"Really, fellows." This was the man who had been on the wagon seat with Steens, maybe because he did not know how to ride. He had that eastern inflection and phraseology that made the language sound foreign to Cord. "Must you be so damned distasteful. Your talk would gag a vulture."

"Gag on this, Mortie," Hank said and gestured at his crotch, and the others laughed, pleased with the easterner's estimation of their roughness, but still uneasy. They had the numbers, and they had Cord and Chi trussed like Christmas turkeys, and still they were somewhat frightened, even Steens, who was supposed to be in charge. Cord reckoned they did not have a lot of experience in this line of work.

They could not be regular law, not from Idaho or anywhere else, not even the easterner. The first lawful step, once they had Cord and Chi wrapped up and ready to go, would have been a trip to the Twin Falls city jail, at least to layover for an early morning start. These men had gotten Cord and Chi away from towns and people—away from the regular authorities—as quickly as possible. This was a kidnapping. Someone wanted them and alive.

It wasn't bounty hunting either, despite the Idaho money on their heads. Any sensible bounty man would know their reputations. He'd deliver them over to the sheriff of Twin Falls, collect his receipt, and spend the night getting a good head start to somewhere Cord would never find.

Cord could smell a rotten deal blowing in the night wind.

"Pull his gag," Steens said, "but be goddamned careful." Hank reached down and ripped the cloth away, and Cord spat and worked his jaws, trying to get the taste of dirty cloth out of his mouth. When he'd worked up enough saliva to talk, he looked up at Steens and said, "Ungag the lady."

Steens gave Cord a leery look, like he'd suggested they run off to Boston together.

"Afraid she'll bite you?" Cord needled.

"I got something she can bite." It was Hank, and Cord turned his head and regarded the man at his leisure. He was short in the legs and trunk and had a way of standing with his chest thrust out in compensation. He looked like the kind of man who had a lifetime of experience in barroom fights over slights that had probably not even been meant, the kind of man who proved he wasn't so small after all by getting the shit kicked out of him a lot. Cord waited until Hank licked at his lips and looked away.

"She will," Cord said solemnly. "She'll bite it off and spit it in a saucepan, and you'll spend the rest of your life playing with a stump and wishing you had some brains and less mouth, dumb cluck."

"Well ain't he a bad one?" Hank said to the man next to him, but that man turned away and wandered off to do something unnecessary with the horses.

"Shut up, all of you," Steens snapped, and for no good reason he pulled his revolver.

Cord looked up at him and laughed.

It was a pleasant starry night, warm even for late spring; the moon, almost full, was falling toward the western horizon. Somewhere off to the south Cord thought he could make out the noise of the Snake River in its canyon. He could smell the ozone in the dry desert air.

To hell with these biscuit eaters, Cord thought. They had been in worse trouble, he and Chi, and by now he was anyway convinced they were in no real danger of being gunned in cold blood. There was a way out of this—there always was—and maybe they needed this kind of death-edge action to bring them out of the morbid thoughts and waking sleepiness that had dogged them all winter. Maybe he was even showing off a little for Chi and what the hell: She was his woman to the degree he would ever have a woman, and these men were pure-D assholes.

Cord looked up at Steens's flushed, anxious face and laughed again.

Steens stepped forward and laid the barrel of his Colt across Cord's cheek, swinging wildly and hard enough to crack jawbone if Cord had not the wit to turn his head with the blow. Still the gunsight split his face like peach peel, and he tasted salty blood.

So much for the sport of showing off.

Steens stepped back and glared down at Cord, his breath a little ragged. He jammed his gun back in its holster like he was angry at what it had done, and growled, "Do her." For a moment no one moved, but then the easterner, Mortie, bent and ripped Chi's gag free. She stared at him until he began twisting the cloth in his fingers, then turned her glare on the rest of these rabbity men. Even Cord could feel the heat of her contempt, and wondered again if some of it was reserved for him. There were so many ways life could go wrong...

"You listen up," Steens said. His breathing was mostly under control. "We still got a day's traveling to come, and nothing for you until it's over. We'll feed you and treat you halfways decent so long as you don't act up. Otherwise we can leave you there in the back of the wagon wishing for water. Up to you."

Steens shut his mouth, like he was waiting for encouragement.

Let him wait on hell, Cord thought.

Steens cleared his throat. "Anyway, we got to deliver you in one piece, or not at all. Fool around and you will get hurt. Some one of these boys might cut off one of your fingers with a jacknife. So you do nice and we'll all get where we're going without any ruckus." Steens smiled, like he had remembered everything.

"Where's that?" Cord said mildly.

Steens started to pull his gun again, and Cord said quickly, "All right, all right." There was no dealing with these chickenshit amateurs. They spooked too easily, and spooked men with guns could be irrational as scorpions. Cord shot a glance at Chi, but she was staring straight ahead at nothing: somewhere else.

Steens turned away, and the others, seeing the fun was over for the moment, went to see to their horses. But the eastern dude, the one called Mortie, crouched beside Cord. He plucked a blade of grass, looked it over, and stuck it between his teeth. "That's a good man, Mister Cord," he said. "Your rewards will follow." He shot a sidelong glance at Chi, but for her he was not there.

And what do you want, Cord thought.

"You need some whiskey for your pain," Mortie said.

"About a gallon," Cord said. The truth of it was, he had forgotten the throbbing in his head until Steens's blow had rocked it once more. He could feel the clotted mess of blood on his cheek.

Mortie pulled a flat silver flask from the inside pocket of his frayed, town-cut jacket, worried out the cork, and held it to Cord's lips. The whiskey was good, smooth and dark and smoky, but even so Cord gagged on it a little, and a dribble ran down the corners of his mouth.

"Don't waste it," the man said. His eyes gleamed with good humor as he sipped at the flask himself. He reached out and traced his fingertips over the ragged wound on Cord's cheek, his touch gentle as a mother's.

"There are ways this could go easier for you," he murmured.

Cord smiled and pointed his chin at the flask in the dude's hand, and Mortie nodded and held it to his mouth. Cord drew a mouthful of the warm whiskey, then spat it full in the man's face. Mortie fell back in surprise. The flask dropped out of his hand, and a little of the whiskey gurgled out onto the ground before he snatched it back up. Cord watched more of it drip from the slopes of the dude's cheeks and the ends of his little neat-trimmed mustache. Even Chi came out of her stony reverie to stare at him.

The easterner drew himself up and slapped the cork into the flask, then wiped the back of a sleeve across his face. "Which is worse, Mister Cord?" he said. "The pain or the humiliation?"

Cord stared up at him impassively. *Queer son of a bitch*, he thought.

Then, surprisingly, the easterner laughed and said, "Well, you'll do." He turned and went off into the shadows.

Whatever that meant. *Little victories*, Cord thought. Well, little victories would do for now.

Their camp was uphill from the road, where a little seep-spring came out of the lava rocks to fill a series of small pools surrounded by a few willows. A couple of the men gathered up armfuls of the heavy sagebrush back of the pools, and when it quickly burned down to ashy coals they set a blackened pot right on it, the cast Dutch oven sizzling as beans began to warm. It was the poorest sort of cooking, but Cord was pleased to find himself hungry. At least he had not been knocked clear out of his senses.

Chi had not spoken a word since they had ungagged her, which worried Cord some. She knew the way of this well as he did: There was no workable play open to them save waiting for possibilities. For now they were got, good and proper. Still, her impotent anger at being bound up and stared at and remarked about by these scum was feeding on her like a tick. Her malice might go beyond reason, and no one—even Cord—could predict what she might do then.

Hank's bandy legs appeared in front of Cord. He crouched, holding a tin plate of beans, scooped up a spoonful and held it out to Chi. "Here you go, puppy bitch."

Chi pulled back her bound legs and planted her heels in the man's chest, arcing her back with the effort of the kick, and the man tumbled back on his ass. Beans arced through the air and cascaded over his face and shirtfront.

"Son of a cunt," the man howled. He pawed at his throat, where the hot paste of recooked food was plastered and burning at him. "Goddamn a black woman," he snarled. He clawed up a handful of dirt and flung it at Chi. She turned her head but otherwise did not move. The man looked around for something else to throw, his face screwed up as if he were about to bawl like a child.

"Enough," Steens said behind him.

Hank scrambled back.

"Leave her be," Steens said.

Hank drew himself to his feet. "She don't need no food, the bitch." He grabbed at his belt buckle with both hands. "I know what she needs."

"I said leave her be," Steens said. For a moment Cord thought Hank was going to swing on his boss, or at least argue. *Jesus*, he thought with disgust. *What a sorry bunch of scum-suckers to get caught up with*. Hank wiped an angry hand across the mess on the front of his shirt and turned away.

Steens retrieved the plate Chi had kicked over and slopped more beans into it, over the dirt that adhered to the gravy of the first scattered serving. "You going to take your food?"

"Like a baby bird," Cord said. He knew from experience that he had to have food to keep up his strength. Chi was different. Over the years he had marveled at the way she could operate for days without food or water, and her ability to endure cold and minor wounds without notice. She had tried once or twice to teach him the trick of distancing pain, but compared to her he only knew the rudiments. Her strength, the way she could subdue the demands of her body by force of will, was uncanny.

But Cord needed food, so he let the lop-gutted man named Steens feed him, a bite at a time. The beans were a thick, glutinous mess, but when they were down they filled his stomach well enough, and afterwards, leaning back against the wagon wheel, Cord felt almost well, wanting only to-bacco.

Chi's shoulder was warm against his. She might have been asleep, and did not move until Hank came back to stand guard over them. He was carrying a Winchester, and the dried mess of beans was a dark stain across his already dirty cotton shirt. Chi raised her head and stared up at him from under the wide brim of her black sombrero, and Hank looked vaguely sheepish, a man with a rifle standing over two incapacitated prisoners, aware he was ridiculous.

Chi turned slowly away, as if for her he no longer existed. *"Qué dice?"* It was the first time she had spoken since they had been manhandled out of their room in the Rancher's Rest.

"We'll see," Cord said.

"Yeah," Chi said and grinned up at the guard. "Sure we will." The implied threat, toothless as it was, frightened the man. He looked away, but then looked back, like they were some abomination of nature that horrified and fascinated all at once.

Chapter Four

THE DAY WAS HOT AND ENDLESS, AND CORD and Chi spent it bound and hidden under the canvas canopy that topped the jolting wagon's deck. But now it was twilight, and they were parked on a high bluff above the middle fork of the Boise River. The tail of the wagon was pointed west, so through the opening above the tailgate Cord could see the garish lights of the territorial prison, and beyond the fainter pinpoints that marked the city of Boise, out where the flatlands started. At least it was cooler. They had not eaten since a predawn breakfast of stale baking powder biscuits and leather-tough jerked beef; Cord had heard one of the horsemen ride ahead to the front of the wagon and suggest a break for lunch and siesta, and Steens's curt refusal. Someone was in a hurry to get somewhere.

When they did stop it was midafternoon. Steens brought around a canteen of warm, brackish water, and even Chi drank, without making a fuss.

"You ain't going to like this," Steens said after pulling the canteen away, "but we are going to bind your mouths again. You don't have to like it. We are coming up on a town pretty soon now, and we can't have you squalling and yelling back here." He produced the two dirty neckerchiefs he had used before. "Open your mouth or we'll open it for you." There had been nothing to do but go along or risk getting some teeth knocked out.

A couple-three more hours of rutted, spring-wrenching travel had brought them to this place outside the territorial capital.

During that time Cord sensed that the guards' edginess was increasing; he could almost get a scent of it in his nostrils. These were men who, from the looks of them, had grown used to the inevitability of failure, and now that they were nearing their destination and the disposal of their cargo, they maybe felt a fatalistic sense of last-minute catastrophe.

So this waiting was wearing on them. No one was saying much, and when they did speak it was in a low, cautious voice. Cord smelled the smoke of their cigarettes. Steens looked in on them every few minutes, and Mortie stood at the end of the wagon and made a show of finishing off what was left in the silver flask, as if that were a way of paying Cord back for the mouthful of whiskey in the face. Chi was curled up within the folds of her serape, her back to Cord. Her black sombrero shaded her face, and the twin braids of her dark, shiny hair hung from below it. Cord listened to her deep rhythmic breathing and studied the curve of her hip. She could sleep anywhere.

There was supposed to be a meet here, Cord guessed, a rendezvous. Steens was waiting to turn them over to someone, the real ringmaster of this circus.

But Cord was wrong. They were only waiting for full dark, and when it came Steens fastened a canvas flap across the rear end of the canopy so they were pitched back into blackness, and the wagon moved on. It jolted a few hundred yards over more bone-wearying ruts and lava-rock ledges and then started down off the bluff, the hand brake squealing against the metal-shod wheel, the team nickering at the weight backed up to them. The wagon cut around a switchback turn, then another, and Cord heard the river close by. The wagon went upstream, away from Boise, turned from the water once more up a more gentle slope, and pulled to a stop.

"You are looking good, my fine boys." The voice was gratingly familiar. "Congratulations. Felicitations. Welcome home."

"Go to hell," Steens muttered from the wagon seat, not very loud.

"Didn't know how you boys would manage, riding herd on a pair of wild horses like those two," the new voice went on, bullyragging the men. "Even if they was tied down, hand, foot, and asshole. Thought they might chew the ropes off each other. Thought they might scare you witless, which wouldn't be so hard considering you boys. Thought you might lose the trail."

"Let's get this done with," Steens snapped.

"Let's do that thing." Footsteps sounded alongside the wagon.

The canvas flap swept back, and Jaeger's round, shiny face stared in at Cord and Chi. He tipped back the brim of his derby with one finger, then let down the tailgate and sat down to regard them, like a man resting after a good meal. He smiled his smartassed smile at Cord and Chi and said, "My, but aren't we looking fine this evening?"

Jaeger stood and took a folding knife from his pants pocket. He made a show of pulling out the blade and testing the keenness of its edge with his thumb, before leaning in and cutting the ropes at Cord's ankles, then Chi's.

Cord crawled out to the tailgate all right, but when he tried to stand he had to grab at the wagon wheel to keep from collapsing. "You ain't gonna be any trouble at all," Jaeger said with satisfaction, but the bastard was right, at least for now. Cord's legs were numb from the long pounding ride and the immobility and the lack of blood, but after thirty seconds on his feet the numbness turned to pinprick pain. In fact he was hurting most everywhere, the blood crusted and cracking over the cut on his cheek when he worked his mouth against the gag. He was tired and losing his tolerance for nonsense.

When Chi came out of the wagon she moved as fluidly as ever, and Jaeger swallowed a wisecrack and looked her over thoughtfully. She was smoldering on a short fuse and ready to go off, and maybe Jaeger figured that out, because he took a short step back from her.

Even in the darkness her eyes seemed to burn with fury, and Cord knew that unless they killed her first, someone— several people maybe—would pay dearly and in painful ways for this two-day ride into humiliation. Chi would not bear this, her forced submission to men such as these. There would be gunwork, Cord knew it, and she would be pitiless.

Strength was seeping back into his legs, and the dizziness of standing erect was leaving him now. Cord looked around. They had come off the road and up a long drive to a big house with wings like flying buttresses. The wagon was parked under a columned portico that faced a vast spring-lush lawn, the grass turned bluish by the moonlight. It swept away along a gentle slope, then steepened down to the river bank. Hedges of high flowering white lilac edged the grounds, and the air was heavy with its rich odor. To Cord it smelled like wealth and slow-growing certitude.

The house was white and solid, two stories in the wings and three in the main central section, its design copied from a tradition of American nobility adapted from England by the planters along the Tidewater in Virginia. Cord had seen only cheap imitations of such houses in his travels in the West, but he knew immediately that this was the real thing. It was solid and oaken and permanent, as if it had grown from the earth from an acorn planted at the beginning of time, as if it had more right to be than the hills. It was home to money older than the West, and power accumulated and passed on over a dozen generations, and absolute willful-

ness. Even the air here was different and smelled thick with
privilege.

Cord liked the smell, and wanted it for himself—and
hated it, because he feared it would never be his.

"Inside." Jaeger prodded Cord roughly in the back with
the snub nose of his little Colt .45. "Folk are waiting on you,
Mister Cord." But even Jaeger seemed a little cowed, now
that whatever this was all about was finally going to be
settled.

The door was dark hardwood with a stained-glass inset
in the shape of a star, red and blue flamebursts shooting out
from a white crystal center. It swung on its hinges smoothly
and silently and reminded Cord of the door to a walk-in bank
safe.

A long Oriental rug ran down the center of the entryway's
parquet hardwood flooring. It was deep and thick in a way
Cord could not recall having felt before, like mossy ground
where you sunk in a little with each step. The walls were
covered in red and purple velvet. From a lighted room near
the end of the hall came mournful, elegant piano music, and
as they passed it Cord caught a glimpse of a middle-aged
woman in a white gown seated at the keyboard of a concert
grand. There were spots of rouge on her pale cheeks, and
her eyes were dreamy and half-closed at her own music. If
she noticed the parade of strange men down her hallway,
she gave no sign.

They were strung out behind Cord, first Chi and then
Jaeger, Steens, and the rest of them, and their uneasiness
was palpable, like that of children called to recite before the
rest of the schoolroom. They shuffled on the rug like they
were the real prisoners in this business, and one of them
sucked at wind like he'd been running a foot race, breathing
quick and shallow into bad lungs, and coughing a little every
few seconds.

The carpeting on the stairs and down the upstairs corridor
was thick as that downstairs, but colored dark, so the dust
from their boots left a trail. "Down there," Jaeger said. He
pushed past Cord and led them to a lighted room at the front,
overlooking the portico.

Cord paused inside the doorway. The room was a library,

or some sort of den. On two walls there were shelves all the way to the high ceiling, the dark wood lined with leather-bound books with gilt lettering stamped on their spines; a third featured a slate-fronted fireplace with a firebox fully four feet wide, in which three massive chunks of split larch stacked neatly on curly-toed andirons burned against the night-chill. Two deep-cushioned leather chairs faced the fire-place on either side. The wall-mounted oil lamps burned with wicks so neatly trimmed that no flickering or sputtering disturbed the dignified, soft-edged illumination of the stately room.

Behind Cord the rest of the party filed in.

The two chairs were high-backed and seemed empty, so Cord was vaguely startled with a man rose from one with slow ceremony. He looked like the cartoons of eastern cap-italists Cord had seen in the newspapers of San Francisco and Denver and Salt Lake. The man was maybe a trifle more closely groomed than the politicians and spoilers that the artist Thomas Nast characterized in his satiric etchings, but his dewlaps were just as thick, and he had that same gross sleekness that told of influence and abundance gained at someone else's disadvantage.

He was in his mid-fifties by Cord's guess, heavy to the edge of obesity, though his clothing was cut to flatter. He wore an immaculately tailored dark banker's suit with ash-gray pinstripes, a matching vest, a boiled white shirt, a cel-luloid collar stiff as horn, and dark four-in-hand with a touch of silver thread running through the fabric. On the end of the gold chain depending from his vest pocket dangled an elk's tooth large as a man's thumb, and the ring on his left hand was set with a single diamond the size of a sweetpea.

The fat man wore his thinning hair combed forward over his pate, which made him look something like a late Roman emperor, dissolute and wearied by everything around him. Yet his face was incongruously free of wrinkles, as if it were inflated. Someday, if he lived long enough, Cord thought, age or the end of his rich man's diet would shrink his gross face into something hideous.

The man cleared his throat and fitted his thumbs into the

pockets of his vest and studied the crowd across the room—
Steens and his men, Jaeger, Cord and Chi.

"What is this"—his voice was deep and grating, like a
rockslide, a voice uneroded by time or cheap whiskey—"a
church social?" He smiled, but sourly, as if he disliked his
own joke.

"Here they are, sir," Steens quavered. He took a step
forward and stood like a pup waiting to be patted.

"Wonderful," the fat man said sourly. "Now get out."

"Huh?"

Jaeger put his hand on Steens's arm. "Go to town, Steens.
This is over for you. Have a drink. Get laid. Take the boys
with you."

Steens looked at him blankly for a moment, as if Jaeger
were speaking in tongues. Then he blinked and turned and
pulled open the door.

"Also," Jaeger said. "Keep your mouth shut. All of you."
When the six of them had filed out he caught the door and
held it open. "You want me out of here too, chief." His tone
was laconic; he was the only one of them not cowed.

"Yes."

Jaeger shrugged to show it made no difference to him.
But then the fat man looked closely at Cord and Chi and
said, "No." Jaeger grinned.

"Ungag them," the fat man ordered.

Jaeger worked the knot at the back of Cord's neck. When
he was ungagged, Cord spat out dirty cloth and said, "The
ropes too."

"How's that?" the fat man said, like he had been challenged. Jaeger was working on Chi's gag.

Cord stared at the fat man. The fat man frowned.

"Untie them," he said finally.

"Wait a minute, chief..."

"Untie them." Here was a man used to making decisions
and giving orders, and not to compromise.

Jaeger crossed behind Cord. "You are going to behave
yourself for the time being." He began sawing at the ropes
around Cord's wrists. "There is going to be some dealing,
and you are going to be a good lad, Mister Cord. You make
any trouble and you are going to die, quick, along with the

lady. You wait out the dealing and you'll maybe come out a lot better than you got a call to hope for." The ropes parted, and Cord began to work life back into his hands, massaging at the fingers of his right, the gunhand.

Chi did not look at him when he went to work on her. "You got no hope at all, little man," she hissed, staring straight ahead, over the fat man's head. "Your hope is running thin, pig bastard. You got lots of pain to look forward to, someday soon."

She spoke with such awful vehemence that Cord suddenly wondered what they might have done to her back in Twin Falls, while he was unconscious and unable to protect her. *Protect her?* There was a new and absurd notion. He was her partner, not her knight. Chi protected herself.

"Yes ma'am," Jaeger said blithely as he cut through Chi's bonds. "But for the time being, you remember what I told you."

Jaeger turned to the fat man, extended his right hand parallel to his waist, palm up, performed a sarcastically elaborate bow, and intoned, "And now, chief, let me present Mister Cord and the redoubtable Miss Chi, ruthless banditos of the great West."

Jaeger grinned over his shoulder at Cord and Chi. "Folk, say howdy to the Honorable William Deane Majors, Colonel of the Army of the United States, retired, and by appointment of the President, Governor of the Territory of Idaho, U.S.A."

Majors looked thoughtfully at Jaeger. "Why is it, Bruno, that so little of your crap goes so far these days?"

"Familiarity breeds contempt," Jaeger said nastily.

"There's a funny sound to your voice," Majors said. "I seem to hear your death rattle."

Jaeger stopped smiling.

Cord had seen men like these two before, bound by a perverse and mutually parasitic relationship that had nothing to do with friendship, and everything to do with fear and hate and resentment. A strong man like Majors tolerated the impertinence of a Jaeger for reasons that ran beyond utility. Jaeger understood the fat man's weaknesses and vulnerabilities and served them, and Majors hated him for his knowledge at the same time that he feared living without his services.

"Are we going to get to that dealing," Cord drawled, "or just stand around watching you boys play kick the can?"

For an excuse to compose himself, Majors turned to the fireplace. The mantelpiece was a thick plank of oak ornately carved with figures of dwarfs and dragons and gargoyles. Majors opened a silver box atop it from which he took a factory-made cigarette. He lit it with a repeating lighter that matched the box. He inhaled deeply, blew out smoke, and finally turned to them again.

But before he could speak Chi started toward him, moving slowly and carefully, her hands out from under her serape, and up and away from her body, posing no threat nor overt challenge beyond that inherent in the unspoken demand that they watch her. All three of them did.

She brushed close to Majors, whose eyes were beginning to betray a startled expression. She watched him while she opened the cigarette box and took out a handful of smokes. She put two in her mouth and used the lighter on them; the othes disappeared under her serape. She turned her back on Majors and crossed back and stuck one of the cigarettes in Cord's mouth. She did all this smooth as an adagio dancer, every motion stylized and full of grace, her anger betrayed only by the slightest trembling of her hands. Cord inhaled smoke deep into his lungs. The cigarette tasted wonderful.

Interest replaced skepticism in Majors's expression; he was seeing something unexpected, like a congregationalist at a faith healing watching an arthritic widow woman slowly straighten her gnarled limbs and then dance an Irish jig. His eyes flicked to Jaeger's and he allowed a small smile of approval to light on his face for a moment.

"Bruno," he said, "maybe you are worth the trouble. You've brought me these fine people." The smile did an encore. "She is a prize. Men will fight over her."

Chi took a long drag on her smoke and glanced at Cord. "Piss-ants," she said, so everyone could hear.

"What say we pow-wow," Cord said. "It's getting a little close in here."

Majors stared at him through a cloud of smoke. He half

turned and tapped ash into the fireplace, and when he looked at them again his face was changed, hard-eyed, his sloppy jowls seemingly frozen into stone.

"Here is my proposition," he said. "It is one you will have to accept."

"I don't think so," Chi said darkly.

"You got some hard days coming, lady," Jaeger said. "I'm going to make myself part of them."

"Your woman is my hostage," Majors cut in, staring at Cord across the big room. "She will not be mistreated"—the fat man shot a warning look at Jaeger—"or molested. She will be in a secret place, at least for a time. If you do what I want, she'll go free. If you don't, or if you run, she will spend the rest of her life in the territorial prison. There is that bank business you transacted in Pocatello some time back."

The threat of further confinement was edging Chi toward the precipice. Her anger was radiant. She held it back by pure force of will.

"You could both die in jail," Majors said. "Pocatello is your ticket. On the other hand, if you do what I say, Mister Cord, I as Governor will grant you both full amnesty. You will walk away clean."

Majors gave Chi an oily smile. "You should urge him to accept, my dear. You'll be eating pheasant."

"You'll be eating shit," Chi snapped.

Majors kept smiling. "Not if this works out. You'll thank me, in the end."

"Who do you want me to kill?" Cord said.

Majors blinked at him. "That's not the job."

"What is the job, *El Gordo*?" Chi put in.

"A simple thing—your kind of work." Majors drew himself up. "You must capture and deliver to me the outlaw Chris Kelly."

And there it was, the part that Cord had been waiting for all along, since that moment in the Rancher's Rest hotel in Twin Falls when men with guns came through the doors and windows. When they did not kill him, he knew it was because they wanted something only he could accomplish, but there had been more to it, something he could see vaguely but could not touch. Until now.

Cord knew the name: Chris Kelly was no stranger to Cord. In a lifetime of drifting along the outlaw trails, Cord had left frayed string-ends of his history in a lot of different caches. It was part of the way of existence he had invented, he and Chi, and usually tolerable. The thing about history, though, was that it had the goddamnedest habit of biting you in the ass when your back was turned.

Chi was looking up at him narrowly. Sure, she remembered Chris Kelly—better than Cord, in some ways.

"You'd kill her, wouldn't you?" Cord said. Chi touched his elbow, but Cord did not react.

"Possibly."

"She'd make you kill her."

"That would be her choice."

Some fine choice. For both of them, some goddamned fine choice.

"You know Chris Kelly," Majors said.

"I've heard the name." That was true enough.

"Tell the rest of your story, Mister Governor," Chi demanded. "Tell us what this is about."

Cord was already trying to think of ways around this. Ideas were not flocking to him.

Majors flicked his half-finished cigarette into the fire. "Eleven days ago," he said, "Chris Kelly and his thugs robbed the First Clearwater Bank in Lewiston of nine thousand dollars in bank notes. On the way out of the bank they shot a bookkeeper, and on the way out of town they killed the marshal and wounded his deputy."

"That is a crock of dogshit," Cord said.

"That's not an issue. It happened." But then Majors's brows furrowed. "Why don't you believe me?"

"Kelly is an old hand at this business," Cord said. "That much I do know. There is one cardinal principle of this business: You do not kill a lawman. Kill a lawman and none of them ever forget. You have stepped over the ditch between robbery and murder, and you can never go back, because they will hunt you until you are dead." It was a long speech for Cord, and he pronounced it precisely.

"You are correct about one thing," Majors said. "We will
pursue him until he is dead." He toyed with the elk's tooth
on his watch chain, as if debating how much to tell them.
"The citizens are in a terrible uproar. Civilization and order
have fairly come to Idaho, and the people do not like to see
it breached."

"Makes you look bad," Chi suggested. "All sorts of outlaws making mischief in your preserve. Makes you look like
shit."

"Not all sorts," Majors said. "Just you and Chris Kelly.
Cord catches Kelly, we will blame the Pocatello job on him,
and you can go free. Your slate is clean, and so is mine."

Chi took a last drag on her cigarette, examined the live
coal, then ground it under the boot heel into the hardwood
floor, surly as a drunk in church. "*Gordo*," she said, "you
are everything I do not like. You are a fat, citified pig, and
you walk on people like you were Pope." She spat out the
words. "All this bullshit finery. This place you live is a cathouse, and you are the biggest *coño.*"

"No need for that." Jaeger held up his hand, palm out.
"We're all some kind of whore, now, aren't we?"

Chi spun around like she was about to come for him,
regardless of the snub-nosed .45 he held trained on her mid-
section.

"I said hold it." He thumbed back the hammer.

Chi stopped.

"All right," Jaeger said. He looked relieved. "Maybe you
don't feel like a whore, and maybe you are right. Because
I know you are right about one thing, and that's the situation
around here." Jaeger cocked his head at the Governor.
"Ain't that right, chief."

"Shut up, Bruno," Majors barked.

Jaeger ignored him. He let down the hammer of his little
Colt and stuck it back inside his jacket, then went to a bookshelf, where newspapers were stacked in neat piles. He rifled
through one, pulled an issue out, and brought it to Cord.
"Read here."

Majors's displeasure was evident, but he did not try to
interfere further. Cord wondered again at the tie that bound
these two men together. There could only be one reason for

Majors to tolerate a man like Jaeger: fear. But fear was a tricky thing: After a time some men could not stand its constant presence; this bond between Majors and Jaeger would be undone only with a gun.

Chi leaned over and read along with Cord. The newspaper was the *Boise Statesman Express*, and the item Jaeger pointed out was an editorial in the second column of the front page.

THE SCANDAL OF DESPERADO DEPREDATIONS
Will Nothing Be Done To Stem the Savagery?

GOVERNOR IMPOTENT IN THE FACE OF CRIME AND RAPINE

by the Editor

There is a plague upon the territory, an epidemic of lawlessness that threatens to infect the moral corpus of the Territory of Idaho. Yet the physician is powerless—indeed, seemingly makes no effort whatsoever—to lance this boil that is festering on the skin of our society.

We make specific reference to the outrageous siege upon the First Clearwater Bank of Lewiston, this Territory, on Thursday last. More than $9,000 of bank funds was liberated by the brigands; Town Marshal Willard Crites was shot dead; Banker Laurence lies moribund with a hole in his lung; and young deputy Boak wears his shattered elbow in a sling these days. The perpetrators are well-known badmen, and were identified by several reliable witnesses, including the brave Boak. They are Chris Kelly, whose damnable outlawry has despoiled towns the length and breadth of the West, and his band of murderous ruffians.

As this newspaper has stated time and again, this Territory will not prosper, nor will its people enjoy full enfranchisement, until we are admitted to the great Union of the United States. We believe statehood could be imminent. However, its cause and promotion is viciously crippled by such as is described above.

The United States is a country of law; the people of the Eastern states embrace orderly society above all else. Therefore, they do not wish to admit into their company a congregation where anarchy rules order, where notoriety overshadows esteem, where gunfire is sovereign over government.

The Union has no use for a place where lawmen are shot dead in daylight by raving criminals.

The cure to this pandemic of crime lies solely with the

ministrations of one man: William Deane Majors, Governor of this Territory. Yet what of Governor Majors, late of Pennsylvania and hero of the War Between the States, appointed by the President to guide us unschooled frontier folk to our destiny? What has Governor Majors done to stem the scourge that is Chris Kelly and his ilk?

The Governor has done nothing, while Master Kelly and his Black Knights have no doubt by now made their way to San Francisco, and are this moment shipboard and halfway to the Sandwich Islands...

The editorial went on for another half column in the same vein. Jaeger watched with pleasure as they read, occasionally glancing at Majors to gauge his reaction. Majors stared darkly at Cord as he read, but his anger was cut by uncertainty.

"Hard to say what this newspaper writer wants more," Cord said when he finished. "Chris Kelly's neck, or your ass."

"I'll be direct," Majors said.

"There's an idea," Chi said.

Majors glanced at her. "I must have Chris Kelly behind bars. I have been Governor of this Territory for eighteen months, and in that time I have not won the hearts and minds of the citizenry. I was not popular when I arrived, and I have not improved the situation. I am a Republican, an appointee of the government in Washington, and a Yankee—worse, I am a retired officer of the Federal Army. As far as these raggedy westerners are concerned, I am a carpetbagger and a scoundrel."

"Wonder where they get their ideas," Chi drawled.

"I don't really care," Majors said. "What they think makes no difference. This appointment is a stepping-stone, something to be endured on the way to achieving my real ambitions."

"You want to be like Chris Kelly," Cord said evenly. "Except instead of a gun you'll use bills of law, and writs, and demand-note mortgages, and instead of robbing banks you'll rob widows." Jaeger was grinning with sadistic pleasure at this accusation, like a demented schoolboy watching a kitten being set on fire.

"I don't wish to debate social systems, Mister Cord. I am telling you the facts. You don't have to like them, or me."

"*Bueno*," Chi said. "I don't like you at all."

"There'll be enough time for you," Jaeger said. "You'll learn to like us all." But then he saw the look she was giving him, and his cocky grin faded a little, like it had stretched his face too taut.

"I expect to be a powerful man in the not-too-distant future," Majors went on. "My destiny lies in the high centers of the Federal Government." He permitted himself a slow smile, savoring his fate. "But first I must control Idaho. I must serve my tenure here from a position of strength if it is to be fruitful. And I will succeed."

Majors stabbed at the air with a forefinger. "I will stand before the people with Chris Kelly beside me, bloodied and bowed and bound. The press will report my instrumental role in the outlaw's capture and will hail my forcefulness, my intolerance of all that is disruptive to the commonweal. I will leave these Idaho buffoons singing my praises and return to the embrace and the high regard of my superiors and cohorts on the Potomac River."

"You better figure on a couple of years." Cord tapped his finger on the newspaper. "From the sounds of this story it will take about that long to track down Kelly, over there on the beach with the pretty girls and his money."

"Could be," Jaeger said casually, as if it didn't matter anyway. "But there ain't no beaches up in Kellogg, unless you count the piles of tailings around the settling ponds. Seems that Kelly and his bunch were spotted by a surveying crew up there in the panhandle, not two days ago. He looked to be headed west, toward Coeur d'Alene."

"Do you know that country?" Majors asked.

"I've seen it."

"You're going to have a chance to see it again."

Cord glanced at Chi and murmured, "*Qué dice?*" She stared back and did not answer. But she was right: There wasn't anything to say. Cord wondered again how much of her simmering anger was reserved for him, how much she blamed him for getting them into this fix.

They had been in greater danger together, but they had

never been so tightly boxed in. Every option open to Cord was a betrayal of some kind.

"You don't want me," he said. "You want regular lawmen, a posse of maybe fifty of them and a remuda of good horses. You want to send them up to that panhandle country to drive Kelly and his bunch into a pen, and then ride all over them like they were gophers. Shoot maybe a dozen holes in each of them, and bring their corpses back so you can lay them out on pallets and pose among them for the photographer, and then charge the people two bits apiece to prod at them and snip off hanks of their hair."

Majors ignored the bait. "I want you, Mister Cord, and I will have you. Nothing you say will change that. You saw the caliber of men at my disposal, the ragtag bullies who brought you here." He looked at Jaeger, so the man would know he was being included in the description. "I learned to judge men during the war, and I judge Steens and the others to be worthless.

"I brought these men with me," Majors said, "because I knew them and could manipulate them. Steens and Hank were soldiers. Mortie and some of the rest were police officers in various eastern cities. They had some expertise with violence and corruption and greed, but they are bewildered and discomfitted by the wilderness. They would be lost within fifty miles of this town, and if by some dumb luck they did find Kelly and his gang they would be massacred."

He glanced at his cohort. "Jaeger here is a little better." Jaeger grinned warily. "He at least knows his limitations."

"Go to hell, chief," Jaeger muttered.

Majors's eyes glittered. "So I need a strong man, Mister Cord. Then there is the old rule—set a thief to catch a thief. Even here in the wild West we are bound to follow the dictates of civilized law. If I were to take your suggestion and send a posse charging in to annihilate Kelly, the editorial writers would have a field day.

"Lawmen are weak because the law is weak," Majors said. "But you are strong, because you are not bound by the law and never have been. You can accomplish alone what other men in a band could not."

Majors steepled his fingers, as if he were about to pray. "You see, there is nothing left to chance in this plan."

"There's one thing," Cord said. "There's me."

Majors shook his head. "You're the most predictable aspect. I've got your partner."

"Once I ride free of here," Cord said, "why do you think I'd care?"

"You are not a savage, Mister Cord. You are trapped by the nobility of your spirit, as it were."

The fat man had him there. Cord did not like the way Majors could look into him; he felt indecently exposed, and the man's perceptions were like clammy unwanted caresses.

"Your silence is your answer," Majors said. "Don't struggle with your nature, because it will win, and then go on to defeat everyone. The woman will lose the most."

"No," Chi hissed.

"You're not part of this," Majors said. "I have hold of you, miss, and I can do what I want with you."

"I got some ideas along that line," Jaeger said.

Cord looked at Chi and felt his skin prickle. Her eyes were dark, burning coals of loathing, opaque as mirrors, hiding a stranger who hardly recognized him.

"I saw it all," Majors said with pride. "When Jaeger wired that he had spotted you in Twin Falls, I could have had you captured and thrown in jail to rot. That would have done something for my repute—but not enough. Pocatello is dim in the memory of most people; Chris Kelly's wanton killing is at the root of the uproar. I recognized the best use for you; I saw my opportunity."

So, Cord thought, *it came to this*. The possibilities were dissolving like mist after sunup, and all that was left was the plan.

"How do you see it?" he asked. "How do you see me doing this business?"

"You ride out at dawn, alone. The sooner you deliver Kelly, the sooner your lady is freed. You won't want her in the nest I've prepared for too long. She is a handsome woman, and things happen to handsome women."

Cord glanced at her. "We'll talk it over."

"You'll do it," Majors said in a hard, cold voice. "You

will go along with my plan, or you will spend the rest of your
life in prison just as she will, living in filth and picking lice
from your hair, listening to your mind talk back to you and
waiting for daylight that never comes. You will pass the time
fighting off other men, and your dreams."

"We'll talk it over."

Majors nodded to Jaeger. "Take care of her." Jaeger
crossed the room in quick strides, keeping away from Chi
and her fiery dark gaze. He opened the door, and immediately Steens and his five men filed in, looking nervous as
ever.

"Take her," Majors ordered.

Steens looked at Cord and Chi and licked his lips.

"A cigarette," Chi said, almost pleasantly. "One cigarette
before you cart me off." She managed a smile at Majors.
"One cigarette to seal the deal."

Majors considered, then returned the smile. "There you
are," he said to Cord, as if announcing some kind of sexual
triumph. "We will all be friends here, while you are going
about your work."

He took two cigarettes from the silver case on the mantelpiece, lighted them with the silver lighter as Chi came to
him. He handed one to her, and Cord recongized a grotesque
parody of the smoking ritual he and Chi observed so many
times. Chi took the cigarette and puffed delicately.

Cord held his breath.

Chi smiled sweetly and stepped toward Majors, and
jammed the glowing tip of the cigarette into Majors's greasy
forehead, grinding the fire in while Majors shrieked and
flopped his arms and clawed ineffectually at her hand. Steens
and his men seemed mesmerized by this show. Cord started
to take a step and felt Jaeger's gun jab into his back. He
held and raised his hands.

The sick sweetish odor of charred flesh permeated the
room, and Cord swallowed air through his mouth. Ten years
of partnering, and still he could be shaken by the extreme
turns her anger could take.

"Goddamn the bitch," Majors roared. "Take her, you
cockless bastards."

Steens and his men broke from their trance, circling warily

toward Chi. She put her back to the wall next to the fireplace, as Majors scuttled away out of the fight's path. She did not look at him again. Steens and the others had fanned out around her, pinning her against the wall but keeping just out of reach.

"Take her!" Majors screamed.

The man on the end, momentarily distracted by Majors's manic yell, glanced over his shoulder, and Chi brought up the pointed toe of her riding boot between the man's legs. The man folded up and fell on his side, mewling like a whipped bitch. Another man stepped in with a drawn gun, and Chi spun and back-kicked the weapon from his hand, twisting at the same time from the grip of another of them. The man got hold of the hem of her serape, and wool ripped.

Jaeger pressed his Colt harder into Cord's back. Cord stiffened and did not move.

Chi was free of the enclosing circle and backed against one of the high bookcases. One man was down, another nursing his shattered gunhand. The remaining four regrouped and came at her again.

Chi reached behind and got hold of a heavy, leather-bound volume. She flung it at Steens and he ducked away, but already she was throwing another book and this one caught him in the chest, knocking out a grunt of wind. Chi was throwing books with both hands now, and the men were stopped, ducking their heads behind crossed arms. Chi kicked a low table into their path, and the easterner called Mortie stumbled and went down on one knee on top of it, the fine delicate hardwood shattering like ice.

"Kill her!" Majors shouted. The men froze, then turned slowly to look at him. Even Chi paused, in the middle of reaching around for more books.

Majors's face was white and sagging, his lips wet with spittle.

Majors drew breath, exhaled, and repeated, "Kill her." This time he sounded rational.

Steens drew his weapon and turned on Chi, and Cord tensed and got ready, knowing he was going through Jaeger's Colt, no matter what else happened.

But it was Jaeger who stopped it. "No."

Steens looked at him.

"Take her but don't kill her," Jaeger ordered. "We need her alive. Without her we have nothing but trouble, every one of us." He was talking to Majors now.

Steens nodded like that was the first sensible thing he'd heard since coming in. But he put the gun on Chi again and edged a half step toward her, flanked by Hank and another man to the right, Mortie on the left. Mortie was rubbing at his shin where the table had caught him.

"I ain't going to kill you, lady," Steens said, talking to himself as much as Chi. "But I'll shoot your ass someplace, without worrying much about it. So you just stop this cutting up."

"Rush her, goddamn it," Jaeger snapped. "You are three men . . ."

"Three cowards," Chi breathed. *"Tres cabrons.* Come ahead, *cabrons."*

Steens and his men hesitated, weight forward on the balls of their feet, ready and yet not willing, maybe waiting for help from some quarter.

"Rush her!" Jaeger ordered.

The one called Hank made the first move, maybe because he thought he owed Chi a payback on humiliation. He came in with shoulders up and head down, so he did not see her boot until it caught him in the chest. But he kept coming anyway, powered by anger or momentum. Chi tried to twist to one side, but Hank grasped at her and caught her wrist, pulling her toward him as he slammed into the bookshelves.

Steens stepped in behind Chi and cracked the barrel of his Colt atop Chi's head. It was a savagely hard blow, and her sombrero couldn't absorb it all. Chi staggered but did not go down. Hank had hold of both her wrists now.

Steens hit her again, on the side of the head this time, knocking off her sombrero so it hung over her back by its neck-thong. A moment later, the one called Mortie got his arms around her waist. Chi kicked at him and got lucky, and Mortie yowled and let go.

Steens hit her with his gun in the middle of the forehead, and again on the crown of her head as she went down.

Each blow made a sound like a mallet striking a gourd. Chi thumped to the floor, and then it was quiet.

Books were scattered all over the room, and pages fluttered in the fireplace's draft. Steens stepped back and stumbled over the remnants of the crushed table. Men started at Chi, breathing heavily and clutching at themselves, wondering if she were dead.

"Kill her," Majors said shrilly.

Steens stared at him for a long moment. He thumbed back the hammer of his revolver, held it out straight in one arm and supported his wrist with his other hand, and sighted on Chi's face, eighteen or twenty inches away.

Behind Cord, Jaeger said, "Goddamn you assholes." He stepped past Cord and held his gun on Steens. "Put up that gun, you damned shit-simple fool." Steens stood there looking like a dog with two masters.

"Put it up or you are dead," Jaeger said in a hard cold voice. "I won't have any of you queering up this deal we got, even if you ain't got brains to see the way it is."

Steens holstered his gun.

Majors bellowed, "Kill the bitch!" He held his handkerchief to the hole burned into his forehead.

Jaeger spun on his heel and crossed the room to Majors. He raised the weapon and let Majors see the view down the barrel from about a foot and a half. Majors took his hand away from his head and stared at the pistol.

"Kill you," Jaeger hissed.

The burn in Majors's forehead gleamed like a third eye. Majors was whimpering softly.

"Stand tall," Jaeger whispered.

Majors stared at him. Carefully, like a man building a house of cards, he drew himself back to the bearing of a leader.

"I follow your command," Jaeger whispered.

Majors became powerful and arrogant once more, hands at his belly in a pose of satisfaction, his eyes glittering with calculation and quick intelligence. He stood a moment remembering his role, gazing around the room as if his look would restore order, finally letting his eyes take casual note of Chi, lying on the carpet up against a bookshelf. "Get her out of here," he rasped.

Steens and Hank took a leg apiece and dragged Chi from the room. Jaeger was back behind Cord, the little handgun a rude finger between Cord's ribs.

The first man Chi had kicked was still curled up on the floor, weeping softly. Majors looked at him as if he were a slug. "Get out."

Mortie and the others edged through the door and disappeared. The man on the floor had to crawl, crabbing along on his side, pulling himself across the thick rug. Majors watched him. When he was out the door, Jaeger pulled it shut.

He stared at Cord for a moment, then put his gun away. "There won't be any trouble from here on," he said, stating facts. "We've got her now, and you know what will happen to her if you don't play our game."

Cord did not trust or believe anything about all this, especially the notion that Chris Kelly had become a killer bandit. These two men could be working from any side of the truth. But for now that did not matter. He had to do as they said, or at least look like he was. It was the only way to stay free, and free was his only chance at getting Chi away from them.

"I'll need a good long-legged horse, and not some easterner's idea of an animal that travels. You assholes wouldn't know horseflesh from tame pigs."

"Watch your mouth," Majors barked.

"Why?" Cord snapped. "What will you do with me?" This was mindless baiting, Cord knew even as he said it, but all the tension that was backed up inside him, along with his impotent horror at the beating Chi had endured, needed an outlet, and Majors was the nearest target.

The fat man glared. The handkerchief was at his wound again, smeared red and black.

"We might pistol-whip you a little," Jaeger said. "Just to soften you up."

"You might make me crazy," Cord said. "You never can tell what will make me crazy. But when it happens you will know. I'll wait until you give me my guns—you have to give me guns. When you do I'll turn backwards, the way a man will sometimes, and come to kill you and fat-ass over there."

Cord had their attention.

"So I need a horse," Cord said, "and I'll do the picking. I need a good broke-in saddle of a size to fit me. And I need my guns back—mine, not some other guns. I can't fight with guns I don't know. It would be like pissing with someone else's dick." Cord smiled hugely and coldly. "You might as well get moving on it."

"You won't need anything until morning."

"I'll decide what I need, and when. You better understand some things. You either have to kill me, this minute, or give me my head. You don't know what you get when you turn me loose. You have to sweat a little. But that's how it is, because from this point on you can't control me. So kill me or get my guns."

"In a few hours," Majors said calmly. "We will restore your weapons as soon as your woman is securely boxed up and awaiting the pleasure of your return." He was in charge again.

"Five hundred dollars," Cord said.

"How's that?"

"Expenses. Just give me the money."

"Two hundred."

"Holy Jesus." Cord snorted his disgust. "You people aren't only fools, you are cheap fools."

Majors inflated with anger. Cord muttered, "Shit," and shook his head.

Majors went to the bookshelves. One row of volumes turned out to be a false front, the book spines pasted to a panel that slid open to reveal a safe. Majors ran through an elaborate combination, pulled open a thick round door, and withdrew a steel box which he opened with a key on his watch chain. The bills inside were crisp and new and looked like they would be cool to the touch. They were mostly $100's, with a few $20's, and they were packaged into sheafs wrapped with paper ribbon. Maybe $20,000 all told, there for the taking.

"Don't even think about it, Mister Cord," Majors said.

He shut the door and twirled the dial. "This safe is invulnerable, and so am I. This is my place."

"Must be nice."

Majors counted five bills from a sheaf of $100's and slapped them into Cord's hand. "There's a room for you down the hall."

"I'll sleep in the stable," Cord said. "The horses got a stink I can stand."

"Good night, Mister Cord."

"Not so far."

But when Cord was at the door, Majors called his name once more.

Cord waited.

Majors took the handkerchief from his forehead and examined the colors staining the white cloth. "Actually, Mister Cord," the fat man said while looking into the cloth, "I lied to you a bit, or rather, I held back. I wanted the job to seem easier than it is. I was hoping you would just give us the woman, without all that trouble." He gingerly fingered the blackened hole in his flesh above his eyes.

"Tell your story."

"I want Kelly alive. I do not care what you do with the others—I'll even pay the bounties on your word they are dead—but I must have Kelly alive."

"Why?"

Majors shook his head.

"You tell me what I'm getting into, you fat tub of shit and lard."

"Kelly," Majors said in a low voice. "Alive. If Kelly dies, so does your woman. Do you understand?"

Cord finally nodded. There was no point in argument. Maybe this sick business would never come to a head, or at least not to gunplay and dying.

He was being set up, lied to, and used, and he knew it, and knew there was nothing for it.

There was no chance, unless he made the opportunity.

"Get my guns," Cord said. "Now."

"No, Mister Cord," Majors said. "You are right. You might go crazy and kill somebody. You might pull a pistol on me for that woman."

"You'll wear it up your ass."

"You'll get your guns when you are on your way, and calmed down, and safely out of this house. We keep the doors locked against the likes of you."

Cord crossed the room, setting his boots carefully in the unsettlingly thick carpeting.

"I'm crazy now." Cord put his nose six inches from Majors's bloated jowly pan. "I'm going to spit in your face, and you're going to let me. Aren't you?"

Majors stood there, white and quivering.

"You can't do a damned thing about it," Cord said. He spat, and watched the spittle drool down the floppy dewlaps, and waited, gave Majors all the time he needed to react. But the fat man only quivered and stood his ground, his flesh greasy with the sweat of his fear, and the black circle on his forehead like the scar left when a horn is removed.

Chapter Five

THE RANGY BLACK GELDING WAS A FINE TRAVeling horse, a pretty animal with three white stockings and a white blaze down the face, and he moved across this rough country with a ground-eating stride. The horse was as easy to sit and move with as a rocking chair, so at least one of Majors's eastern bully-boys must have picked up some regard for animals. Among the dozen saddle horses in Majors's livery barn, this crossbred working animal from the high desert country stood out like a nun in a whorehouse.

Cord felt halfway good, considering his purposes and his distance from Chi. It was the getting back out into the country; it always filled him out again, especially after being held against his will.

And this Idaho country was pretty as it came, with enough

change packed into a relatively small area to please anyone at some point along the trail. The hills of the Palouse rolled along the shelf-land north of the Clearwater and east of the Snake, fine and freshly green with the spring season, and the trail cut easily between the hills' undulations. This looked to be some of the richest farming ground Cord had seen in his travels. The sodbusters who had come into the country now that the Nez Percé were pretty much broken were opening up large tracts. The ground was worked and seeded in the fall to a variety of grain which came up and then lay dormant under the winter snows, to grow again when the spring sun warmed the soil. Already the wheat through which Cord rode was stirrup high and well into forming seed-heads. A man could settle in this fertile country and make a prosperous life.

But Cord knew something of working the ground from his East Texas childhood, and he knew enough about himself to understand he would never find contentment in being tied to the earth, and the weather and the ergot and the 'hoppers, and breaking your back every hour of the day coaxing life from the endless brown furrows.

The ones Cord envied lived in white-painted houses up in the draws of this country, alongside their windbreak rows and Lombardy poplar, newly planted and still small. He was starting to feel sorry for himself, contemplating the ache of traveling too long, too many years, and of being alone.

Riding through a grove of cottonwood along a little creek running clean with late spring, Cord reined in the black gelding and pulled his Peacemaker. He rested his right wrist on his left forearm, carefully framed the open sights, and shot a squirrel from a limb, blowing the little animal to nothing for no reason he could think of once it was done. It didn't make him feel better, but demonstrated the ache of loneliness was turning to anger.

Well, there was nothing wrong with anger, so long as you kept it controlled, and did not start in shooting humans like they were squirrels. This was going to be a balancing act, so Cord had instructions for himself: Do not sink away into sadness and might-have-beens, because eventually it will turn to blind unharnessed fury. Look at the country and stay light-footed, and at least at the outer fringes of your mind, keep loose and keep quick.

North of the Palouse the land would turn to piney woods, along up toward the tail end of Lake Coeur d'Alene. He would cut up the west side of the lake at the fork, which would take him to the town. The other way led over to the Kellogg-Wallace region less than a hundred miles to the east, where the mountains were laced with silver and lead and gold and zinc. They said the silver strike out of Wallace was the richest in the world. Those were hard towns, populated by miners and grifters and coolie Chinese who were worked like slaves. Boom towns, and mean ones.

Cord had heard of Chinese killed for sport—like they were squirrels.

On his third morning on the trail, Cord ran out of coffee. He tried not to let it bother him as he broke camp, gnawing on a strip of jerked beef. He strapped his bedroll on the gelding's back and stood a moment listening to the birds flying and mating in the flowering bushes nearby. He took a deep breath of fresh, sweet morning air. It tasted fine— and, dammit, he wished he had a cup of coffee. He could taste it, boiled strong and black. At least there should be coffee. A man should be able to count on coffee, sure as sunrise, more surely than any woman.

Cord rolled a lopsided cigarette and smoked it and made himself get calm again. When he was, he saddled the gelding and rode on, easy-like, composed.

A few miles along, he was rewarded. He followed the smell of strong coffee through a break of cottonwoods and into a little clearing by a creek-run no more than a yard wide. Cord rode in slowly and smiling, working on looking friendly and no threat, like a man approaching honeybees. A roan saddle gelding and a pack mule were tethered by the water, and a little man in denim coveralls was sitting by the fire. The black coffeepot sat steaming in the coals. The little man took a celluloid toothpick out of the corner of his mouth and returned Cord's smile.

"Coffee?" he offered. "Pot's on."

"Yeah," Cord said, climbing down. "There is a good idea."

The coffee was wonderful, good as any Cord had tasted

in the fanciest San Francisco hotels, and he said so. "Ought to be," the little man said. "Imported all the way from Hawaii, so it costs, but that doesn't matter. A man on the road must carry a decent bait of coffee. Reckon you've learned that."

"Drummer?"

The little man nodded. "Ladies' undergarments. My daddy had a store in St. Louis, and I learned the business there, but I had a hankering to see the country. It's a going business, ladies' unmentionables. Good times or bad, ladies will have their corsets and step-ins and chemises. Maybe they will make do with homespun when push comes up to shove, but they like their pretties, and the shopkeepers know it. I spread out my wares there on the counter, and before the wrinkles are shook out there is a crowd of ladies around me."

Cord sipped at the good Hawaiian coffee. "Must be cozy."

"I'm the right sort for the job," the drummer said. "My daddy told me, 'Son, you will always be at home in ladies' frillies.' You see, I got the build for it. A decent woman gets embarrassed talking knickers and bloomers. A big man is going to make her blush and stammer, but a woman can talk to a little man like a sister. These are my trail clothes"—the drummer swept a deprecating hand down his coveralls—"but when I get near town I'll dig out my church suit and my four-in-hand and my silk derby hat, and slap a little of that oh-de-toilet on my cheeks. The women will flock to me and my wares like I was one of their own. It don't eat at your stomach. Notice that?"

"Huh?" Cord said.

"The coffee. It don't burn a hole in your gut. It's the lava."

"The lava," Cord repeated.

"Them Hawaiians grow their coffee on the side of volcanic mountains. Plant 'em in the lava, so the ash keeps the acid out of the beans."

"That so?"

"Don't get the idea I'm anyone's weak sister," the drummer said, veering back to the main trail again. "I had a wife and three children in St. Louis. But me for the open road.

I have my share of women. They get to talking to you about their intimate apparel, and before you know it they are telling you about all sorts of personal business, like you was a doctor or a padre. One thing leads to another, you get my drift."

"You sure like to talk."

"I don't get much chance, not with men. A little fellow in a silk derby and perfume goes into some backwater saloon, there is liable to be trouble. I don't mind a fair fight, but I don't see any profit in getting the shit kicked out of me by a bunch of drunken cowboys whose idea of a good time has got four legs and goes, 'baa.'"

Cord laughed. "I can't argue with that."

The drummer was eyeing him speculatively. "You want to ride on with me? The name is Charlie Dutch, and I don't mind having a gun-toter riding friendly with me in the mining country, a man who has been drinking down my good coffee."

"A gun-toter?"

"I think I know you," Charlie Dutch said. "But never mind that. I judge a man by what I see of him, and nothing more."

Cord helped the little drummer cinch the mule's sawbuck saddle and then wrestle on the panniers and loop them over the saddle forks, two balanced bundles each the size of a hundred-pound sack of meal, the woman's dainties wrapped over with oilcloth. They split the last of the coffee and were trailing north ten minutes later.

Charlie Dutch had been around. He knew the gossip, and as Cord had already figured out, he loved to talk. Cord only had to mention the name Chris Kelly, then drowse back in the saddle and listen to a digest of what folk all over the territory were saying about him and his gang.

Chris Kelly, it was said, ran a nasty bunch of hardcase riders, gunslingers, and general ruffians. They were supposed to be the worst kind of scum, men who would have been wolfers up north of the Missouri breaks in Montana, or scalp hunters along the Mexican border, if they had been on hand for those sorts of nastiness.

"One of the gang is a woman," Charlie Dutch said. "That's

gospel—lots of folks have seen her. Think of that, a woman on the outlaw trail, holding her own with those murdering hellions. You ever hear of such a thing?" The drummer shot Cord a narrow look.

"Once or twice," Cord drawled.

"Yes indeed," the drummer said. "We hear of it, but we don't usually credit such stories."

The news that Charlie Dutch had picked up heading north across Idaho was that the Kelly gang was still in the territory, holed up somewhere in the panhandle, hidden among the miners and timbermen and other rough trade in the remote country. Some people said that there was personal trouble between Kelly and Governor Majors.

"Having humiliated the Governor once," Charlie Dutch said, "Chris Kelly is sworn to ravish his bailiwick again and again, while thumbing his nose in that fat man's face."

"You believe that?"

"Nope. Kelly probably has all the money he needs. I figure he would strike out for better living than he could find in the panhandle country. For one thing, it's the worst food you ever ate up there, and it costs twice what it's worth because it's all trucked in by freight wagon."

Cord had already figured that part out; at the root of his discomfort was the notion that Chris Kelly had lit out for parts far away and unknown a week ago, that he was long out of Cord's reach. In a way Cord hoped that was true— but then he came back to thinking of Chi, where she was and what they might be doing to her. So he would find Kelly wherever he was, and nothing—including betrayal—would stop him from redeeming his partner.

"On the other hand," Charlie Dutch said, "I was in Moscow yesterday afternoon and I heard that Chris Kelly was seen only two days ago. A sheep rancher up in the hills east of the lake is claiming Kelly put up at his place for a night. Damned fool was bragging about it. But you see, there's where that business about personal bad blood between Kelly and the Governor comes from."

"How's that?"

"Not too many people in these parts have much use for Majors. He's an eastern Yankee and looks and acts like one, and folks don't like his kind telling them how to live. When Kelly pulled that Lewiston job, he put egg on Majors's face, and any humiliation of Majors pleasures those who despise him. It isn't so much more of a step for some folk to whip up some make-believe about Kelly out to drive Majors from the territory, and get rich on eastern bankers' money at the same time."

Charlie Dutch crossed his arms on his saddle horn and grinned across at Cord. "Maybe there will be a full-blown showdown pretty soon. There would be a story for the romancers and the book writers."

Cord wondered how much all of this came from Charlie Dutch's imagination, maybe fueled by just the kind of yellow-back dime novels he was talking about.

"You can see it," the drummer said. "Majors hiring some gunslingers to track down Kelly, and then a shootout in the street, and Majors getting so lathered up with excitement he dies of a burst heart."

"You ought to be writing those books," Cord said.

"Maybe I will."

They rode on in companionable silence for a while. There was no dime-novel Robin-Hood rivalry between Kelly and the oily Governor, Cord was pretty sure of that. Yet he remembered the man's vehement insistence: He must have Kelly alive. Maybe their relationship did run trickier than anyone knew.

Or maybe Cord's imagination was running a trifle strong to fantasy, and like Charlie Dutch he was seeing make-believe.

"Chris Kelly is going to take the money from the bankers and give it to the people." Charlie Dutch snorted in disgust. "I actually heard someone suggest that in earnest."

The Governor wanted to show off his captive, Cord figured, wanted to pillory him before the rabid crowd. Majors was just the sort of man to feed on another's fall from grace.

Yet some hunch in the back of Cord's mind kept tickling at the idea that there was more to it. Kelly had something Majors wanted, bad enough so he could taste it, bad enough to kill.

Charlie Dutch split off at the crossroads to Saint Maries.

The mercantilist there was a good customer, he said, though a little strange. "I think he's saving some of those ladies' silkies for his own amusement, if you know what I mean," he said. Cord thanked him for the coffee and company and rode on alone toward Coeur d'Alene.

The trail curved around the thumb of Lake Coeur d'Alene on a high wooded bluff above the water, and from up there Cord could see all the way across the east bank. There was some sort of mill there, but all Cord could make out was a stream of smoke billowing up into the breeze. Lumber, Cord guessed, the smoke from slash and sawdust fired up in a teepee burner.

Cord watched it curl up into the air, gave the gelding its head, and let his mind run to a track he had been avoiding— Chris Kelly, the interweavings of their paths in the long-ago, and the last time Cord had seen the man, six years back, a thousand miles away.

They had been partners of a sort, maybe even friends, though Cord could not recall for sure. The only person he could for sure call friend was Chi—caged up now in some hole by Majors and that bastard Jaeger, helpless and waiting on Cord...

Chris Kelly—Cord pulled his thoughts back to Chris Kelly. He had to work through that time in the past when they had been together for a while. Perhaps he would find some loophole in the moral law he seemed bound to break.

He was an equal; there were damned few men Cord called peers, and Chris Kelly was one. But there was trouble, as there will be sooner or later when men of equal strength and confidence and skill run together.

Chi had been there with them, part of the trouble. What had she recalled, that moment in Majors's gaudy den when the fat man pronounced their old pard's name?

At least he and Chris Kelly had managed to part without a showdown—which had probably been good sense on both sides. With most men, you could be pretty sure of walking away from a showdown, because most men did not have much experience with the business of shooting at a living target, of taking time and ignoring the thumping in the middle of the chest and firing to kill, and you did. But when you faced an equal, you needed all that plus unshakable grit, and luck, and maybe the beneficence of fate as well, whatever that was.

He wished there was a way to talk it out with Chi. She understood him, and the tangled twists his thinking could take, and she had the intuition to unravel his concerns and set them straight. He needed that. This was no job for a man with doubts, complicated as it was already by old bloody loyalties and angers.

Cord felt the realization of his isolation creep over him like possession.

It had been nearly ten years since he had ridden into trouble alone, and in those days he was armed with the strength of boyish ignorance and bravado. Now he was lonely, not frightened but fatalistically aware that the defeat of Chris Kelly was no sure thing.

Bringing the man in alive could be impossible.

Cord shook his head, and the gelding pricked its ears, sensing the sudden uncharacteristic movement. It could not be impossible, because his life with Chi was on the line, and that was the only tolerable life there was. If he did not bring in Kelly, there would never be any settling down to an endurable existence.

Chi was the safety net under him, and without her the chances would eat him up. His future would be a quick, stupid death in a showdown with some kid, or the long shaking old age of a drunkard, because the day he lost her would be the day he had no reason to quit drinking.

They had been apart some time, between jobs and such. Once Chi had left him for nearly three months, a whole winter season. He got the idea she had been down with her people, in Sonora in Old Mexico, seeing to some business, though she did not talk about it. That time they had separated easily enough, but other times the split had come out of one of his drinking bouts. Alone, he would hole up and turn ugly in some little town, seeking out and always finding the mindless trouble he seemed to need every once in a while. But always a part of him knew they would get back together, and after the hard whiskey drinking and the brawling had gone on for a time, after Cord's head and eyes cleared and his stomach stopped spasming in reaction to gut-eating whiskey and days without food—after all that nonsense the knowledge that it was time to get back together gave direction to his maundering thoughts and pulled him back together. She was always there for him and back at his side when the time came.

Cord hated this riding alone. For the first time he flat-out admitted it to himself, in a way that stood open and honest at the front of his brain.

Well then, he thought. *If that was the way of it . . .*

Cord spurred the black gelding into a long trot. The sooner this was done with, the better for everyone. Just believe that, Cord told himself. Do not think of the past, and stay tuned and quick-handed and ready in your heart. Keep the eye of your mind on what comes next, one thing and then the next. See to business: Kelly, and then Chi, and riding to find a place in some country like the springtime Palouse hills.

Chapter Six

THE RAILROAD HAD COME THROUGH COEUR d'Alene. Here was a town with plans for the future.

Not so many years back this was a mining camp, ramshackle and temporary as any of them, more pleasant than some only by virtue of its site at the head of the lake. But with the railroad its permanence was assured, and like a washerwoman dressing to meet high-born visiting relations, the town had taken on trappings of civilization and society. There were brick buildings housing shops, a twenty-room travelers hotel where rooms cost four dollars a night, and a granite-walled two-story bank on a Main Street three full blocks long, set above the lakeshore where log-booms rode the lapping waves. The citizens looked proper as the town, clean and dressed for commerce, and willing to brook no wild-West hooligans. There would be no six-shooter cutting up on any night of this town's week.

Yet the citizens shared the streets with the roughest sort of transient working men: drifters employed busting underground rock for the big mining companies; single-jack prospectors come to town for provisions, a week-long drunk, and if there was money to burn, a bath; independent tree-fallers who contracted with the mills and the mines, in checkered-wool shirts from which extended arms big as pot roasts. The presence of these men overlaid a vision of the old-time camp life on the spanking-new and frantically decent town.

The good folk appreciated the business of these men but had no wish to witness their more gross pleasures, so for recreation the working men were herded into the place called Minertown. Laid out north of the tracks, far from the lake and the tree-shaded side-street homes of the good folk, Minertown was two blocks of saloons and gambling hells and cheap whorehouse hotels, offering the finest variety of vice and sin and Oriental bondage the rough trade could desire.

It was to Minertown that Cord headed for information.

The Galena looked like the most popular of the barrooms. This was a solid place, with a long brass-railed bar, matching spittoons set every ten feet along its length, a dozen well-worn but sturdy hardwood tables with mostly matching chairs, and bottles on the back shelf with labels that looked authentic. It was a little past suppertime, and the place was beginning to fill. The customers were mostly working men come straight from the job for a settle-down drink. They were neither seedy nor broke and had pride in themselves, not much like the ragtag alcoholics Cord was used to seeing on the outskirts of camp life. A dice game in the corner had the attention of half a dozen Chinese, chattering out their bets quietly in their own singsong language, and the presence of yellow folk mixing in with white didn't seem to bother anyone. The half-dozen women in facepaint and short skirts sat quietly and almost modestly at a table by themselves

until approached, and two of them—a plump, shiny-haired
Indian and a pale, long-necked redhead—were almost pretty.

Cord found a spot around the corner at the end of the bar
and ordered a shot of Jim Beam bourbon and a glass of water
back from a middle-aged white-shirted bartender. The bourbon had the smooth smoky flavor of its Kentucky pedigree,
and Cord sipped at it slowly and carefully, and tried not to
be obvious as he looked things over.

The one man who did not fit in sat alone at the corner
table opposite the dice game, his back to the wall. He was
a halfway elegant looking hombre, at least among this company: He wore a black swallowtail coat, matching britches
tucked into black riding boots, a white shirt under a vest,
and a black, flat-brimmed Stetson sombrero. He looked to
be a few years older than Cord, maybe thirty-eight or forty,
and he sat erect and a little canted to his left, to favor the
revolver Cord figured was on his right hip. Facing the man
in black, so his back was to Cord, was a miner, in dusty
canvas pants and an overshirt. There was a three-quarters-
full bottle in the center of the table, and a glass in front of
each man. The miner picked up the bottle by the neck and
filled both glasses, then tossed his shot back. The man in
black let his drink sit.

Some maverick-sect preacher? Cord speculated, or maybe
a gravedigger or embalmer. Or maybe someone more intimately involved with death, because Cord felt the aura of it
about him, in the way he sat motionless and in his eyes,
focused on distant events at the same time he listened to the
man across from him.

Cord sipped his drink and chased it with a swallow of the
water. It was warm but sweet. From the corner of his eye
he watched the man in black take a gold coin from his vest
pocket, hold it edge-up on the tabletop with his forefinger,
and flick it so it went spinning off across the table toward
the miner. The miner watched it approach and then his hand
darted out and snatched up the coin. He nodded at the man
in black and made his way steadily to the door, not drunk
at all.

Cord turned back to the bar in time to see a familiar face
in the mirror above it. The doors were still swinging from

the miner's exit as the man came in and made for the bar. Cord pondered and came up with a name: Jimbo Sundown, the man called himself. He was dark-looking and liked to let slip he was half-breed son to a Comanchero chief and a captured Englishwoman. He thought it would bring an automatic reputation for mystery and cunning and quick killer instincts.

That sort of posturing might have worked among the working men of a place like Minertown, but on the outlaw trail it was common knowledge that Jimbo Sundown's real name was a goulash of *o*'s and *i*'s that no one could remember. He was a second-generation Bohemian from Hartford, Connecticut, who had come West on the run and had never been more than a petty sort of conman, occasional horse thief, and would-be whoremonger. Cord wondered which of his trades Sundown was currently pursuing. He could not feature the kid doing any real work, especially something as demanding as digging or lumberjacking.

The saloon was filling more rapidly now, and one of the few open spaces at the bar was next to Cord. Sundown came up to it, licking his lips like a man with a powerful taste for alcoholic beverage. When the bartender had splashed whiskey into a shot glass, Sundown raised it to his lips, threw back his head—and recognized Cord in the mirror. He froze for a moment, then put down his drink without tasting it.

"'Lo, Jimbo," Cord said to the mirror in a low voice. "I see you're buying your own drinks."

Jimbo Sundown was in no way pleased at this encounter. He started to turn away, but Cord grabbed his elbow, deliberately digging his fingers into the joint tendons, where he knew it would hurt. "Drink your drink, Jimbo. You're not so prosperous you can walk away from whiskey."

"What do you want?" Sundown had been whipped back in Hartford and chased out of his family home, and he'd been whipped again periodically since his arrival on the frontier. Cord could hear the whippings in the whine of his voice.

"Want to buy you a drink, Jimbo," Cord said.

"The name ain't Jimbo anymore. It's Duke."

Cord laughed, not pleasantly. "Jimbo suits you."

"I got tired of Jimbo. I needed a change."

"You haven't changed, Jimbo," Cord said. "Boys like you never do." He tossed a five-dollar gold piece on the bar and picked up the Beam bottle and glasses, squeezing a bit more pain into Sundown's elbow to gentle him down.

Cord led the kid to a table near the wall. When they were seated, Cord shot a glance at the man in black two tables away, but he was staring straight ahead, his drink glass still full in front of him. If he had picked out Cord as the only other stranger in this saloon—and Cord had a hunch he had—he gave no sign of it.

Cord refilled his own glass and turned it between two fingers. "Tell me some news, Jimbo," he said. "Old pals like us, we ought to share the news."

Jimbo Sundown smiled weakly.

"Talk to me, Jimbo," Cord said in the same tone he might use on a green-broke colt.

"Nothing much to say. Good times. You know."

"Yeah, I know. I know something else too. I hear an old pal of mine is got real good times. I'd like to look him up."

"What for?"

"I loaned him ten bucks."

Jimbo Sundown's dark complexion was turning ashy.

"You coming down with the influenza, Jimbo? You too sick to talk?"

But Sundown had already figured out that talking and his health were intimately entwined. "I'm fine. I'm having a high time, sitting and passing the bacon with you."

"You know the old pal I'm talking about."

"Maybe."

But Cord had pulled back, tipped his chair against the wall. The man in black finally drank his drink, rose and went past on the way to the swinging doors. Cord flicked his eyes at the man and said, "Mark him," and Jimbo Sundown turned to look at the dark man too.

"Who is he?" Cord said when the man had gone out.

"Don't know. Some stranger, like you. I never seen him before."

"You could find out."

"I ain't working for you," Jimbo Sundown said sullenly.

Cord pointed a finger at him. "You'll do any goddamned

thing I tell you to. You'll do it and you'll like it. Tell me that you will."

"All right," Sundown muttered. "Take it easy."

"Now—" Cord said. "You tell me about Chris Kelly."

Jimmy Sundown turned a shade grayer, and his eyes screwed up, almost like he was fixing to cry. "Don't know nothing about Chris Kelly," he grumbled, petulant as a child.

"Don't you lie to me, Jimbo. Sometimes when people lie to me I just go batshit. You know about that, don't you, Jimbo?"

"I heard."

"Then save us both some craziness."

Jimbo drank his drink and coughed. Cord refilled the glass.

"I hear Chris ain't doing so good these days."

"How's that?"

Jimbo Sundown drank again and sat a moment basking in the liquor's warmth. He was a shot braver when he went on. "He ain't doing so good after all. He's fallen in with strangers."

Cord took out his makings from his shirt pocket, started to worry open the drawstring pouch, then changed his mind. He never had been worth a damn at building cigarettes, and he realized that without Chi around to roll them for him, he had cut down on his smoking. Jimbo Sundown looked hungrily at the tobacco. Cord put it back in his pocket.

"That bunch at Lewiston," Jimbo Sundown said, "they wasn't his regular gang. He don't have no regular gang these days, and has to settle for just boys, and sometimes downheel scum. He shoulda known better. We know better, don't we." He was behind his third drink now, and feeling tougher, staring bright-eyed at Cord and talking like they were cronies.

"Which boys?"

"You ever hear of Pete Hake? Little skinny drink of beer, crabbed legs, did a few years in Yuma for raping and killing some squawman's Indian bitch. He behaved hisself in the hole, so after a time they put him on a work crew, and he beat two guards half to death with a flat-blade shovel and lit out."

Jimbo Sundown smiled at his drink. People didn't listen

to him that often, so this was a treat. "There's one named Jonnie Frye, an Aussie. They shipped him from England to Sydney for something or another and lost him over the mountains and into the outback in about a week. He came back to San Francisco—said the London streets were too dangerous these days. He made enough to get back on his feet by pulling citizens into alleys and taking their watches and pocketbooks. I heard he didn't hurt the ones that played along, but the ones who lipped off got their skulls cracked on the paving stones."

Jimbo Sundown was hearing how important he sounded, and liking it. "About the only one seems able to keep any kind of rein on those two boys—besides Chris hisself, I mean—is the one they call the Chief. Comanche, but his own people ran him out of the Indian territories for horse thievery, introducing, and this habit he has of killing folk in bar fights. Mean as a starved dog when he drinks. He'd chew your leg off, strip it of meat, and beat in your face with the bones."

Cord wondered how the Comanche got along with Pete Hake, the squaw-killer. But he had seen stranger alliances among the community of crooks. There was Jaeger and Governor Majors, for one . . .

Jimbo Sundown drank again. "Those are the stories I hear. I don't really know nothing." He grinned at Cord like he was being really clever.

"What about the woman?" Cord asked in a low voice.

Jimbo Sundown's grin blinked out like a grass fire in a cloudburst. "Don't know any women."

"I wonder why," Cord needled. But here was clearly a dangerous topic, more dangerous in Sundown's mind than the immediate threat Cord was posing. Cord sensed he had pushed the kid about as far as he would go without pain, and just now Cord did not have the taste for that.

"Where are they now?" Cord said.

"I heard talk. Rumor is they were sighted in the panhandle country a couple times this week."

"Whereabouts?"

Jimbo Sundown considered. "Rathdrum." He gave Cord a shy grin. "My honor, that is all I know."

"I trust you." Cord smiled back. "'Course I do, because you know how I get when people lie to me."

"Right," Jimbo Sundown said quickly. "I know."

"You find out about that man in black," Cord told him. "If I happen to come back and ask you about him, I want ready answers." Cord pushed back his chair and stood. "Have a good time with this bottle. You deserve it."

"That's right," Jimbo Sundown said defiantly. "I do." He grabbed it with both hands, as if willing to fight for the whiskey if Cord changed his mind.

On the street in front of the Galena, Cord retightened the cinch of the gelding's saddle. The night was just touching twilight, and as Cord straightened he caught movement in the shadow of the marquee of the shabby hotel across the street.

A figure stepped from the shadow: the man in black. This time he openly met Cord's gaze, barely nodding in acknowledgment of the mutual recognition. But any taste Cord might have had for this sort of bluff-and-bluster game had been spent on Jimbo Sundown. Cord turned away, swung into the saddle, and headed up the street away from the main part of town.

Full dark was still at least an hour away, and Rathdrum wasn't much more of a ride than that. Cord thumped the gelding and headed him up-country, away from the lakeside meadows and into the timber.

Chapter Seven

RATHDRUM WAS A WORKING TOWN, AND STILL halfway a camp. It existed for the service of the loggers and trimmers and teamsters and sawmill hands. There was not a job of work among the spectrum of lumbering that did not make urgent demands on a man's muscles and bones and stamina, so even those who were not out in the timber camps were generally too exhausted for nightly carousing. It was ten o'clock by the time Cord passed the first camp on the outskirts, and he saw plenty of tents but few lights. These men had not been back in the forest more than a week since the end of spring break-up. They were paid by the tree-foot, and would not likely waste daylight with sleep.

Cord was tired himself. He had been riding hard for three days out of Boise and felt like he had gotten nowhere. When he came into Rathdrum, the few lights that showed above the little street's storefronts threw weary shadows over hard-pan dust pavement where nothing moved.

There was only one hotel, and it looked to have four rooms and no name. The lobby was dark; he'd have to roust someone up before he got a bed. He'd try the saloon first. Cord had been in small towns like this where the hotel man drank and drifted off early, leaving the keys and register book with the barkeep. Cord tethered the black, stocking-footed gelding in front of the shadowy hotel, which was across from the saloon. He turned to untie his saddlebags and saw a figure come out of the saloon and stand silhouetted in its doorway.

Cord squinted and made out it was the man in black, from the Galena in Coeur d'Alene.

The son of a bitch must have made a hard ride to beat

him here. Which suggested to Cord another mystery: How did the bastard know where he was heading?

Cord considered coincidence, and while he pondered the man across the street stood holding a whiskey glass but not drinking, and sure as hell staring straight at Cord, who decided this was no coincidence, after all. All this—the backlighting that deliberately made the man an easy target, the rude scrutiny—this was some sort of cock-of-the-rock dare. The man was building a case for pointless trouble.

But Cord needed to know why the other man was latching on. It might be a lead, and he was plenty shy of those.

So Cord left the saddlebags and his Winchester where they were, and crossed the quiet street toward the barroom, moving with neither haste nor leisure, his right hand loose at his side and inches from the butt of his Colt, the picture of a man who was interested in being careful without stirring needless trouble.

Cord stepped up on the boardwalk, moving soft-footed and casual.

"Hold up," the man said, his voice soft and not so much deep as rich in timbre, flowing out in an easy southern drawl. It was the voice of a deliberate and confident man.

Cord stopped. The man was facing him, a couple steps off to the left, leaving Cord a clear line to the saloon doorway—if he wanted to try to take it.

Cord looked at the man and took a step past.

The man in black took hold of Cord's left bicep. "Hold up, I said."

Five nerveless seconds passed—and Cord shrugged free.

Before he could make another move, the man slipped a little Remington over-and-under .22 derringer into Cord's navel.

"These little slugs burn as fiery as their big brothers," the man in black said. "Hold up is what I said, and hold up is what I mean."

"Put up the gun."

"We want to talk."

"Fine," Cord said. "Put up the goddamned gun."

In minute degrees the derringer stopped exerting pressure against Cord's gut. Cord shook himself a little, as if he were trying to relax after a serious fright, and then he turned just slightly and hooked a short hard blow that connected perfectly with the man's chin. The man in black let go of Cord's arm and slammed back into the wall of the saloon. He fought to keep his feet, but his knees went rubbery and he slid down the wall and sat against it, his legs splayed out in front of him like a doll's. Cord started to kick in a couple of the man's ribs, then checked himself. He stared down into the man's glazed eyes for a moment, then pushed into the saloon.

One drink would do more good than harm. It was an old orthodoxy, and as such had caused its share of trouble, but in this case it seemed to Cord it applied aptly enough. The day had been longer and more frustrating than he would have liked, and surely it was no time to sink his angers in a long, hard boozing session. But one drink?

This saloon was rough-hewn and contained nothing that did not contribute to its purpose, which was whiskey drinking and the desperate sort of fun that went with it. There was a plank counter laid over four empty nail kegs, a back-shelf with two dozen bottles and about the same number of glasses, four or five tired customers at two tables and three at the bar, one sad-faced fat whore playing solitaire, and a middle-aged barkeep with a nose the size and color of a yam.

Cord crossed to the barman, put both hands on the bar where everyone could watch them, smiled cordially, and laid a finger alongside his own nose, like Saint Nick in the poem. "You must have been a box-fighter in your younger days," Cord said, companionable as he could.

The bartender shook his head no. "I got this by sticking it into business that wasn't mine," he said. "It's a habit I broke a long time ago."

"Along with your nose." Cord smiled. "Bourbon. Water back if it's fresh."

"Gettysburg," the bartender said.

"Say what?"

"That was the last time anything in here was fresh."

The bartender brought a bottle and shot glass, and a tumbler of water. Cord poured his whiskey carefully and was fixing to drink when he heard a sudden chorus of chairs scraping back behind him.

Cord turned in time to see the man in black standing inside the door. Cord saw him bring up the derringer in both hands from a range of maybe five yards. Cord saw him cock and squeeze the trigger and heard the thin report, and thought he saw the explosion of fire.

Cord's Stetson jostled, and the tips of his hair felt the passage of the little lead slug, yet he was untouched. Cord managed to hold still, frozen like an arch-backed cat facing down a mongrel dog.

The man in black resighted down the two inches of the derringer's length, squinting judiciously. The stacked barrels looked dark, as if monsters lurked within.

The little gun exploded in Cord's face again.

Cord's hat flipped backwards, turned a somersault in the air, and landed atop the whiskey bottle behind him. The man in black smiled pleasantly and said, "Ringer."

"Two shots is what that popgun holds." Cord's voice sounded strange, even to himself. The fingers holding the shot glass were a little wet. Cord drank what was left, sat the glass on the bartop without looking back, then eased his Peacemaker from its holster. "What are you figuring on now?"

"Like I said," the man drawled in his round-edged southern tones. "We want to talk."

Cord stared at the man in amazement—and could not suppress a bark of laughter. He holstered his revolver and shook his head, grinning. "You sure seem to be dying for a conversation."

Behind Cord, the bartender said, "There is just one thing."

The bartender held a double-barrel, the side-by-side pipes sawed off so the whole thing was no more than a foot and a half long. A gun like that would be useless as a handful of dirt in a street shoot-out, but for short-range work—like keeping indoor order—it could chew a man to stew meat and still retain a load for anyone who missed the point. The bartender stood three steps down from Cord, where he could cover him, the man in black, and whoever else had a notion to act up.

No one moved, until one of the men at the tables pushed back his chair and stood, shaking his head in disgust. "Shit," he said to no one, "what in hell do you have to do for some quiet relaxation in this goddamned town?"

The painted girl at the side table stopped her endless card playing. "You got five bucks, I'll show you a place." She said it so solemnly that no one else laughed, and her laughing was a wheezing sad business.

"Guns on the bar, gents," the ex-pug bartender ordered, waggling the cut-off double-barreled scattergun.

The man in black reached carefully into his vest pocket, using two fingers only, and came out with a twenty-dollar gold piece. He flicked it into the air, and it arced lazily past Cord's head to hit the planking in front of the bartender. The coin landed perfectly flat, so it did not roll, did not move at all while the echo of its clink faded in the room. Cord frowned at the coin, looked up again at the man in black. Here was someone who could do certain kinds of sorcery with his hands. It was a skill only partially learned: It began with lots of practice, but when the practice was put to work, the strange quick shots of men like these did not seem so much a result of that practice as of force of will, and some impossible gun-trick came sure and easy. Cord knew something about such fast-handed spell casting.

The bartender picked up the gold piece and put down the shotgun. "What're you drinking, gents?" he asked with no irony at all.

The man in black broke open the breech of his sneak-gun, seated two pencil-thin cartridges, and snapped the gun shut. He looked around and smiled at the eyes that were fixed on him. "Nothing more dangerous than an empty gun." He crossed to the bar and lifted Cord's Stetson so he could look over the bottle, nodded his approval, and said to the bartender, "I'll share with my friend here." Almost as an afterthought he handed the hat to Cord.

Cord stared at the two little holes in the crown, one a half-inch from the other. "Only had this hat six months," Cord said.

"Too bad," the man drawled. The bartender brought another glass, and the man in black took it and the bottle to a vacant table, next to a battered piano with no front panel and a half-dozen broken strings. The other men in the room were back to their quiet drinking, like the floor show was over. These men had drifted through the logging West, and had seen some things. Some men got killed and others did not, and either way their work in the woods would be just as arduous and dangerous the next day.

"You are going to have to get a new one," the man in black said. "Fellow in your business can't go around with bullet holes in any part of his wardrobe. Holes like that, they let in the ghosts."

Cord wondered what manner of ghosts pursued this man; he had a hunch he had turned a few men into shades at one time or another. But they were not here to discuss gunman metaphysics.

"I didn't break your jaw, looks like," Cord said, "and you didn't put a bullet in my brainpan. So the foolishness is over and we are even up. Now—state your business."

The man offered his hand across the rough tabletop. "Lanett Sayre," he announced. "You are Cord."

"Lanett?"

"A kinfolk name—my mother's side of the family. She loved it, and I can't befriend a man who finds it humorous."

Cord poured drinks. Sayre watched his hands, accepted his full glass, and let it sit. "How do you know me?" Cord asked.

"My business. I also know you are seeking Chris Kelly."

"So?"

"So—so am I."

"Your business," Cord guessed. He was adding up some ideas.

Sayre shrugged. "People will pay me money for that man, people who want him stopped. That's my profession: making bad men stop." The corners of his mouth turned upward a little. "I do it for money."

"You fixing on taking in my pelt, bounty man?"

"You're not worth so much as you once were. You needn't worry."

"Actually," Cord said, "I wasn't that worried." He drank, and the two men traded cold smiles. After a moment Cord took Sayre's proffered hand, and they shook.

"We are hunting the same man," Sayre said. "We can side each other."

Cord stared at the man in disbelief. "Why would I help a bounty hunter?" He kept his voice low and even, and mostly free of anger. "For years I was waiting for some bounty hunter to put a hole in my spine. Nobody holds dead-or-alive paper on me now, but I remember how it felt."

"We got a common enemy."

"We do like hell," Cord snapped. Tracking down Chris Kelly, a man who had shared his past, had already rubbed Cord's sensibilities raw. The notion of teaming up with someone like this Sayre, who sold corpses like a butcher sold sides of beef, was salt on Cord's exposed nerve ends.

"You got some high-blown notions, Mister Cord," Sayre said stiffly, and Cord wondered just how much the bounty hunter did know about him and Kelly, and maybe Chi. "I am going after Kelly, with you or through you. Guess you feel the same way. It is going to happen, nothing to stop it. The only question is, are we going to fight each other first? It would be a damned fool business to kill over the man, seeing as how he is already condemned."

Sayre smiled into Cord's scowl. "I am willing to deal. This can accrue to both of our benefits. We do not have to be friends, but we can be partners for our purpose. I give my word to be true to our bargain, and that's it. I don't go back on my word. People cheat on me, and the war starts, but I do not cheat first."

"State your bargain," Cord said. "This talk is going nowhere." The man impressed and horrified Cord at the same time. He wondered if Sayre wasn't ignoring about half of life, the best half at that. Trailing through life on the edge of law made many men bitter, and then gunhand hardness became a defense not only against other men's bullets but against emotion as well. For bitter men, emotion could cripple as badly as lead.

"No," Sayre drawled. "Talk never won battles."

"You'd know."

"I won all my battles." Sayre's eyes softened a bit. "I did not lose the war. I would have fought them until every Blue was dead."

"Carolina?" Cord guessed.

"Georgia. Which is where I would be buried, if they had not surrendered."

"But they did."

Sayre finally drank, putting down his shot in one neat gulp. "I learned a rule at my father's table: Never move from that which you know is correct. I could not live by that rule in Georgia, so I came West, where I could. Men commit depredations, the law puts money on them, I collect that money. These men are fair game—so says the law, and the law is right. Our law in the South was right, but the masses would not defend it in the end. Here a man only needs himself to defend the right law."

"You're a lucky man," Cord said. "You've never got to wrestle with decisions. Your choices are already made, a whole lifetime of them."

Sayre refilled his glass and let it sit, staring at the oily surface of the whiskey as if he had momentarily lost the thread of the conversation. "You listen to me, Mister Cord," he said finally. "There is three thousand dollars on Chris Kelly, dead or alive, since he started shooting bankers and killing town marshalls."

"You sure he is the murderer?"

"Nope. Doesn't matter. We are talking dollars and the law, which is not necessarily the same as facts. Three thousand on Kelly, one thousand a man on Pete Hake and the Australian. There is California and Federal money both on the Comanchero, two thousand total. One story has a boy named Billy Pate riding with them, worth five hundred in Texas. Normally that ain't hardly enough to justify rail-shipping his carcass to Austin, but in this case he won't be much trouble to add to the rest." All this in the same unhurried, neutral Georgia drawl.

"Then there is the woman," Cord said with the same neutrality. "What is she worth to a bounty man?"

"They call her Jewel," Sayre said. "Talk is that she rides and shoots sharp as any man. But then, you'd know about hard-riding women, wouldn't you?"

Cord ignored the bait. "Seven thousand five hundred dollars," he said.

"Plus a thousand for her," Sayre admitted. He grinned. "Maybe after I get a-holt of her I can figure ways to make more."

Cord did not like that crack, but it fit what he could see of Sayre. Actually Sayre did not make a distinction between the woman and the rest of them: They were all worth money to him.

"So what is your plan?" Cord said. He was coming to hate this conversation. What he proposed to do was bad enough; making pacts with someone like Sayre was downright unnatural. It was like a sheep making love to a coyote.

Yet Sayre was right: They were both bound to seek and subdue Chris Kelly, and no way around it but partnering. Unless Cord killed this man, right here and now. But even as he had the notion, he knew he would not. There was too much killing ahead, probably, and already Cord had lost whatever taste he might ever have had for that sort of business.

"Talking to you, first off," Sayre said. "Trying to figure some way I can collect for Chris Kelly without having to gun it out with you." Sayre smiled. "You are thinking along the same lines."

"You got an offer in mind?"

"Something to do with teaming up. Maybe you can get inside the gang, you being what you are." Sayre snapped his fingers, like something had just come to mind. "Sure. You and Mister Chris Kelly were close partners once."

Cord did not like hearing this. His time with Chris Kelly was brief, and not common knowledge now. This Sayre was good at his work. He listened and remembered what he heard. Probably paid attention to old posters, knew the outlaw histories as they were told around campfires, and which parts were likely true. He knew who rode with whom, and who got damaged when it came apart.

"So what do you want, Mister Cord, aside from the assistance of one who knows man-hunting."

It was about time this came to a point. "I want Chris Kelly. You can have the others."

Sayre considered. "The money works out—three thousand for you, near twice as much for me—only you're not in this for money." Sayre folded his arms around his full drink and leaned forward, smiling, inviting confidences between men. "What do you want with Kelly? Are you planning on preaching to him until he agrees to walk the Lord's path from here on? Are you planning on saving your old partner's soul and ass?"

"I'm planning on turning him up to the law," Cord said coldly. He fished his makings from his shirt pocket. He hated saying it right out like that. The pronouncement of it seemed to set his course, and it was a slimy trail he was headed down. Cord creased a square of brown cigarette paper, and it ripped between his fingers. He wished he had not spoken— and wondered how he would ever force himself to engineer this betrayal, when just the speaking of it rattled him so. He shoved the pouch angrily back where it belonged.

Even Sayre seemed startled. "You mean give him up straight, so they can send him to that prison they got on the east side of Boise for what time they let him live? You must have some real trouble between you." But then a light came into the bounty hunter's eyes. "No trouble," he corrected himself. "Your woman, the one they call Chi. Where is your woman?"

Cord slammed a fist down on the table, hard enough to draw the eye of everyone in the place. The bartender turned and let his hand rest on the stock of the racked shotgun.

"You stick to your business," Cord said in a low voice, "and you keep your nose out of mine. Reasons don't pull the trigger. I want Chris Kelly, alive. You know that and you know me, and you don't need to know anything else."

"All right," Sayre said mildly. "You have yourself a deal." He poured two more shots of bourbon and pushed one in front of Cord, then raised his glass. Cord blinked. This wasn't going as he figured—but then, nothing was, since that bastard Jaeger had bushwhacked them in Twin Falls. Ever since that night Cord had felt like a bug under a microscope, seemingly given his head, but really under close scrutiny.

Well, here was another time when the choices had been pruned out for him, and nothing to do for it. Cord raised his glass, nodded, and drank. The bourbon was starting to touch him; he'd either sleep dreamless that night or be knocked cold in some whiskey-driven trouble.

"First off," Cord said, "the pushing is done with. We've both got it out of our systems."

Sayre smiled. "Yes sir."

"Next thing: You got any line on Kelly?"

"As it happens," Sayre drawled, "I do. You would tend to figure that he'd want out of this territory, what with bounty hunters and the Governor and even the odd outlaw on his trail. But it turns out that there is a place right here in Idaho that is safe for them as Tibet. When were you in these parts last?"

"Not for six or seven years."

"Then I guess you never heard of Lord."

"Lord?"

Sayre refilled Cord's glass. "You might want to try building that cigarette once more," he said. "I have a tale to tell."

It was three springs earlier, Sayre told Cord, when the man named Dunraven went prospecting in the timberline country northwest of Sandpoint and north of Priest Lake, not far from the Canadian border. It was rugged, isolated country, the low draws filled with blown-down trees and the ridges sharp rocky knife-edges, and it had been prospected by others years before, without much luck.

But Dunraven was an educated man with some book knowledge of geology, and besides, he had a hunch. He followed it up a trickle-creek above a bigger drainage that ran into the Priest.

Dunraven had made a life of long-odds ventures. At the time of his prospect he was a man without family, future, or much pride. He had nothing going for him with the possible exception of chance, and he knew it.

His was a prominent English family from Tunbridge Wells, the second son of a Member of the House of Lords, according to one story that might have been true. His older brother prepared to take over the administration of the family estate, fortune, and reputation. Dunraven had none of the responsibilities, and, said Sayre with a smile, his idle hands became the devil's playthings.

There was an indiscretion, and a bulging-bellied servant girl who demanded payment of a fair sum of money, followed swiftly by one-way passage to Boston for Dunraven. His father the Earl was a civilized man, though. Dunraven carried to the New World a letter to a second cousin with attorney's chambers on Beacon Street, requesting that he assist his exiled relative in reading for the bar. Dunraven also had his father's promise of a monthly remittance large enough to allow him to live like a gentleman—provided that he make no attempt to contact any member of his immediate family for the rest of his life.

Boston did not suit Dunraven. The law struck him as codified sophistry. Also, there were too many like him, and when he began to despise them as parasites he despised himself as well. For two consecutive months he did not visit the Shipper's Express to pick up his remittance, and in the third month he left Boston. It was after the war, and he joined the host of drifters going West. Dunraven went on drifting and ended up trailing a single jackass up some headwater rill of the Priest.

He spent most of the summer working his way up the stream, and on a sand bar on a little shelf above a three-foot waterfall, he brought in a strike. In the first week of working it Dunraven panned about fifty ounces, which was anyway better than a summer's worth of day wages, but after that the pickings dropped off, until he was barely panning color. When another prospector drifted over from the next gully and offered $2,000 in dust for the claim, Dunraven took it before the man could change his mind.

No more than four feet downstream from where Dunraven had been panning there was a little whirlpool. The new owner figured that it would settle out anything heavy churned up by the water-drop, and he was right. Within two days he had panned 107 ounces, and within two weeks he had one thousand ounces of clean dust, flake gold, and even a few pea-sized nuggets—nearly $20,000 dollars' worth in all.

Dunraven was in Sandpoint when the news came in. Understandably chagrined, he reacted by drinking up his $2,000 and then heading back upriver. By the time he got back, a mining camp of sorts had sprung up around his one-time

claim. They named the rill after him—Dunraven Creek, it
became—because that was tradition, and men depending on
Fate's whimsies do not lightly ignore tradition. But they
called the camp Lord, after the ironic tag "m'Lord" they
had hung on Dunraven himself.

Another man would have been beaten, but in comparison
to the rest of Dunraven's life this misfortune did not stand
out. He took himself further up the creek and found another
place, not so rich as the other but paying colors for certain.
In a month of lonely back-breaking work, with fall coming
up strong, he took out $5,000. This time he sold out on
shares, taking $500 against a fifty percent absentee owner-
ship. That fall before the snows, and through the next spring,
the outstanding shares changed hands several times, but each
new claim-holder managed to pass on to Dunraven a few
hundred or a thousand dollars.

For reasons known only to himself, Dunraven determined
to put down his roots in Lord. Perhaps it was because it was
the first place he'd enjoyed anything like success and esteem;
perhaps he had become convinced of the blackness of his
soul and felt that he belonged in the company of miners,
grifters, gamblers, and whores who made up camptown society; perhaps he had simply learned the surest way to mine
gold, which was out of other diggers' pockets. Whichever,
he bought up the faro tent and the shanty saloon and the
Chinese opium hole, and he paid the camp's two pimps to
leave and its eight whores to stay. He built cabins and re-
covered in two months' rent the cost of construction. He
grubstaked likely miners, and though only one in ten hit
paydirt, Dunraven made more than he spent. A year after
he'd hit and lost his first strike, he built a three-story hotel,
with a saloon and casino on the first floor, offices and whore-
cribs on the second, and hotel rooms on the third. He put
his name on it and told the diggers it was the grandest place
north of Coeur d'Alene and west of Missoula, and maybe it
was.

That summer, the strike on Dunraven Creek played out.
A few men, too broke to buy wagon-space out on the valley,
stayed on through August working the tailings, but by first
snow Dunraven was alone, watching from the window of his

pleasure palace as thick, wind-driven flakes billowed through the open doors of abandoned shacks as the last man left.

"The way I figure," Sayre told Cord across the table of the saloon in Rathdrum, "it was because for the only time in his life Dunraven had a place of his own. The family home back in England, that was his pappy's while he lived and his brother's after that. In Lord he was alone, but at least he was on a piece of ground that was no one's but his."

Cord wondered if Sayre had been disenfranchised in something like the same way. Cord imagined a white mansion, back from the road and half-hidden in a stand of pecan trees and spiky palmetto, a formal garden of roses, tulips, irises, and flowering kale, with walkways paved with crushed oyster shells. Cord saw green meadows fenced by a boxwood hedge trimmed flat as a tabletop, broken by a gateway arch displaying the family name. Within the mansion were house servants in livery, speaking fine as any white man, and beyond the hedge, out of sight of the house, the field niggers working the crops.

And then the Union troops coming through, giddy with power because the war was as good as won and the Rebels subdued: Cord saw the burned remnants of the plantation as Sayre must have seen it when he came home, the women bereft, the slaves gone, the grounds bare as desert.

"Dark Tom, they called him."

Cord was jerked out of his reverie. Why was he suddenly feeling sorry for this bitter bounty hunter? Cord's people had lived not so far away, as distances were measured in the West, and all he knew about niggers is that he'd worked like one every day of his growing-up life.

"Dark Tom McVey," Sayre said, like he enjoyed the way the name filled his mouth, and waited for Cord's full attention to return to the matter at hand before going on with his story.

Dark Tom McVey was a badman of minor repute, and he rode into the ghost town of Lord during an early November Indian summer thaw a year and a half back, after Dunraven had been by himself in his domain for a couple of long months. There were five rough men with him, and they were all on the run from a failed bank job in Spokane. "They made Washington a goddamned state since I was there last," McVey declared. "They shoulda put up signs. Ain't never had luck with banks outside the territories. They make a state and everything goes to hell." At the time they came upon Lord, McVey and his bunch were hightailing it for Canada and looking for provisions and a place to rest their horses, or preferably steal new ones.

McVey reined up in front of Dunraven's place, hollered, "Hello, the cathouse!" and put a couple of shots in the sign with Dunraven's name on it. When Dunraven came out the door to investigate, McVey lowered his revolver on the dude and announced his intention to kill him and loot his town.

"I dare say that would be a mistake," Dunraven said coolly.

McVey showed black rotted teeth in a grin. "What would you do if you was us, m'Lord?"

"I would pay me for my whiskey, my provender, and the clean linen of my bedrooms."

Dunraven waited with icy politeness until McVey and his men stopped guffawing. Then he explained: If they killed him they would never discover his best liquor or the butchered beef stored up in the snow caves above town or the glen below where he autumn-grazed his horses—and they would face a charge of murder. On the other hand, if they became paying guests they would be most welcome and guaranteed an unmolested sojourn, assured of his discretion now and after they left.

Lastly Dunraven played his hole card: As valued clients, Lord would always be open to them and their colleagues as an outlaw hole-up, a robbers' roost.

Dark Tom McVey was not a smart man, but he had spent enough months of his life shivering in some high-country lean-to or sweating out a desert's quiet summer fury, waiting for the law to lose interest in him. His joints were stiffening and less tolerant of bed-roll nights. He dug out the few hundred dollars he and his boys had managed to take from the Spokane bank before the Pinkertons started firing from across the street, handed the currency to Dunraven, and said, "Bring on the cancan girls, m'Lord."

"Ever since," Sayre told Cord in the saloon, "that Lord

town has been temporary home to road agents and murderers and horse thiefs and so forth from all over the West. A lifetime of black-sheep orphancy, and now old Dunraven has found his home at last."

Cord knew of such places, such as Hole-in-the-Wall over in Wyoming, where Kid Curry and his brothers the Logan boys and Butch Cassidy and his Wild Bunch were reputed to hang out. Cord and Chi had always steered clear of such congregations. A community of criminals like that could draw the law like shit draws flies, and would one of these days as the crush of society closed down the old, free outlaw ways.

"You figure that's where we'll find Chris Kelly, in Lord," Cord said. Sayre had not told the long story just to pass the drinking time.

"I figure it's a strong possibility. There's been too many sightings of his gang in these parts for them all to be made up by bored farmers. If they are nearby, Lord is the likely place."

"How do you figure to find out for sure?"

Sayre smiled as if he had been anticipating the question with pleasure. "I figure on you riding in for a look-see."

"How's that?"

"I can't do it," Sayre said reasonably. "I been living off bounties almost since the war, and not everyone I brought in was cold, neither. There are living outlaws who know my face, and if one of them is there in Lord, they will kill me faster than a deacon can eat a free meal."

"I am disappointed in you." Cord shook his head. "Talking so tough a few minutes ago." He poured another drink.

"That place is running with hard men, as many as twenty at one time, sitting down for food together, sharing the same bottles."

"I've got a better chance of being known."

"That's right," Sayre said. "That's the point. Dunraven will know who you are, because part of his business is reading the posters, like me. It will count to your credit. You are a wanted desperado, exactly the sort of client Dunraven seeks."

Sayre was right, which did not mean Cord liked it. He

was tired of other people's being right, when what he was doing was so for-sure wrong.

"Something eating you?" Sayre inquired.

"This whole damned thing." Cord drank and ran his tongue along the edges of his teeth. "You know I was one-time partners with Kelly, and here I am fixing to turn him in."

"You had better get your mind settled right now."

"That's right," Cord said thickly.

"You had better be dead solid in how you see this," Sayre pressed. "You got to go in with a clear head, you know that good as I do. Otherwise you'll be bait for their dogs soon as you climb down from the saddle. You got to forget who Chris Kelly is, and you got to want him bad enough to taste the salt-blood flavor in the back of your mouth. When it is time to take him, you'd better not be thinking about anything else, especially muddled-up notions of right and wrong."

Cord hated what he was hearing, and knew it was true. And still he was miles from committed to all this.

"I'll ride out in the morning," he said. That would have to be answer enough. "How do you find this hideout town?"

"I'll get you on the trail come daylight."

"You got a plan for me, once I'm there?"

"Simple enough. You cut Kelly and his bunch out from the crowd—just like sorting cattle, except these got my brand. You get them out of town, where you and I can ambush them."

"Pretty," Cord said. "I can see it. Us riding alone like best pals, until you start shooting from out of some rockpile. Me in the middle of it, bullets flying everywhere, and you out of sight. My part sounds a little dangerous."

"You worry about taking Kelly alive, if you got to have him that way. The rest will go down, all around you. I don't miss."

"Neither do I," Cord said. "The first whiff of double-cross, and I get deadly accurate. Shoot the head off a snake at fifty steps."

"Good for you," Sayre said mildly.

"Once I get them set up, how do I tip you?"

"I'll be at the Timberjack House in Sandpoint. You'll think of something. Don't you always?"

Cord was weary of the man and his petty, jackass remarks. He tossed back his drink and poured one more, a nightcap.

"Tomorrow's your big day," Sayre said. "You might want to go easy on the juice."

Cord leaned forward. "I might want to rip off that grin of yours like it was a false mustache," he said in a low voice. "But I'm not going to do that, either."

He swallowed the second drink, stood a little awkwardly, and turned his back on the bounty man.

"Gets a little cold and lonely," Sayre murmured, "riding by yourself."

Cord spun around. "What the hell is that supposed to mean?" he said savagely.

Sayre pushed back his hat a little. "Just a thing to say."

But it was no thing to say, and Cord was going to prove that to the bounty man, right now.

Before he had a chance, someone tapped him on the shoulder.

It was the loudmouth who had complained after Sayre's demonstration of hat-shooting. "This was a quiet sort of place, bud," he said, "until you come in. Maybe you ought to leave."

The logger was tall as Cord and fifty pounds heavier, in heavy layers of thick wool that smelled of sweat and mildew. His hands were big, calloused, and gnarled as oak bark. He looked big and mean as a bear.

Cord grinned sheepishly. "Maybe you're right."

Cord feinted at moving past the man, then interlaced his fingers into a double fist and swung his arms around and hit the man at the point of his jaw, hard enough so Cord felt the shock all the way into his shoulders.

The logger's head moved maybe two inches. He looked at Cord through small dark pig eyes, grinned, and came at Cord with a lethal overhand right.

Cord was ahead of him. As the logger swung, Cord's Colt swept from his holster, and Cord stepped inside the blow and caught the logger alongside the head with the long gun barrel, hard as he could swing. It made a crack like a board breaking.

Everything stopped.

The logger stood there and swayed a little. His tiny eyes were glassy, but he did not go down.

Cord holstered the Colt. He double-cupped his hands again and reared back, putting all his weight behind this one. He came around from the right so his left hand absorbed most of the shock. It was instinct: Do not hit people with your gunhand, not if you plan on using it again soon.

The logger blinked and staggered a half step forward. Cord hit him again, coming up from under this time, and the logger stumbled back and tripped over a chair leg and went down atop the table where his buddies still sat. The tabletop shattered and its legs buckled and splayed, and the logger lay sprawled at his friends' feet in a jumble of arms and legs and kindling.

Cord stood over him, swaying a little and feeling better already. It was an old story with him: Contrary news would build up, one thing after another, until he lashed out. After that it was all right, at least for a time. He was no longer much interested in kicking in Lanett Sayre's face, so he turned to the bounty man, nodded at him, and touched two jaunty fingers to the brim of his hat, then went past the other men and out into the Idaho night.

Chapter Eight

THE MAN ON SENTRY DUTY DIDN'T HAVE MUCH to do. He was posted at the head of the gorge overlooking the only trail, which ran upstream along the drainage to dead-end at Lord. Few wandering strangers would appear in these parts, and those who did, out of curiosity or bad luck, would have to take the trail. The sentry could turn them back easily enough; if he had any wit, he could do it without raising suspicion or anger.

Still, he should have stayed halfway alert.

Instead he was taking it easy, sitting half-asleep in the saddle this drowsy morning, hands folded one atop the other over the horn and a cigarette dangling forgotten between his fingers. He was probably dreaming about his next time in a real town, or listening to his mind exaggerate some long-ago woman and how she had done him.

Cord hobbled the black gelding and made the last downhill stretch through the woods on foot, circling to keep behind the man and cursing silently each time a twig broke beneath his boot. But the guard was lost in his dozing, and Cord almost made it. A slip of rockfall slid loose under his feet as he braced to jump. The guard sat up, chucked away his forgotten cigarette, and looked around. He saw Cord, and his hand was jerking to the Colt on his left hip when Cord vaulted up on the saddle behind him.

"Son of a bitch," the man grunted. Cord got his left hand over the man's mouth, and he clamped down with his teeth on the fleshy ball of Cord's thumb. Cord drew his own revolver and clubbed the guard with the barrel. The man went limp, and Cord threw him out of the saddle and sat there, shaking his arm up and down, whipping the pain out of his thumb. It wasn't cut too bad. The guard's horse raised its head and looked around incuriously at Cord, the first time in all this that the animal had moved.

Cord slid down, got the unconscious guard under the arms, and managed to wrestle him up so he was draped over the saddle. He used the man's own rope to tie his wrists together, then his ankles, looping the two knots together on a tether so he would not roll off the horse while he was out, nor raise a ruckus when he came to.

He led the guard's burdened horse back up through the trees. The hobbled gelding nickered when it scented the other animal. When Cord reached it he tossed the other horse's reins over a branch. He took care rolling a cigarette, but he still came up with something thick and raggedy.

It was nearly time.

Time for Cord to go in and play his charade. He had

always hated acting out roles. Cord's most stony contempt was reserved for men who pretended to be what they were not, so now he seethed with contempt for himself. And this was no make-believe or even some conman grift; this was perjury, deceit, the basest sort of dishonesty.

From where he stood, near the top of the right-hand ridge above Dunraven Creek, he could see most of the little town of Lord. Dunraven must have had some prospector's luck after all, because his place was made for its present purpose, a natural fortress.

The dug-up flatland where Dunraven made his original strike was an ancient riverbar of gravel and sand, now littered with old flumes and timbering. But at its downstream end it cascaded nearly fifty feet into a steep-walled, rock-rimmed gorge, where the creek had cut its way down between high cliffs. The mountains rose directly from the cliffs, steep and dense with Douglas fir and ponderosa pine—except for about fifty yards along one side, below the flatland. Lord perched on this isolated natural shelf. It was a place where the sun would come up late and go down early.

The town was scattered about on the boulder-strewn clearing at the foot of the steep walls. No one had built down on the flats where the gold was mined, and the result was a town which could be defended like an old-time castle. From far above where he stood, Cord could hear the constant rush of the spring, swollen in its gorge by spring runoff from the huge snowfields above the treeline.

The only substantial building in the town was Dunraven's three-story monument. It was not so fine as Cord had expected. It looked to have never been painted, part of it built of rough whip-saw lumber and the rest of logs; additions looked to have been tacked on a half-dozen times. Around it in no particular order was a cluster of cabins, shanties, and a few tents; a faintly visible network of trails worn into the rock by usage ran between them.

Cord descended through the woods, leading the two horses. He came out of the rimrock a hundred yards downstream from Lord, meeting up with the trail near a crumbling point of rock hidden by a bend. The ledge was narrow and treacherous, only a few feet wide, with the cliff dropping off almost a hundred feet to the mud-thick creekflow surging past the boulders in the canyon below, and this would be the last cover. More of the town's natural barricades: Anyone riding this trail would be paying attention to where his mount set its foot down, not the possibility of ambush.

Well, that was all right. It was time to stand out and be seen.

But for a moment Cord stayed where he was, trying to pretend himself into the game he was about to play. He thought: *Just another thief in need of a layout for a while, paying his own way and dangerous as anybody, but all right, a good and true enough member of the owlhoot world.* The notion did not rest easy on his mind.

Yet when he came around into the open, riding the gelding and leading the guard's horse with his corpse in the saddle, he was a man with nothing but the time of day on his mind. They spotted him right away, it looked like. Men began to file out of the saloon that occupied the lower floor of Dunraven's place. They ranked themsleves out across the street, not blocking the hitching rail but almost. This was a somber and stiffly formal welcoming party, two dozen gunhands, some holding drinks and all of them silent and staring and waiting, ready to kill without many questions. The man on the horse was enough; maybe they did not even need that excuse. Each man stood with his working hand empty and loose and close to the holster.

A finer-looking crowd of hoodlums you would never see. It was strange, this many of them together, and Cord, seeing these dirty, squinting men who practiced his own trade, wondered at himself. A number of the men were fat and slack from too much time holing up and no daytime work for years—but maybe that was the price you paid for assurance you would not live your life as a farmer. Cord considered whether he was looking at his future.

And decided he was not. He was different from these men. He had gone outlaw in search of freedom, but these men wanted nothing but one easy gratification after another and no responsibilities, one more woman and one more drink and more of the same later on. These men did not care about freedom so much as taking, easy cruelty, and eating whatever was to hand.

All right, so he was not one of them—and it was time to stop daydreaming.

Because however yellow skinned and flaccid looking, these men were dangerous—despite grimy-rimmed bloodshot eyes and bulbous noses chased with broken capillaries, missing fingers and mouthsful of dark, rotten teeth, these men could shoot and would kill. They could not have survived without such abilities and inclinations.

Then the men all turned their heads. Cord stopped maybe thirty yards from the crowd and followed their gaze. The woman had come out of the saloon: Jewel, the one who was supposed to ride with Chris Kelly. It had to be.

Her hair was stuffed up into a high-crowned, dirty-brimmed Stetson. The hat had once been a rich palomino color, and probably expensive. The wisps that showed were dirty blond. Her features were regular—not striking, but somewhere on the outer edge of handsome. Once upon a time she was probably a girl run off from a Scandinavian sodbuster home somewhere on the plains, Cord guessed, strong enough to go her own way, which ended here.

She was tall, taller than most men in the crowd and only an inch or two shorter than Cord, and long-legged, with leather britches pulled tight into her crotch. She wore a matching leather vest. Her breasts, under a loose flannel shirt, were almost virginally high, and girlish more than sizable. Cord was weeks from a woman, and found himself watching her move and ignoring the men ranked before him.

She wore a Peacemaker on her hip, the same gun as Cord's, but it was not that alone that gave her a flavor of toughness and something like masculinity. Cord imagined some men would call her a name, as they did Chi, and wondered if she cared. Probably not. The remarks such men made when they thought she could not hear were masks over their own insecurities, and she would have little interest in insecure men. A few, stronger and more self-reliant, would find her a challenge. There was something to the way she moved that almost made Cord think it was just for him. Cord licked his dry lips: Well, yes, it figured that she would have learned that trick.

The men stood there ranked before him, watching Cord ride up and dismount and hitch the black gelding at the rail in front of the garish pleasure palace. The guard, sprawled and tied over his saddle, began to stir, moaning and trying to shake the ache out of his head. Cord drew his thin-bladed Stockman's knife and slit the ropes at the guard's wrist and ankles. The man slid himself off the saddle, and went down on one knee. The assembled mob looked at him incuriously, like stagehands at a long-running show.

"He isn't hurt bad," Cord said. The men looked up at him. "Coming in quiet, that seemed the right way." He gazed over the crowd, meeting the look of one man after another, and ended with Jewel. She returned the look, staring out from under the brim of her Stetson. She had very pale blue eyes. Cord grinned suddenly, insolent and almost crudely, and turned his back on all of them and went into the saloon. He left his saddlebags over the gelding's haunch and his Winchester in its saddle scabbard. There was no thievery where all men are thieves.

The interior gave Cord another insight into Dunraven: The Englishman had not wasted time and money with the facade of his establishment, but some care had been taken with the appointments of the barroom, the place where drinking men would be spending their time and money. There had probably been something close to opulence here during the boom, but now it had gone to seed. A wagon-wheel chandelier of coal-oil lamps hung over the center of the big room, but all the glass chimneys had long ago been shot off. There were bullet holes in the breasts of the naked women in the framed painting over the back bar, and the gaudy-colored six-foot wheel of fortune was permanently canted to one side and shoved back against the far wall. Incongruously, the bedsheet-sized mirror over the whiskey bottles was intact; Cord wondered who in this pug-ugly crew would want to see himself. There were nearly two dozen tables that had once been a matching set, now scarred with cigarette burns and the carved initials and obscenities of men who had nothing better to do with their time. The spittoons were real brass but pocked with dents, and cobwebs hung from a neglected piano which must have been freighted in at incredible effort and expense. All the usual trappings, but dirty and hard-worn and beat up, the tawdry decadence showing everywhere through the veneer of elegance.

Cord released the batwing doors, and they swung shut behind him on hinges that creaked for oil. Two men had stayed inside while the welcoming committee came out into the street. The bartender was a boy, maybe eighteen or nineteen, with sandy hair and dark, suspicious eyes. His open features were contorted into a scowl, which he seemed to consider the proper expression for greeting a stranger. His barman's shirt was graying but clean, and he wore a bow tie of black velvet. His left sleeve was folded at the elbow and pinned neatly to his shoulder; his right was rolled up above a huge lump of bicep, developed in compensation and out of all proportion to the rest of his slim body. The sleeve was held up by a royal blue satin garter: the one-armed man showing his pride.

The other man in the saloon was about Cord's age, and utterly grotesque, a cautionary case. His features were wrinkled far beyond his years, and his nose was a soft, lopsided lump, formless as melted wax. There was an obscene black-edged hole in his forehead at the bridge of his nose, as if acid had eaten into his flesh, and it gaped when he sucked breath. The man's hair and whiskers were spiky and prematurely gray, thin as dying plants. His feet were bare and calloused and filthy—Cord thought he could smell them from where he stood—and the man's britches, held up by suspenders over a filthy union suit, were so baggy he might have been carrying a load.

The man carried a broom, which would have made him the swamper, had he been able to sweep in a coherent fashion. Instead he seemed intent in rearranging the dust, which he went on doing for several moments after Cord came in. When he finally caught sight of the newcomer, he scuttled toward Cord in an awkward gimping walk which was not quite a limp, but more a lopsided hunched-over shuffle—and when he reached Cord he circled him like a dog sniffing a stump. Then he stepped back and said, "Howdy, howdy, howdy," in a lunatic singsong. Spittle sprayed from his mouth.

Cord found a coin in his pocket and flipped it in the air, and the swamper flailed at it with both hands and managed to bat it into the corner. He dropped his broom and fell to hands and knees and crabbed after it. The poor son of a bitch. Cord turned away and realized he had been breathing shallowly through his mouth to avoid the odor. Cord had seen the same sort of pox-eaten features and brain-soft lunacy in other barrooms in his day, and he knew what it meant: early death and no sorrow.

Cord left the swamper clawing for his coin and crossed to the bar. Behind him the swinging door screeched and moaned as the outlaw citizenry of Lord filed back into the room. They were still mostly silent, and they went to various tables as if seating had been assigned, watching Cord like playgoers awaiting the first curtain. Cord didn't see Jewel among them, nor Chris Kelly. He did catch sight of the guard he had cold-cocked, and curiously enough the man was watching him with as neutral an expression as the others, as if being ambushed and knocked out from behind was part of a normal day's business.

The bartender was the only one of the company who seemed to have any opinion on the goings-on: He scowled at Cord as if his presence was a deliberate and personal slur. Cord put both hands on the bar and smiled.

"Up them stairs." The bartender nodded in the direction of a flight of steps along the right-hand wall. His voice was unnaturally guttural, despite his efforts: the voice of a young man trying to sound tough. "Second door down the hall, the one with the sign."

"How's that?" Cord inquired.

"Up them stairs," the bartender recited. "Second door down the hall, the one w—"

"You got some creek water back there?"

"You gotta see Dunraven."

Cord broadened his grin. He looked over his shoulder and showed it to the assembled company. No one seemed much interested. "I've got to see Dunraven to get a drink of water?" he asked the bartender.

"Got to see Dunraven to get anything. This is his town."

"Must be nice, having your own town."

The bartender sighed. "Up them stairs," he began, as if he only knew one speech but was practiced at the recitation.

"Got it," Cord cut in. "Up them stairs." He turned toward them.

"One other thing," the bartender said.

Cord turned back. "What's that?"

"You want to keep in mind—" the bartender said, "anything happens up there that shouldn't, you are a dead man. You'll be in that creek you hear running way down below out there. There'll be plenty of lead to weigh you down, and nothing left for your kin to read over, if you got kin. You ever see anybody get et by fish? Your bones will wash up on a beach in Oregon." The bartender was grinning his toughman grin. He liked this speech even better than the one about the stairs.

"This is a bad town to get thirsty in," Cord said, but that didn't buy him any slack either, not from the hard-boy bartender or the crowd. He shook his head and turned and headed up the stairs. He was almost at the top when the barroom doors creaked again, and he looked down in time to see the blond woman, Jewel, come in. She glanced up at him and Cord thought he saw a rush of color rising over her long neck—but the light was dim for observing such subtleties, and it was probably his imagination. This town of Lord, with its sullen society of outlaws, was a place that promoted second thoughts. Cord grinned to himself.

You keep your mind on business, he thought. *And your hands off that woman.*

The sign on the second door read CHARLES STUART DUNRAVEN, PROP., CITY OF LORD. Cord knocked once and went in without waiting for a response.

The man behind the heavy oak desk was a duded-up toff, as if to establish immediately and beyond a shadow of a doubt that he was not of the grubby crew he served. Dunraven was around fifty, a slim, long-fingered, delicate-featured man who looked more like a concert pianist than the proprietor of an outlaw hole-up. He wore a fawn-colored suit, and a black-and-gold checkered necktie over a stiff white shirt. His hair, black and gray in equal parts, was slicked straight back, and his mustache was trimmed precisely and symmetrically.

"Yes?" he murmured. He executed even as simple a move as looking up with doll-like precision. His manner was polite, proper, but in no way familiar. Here was a man who kept all others at some distance, a top cock who meant to stay one.

A cut-glass decanter and a multifaceted matching tumbler, half-full of whiskey, sat on the desk before him, but only the vague cast of his eyes revealed that he was halfways drunk. Cord guessed he was always that way, never shit-faced and never dead-cold sober. Dunraven had been kicked in the ass all his life—out of England, out of Boston, out of his first paying gold claim—and had finally found a life he could abide. Yet he had paid the price with his humanity, and Cord sensed in him the constant anxiety that full-time drinking breeds.

"A glass of water," Cord said genially.

"I beg your pardon."

"I'd like a glass of water. The kid downstairs said I needed your say-so."

"I see." Dunraven stared at Cord and pondered this puzzle for a moment. Then he stood, went to a sideboard, and poured from a pitcher, offering the glass to Cord without taking it to him. Cord drank, sighed, and smacked his lips appreciatively. If Dunraven thought anything of this performance he gave no indication. He went back behind his desk and sank into his swivel chair. "Now then—" he said, "was there anything besides the salubriousness of our waters that brought you to Lord, Mister Cord?"

Dunraven smiled without warmth, opened the middle desk drawer, and took out a thick sheaf of paper, which he flopped on the desk next to his untouched drink. He shuffled through the pages, pulled out one, and reversed it toward Cord, so Cord could see it was a copy of the poster on him and Chi from the Pocatello job, offering a thousand dollars on each of them and signed by Governor William Deane Majors.

"My business requires me to maintain familiarity with present and potential customers," Dunraven said. "I dare say, though, that from what I have heard I did not expect to make your acquaintance, at least not here. They say you are not a chap to mob up with large groups of men." Dunraven shot a look at his glass, as if he wanted a drink but was shy about taking it in front of someone else. "In fact," he said, "I will be frank: You make me uneasy. I have lived among rough men for almost twenty years, and in intimate contact with arrant outlaws for the last two. It may surprise you to know that I find such company congenial."

Cord watched Dunraven's almost-girlish hands flutter in the air like birds.

Dunraven noticed the scrutiny and colored. He squared his shoulders and said, "I don't judge men by their differences. You meet the requirements for admission to our little family, and you may stay if you wish. Do you have any questions?"

"Yeah," Cord said. "How does that one-handed bartender of yours tie his bow tie?"

Dunraven laughed politely, then looked pointedly past Cord at the door. "Was there something else?"

"One thing: Where do I find Chris Kelly?"

"What leads you to believe Mister Kelly is in Lord?"

"Is he?"

Dunraven touched at the knot of his necktie with his long, tapering fingers. "What do you want with Mister Kelly?"

"I'll tell that to him."

"You could," Dunraven said deliberately. "There's no harm to it, is there?" Dunraven seemed to be talking to himself, but then he leaned far back in his oaken swivel chair and rapped his knuckles twice on the wall.

"You shall have your opportunity, sir." Dunraven dry-washed his fine hands vigorously. "Yes, you shall."

Behind Cord the door opened, but Cord did not turn right away. Here in this spa for desperadoes it was vital to show good faith and no fear. Instead Cord watched Dunraven's patrician weariness drift into a slight sad smile.

"Mister Kelly," Dunraven announced, "may I present Mister Cord."

Cord turned, and Chris Kelly smiled and said, "We've met."

It was like looking into a mirror, or rather a memory of what the mirror once showed. Chris Kelly was about Cord's age, but Cord saw a younger version of himself, before he began brooding about his future and Chi, before the long high-dives into the bourbon became something like habit. Cord had passed too many days considering the ways the West was changing and wondering how much longer the thin wire of code he walked would bear his weight. But these concerns did not seem to have touched Chris Kelly.

Looking at Chris Kelly showed Cord the changes in himself, and he was shocked.

Chris Kelly stood loose and easy and grinning, and judging from his looks he had not gone near as deep into the dark side of things. Cord felt like a somber, cranky old man, given to biting wisecracks and quick irritation over small things, and Chris Kelly was the man he had been.

He was clean-shaven and had a rangy, horseman's build and smooth, graceful movements, and his hands radiated quickness even at rest. Near to Cord's height and build but fair rather than dark, Chris Kelly wore his sandy blond hair wavy and long and brushed back under a battered light-colored Stetson. He was dressed in trail clothes, leather vest over a woolen shirt, a bright orange neckerchief, gabardine trousers over cowhide boots, and a smooth-worn, tie-down holster carrying a Colt .45 Peacemaker revolver.

Cord nodded and said, "'Lo, Chris."

Kelly lifted a hand to Cord in mock salute, held it a moment. "Hey there," he said easily. "It's been a time, partner."

Partner, Cord thought. The word ate at him. Well, hell, he was no partner to Chris Kelly, not anymore. He was responsible in that way to no one but Chi, and she was lost if he started thinking different. That was all that mattered; that decided everything, including this deception.

Yet there had been a time, enough of a time to give Chris Kelly the right to use the word that rankled Cord so, and Cord had to concentrate to meet Chris Kelly's eyes.

Chris Kelly did not offer his hand, and Cord was glad. Shaking with the man would have been like the kiss of Judas.

Behind Cord, Dunraven's chair scraped along the floorboards. The Englishman did offer his hand, and Cord took it; his fingers were cool as snakes.

"Welcome to Lord, sir," Dunraven said, pompous as any small-town mayor. "The sponsorship of Mister Kelly is more than sufficient to establish your bona fides." He gave Cord back his hand.

"Now then, the hospitality of my public house is yours." Dunraven cleared his throat importantly. "I daresay you two gentlemen have much to discuss."

Chris Kelly gave Cord a wide, pleasant grin. "Yeah," he said. "I daresay we do."

Chapter Nine

"THERE WAS SOME TROUBLE," CORD MUMbled, toying with a glass of beer.

Kelly did not press. He had only asked one question so far, carefully phrased, casually voiced, and accompanied with a grin: "How is that hell-raising spitfire pard of yours?" Which was a polite way of giving Cord a chance to say whatever he wanted, or nothing of substance at all. Still, Cord thought he heard a note of challenge. There were days when he would have filled Chris Kelly in on all his doings in a second, but now he just stared down into his glass.

"Well, Chris," Cord said lamely, "there was a time."

"Women," Kelly said and shook his head ruefully.

"Sure as hell," Cord agreed. They raised glasses and drank. Chris Kelly was drinking bourbon, and Cord had a mug of draft. He was not generally partial to beer, but it would not have been mannerly to refuse Chris Kelly's offer of a drink, and Lord surely had to be one of the all-time worst towns in the West for a man to guzzle down a great deal of bourbon whiskey and then howl for trouble.

So Cord was sober, which did not mean he was clear-headed. He felt that Chris Kelly could see through him like window glass. When Kelly toasted his coming the first time, Cord was jolted by something like panic: Chris Kelly knew the whole story, of Chi's entrapment and Cord's intention to betray him to save her. Chris Kelly was playing him like a fish, waiting for the kill.

Cord got himself calmed and hoped Kelly noticed nothing. *Act normal, for Christ's sake*, Cord told himself. Kelly was not prescient, and the fear that he was came out of Cord's own guilt.

But surely Kelly recognized subtle differences in Cord's demeanor and was a mite cautious. In the outlaw life you learned to be suspicious of any deviation, if you wanted to stay healthy and whole.

"She was a one," Chris Kelly said, and Cord sure as hell knew who he meant.

He drank a couple of swallows of the beer, which was cool enough so the bubbles bit at Cord's throat. When he'd ordered it he'd expected the piss-warm flat brew that was usually served in backwoods bars with no competition. It turned out the bartender had rigged up a pulley contraption with a rope net, mounted on the edge of the gorge and anchored to steel spikes driven into the rock. The netting held two kegs, which the bartender winched down into the creek-water for cooling. That went a ways toward explaining the double-helping of muscle on the man's good arm.

"I made a mistake," Cord said.

"You sure as hell did," Kelly said without rancor. "But what the hell. The whole damned business looked bad, back then."

Cord stared at the tabletop as if it were a window on the long-ago. "You ever see that German, Oosterbahn?"

"I heard he was dead."

"Well, the way he drank, they always said it would get him."

"It did," Chris Kelly said. "He got run down by a beer wagon."

Cord laughed at the old joke and felt better. All right, he had come this far. Thanks to the bounty hunter Lanett Sayre, he had found Chris Kelly with no waste of time, and there was no point now in dragging this affair out. Forget guilt and suspicion, and get on with it.

They were seated at a corner table in Dunraven's barroom, and now there was no more tension in the air than there would be in any other drinking establishment. The other men had returned to their glasses and conversation: Cord was with Chris Kelly, and that was enough. From the way they were careful not to stare, and the corner-protected table left vacant for them, Cord got the idea that Chris Kelly would be one of the leaders among this company. They by and large respected him, or at least feared him, which was good as the same thing.

In any case, no one wanted any confrontations. After he and Chris Kelly had drinks in front of them, the guard Cord had knocked cold and brought in like a delivery of grain came to the table. Cord got his hands empty and tensed for action, but it turned out the man, whose name was Marley, only wanted to tell Cord there were no hard feelings.

"Don't blame you," Marley said. "A man's got to be cautious, Mister Cord."

So they all knew who he was. Maybe that was not so bad.

"Anyway, you did hold back from hitting me harder," Marley said, like he was the one who owed an apology. "You didn't scramble my brains or nothing."

A man at a nearby table laughed and said, "How would you know the difference?" Marley grinned back, so it was okay.

What a pretty bunch of roisterers, Cord thought. The only one missing was the woman, Jewel, and Cord was sorry she was. Cord liked the idea of women nearby, not necessarily women you even thought of going after, just women. They gave the air a scent of potential.

Instead of women they had the dim-brained swamper. His name was Dicker, and he wandered among the tables with his broom, sweeping randomly and chanting his endless "Howdy, howdy, howdy..." like a rosary. Holing up was never a fine time, but Cord could not imagine spending long weeks in this place, crowded by the smell of these men, nothing to pass the time but drinking, nothing to eat but the greasy food served up by the one-armed kid bartender. There was a cookstove at the far end of the bar, with a griddle kept hot and a cauldron of simmering stew that gave off a faint odor that was not savory. Cord had watched the bartender serve up sandwiches of hard-fried eggs and ham. He wondered where the eggs came from, and who would eat the stew.

"So Oosterbahn is dead," Cord said to Chris Kelly. "Never thought I would be sorry to see him gone, and I'm not."

They had been sticking to the old days, which was a safe enough topic so long as they kept it general, but now Chris Kelly changed the subject. "Run into a wildcat, pard?"

For a moment, drifting in memories, Cord had no idea what Kelly was talking about. Kelly gestured at his own cheek, and Cord touched at the cut opened by Steens's gunsight. It was almost a week old, scabbed over and forgotten. This was Kelly's cautious way of asking if there was another woman.

"There was a fight," Cord said.

"Who won?"

Cord shook his head. "Maybe next time."

"And there's always a next time, isn't there, pard? Who would have thought of us coming together after all these years, smiling and sitting down to drink together."

"High time," Cord agreed, and raised his glass, but he was thinking, *That tears it. Kelly would use anything, including old friendship, to trap him.* Cord tasted the nastiness of it in his beer.

But Chris Kelly raised his own drink, smiling in his open way, looking only guileless and pleasured at Cord's company. He drank, then cocked his head sideways and looked past Cord.

Cord had seen the three men at the bar when he'd come downstairs. Now they were standing at the table, holding empty shot glasses and looking resolute, as if they had conferred at some length on the plan they were acting out.

"Well, hey there, boss," one of them said. He was runty and missing all four front teeth, so there was a whistle in his voice. "How's for us having a drink with you and your pal here?"

It was another of the pointless challenges that must have been issued by the dozens in a town inhabited by men with few standards and too much inner anger. But Chris Kelly handled it, as Cord figured he would.

"Pull up some chairs, boys," he said. "Wondered what was keeping you over there to yourselves when we had this bottle." Chris Kelly grinned like the good-natured victim of a harmless joke and poured all around.

"This hombre is Pete Hake." Chris Kelly nodded toward the runty man. Pete Hake wore a permanent scowl, as if he were born small and had been pissed-off ever since.

"Yeah," Hake grunted. He gunned back his shot.

"This big drink of water is called the Chief." He looked to be full-blooded Comanche all right, and mean enough to call himself any damned thing he pleased. Cord remembered seeing a few of the last of the free Comanche ride by his peoples' Texas farm, and being a little frightened, and impressed beyond his child's years. This man should have been riding among them, hunting buffalo and returning to camp to smoke while the women dressed the hides—back there he would have been a natural man. Here he smelled of danger, a warrior gone wrong. His hair, black as obsidian, was greased and plaited into two braids that hung halfway down his bare chest, where great welts of scar crisscrossed. The Indian stared expressionlessly at Cord and did not speak.

"Last but never least," Chris Kelly said lightly, "we have got the Aussie, Mister Jonnie Frye."

"Aye, mate, you've got me." Frye smiled at Cord without wasting any warmth. "Let's see if you can keep me."

"Jonnie Frye, you have got to keep yourself."

"I can do that, mate, Bob's your uncle." This Jonnie Frye was the kind who had to have the last gibe, who needled folks indiscriminately for the fun of the trouble it might cause. "Who is your friend?" Frye jerked a thumb at Cord without looking at him.

"An old-time trailmate," Chris Kelly said. "I reckon you heard his name by now."

"I heard all about this man. I heard he rode with a woman."

"Anything good?" Cord smiled deep into the Aussie's dark brown eyes. "You hear anything good except for riding with a woman? Anything about what happens to some sweet fellow who makes sport of riding with a woman."

Frye looked away. "Nothing wrong with it," he muttered.

"That's nice," Cord said.

"Speaking of women," Chris Kelly cut in, "where is Billy Pate?"

"Upstairs," Hake said. "With *her*." He gave the word a lewd twist, and Frye laughed. The Chief's face could have been carved from granite.

Kelly raised his glass. "Well, boys, down the hatch. Nice drinking with you, but it is over. Mister Cord and I have business to discuss."

"Money business?" Hake demanded.

"Any damned business we think of. We go back a ways."

"If it's money," Hake lisped, "I am here to listen. We are in this together, and you can't just send us away."

"I just did," Chris Kelly said. "There will be your turn, but right now you are gone, so ease off, Hake. No one but you is making a fuss."

Hake said, "Yeah. Sure thing," and reached for the bottle.

The Chief grabbed Hake's forearm and stood, upsetting his chair. Hake had to stand too. He looked up at the Chief's stone face and turned a little white under the unwashed windburn redness of his face.

Jonnie Frye stood quickly. "Been a pleasure meeting you, mate. Thanks for the drinks. Don't get lost."

Cord watched them back to the bar. "Fine bunch of boys."

"They are trash, pard."

"But they're riding with you."

Kelly shrugged. "You know how it goes. I was flat-assed, out-at-the-knees broke, and no prospects. Those boys come up to me in a bar, down in Ketchum, and tell me they got a bank they could rob. They also got just enough sense to know they can't do the job on their own. They need a leader, someone with a plan. Same old story."

"Not all the way the same," Cord said. "I hear some marshal got killed. That's not your way."

"Not my way!" Chris Kelly exploded. "You know me, Cord. Was I ever stupid enough to kill a lawman or anyone else during a job?"

"Sorry," Cord muttered. "Didn't mean to get into it."

"Goddamn the stupid motherless sons," Chris Kelly said, like he was trying to turn his anger where it belonged. "Look at them over there, buying drinks like they had good sense." He shook his head. "I wouldn't have come within three counties of them, but I needed the work. I told them: I call the shots, every inch of the way. My word is the law. Sure, they said. We are looking for a bossman and you are it."

The one-armed bartender came over and set another glass of the cold beer in front of Cord. "From the Aussie," the bartender said, scowling over his shoulder. "Said to tell you, 'Drink hearty.'" From the bar, the Aussie grinned his wiseacre grin.

"We picked up the kid, Billy Pate," Chris Kelly said. "You'll see him, trailing after the woman most likely."

"Figured the woman was yours."

"Not ever," Kelly said. "I learned my lesson."

Cord let that one pass.

"Anyway," Kelly said, "we got in a tight spot and the kid went squirrelly and started firing, and that queered it for sure. Nobody knows who shot the lawman except the man who did it, which sure as hell was not me."

"Doesn't matter now."

"That's for damned straight. We are all wanted for murder, free and equal. So we are stuck with each other in this place—until we run out of money."

"You got bank money. Nine thousand dollars is what I heard."

Chris Kelly snorted. "Them bankers, they've got insurance from the Wells, Fargo now. They pick a number out of the air, long as it's a big number, and the insurance pays them. Hell, they like getting raided now—they make money on the deal."

"I guess that's why we always went for the banks, you and me," Cord said lightly. "I guess we figured it was just crooks robbing crooks."

"Two thousand is closer to the real mark," Kelly went on, "and split into six shares too."

"What's your play?"

"I'm sticking for now, long as the money holds up and I

can stomach the company. After a time folks forget. I been thinking of drifting south to Arizona. I know some people down there who used to rustle Mexican horses and cattle, before they give it up for legitimate ranching. I could get on as a hand."

It was not the answer Cord had expected. "Think you could stand it?"

"Working?"

"The life. The same country and the same cows, the rest of your days."

"Who could?" He pulled the bottle to him but did not pour. "Best thing would be one quick good bank job with these boys, so I can pay them off and get rid of them, everybody riding with some money. All I need is a plan."

"Got an idea?"

Chris Kelly showed Cord a wide grin. "Yeah," he said. "I got an idea that you got a plan."

There it was; Chris Kelly could not have made it easier. He had broken a trail wide as a locomotive, and all Cord had to do was ride down to its end. Tell his story and make it sound right, and Chris Kelly was good as nailed.

Cord hesitated. Once he took this step there was nowhere but forward; until he did, though, he could still ride out. *Ride out to where?* he asked himself furiously. To a life without Chi, and the constant erosive knowledge of her confinement and horror because of him.

Cord leaned forward, lowered his voice, and said confidentially, "I know a job."

Kelly nodded and waited.

"It'll take a gang. That's why I'm here—I came looking for you. There's all kinds of talk that you are in the country, and then I heard about this place and it seemed likely."

There was some noise near the door, and Cord turned that way, immediately thinking about the woman. But it was only the Aussie Jonnie Frye, having a cruel joke at the expense of Dicker, the deformed swamper.

"Looking for somebody?" Chris Kelly asked.

Cord turned back. "You," he said.

"Okay," Kelly said, "you are on."

"Just like that?"

"If it is your plan, that's good enough for me; and it will work, if we can keep these dog-shits from killing somebody." Chris Kelly leaned close. "What is the plan?"

There was a damned good question. Cord cursed himself in his mind; he had been in a muddle for too long, which had to account for the stupid mistake of not making up a story. Or maybe he had forgotten on purpose, in denial of the treachery the phony plan would make possible.

"We ride out in the morning," Cord temporized, "ride back before midnight. One day, two at the outside."

"Where we riding?"

"Rathdrum." It was the first place that came to mind.

Chris Kelly's face clouded. "That's strange. Unless they built one since I rode through there last week, there is no bank in Rathdrum."

Cord felt like he'd been kicked in the chest, because Chris Kelly was right.

"They got one," Cord said. He recalled a story he had heard years back, and hoped to hell Chris Kelly had not heard the same story. "It doesn't look like a bank. It looks like a bar."

"You telling me a joke?"

No, Cord thought, *I am telling you a lie.*

"No joke," he said aloud, and thought of why. "There is plenty enough money in that country, from the timber business, and there was no good place to keep it safe between the times they could round up enough men with guns to run it down to the bank in Coeur d'Alene. Until they rigged up a secret cache under the floorboards in the saloon. There is a laminated-steel strongbox they ordered from Chicago, and it is set in stonework, with a steel plate under a trap in one corner of the oak flooring. There is a broken-down piano that no one ever plays, and they set that over the cut-out in the floor."

Cord was warming to his own story. "The only ones who know all about it are the barman and a tree-faller who was elected by the others to keep the accounts, because he had once clerked in a shoe store back East. The rest of 'em just know their money is safe. When one of the big men from the mines over in Kellogg comes with a payment for timbers, the money goes in the box, less the draws the men take for necessaries. Sometimes the proceeds of three or four sales pile up before it gets cleaned out and taken to town."

"This is one of those times?"

"That's right."

"Who told you the secret?"

Cord grinned, working on looking sheepish. "The man who owns the saloon has got a wife. I tickled the secret out of her. The barman beats hell out of her, so I told her she could ride off with us."

"We got enough women," Chris Kelly said. "God knows."

"Well, she is not riding with us," Cord said. "We get the money, and she gets left. We'll tie her to her husband and leave them to talk it over. What do you think?"

"I think I need to know plenty more. For starters, what do you need us for? Why not just saddle up on that old girl, talk the key out of her, and go your way?"

"Her husband wears the key on a string around his neck. Never takes it off, and he's never alone except for after the bar closes, and then he forts up with his wife and does his business." Cord grinned. "She says he doesn't take off his union suit, just drops the flap and pulls it out. She says it takes him maybe half a minute to finish up, and after that he falls asleep on top of her."

Chris Kelly was looking at Cord like he was crazy.

"Believe me," Cord said and felt the beer sour in his stomach. "Three men on the husband, so we can be sure of taking him out of action and getting the ropes on him without having to cold-cock him. Hit a man too hard or in the wrong place and there is your killing problem again. Two men on the wife in case she forgets who she is siding with and tries to raise a holler. And that steel plate over the strongbox is heavy. She says it takes both her and her husband and the bookkeeper to get it lifted."

"You sure you know what you are doing?"

"What I am doing," Cord said, "is offering you the easiest money you'll see in some time."

"How much of this easy money are we fixing to get?"

"Don't know exactly. More than plenty. Enough anyway

so you can pay off those boys of yours and get them out of your sight."

The skeptical look still creased Chris Kelly's face, and for a moment Cord thought he would turn the deal down. He'd seemed to come to some resolve.

"Fine," he said. "So we ride at sunup?"

Cord realized his lying had led him into a box canyon again, as lying will. He needed time to get word out to Sayre.

"You said the money is there," Chris Kelly pushed. "So is there something wrong with tomorrow?"

"Sure," Cord said with forced enthusiasm. "Might as well get it done with."

"Sounds real perfect," Chris Kelly said with a note of something that might have been sarcasm. But then he looked to the bar, where his dirty crew was arguing about something. His eyes cut back to Cord, and he smiled a bitter ironic smile.

Cord did not like the smile, and again had the uncomfortable feeling Kelly was ahead of him, that he recognized this foolish make-believe for what it was. Cord wondered who was setting up whom, and for what.

There were too many mysteries to this business. Cord had understood that the Governor was somehow bound up in trouble with his bully-boy Jaeger, but it had not occurred to him that Chris Kelly was mixed in as well. But otherwise, why the Governor's insistence on taking Kelly alive? Way in back of everything sat the regal William Deane Majors, playing them like a puppet master, and to what end?

"We'll tell the boys," Chris Kelly said. "We'll draw them maps and walk them through it, so's they mind their manners and don't panic."

Cord could not shake the thought: Kelly had come around too easily.

He sat back and rubbed his eyes. By nightfall tomorrow he would be in Rathdrum with this bunch, and there would be no woman, no secret bank, no money, no Sayre, and no way out, short of back-shooting them all.

"Fine," Cord said. "We ride."

He was raising his glass to seal the bargain when he felt a change in the room, as if the floor had tilted a fraction of a degree, or the air pressure had dropped. Men drew loud breath, and the talking slowed and then stopped. Cord knew: The woman had come in. Her presence drifted across the room like a ghost.

Jewel crossed the room slowly, moving their way like a challenge, a big girl with business on her mind. Sexuality swirled around her; she looked like she might glow in the dark. She moved like she had been laid in the last half-hour and could still feel it, wet and confident.

The man following her had to be Billy Pate—a boy, really: her bedtime boy, maybe seventeen and not all the way filled out yet, a skinny, gawky, chicken-necked lad with a patchy mustache that was worse than no mustache at all. He trailed her like a consort to royalty, privileged to be the cock-robin in her life for the time being but aware of his place.

At the bar Pete Hake said something low to the other two. The Aussie sniggered and even the Chief cracked a faint smile. They were making sport of the kid, who knew it and reddened and scowled at them. The woman paid no notice, but sailed toward Cord and Chris Kelly like a great ship coming to dock.

Despite himself, Cord was smiling as he stood. Chris Kelly, taken by surprise, followed suit. "This here is Cord," Kelly said.

"I know who he is," Jewel said to Cord.

"Here you got Jewel," Kelly said. "She rides with us."

"All of you?" Cord could have bit off his tongue. To his relief the woman grinned, and when he saw that so did Chris Kelly.

"Not all of them," Jewel said, nodding toward the bar. "No big, dirty fellows. I like a man who is about an armful."

Billy Pate flushed darker. Cord shot a look at Kelly, searching for a giveaway. He couldn't imagine Chris Kelly sending Jewel off to bed with Billy Pate if she was his on any more than a one-time basis, but Kelly was grinning and Cord couldn't tell.

"Here," Billy Pate said awkwardly, and he pulled out a chair for the woman and another for himself.

Chris Kelly put out a hand. "Get yourself a drink with the boys, Billy," he said, not unkindly.

"I don't—"

"You do what I say, Billy." Chris Kelly's tone had not changed, but his smile had turned a few degrees colder.

Billy Pate tossed his head like this was all a matter of indifference to him and turned on his heel.

"Get over here," Hake called from the bar. "You're too little for those folks."

"But not too little for her." The Aussie laughed. "You must be a dog for punishment, Billy boy."

Other men were following all this from the tables.

"Charming Billy," Hake called. Several men laughed.

None of this was happening for Jewel. She was watching Cord, waiting on him as if she were a courtesan but might turn gunfighter at any moment. Her clear blue eyes were open wide and seemed to absorb everything. They pulled at Cord while Chris Kelly talked.

"Jewel come out of the Dakotas," he said. "Shipped steerage from Sweden when she was a baby, and then out across the plains with her folks. She grew up in time to see her mother go shithouse crazy." He and the woman exchanged looks. "So she says."

The woman did not contradict him.

"We been riding together," Kelly said. "Trying it on for size. We were teamed up when those boys came looking for a leader. We'd wintered together down the Rio Grande, and we came north with spring, following the snow-melt. Jewel likes to keep moving, and I always have, so we tried covering for one another. We still are."

Like himself and Chi, Cord thought. But there was a difference. Chi would never go off with some boy like Billy Pate—not more than once. Even if she did, she would never flaunt her ass the way this woman did.

Chris Kelly shrugged. "I figured . . ." Cord thought he was going to point out the obvious parallel, and maybe use it to finally get around to asking about Chi, but just then Kelly was interrupted by a shout from the bar.

"Don't you ever shut up, you fucking moron?" It was Pete Hake's bullying, sibilant voice.

Billy Pate edged away from his three partners. He was not a part of this.

The stumbling, cheese-brained swamper Dicker had been working his broom around the men at the bar, mostly raising dust. He looked up with a wide vacant smile, as if he had been paid a fine compliment.

"Howdy, howdy, howdy," he said to Hake.

Hake backhanded him across the face. The Chief and Jonnie Frye watched with glowing eyes, as if this sort of viciousness recharged their own inner brutality.

Dicker swayed and Hake hit him with his fist, catching him on the point of his chin and knocking him on his seat. For a few moments Dicker flopped there, shaking his head slowly. Then he spotted his broom, lying a couple feet out of reach. Laboriously, and with bewilderment creasing his lopsided face, he got to hands and knees and reached for it.

Jonnie Frye drew and fired, the shot overly loud in the crowded room. The handle of the broom splintered and it skittered off across the floor.

Except for turning his chair so he was sitting straight and his holster was not twisted under him, Cord kept his counsel. Frye was quick and he could shoot, no doubt about that. But bullying gimped-up swampers was one thing, and facing a whole man was another.

Dicker watched his broom fly away from him, frowning with uncomprehending concentration. He looked up at the gun in Frye's hand, and then at Frye's smile, and reached for the broom again. Frye fired, hitting the handle in almost exactly the same place, so it cracked and bent but did not quite break.

In the silence that followed the echoing shot, Cord sensed a new presence. Dunraven stood at the top of the stairs, his face gray and his fine, long-fingered hands raised to his breast. His thin, epicene figure trembled, and he looked old and haggard, lost in this world of his own invention. Dunraven looked to Cord, and then past him, but in the moment their eyes met Cord saw into a place he never wanted to inhabit. Dunraven was no lord; he was an impotent middle-aged alcoholic who had built a cage and locked himself within it; and worst of all he knew it, in the depths of his soul.

At the bar, Dicker was trying for his broom once more. Jonnie Frye fired a third time. Dicker yowled like an animal and sat down on the floor again. He held up his right hand and stared at it in pain and puzzlement and curiosity. Frye had put a bullet through the middle of his palm at a range of five feet, the big .45 slug drilling a half-inch-wide hole through flesh and muscle and bone, neat as an auger.

Three tables down from Cord a man stood, the raw scrape of his chair on floorboards cutting the silence. "That's enough, Jonnie Frye," he said.

Some animal instinct told Dicker these men were finished sporting with him. He grabbed what was left of his broom in his good hand and scuttled toward the stairs and Dunraven. Blood made a stipple-trail in his wake, but Dicker let out not so much as a whimpering sound.

The one-armed bartender stood down aways from Frye, watching all this through his perpetual scowl. Working in this place, Cord figured, he must have learned young about the patterns of gunplay, and shooting odds. His sawed-off double-barrel was racked next to the cashbox, and Jonnie Frye was sided by Hake and the Chief. The bartender folded his good arm across his chest and stayed put.

Jonnie Frye smiled cruelly at the man who had stood. "Tell me, mate. Tell me what enough is."

At the bottom of the stairs, Dunraven was crouched over Dicker, wrapping his shattered hand in a clean white handkerchief that immediately began soaking up blood. When that was done, the Englishman put an arm around the other man's shoulders, tender as a lover.

Frye said to the man across the room, "I'm waiting on you, mate. Talk to me."

The man who had intervened wore clothes that had at least been recently brushed, and his face was shaved fresh that morning. A worried man, Cord guessed, so he seeks relief in routine, like shaving every day. Facing Jonnie Frye, he surely looked worried enough.

Frye flipped his revolver into its holster and stood legs apart, hands free and loose. "You got the floor, mate. You got every man waiting on you." Frye waggled the fingers on his gunhand. "'Specially me."

Beside Cord, the woman Jewel watched through eyes gone dead. She sat perfectly still, as if to feel the harmonic vibrations of this impending violence, staring as if at something often seen but still fascinating, like a dog walking on his forefeet.

The clean-shaven man raised a placating hand. "Take it easy, Frye. Just let it lie."

"Sure, mate," Frye said. "Except you are the one who should have let it lie."

"There is no sense to this." But the man looked uncertain. He licked at dry lips, then turned toward the door.

Jonnie Frye put a bullet into the floorboards a few inches from the man's heels. Black-powder smoke swirled lazily toward the wagon-wheel chandelier. The man froze but did not turn.

He took a step, and Frye planted another slug in the floor, this time between the man's legs.

Five shots, Cord thought.

And everyone else in the room could also count to six, especially the clean-shaven man, who knew Frye would not put his last bullet in wood. The man turned and showed his face, and his fright was written clear across it, along with the foreknowledge of the quick clench of pain that was coming.

Other men sat straighter and held their breath, eyes bright. The moment went on, and no one moved.

The clean-shaven man went for his gun, and Jonnie Frye shot him in the chest. The man stepped back and flailed with both arms, and one got caught over a panel of the batwing doors. The man died that way, hanging awkwardly and swinging under his own limp weight, boot heels scratching along the floor.

Then wood ripped as the door hinges finally tore out of the jamb, and the corpse crumpled to the floor. All around the room men let out breath in a great sigh.

Jonnie Frye laughed, cracked the cylinder of his revolver, and began to fill the chambers with cartridges from his belt loops.

Under the table, Jewel put her hand high up on Cord's thigh and squeezed. Cord looked at her, and felt a faint wave of nausea. He pushed back his chair and her hand fell away. Chris Kelly looked up at him when he stood.

"Later," Cord said, and started for the door.

Behind him Jonnie Frye said, "Where you going, mate?"

Cord heard Frye snap home the full cylinder. He waited several heartbeats and then turned. "I need fresh air," he said levelly. "The smell in here sets hard on my stomach." From the corner of his eye he saw Jewel watching him. Now she was smiling.

"Not just yet, mate," the Aussie said and assumed his stylized gunfighter ready-stance again.

Cord snorted and turned his back and moved for the door.

This shit was not his game, not this time, even if he were dangerously close to dealing in anyway. The Aussie would not back-shoot a man, even amid this crew—at least that was the lethal gamble Cord was taking.

This was a test as well: If Frye did try anything, would Chris Kelly cover Cord's back? His boot heels made soft, hollow, lonesome sounds as he walked toward the door.

But nobody shot him in the back, and near as he could tell nobody tried to, so Cord got no good answer to his question. The hell with it; he needed to cool his head.

He crossed the five yards of flat rock apron to the creek-gorge and took a deep breath of the water-chilled air rising from it. It was afternoon of a grand spring day in the high northern Rockies, and Cord tasted the sweet air and felt better for it. He rolled another ill-made cigarette and smoked it, staring down at the rushing water coursing between the boulders far below.

No one bothered him while he finished the smoke, and no one tried to stop him when he went back into the barroom. He drew gazes but no comments when he crossed through the crowd to the stairway. He headed up to Dunraven's office, at this moment wanting nothing except a room of his own.

Chapter Ten

"I DON'T SEE IT," PETE HAKE WAS SAYING IN his whistly voice. "I don't see you coming in here like Santa Claus at Christmas, giving us something for no good reason."

"How could you?" Cord said. "You can't get through a simple bank job without somebody killing a marshal, so now you all got Federal paper on your heads for life. How could someone like you see the sense of this kind of job?"

"You don't talk to me like that," Hake bristled. "You understand, I'll . . ."

"Hake," Chris Kelly said, "shut up."

"The two of you," Hake said, "you bastards think you have got something the rest of us don't. But you'll see."

The third-floor room was walled in rough lumber, and the knots had fallen out and left holes for the rats to home in. The stained mattress smelled of urine and nervous nightsweats, alcohol and ghosts. Cord sat on the only chair, and Chris Kelly was hunkered down with his back against the closed door. This was a planning session, and nobody wanted any strangers wandering in.

The rest of them were crowded around. Jonnie Frye was sprawled on the bed with his boots up on the filthy mattress, and Pete Hake sat on its edge. The Chief was hunkered down on his haunches, not leaning against anything and not moving, like his muscles were fluid instead of tissue. Jewel and her boy Billy Pate—her sad knight whose only armor was the protective innocence of getting fucked steady for the first time in his life—the two of them sat on the floor with their backs against the wall and their shoulders touching. It was too many people in too small a space for Cord's taste, and he recalled the other hotel room, the one in Twin Falls that had erupted with gunmen, the room where all this deception began.

Cord had been telling them about Rathdrum, and the make-believe barman and his make-believe strongbox.

"Two big men." Pete Hake spit, and his sputum quivered on the floor like an oyster on the half-shell. "Think you got it over everybody."

"Truth is," Chris Kelly said, "we have plenty you don't." He spoke calmly and without raising his voice, as if he were explaining to a child. "You stop to think about it, you realize we don't need you near so much." Kelly looked away as he finished his speech, as if he bored himself.

Hake coughed. "Well," he said, "it's the shits."

"Right," Chris Kelly said cheerfully. "It always is."

Jonnie Frye was nursing a whiskey bottle, and now he sat up to pass it to Hake. "Have a tipple, mate. It'll clear your tubes." Frye winked at Cord, like they were cronies in all this and the near showdown earlier in the afternoon was merely a trifle among friends. To Cord the wink felt like a lewd proposition.

"That's the ticket," Chris Kelly said. If he had to be mixed up with these men for another day or so, he wanted peace. Jewel had not said anything since they had all filed into Cord's room. She sat with her knees drawn up and her elbows resting on them, her legs slightly splayed so anyone who wanted to could see how the leather pulled taut over her crotch. She looked drowsy, like she'd logged too much bed time in the last day or so. Mostly she regarded Cord, cool and faintly smiling.

Here was a different sort of proposition.

But Billy Pate was watching Cord too, furious as a frustrated chicken hawk. When Cord looked at him the boy met his stare. His eyes were hard and dark and hurt; what had driven this kid from kinfolk who regarded him with affection? He was probably as good a boy as any, not so long ago, but now this woman would probably get him killed before he grew to true manhood.

"So you see how it is," Chris Kelly finished. He had been going over the details of the job for a third time. "We ride in smiling, we ride out smiling. We get the money, no one gets hurt. We don't break any barroom windows or steal any whiskey. We split up the take on even shares, and we tip out hats to one another."

"Sure, mate." Jonnie Frye looked at Cord. "Only what if there ain't no money, nor even a strongbox? What then?"

"You always take that chance," Cord said, as if Frye should have known. "Maybe they are cleaning out that strongbox right now for a trip to the bank. Maybe the barman's wife was telling me a tale, for who knows what reason. But we don't lose anything by it—long as nobody gets hurt. A half-assed scuffle in a one-saloon town, and who cares? Not the law—they got killers to worry about." Cord gave Frye a hard, humorless grin. "Killers like you boys. Anyway, this time we ride masked, on strange horses—Dunraven will fix us up. The worst thing that can happen is a waste of a day."

Frye nodded, as if coming finally to the sense that this was a reasonable proposition. Cord felt relief. Since he'd made up the Rathdrum story on the spot that afternoon, he'd taken time to figure out the details, and this placating theory.

"You got to go along with Cord quite a distance," Chris Kelly said. "He's done more jobs than you've thought about, and he's sitting here."

"Sure is." Jewel spoke for the first time. "He's sitting pretty." She looked at Cord and ran the tip of her tongue over her upper lip, aiming the invitation at him and not caring if anyone else saw it.

"Then it's set." Chris Kelly stood and stretched a kink out of one leg. "We leave a half-hour before morning light. Be sober by then, or get left behind." He moved a little stiffly. "But I guess one last drink won't hurt, to seal the bargain. I'm buying."

Jonnie Frye took a last pull from the half-full bottle he held, then handed it to Hake before unfolding himself from the bed. Hake tilted it back as he followed Frye to the door. Billy Pate climbed to his feet too, but Jewel stayed where she was. The boy looked down at her with a clouded expression, and even Chris Kelly was regarding her with a frown.

"You all go ahead," she said in their direction. "I'll be right along."

Hake sniggered, automatic and meaningless as a dog's bark. Chris Kelly shrugged, then turned abruptly and went out into the hall. The other three hung back. Billy Pate leaned himself against the opposite wall and crossed his arms over his chest.

"Leave us be, boys," Jewel said mildly. "You too, Billy. I'll be downstairs directly, but first there are things to talk about here." She raised her hand as if to gently push him from the room, but she smiled.

"Your thing, Billy," Hake muttered. "Gonna talk about your little thing."

The kid whipped his head around to Hake and then back to Cord. For an awful moment Cord thought he was going to weep, but then Billy Pate turned on his heel and sauntered through the press of men at the door, a boy's imitation of being full-grown.

"Leave the bottle, Hake," Jewel said in her cool voice.

Hake hesitated in the doorway. "Belongs to the Chief."

"The Chief don't mind."

Hake grinned his lickerish grin. "Nobody does, 'cept for Billy."

Jewel got languidly to her feet and took the bottle. She was easily a half-foot taller than Hake. He went out empty-handed, and she shut the door behind him.

She leaned back against it, uncorked the bottle, and took a healthy slug, then offered it to Cord. Cord stayed in the chair and shook his head. He wondered how much she knew about this deception, and if he were destined to be the final sucker.

"Well, all right," Jewel said. She popped the cork back into the bottle with the heel of her hand. She sat on the end of the bed, facing him from maybe five feet, sat like a man, hunched over with her forearms on her thighs and the bottle dangling between her parted legs.

"Now then," Jewel said. "Just what the hell is this all about?"

"How's that?" This woman took some dizzying turns.

They were on yet another level of confrontation here, and Cord did not like or need it.

"Where is your woman?"

"That's no question to ask."

They stared at each other. Cord reached out and she handed him the bottle, grinning as if his drinking was her victory. The bourbon slugged into Cord's stomach, and then the warmth started back up, from his belly toward his heart. He drank again.

"What about you and Chris?" he blurted. "How are you two tied up?"

"That doesn't concern you."

"That's right," Cord snapped. "Nothing about you concerns me, lady." He stood and made for the door. What he wanted from this conversation was out.

"Wait up," Jewel said from the bed.

Cord swore at himself and turned.

"Maybe we started this off wrong," Jewel said.

"Maybe. But it isn't me who is too easy."

"Is that so? I thought you were interested."

"Where did you get that idea?"

"From you," she said.

Well, far as that went she was right, and a handsome piece of work as well. Here we go again, Cord thought. He tasted more whiskey and wished the door had a lock.

"You're going to like it," she said. She began undoing the buttons of her shirt. "I got you, and you will take it like a man."

"This your way of getting information?"

"One way," she said readily. Cord could see the slope of white skin between her breasts. "You worry me, Cord. Something is not right. You came riding in with this fine setup for us, and without your woman. I don't . . . I need to figure on it."

She pulled the tails of her shirt free of her britches and peeled it back. Cord looked at her high breasts and thought he could feel the weight of them in his hands.

"You'll like it and I'll know you." She lay back on the dirty mattress. "I'll find out things."

"You learn that in the Dakotas?"

"From my mother, before she started crying all day."

"Maybe she didn't like what she found out." He watched her undo the metal buttons down the front of her tight leather trail-pants, and hook her thumbs in the waistband to skin them down over her hips.

Cord threw the shirt back at her. "You'll have to get your news somewhere else."

"Don't be that way," she murmured. "Why not?"

Cord had no good answer. Maybe he believed her, that she could read his mind if he were inside her. "I got enough trouble," he mumbled.

"Do it," she said. "Just once."

"Not with Kelly's woman."

She did not contradict him.

"Put your damned shirt on," Cord growled and turned away while she did, pulling angrily at the bourbon. He wondered if he had just made another fine, mindless mistake. They'd already been holed up in here for ten minutes— anyway long enough. Cord guessed that she'd tell the others a lie, or at least not contradict their crude assumptions. There was no profit in rectitude...

"You got makings?" Jewel asked. Cord tossed them to her; she was dressed again. He watched two cigarettes take shape between the blond woman's strong fingers and thought of Chi.

She passed one of the smokes to him, and he lighted both with a kitchen lucifer snapped off his thumbnail. Jewel took the bottle and drank. "We'll have whiskey and a smoke together," she said. "Maybe I'll find out something this way."

"You never know."

"You start off." She offered the bottle. "First tell me why I should trust you."

Cord was tempted to try, but there was impasse and ambush up that trail. So he told her about Chris Kelly instead.

It went back some six years, to a little California foothill town called San Esteban, a one-time mission that was enjoying a few months of boom from a minor silver strike nearby in the Sierra Nevadas. There was a fight, a brawl really, a dozen men swinging on each other and no winning, just a lot of aches and scratches the next morning for every-one. "This was the stuff that did it." Cord held out the bottle of bourbon. "Just a lot of drunken cock-rooster punching out."

"I could stand some of that," Jewel said. "Get you sooner or later." She laughed easily.

"The barkeep was this giant German named Oosterbahn. He was famous up and down the coast for two things. One was that he could outdrink any man and still keep his feet, and the other was that he countenanced no nonsense in his drinking establishment. He was tough and he could make it stick, but the son of a bitch always carried it too far.

"He waded into the fight and got hold of me and this other fellow first, and threw us out into the street. That was all right, but then he kicked in my ribs for good measure."

"Hurt bad?"

"Felt like the bone was sticking me in the heart, most of the next month. But right at that moment the whiskey masked the pain. The other fellow and I got up out of the dirt and horseshit. I'm coughing and holding my side, and his nose looks to be mashed all over one cheek, but he grins and says, 'Let's get that kraut bastard.'"

Cord grinned now at the recollection. "Just then the doors swing open and out comes Oosterbahn with a couple more half-bloody fistfighters. We step out of the way as they go flying into the street, and then we jumped that German and we kicked his ass hard enough to lay him up in bed for a couple of weeks, or so we heard later. When that was done we went back into his place and had a few drinks together. Me and Chris Kelly."

Cord took another hit of bourbon and offered the bottle, as if this was a formal toast to old times she had better want to join. "I can drink with you," she said, "on wishing I'd been there."

"A couple days later," Cord said, "laying up in a hotel room to heal up and dry out, Chris and I come to find we were in the same business. Chris had an idea about a bank outside Sacramento that sounded like easy work. The only question was Chi."

"Your woman." A touch of the challenge returned to Jewel's voice.

"You know she is," Cord said. "Anyway, she had been gone for a week seeing to some business—might be part of why I got into a bar brawl—but she was meeting me that night. So I set it up for us three to take supper together, and she surprised me by agreeing to a trial team-up. First time she'd ever been purely willing to do a job with a stranger."

"A careful lady."

"Compared to you"—Cord grinned—"all ladies are. Well," he went on, "the bank business worked slick as fish in water. We finished up in minutes, got away clean, and made some money, not much but enough for a summer of resting easy. We rode together for a time longer, and did some other little business to keep busy and fresh. We got on fine, especially me and Chris."

When he'd started in on it, he'd meant the story to end here. "I've got a brother," he said to the floor, "but Chris Kelly was more brother to me than Jim ever could be."

Cord took the pouch from his shirt pocket once more. His fingers were thickening with drink. Jewel got up and plucked away the makings, the gesture eerily like Chi.

"Then it got tricky," Cord said, watching her fingers. "The three of us were drinking one night, somewhere in Oregon timber country, and Chris and Chi got to talking and didn't seem to have much to say to me. I must have been irked, because I went off to play cards, and I've never been much of a gambling hand. Anyway, when I got back they were gone. The next several nights they shared a room."

"Well," Jewel said.

"We had our arrangement, me and Chi. We were partnered up to ride together and nothing else. You can do the rest with who you please."

"I usually do," Jewel said. "I got to have it."

"Well, that's how it was with us," Cord insisted.

"Okay."

"The only trouble was I couldn't stand it, especially when she did it more than once, and with Chris."

"Nothing tricky about that."

"Nothing tricky about anything," Cord snapped. "Except couldn't stand it."

"You had a fight," Jewel guessed.

"Chris didn't want to—so I pushed him into it and he whaled the living tar out of me."

Jewel laughed.

"All right," Cord said mildly, "but it wasn't funny then. The next morning when the two of us were cold sober again, Chris and I had a talk. One of us was going to kill the other if it went on this way, and Chi was still my partner, so Chris saddled up and took off. I never saw him again, until today.

"What made Chi the angriest," Cord said, "was finding out we'd come to a decision without talking to her, like she wasn't part of it. She didn't speak to me like a real friend for weeks, and I was scared it was through for us, after all. But then she told me to from then on just keep my mouth shut and out of her business, and it worked out again."

"So," Jewel said, "where is she now?"

"Just gone for a time. Nothing serious."

"I wasn't offering nothing serious. Nothing overnight."

Cord shook his head. "I told you that story so you could see the kind of trouble I'm working to say clear of."

"Sometimes you can't do it. Sometimes trouble will not leave you be."

Cord stood. "We'd better get down those stairs," he said, "or it's going to jump us right now."

But it turned out to be too late. Cord knew it as soon as he saw Billy Pate, waiting at the bar and staring hatred.

The boy came across the room to meet them at the foot of the stairs. Jewel kept on going, making for the corner table where Chris Kelly and the others were having their nightcap. Billy Pate hardly looked at her; his business was with Cord. He looked to have decided that he was going to be a man, starting this second.

Nothing wrong with the notion, Cord thought—but right at the moment the kid was making a mistake.

Billy Pate stood blocking Cord's way. "You lousy dog-piss bastard," he said and tried to swing on Cord.

Cord caught his fist in midair and held it, but the kid

would not give up straining. Cord tried to figure a way t
turn him loose.

"Take it outside." This time the bartender had no troubl
or risk in getting the drop. He held the double-barrel in th
crook of his good arm, cocked, his finger on the triggers.

"I don't want to fight you, boy." Cord let go the fist bu
kept his guard up.

"You are going to, though, Mister Slick. You owe me."
Billy Pate spun on his boot heel, and men at tables bega
pushing back their chairs. Looking around at them, Cor
saw Dicker the swamper, his mangled hand wrapped in
bloody hank of gray bedsheet.

At the door, Billy Pate turned and waited a moment. The
kid had seen men face-down enough times, but seeing an
understanding were different things. He thought he was doing
the pushing and holding the high hand, but Cord knew he
was vulnerable as a lambkin staked out for coyote bait.

"I offer a fair chance," Billy Pate announced across the
room, "but I want what is due me." He drew his revolver
and aimed it at Cord. "You come out and fight, or I will
shoot you dead where you stand."

The range was the length of the room, a long shot unless
a man had a good hand and years of practice. Cord had, and
could quick-draw and still score a fist-sized cluster at that
distance—in a target or a man. He knew he could probably
beat the kid now and hit his shoulder or arm—anyway not
kill him. Then again, maybe the kid would get lucky and drill
Cord right through the pump—and what did this kid mean
to Cord anyway? Cord had not started this trouble.

Sure as hell no one else in the room would interfere. Even
Chris Kelly showed no inclination different from the men he
sat with. But then, maybe there was satisfaction in this for
Kelly too, having to do with Jewel—and could be with Chi.

What a goddamned muddle, Cord thought, and wished
only for one more gargle of bourbon. But this was not going
to blow by.

While Cord crossed the room the kid kept the gun on him,
which was a mistake and an insult. In Cord's wake men
jostled and got to their feet.

"All right, kid," Cord said. "You got it. I hope you love t."

The rock apron in front of the saloon was washed by moonlight bright enough to make embedded chips of isinglass and pyrite glimmer in its surface. Cord moved to the middle of the flat open space and turned. Billy Pate stepped out on the boardwalk and down onto the rock, and men fanned out behind him. From Cord's back came the rush of water through the gorge, maybe three yards separating him from the cliff edge.

"All right, Mister Badass," the boy said. He was grinning whitely, because he thought he was acting with correctness, and because he had the attention of every badman in Lord, and because he thought the grin hid his fear. But he was three times wrong.

Cord looked past him and up to the second story of the building. Dunraven stood silhouetted in the lighted window of his office, watching, waiting.

"Come ahead, Billy Pate," Cord said.

The kid dropped his shoulder and swung. He was quick, and the solid right hook that slammed into Cord's stomach made Cord gasp. He felt his restraint slip and anger take its place. Cord closed the boy's mouth hard with an underhand right and felt teeth break. Blood exploded over his forearm.

Cord stepped back. The kid tried to shake the clouds out of his head; his eyes were unfocused. Time to finish him up, Cord reckoned.

But Billy Pate came in under his feint, and the follow-up punch only grazed his jaw. He caught Cord's wrist, which was a stupid move. The boy was outweighed by maybe forty pounds, and if they went to the ground he was finished.

They went down anyway, and then the boy was rubbing dirt and gravel in Cord's face, and Cord snarled and gave up the notion of letting this boy out of anything but a goddamned good lesson about fistfighter matchups and pain. They rolled and Cord got his feet under him. He grabbed a handful of the boy's shirt with his left and dragged him to his feet. Cord released him at the same moment he slammed a vicious jab into the middle of his face.

That finished it.

Billy Pate staggered two steps backwards; Cord saw hi
eyes turn up in his head, and then he was good as gone. Fo
a frozen moment he hung there on the edge of the creek'
deep canyon, and he might have known what was happening
because he let out a low moan of terror.

Cord lunged for his hand and missed. From the lip of the
drop-off, Cord saw the kid turn once in the air and hit the
rocks. Cord heard the thump of the impact and the boy's
tormented scream. He saw the water catch the broken body
and sweep it headfirst into a boulder. The screaming stopped
and the body vanished.

Cord gasped air into burning lungs. From the boardwalk
the men regarded him expressionlessly; the fun was over,
and one ending served well as the next. Chris Kelly was
looking at his boots and shaking his head, for reasons Cord
could not know. Jewel was beside him. Cord peered at her
and saw she wore a vague smile.

Chris Kelly frowned at her, and Cord got a sense of what
he was thinking after all. She would not do, not as a lover
nor a partner, at least not in any long-term way. She was
flawed by perverse appetites and would never be right.

Cord walked toward the line of men, and ones near the
door parted slightly to let him by. But Jewel held her ground,
so Cord had to brush roughly past to get into the barroom.
She tried to grab his arm and he pulled free. Inside he bought
a bottle from the one-armed youth. The barkeep did not meet
his eyes.

But then men started filing back inside, and Cord knew
immediately that this Lord town had become too close and
confining for right now, so he took his bottle and walked
through their midst again and went out of there.

Chapter Eleven

LIGHT CAME FROM THE DOOR OF THE SALOON, Dunraven's office above and two of the shanties around back, but there was no one out on the trail, and the town of Lord was quiet. Cord sat with his knees drawn up and his back against a lodgepole pine, near where he'd taken out the guard earlier that day. He was trying to make up ways in his head that this business might conclude okay, but each was flawed. Beyond the intermediate turns, the equation always came to one of two solutions. In each one, someone close to him was going to spend a lifetime in jail, and not a long one either, if Cord had the measure of Governor Majors and his henchman Jaeger.

Yet Cord had to follow through. Chi was the only one of them who mattered—and so what if the way to her freedom were impossible to stomach. Over time, years maybe, he would learn to live with it.

But then, all that could go wrong invaded his thoughts: ambush by Jaeger and Steens and his boys, a double-cross at the hands of the fat Governor, or worse. Chi could already be dead, or raped beyond sensibility.

She had better not be; Cord had plans.

These were no days to ride outside the law. The men Cord knew once were mostly out of the life now; these vermin in Lord were representative of the leftovers. Cord wondered how he would go about bringing Chi in from the way they had lived for nearly ten years, and still keep her at his side.

One sure thing: He'd have to offer her something she wanted. Chi could not be talked into much, and she could surely be forced into nothing. But they would pull one more job, Cord decided, one job for adult money, and then vanish; it would work out.

A twig cracked and a bush rustled, and Cord's fantasy dissolved. He snuffed out his cigarette, stood noiselessly, drew his Colt, and stepped back into shadow to wait.

A man was coming toward him, leading a horse.

Then, in the moonlight filtering through the trees, Cord made out it was Lanett Sayre. He was making deliberate noise as he came on, which meant he'd already recognized Cord and wanted to announce his own presence before any stray shooting got started. He stopped twenty feet up the hill.

"Cord?"

Cord knew the bounty hunter could not see into the shadow.

"I saw you smoking," Sayre called. "It has to be you, Cord. Nobody else would climb this mountain." There was a pause. "Nobody else down there knows how to feel bad."

"I know something," Cord called. "I know how little I like being watched."

"Can I come down?"

Cord drank some bourbon. "Come ahead, bounty man."

Sayre led his horse down the rest of the way and looped the reins around a tree trunk. There was a body slung over the saddle. The clothes on it were wet, but Cord took a handful of hair and lifted the head anyway, as if he had to be certain. The battered face of Billy Pate twisted up toward the moon.

"Five hundred dollars," Sayre said. "It is a start."

"Good for you," Cord said savagely.

Sayre looked him over judiciously. "You are drunk, Mister Cord."

"I'm working on it."

"And you are in a sorry temper." Sayre sounded amused.

Cord drank again. He knew he'd never get his fingers to do delicate tasks now, so he fished out his pouch and tossed it to Sayre.

"You been up here all this time," Cord said. "Spying on me."

"That's right." Sayre creased a paper and shook tobacco

flakes into it. "Protecting my investment, you might say. We can't have any of them slipping off into the night."

"Nobody trusts nobody," Cord said.

"Why should anyone trust you, Cord? You are betraying your friend Kelly, fast as you can." He handed over the cigarette and began on another for himself. "What have you accomplished so far, beyond kicking this kid into the river?"

Cord lit a lucifer on the seat of his britches. "You watch yourself, bounty man."

"Have you worked out anything of substance yet?" Sayre pressed. "Are you any closer to seeing your partner free again?"

"You son of a bitch."

"Did you spend your day in anything beyond drinking?"

"We are going into Rathdrum," Cord said evenly. "To-morrow, about one o'clock afternoon, when the timberjacks are working the woods."

"What is there to rob in Rathdrum?"

"Not a goddamned thing—but we're never going to get there, are we. You find a place on the trail this side of town, and we see to business. I'll take Kelly out, you get the rest. Simple as shooting pigs in a pen."

"That couldn't be finer." Sayre lit his own cigarette and blew out smoke. "There is a little draw about five miles short of Rathdrum, far enough out so we won't attract any unwanted attention while we see to business. I'll leave a forked stick in the ground off the left side of the trail. When you see it, be ready."

"One more thing," Cord said. "I get the woman."

Sayre laughed.

"Alive," Cord said. "If she dies so do you."

"Is that right?"

Cord drew on him, knowing he was fast as ever despite the whiskey in him, but run to sudden bad anger. "Maybe I'll shoot you right now, take care of all my problems with one bullet."

"You'd still need Kelly," Sayre said calmly.

"You listen to me: I want the woman too."

"Well, hell," Sayre said. "Calm down. You get the woman. But how about if you cut me in on any money coming from her, if you get it? I'll make you the deal on honor. That way we got some trust back and forth between us."

"Drink on it." Cord offered the bottle.

"Not me," Sayre said. "I got work in the morning." The bounty hunter led his burdened horse off into the darkness. Cord did not say so long or watch him go. Instead he reholstered his Colt and sat back against the same pine, and set his attention to finishing the bourbon.

When that had been taken care of, he flung the bottle into the darkness, in the direction Sayre had gone. He heard it shatter against a rock or tree trunk, the noise a harsh violation of the night's black serenity. Cord let his chin drop onto his chest and toyed with the notion of letting himself drift off where he was.

But there was a bad idea. He was already courting a brain-wracking hangover, and he didn't need a body full of stiff muscles to go with it. So he pulled himself to his feet and went down to the little run-off rill where he'd picketed the black stocking-footed gelding. The animal nickered softly when Cord lurched into the saddle, then began to pick its way carefully down toward the little town below.

Dunraven's saloon was nearly empty. Two men were playing euchre at one of the tables, and a couple more were hunched over glasses at the bar, not speaking to each other or much moving, except to take a drink. The bartender was sitting at a stool at the far end, reading a yellow-backed dime novel. As Cord glanced at him, he flicked a page over with his thumb, looked up, and nodded. No one else paid Cord any attention.

But then a door at the other end of the bar opened and Jewel came in, hitching up her leather britches. She saw Cord headed for the stairs, and set a course to intercept him. Cord had a sudden irrational instinct of flight.

Jewel put a hand on Cord's arm. "I need to talk," she said.

"Look," Cord said thickly. "Not right now, all right?" It sounded like a plea, and maybe it was. Cord had the eerie feeling of being sucked into the vortex of Jewel's control; if he did not get away from her she would have him turning flip-flops like a trained ape and babbling out his darkest fears.

"Gotta go," Cord said stupidly and pulled away. He felt eyes burning his back as he went up the stairs. He needed his room, a chair bracing the doorknob, and a bed under him before he passed out.

But this night was not yet over.

The door to Dunraven's office was ajar, and light from it spilled into the hallway like a boiling creek Cord had to ford to make the second staircase. Before he reached it, Dunraven's voice called, "Dear Mister Cord, come in here, please." The fop son of a bitch must have watched him ride in.

Which was okay. Dunraven did not pull his strings, Cord thought with a crooked grin—and went into the office. Everyone pulled his strings these days.

Dunraven sat behind his desk, framed in the light of twin oil lamps. The omnipresent decanter of whiskey showed golden in the light. His face was flushed with drink and his speech vaguely slurred, but otherwise he was no more besotted than he'd been twelve hours earlier, at midday.

Dicker the swamper was there too, sitting in a stuffed armchair with one of Dunraven's cut-glass tumblers in one hand and a big cigar between the fingers of the one that had been shot, a grotesque deformed parody of Dunraven, or an idiot relation. Dicker gave Cord a shrewd demented grin.

Dunraven leafed through a neatly stacked pile of papers, made a show of finding the one he wanted, and held it out. "Your bill, Mister Cord." His long fragile fingers trembled slightly, with some unnamed apprehension, or the palsy of lifelong drinking. Cord snatched it and looked it over dully. It was a shop-printed account-due form, with ornate curlicue scrolling at the top framing the words "*Charles Stuart Dunraven, Prop., City of Lord.*" In smaller print below Cord read "PUBLIC HOUSE AND HOSTELRY—SPECIAL SERVICES ON APPLICATION TO MANAGEMENT." Handwritten on the first blank line was "*For beverage service, lodging, and the forbearance of the house: Fifty and 00/100 dollars ($50.00).*"

"What the hell is this?"

"My fee, Mister Cord. The standard tariff for one day in Lord. I understand you are leaving before sunrise, and—"

"You're a nosy bastard, aren't you?"

"—and," Dunraven went on, "I do not wish you to overlook your obligation in the press of your travel preparations." Dunraven smiled his slightly drunken smile. "I cannot say I am entirely sorry to see you go. In certain ways your presence has been disruptive."

"You mean 'cause I killed a paying customer?"

"Accidents happen," Dunraven said neutrally.

Dicker sat up suddenly. "Gonna be trouble," he cackled in a thin voice. "Sure as shooting, gonna be trouble."

"Didn't know your buddy-boy could talk," Cord snapped. He felt drawn and scraped raw.

Dunraven's smile went chill around the eyes, as if he could see something about to happen that he did not much like. He stood and held out a hand, palm up. "Your payment in full, please, Mister Cord."

Cord fished a roll of currency from his britches pocket. He peeled off fifty dollars and threw the bills on the desk—then counted another fifty and added it to the pile. "For the kid," he snarled. "If I hadn't killed him he would've stayed another night." He reached past Dunraven's hand, grabbed the decanter by the neck, and took a long swig. Drunk as he was, he recognized this was not the rotgut Dunraven served downstairs.

"Shooting and killing," Dicker said happily. He held up his wounded hand; cigar ash was smeared into the sticky blood staining the filthy bandage. "Bleeding and broken, blood of the lamb and blood of the wolf."

Dunraven stared at the mound of wrinkled bills scattered in front of him. "Do get an early start, Mister Cord, and do not come back. You are not welcome here."

Cord drank again from the decanter and resisted the urge to plant it about two inches deep into Dunraven's skull. He looked at the broken-minded Dicker, and back to Dunraven, and laughed instead.

"That's a compliment," Cord said, "not being welcome here. You got some town, just right for a fine-handed son of a bitch like you, a pretty congregation of cutthroats and pimps and cocksuckers—one whore—" Cord tried to shut himself down. The woman was no more whore than he was murderer—and he did not like that thought either. The one corner of his brain that was still lucid told him he was full of whiskey and soul-weariness, and angry as he ever got.

"So I'm leaving, all right," he went on, "but you and this pig-nosed idiot got to stay here forever, living at the whim of trash. You are a broken-down, useless remittance man, Lord Dunraven, and your only friend is a syphilitic butter-brain with a hole in his face, but you make a perfect pair and you ought to be happy forever, here in this place." Cord finally got himself stopped. This was mindless bullying, pointless and cruel as kicking the crutches out from under a cripple.

Dicker did not understand the words but he recognized the tone, and he was shrunk back into the velvet-covered armchair, clutching his glass of whiskey to his chest. Dunraven was white, and the smile was fixed on his face like a rictus.

"Such fine sentiments," he said with surprising viciousness. "So handsomely expressed—and so unexpected from the mouth of a man like you." Dunraven pointed a long, thin finger at Cord, posing like a stage actor. "'This above all,'" he recited, "'to thine own self be true/And it must follow, as the night the day/Thou canst not be false to any man.' What do you suppose the Bard meant by those words, Mister Cord?"

Cord had no answer, and quickly as he'd blown up into anger he deflated and came down. Dunraven saw through him like all the rest—Majors, Lanett Sayre, Jewel, and God forbid, probably Chris Kelly as well. He knew Cord had been false—to Chris, to himself; there were simply rules of decency, and Cord had violated them utterly.

He would be just as haunted as the broken, drunken Englishman, for the rest of his life, just as great a failure, and lucky to be better off than Dicker.

Dunraven sank into his chair. "Good night, Mister Cord," he muttered. "Good night, and good-bye."

Cord went out of there, away from this face-down where there were no winners, a showdown between men already condemned. He felt a chill through his bones and feared the next day. He had brought a curse upon them, him and Chi, and he could not break loose of it. He blundered into walls as he climbed the second flight of stairs and kicked open the door of his room. He did not have the wherewithal to pull his boots, only to flop onto the stinking bare mattress, where he fell immediately into dreamless, snuffling sleep.

Chapter Twelve

THIS DAY WAS TOO HANDSOME FOR DYING. IT was nearing noon, and the sun was high enough to have burned off the high mountain chill from the bright air. There was no breeze and it was perfectly quiet except for the clomping of their horses along the dusty hardpack trail.

Cord had just seen the forked stick.

He felt a jolt in the pit of his stomach, as if all his gut muscles had spasmed together; sweat soaked into his hat brim. He had never felt this way before a fight; to the contrary, imminent and inevitable violence usually put Cord into an icy, calm concentration, where survival became the only focus. His joints were stiff, half-frozen, and Cord wondered if this day was his last.

He kicked the black gelding, harder than he meant, and the animal snorted and moved up beside Chris Kelly. Just ahead the road to Rathdrum narrowed to pass through a dry canyon. Kelly glanced over and nodded companionably, but at his other side Jewel stared straight ahead—as if she were considering the chance of ambush. Cord breathed through his nose, and tried to stop his imagination from taking off like a runaway steam engine.

Hake, the Chief, and the smartass Aussie Jonnie Frye were up ahead a couple-three horselengths and nearing the canyon mouth. Jonnie Frye had a pint bottle of whiskey— more to show them all that he could do what he damned well

pleased than from an early-day desire for liquor—and he
passed it to Pete Hake.

It didn't matter, Cord thought. Dead drunk or dead sober,
they were still dead.

It came to him then, a jolt of insight: Sayre was planning
a double-cross. He had protection and position and for sure
an accurate rifle and plenty of ammo. Once they were trapped
between rock walls he would kill them all. Dead, Cord was
worth money; alive he was only trouble. Imagination or no,
Cord was not riding blindly into that defile.

He spurred the gelding again and jumped the animal out
ahead of Chris Kelly and Jewel, set the horse sideways in
the road—and there he was with the Peacemaker in his hand,
and Chris Kelly and Jewel covered cold. Chris Kelly did not
put up his hands but folded them on the saddle horn, but
that was all right. Even he would not try games on a shootist
of Cord's skill, not with a gun already on him.

"What is it, you bastard?" Jewel hissed. "What the hell
is it?"

Cord sidestepped the gelding around to where he could
watch them and the road ahead. Chris Kelly regarded him
with a curious frown but no evident fear.

Jewel looked at Cord's gun, took a deep breath, and hollered, "Hold up, you men."

Hake looked over his shoulder at her, and finally the
gunfire came.

Three rifle shots a second apart, flat cracks deadened by
the rocks: Hake, already twisted in the saddle, went over
first, sliding face-first off the back of his mount. Jonnie Frye
threw up both hands and rolled sideways, one foot caught
in the stirrups and his body dragging over gravel a few yards
before his mount calmed. The Chief managed to get his revolver drawn, but there was no one to shoot and nowhere
to ride, and as he realized this the third shot slammed into
his hard, scarred bare chest and tumbled him into the dirt.

They were dead, the three of them. They had fallen like
dead men and they rested like dead men. Cord had seen
enough to know.

"Sayre! Show yourself, right now." Cord scanned the
rocks before them.

"You stinking son of a bitch," Jewel said and went on cursing in a low monotone.

"Shut up, lady," Cord said, but without much force.

"You don't tell me what to do, you bastard."

"Easy," Chris Kelly said without looking at her. "Save it."

Up on the rimrock above the canyon and the three dead men, the bounty hunter Lanett Sayre stood, his rifle cradled in his arms. He was smiling, which seemed the gravest and most gratuitous of insults to Cord, and he gave thought to the idea of shooting him dead, toppling him off his mountain to crash among the other dead scum—and what would that accomplish? Sayre's figure was black against the sun.

"Are they controlled?" he called.

"Deader than hell, looks to me," Chris Kelly hollered.

Cord looked sideways at him. Kelly should have been cursing him as Jewel was, or at least sullen, anything but this resigned disappointment. Cord could not have felt lower if Kelly had spit in his face.

"Cord," Sayre called. "Are your people under control?"

"They are," Cord answered finally. "Climb down here."

Sayre disappeared toward the back of the little cliff. Cord worked at keeping his attention on his prisoners, but Chris Kelly's sad patience and Jewel's fiery glaze were like a blinding light in his eyes.

"You'll want us to throw down our guns," Chris Kelly said, and without waiting for an answer he pulled his Colt and let it drop to the ground. Then he leaned in the saddle and plucked Jewel's revolver from its holster. She spun around and gave him a furious gaze. Chris Kelly shrugged and let the gun drop.

The high sun was too hot, and Cord fought a sudden spasm of vertiginous dizziness.

Sayre came out from the tall scrub brush down the draw, near where the corpses were sprawled. "Get your prisoners off their horses and march them down here," he called and walked up the road into the canyon.

"You and that bounty-hunting maggot," Jewel spat. "Two of a kind, living on spoiled meat."

"Dismount," Cord ordered and waved his Colt.

"Do it," Chris Kelly said and swung out of the saddle. Jewel looked like she would argue again, but then she did what she was told.

Cord followed them up the trail. He stood over Pete Hake and Jonnie Frye and the Chief, studying them carefully. When you get a man killed, you owe him the guts to witness his looks after he is dead. You made yourself look at death up close, and you saw it was no joke and no sport, and maybe it helped you keep from killing without damned good reason.

Each man had gone down with a single killing bullet in the center of the trunk, the widest, easiest target. Cord could not grieve for these men, but still he was some shocked at the coldness with which Sayre had carried out their executions. It had been an effortless harvest.

"What about us?" Jewel demanded. "You going to take us alive, you two murdering, motherless pricks? You figure there's better money on us alive—that's it, isn't it?"

"I'm taking you," Cord said. "He's taking them."

"Shut up, Jewel," Chris Kelly said.

Sayre came out of the canyon mouth, driving an uncovered buckboard wagon fitted out with a fresh-looking, high-blooded team. It figured that the bounty man would leave little as possible to chance; he'd parked the wagon where it would plug one end of the defile. Hake and the Aussie and the Comanche were deader than Lincoln, soon as they came within fifty yards of this place.

Sayre pulled the wagon up beside the bodies. He fixed the hand-brake and looked at Chris Kelly, a long, level exchange during which neither man's eye flickered.

"Load 'em," Sayre said.

Kelly did not move.

"Mister Kelly," Sayre said. "Dump them dead boys in the back end of this wagon, then shake out that tarp there and cover 'em over and tie it down secure. I don't want the magpies and buzzards following me all the way to Coeur d'Alene."

"Do it," Cord said, gesturing with the Colt.

"I will like hell," Chris Kelly said. "I have gone along

with you so far, pard"—and the word twisted into Cord like a red-hot needle—"but there are a few things I will not touch."

"Mister Kelly," Sayre began in the same cold calm voice, but Cord cut in. "Forget it. Cover them." Cord holstered his gun and began wrestling the bodies into the wagon.

Chris Kelly watched him and that's how it should have been, because maybe this was like penance. Cord got one of them under the arms and felt the nausea rising in the pit of his belly. He had come awake with no more sign of hangover than usual, and coffee had chased off the first fuzziness in his mind, but all morning he had felt hollow. Now he was close to puking.

It was not these dead men; the world was a better place without them. It was Jewel's hatred, because he merited it, and Lanett Sayre and the way he looked at the three cadavers like a banker looks at his vault, and most of all it was what came next, the long ride down through Idaho with Chris Kelly, both of them knowing that at the end Cord would turn his one-time partner over like beef on the hoof at a stockyard auction.

Nothing was more awkward to lift than a dead body, and the carcasses thumped and flopped into the buckboard, leaking red onto the unvarnished planks. Cord flipped the tarp over them and cinched down the ties.

"You are going to leave a trail of blood." Chris Kelly grinned up at Sayre. "All the rest of your life. You'll be easy to track."

"Not by the likes of you." Sayre nodded to Cord and touched two fingers to the flat brim of his black hat. "We got along real fine, Mister Cord, didn't even have to cuss each other. Maybe we'll work together again some time. Business gets better with each passing year."

Sayre snapped the reins, and the wagon was gone into the canyon and south in clatter and dust.

Cord turned and Chris Kelly was watching him. Cord knew what he was waiting for. Kelly wanted to hear it aloud, from Cord's lips.

"Chris," Cord said. "I am taking you in."

"Judas," Jewel muttered. "Scum-assed Judas Priest."

"Shut your mouth, Jewel," Kelly said.

"Fuck you." She stared from one to the other, dividing her contempt equally. "You chickenshit," she said to Kelly.

"Jewel," Kelly said patiently, "he saved your life, whether you know it or not."

"In a pig's ass."

"It's not how you think," Kelly said. "He's not taking me to the law—leastways not directly." He looked at Cord. "Ain't that right?"

Cord stared. All along he had dismissed the idea that Chris Kelly was ahead of him right down the line, and yet here they were.

"Got you, you back-stabbing bastard."

Cord had taken his eyes off her, and now Jewel edged a step away. She held a little woman's pistol brought out from somewhere, with mother-of-pearl grips and plenty enough lead and powder-load to kill at this range.

"You are dead," Jewel said.

And he was, if that's the way she wanted him.

"Jewel," Chris Kelly said, almost gently, "put up the gun. Fetch your Colt and catch your horse and ride out of here. He doesn't want you, and you don't want him dead."

Jewel hesitated.

"He's got your woman, doesn't he?" Kelly said to Cord. "Yeah."

"Who are you talking about?" Jewel said. "What has all this to do with?"

"Ride out," Kelly said again. "This is old business between us, and you got no part in it. You and me will be back together when it's finished. I'm asking you."

Jewel looked all at once like a child, her lips quivering.

"Mount up," Kelly urged, and he was asking, not telling. "I'll get word to you, back at the home place. Go see your brother."

She looked back to Cord. "If he's wrong, if this doesn't work out, I'll kill you. One day while you are having a drink, this blond woman will shoot you in the back of the head. Your brains will splatter the mirror back of the bar. Don't you forget." The little pistol disappeared inside her shirt.

"I'll remember," Cord promised.

Both men watched her walk away, the only fine thing left

of this morning. They watched her pick up her Colt and put
it where it belonged, then loop the reins over her horse,
grazing off the trail in the scrub grass, and they watched her
canter away, back in the direction she'd come.

"That's where I ought to be," Chris Kelly said. "Working
for her brother."

"What brother?"

"Any brother."

Cord knew what he meant.

Chris Kelly squinted up at the noon sun. "Well, pard,"
he said. "Let's get this done with."

Chapter Thirteen

THAT NIGHT THEY CAMPED SOUTH OF COEUR
d'Alene, by the lakeshore. Cord had no intention of going
near a town. But Chris Kelly had tried no foolish bravado
moves, had made nothing near to trouble. He rode along in
front of Cord, his hands bound loosely with rawhide, and
when he talked it was only about an elk they jumped or the
look of the weather in the western sky. "Just like them days,"
he said once. "Old partners on the trail again."

Cord felt like the prize heel of the world.

Chris Kelly sat against a stump and watched Cord go
about the business of making a minimal camp. After bedrolls
were laid out and deadfall branches gathered and set aflame,
Cord mixed beans with bacon fat and a dipper of lake water
in a hot skillet and set coffee on to boil. Dinner on the trail
for Cord was usually something of a ritual, to be done carefully and precisely, but this night he hardly paid attention.
He put a plate in front of Chris Kelly, who had to raise both
hands to get his spoon to his mouth.

Cord concentrated on shoveling warm, mushy beans into

his mouth. He was committed beyond redemption. What happened from here on was as irreversible as a boulder rolling down hill. The betrayal was good as accomplished, and absolute, and to Cord it seemed more inestimably horrible than ever.

And dammit, Cord thought viciously, it could not be. Once that murdering bastard Majors had Chris Kelly, everything was done with, and dead, including himself—especially himself, Cord realized, dead or good as. Maybe this wasn't even so much concerned with Kelly; maybe what counted was himself, and accepting such total defeat for the first time and without anything beyond a self-pitying whimper. He wouldn't have Chi either after Kelly was gone, never would, because she knew him and would see the constant haunted fear in his eyes, and smell the stink of it on him as if he were a skunk-sprayed mongrel.

Cord had pushed this close to lots of other edges in his time, and he had not let them crowd him over, nor had he bolted and run for the quick escape. He would not now. He did not need to look for reasons. Dancing to Majors's tune was dead wrong: There was reason enough.

He'd figure some other way to bust Chi loose. There were always possibilities, if a man wasn't too narrow-visioned to see them. Maybe Chris Kelly could help out, throw in with him once more before they put the old days to rest for good.

Cord put his plate aside and fished out his makings. His head seemed suddenly clear, as if he were emerging from weeks of dull stupor. He was not as a habit quick to speak, especially when the speech was important and required working out to be said precisely. There was time. It was all right now.

Chris Kelly finished his own meal and gestured at Cord's neglected dish. "You done with that mush?" Cord passed the plate over and cleared bean phlegm from his throat.

"A second son," Kelly said through a mess of beans. He chewed. "Probably that's his trouble. Second sons are always a problem, because they got ambitions no one can live with, least of all themselves. Same problem Dunraven's got."

"Listen, Chris," Cord said and stopped abruptly in delayed reaction. This was not idle prattle; Kelly had something to tell him. "What are you talking about?" Cord asked, a trifle sharply.

"William Deane Majors," Chris Kelly said. "Governor of this territory. The man you are delivering me to." He spooned more beans into his mouth and shook his head, as if the meal were so fine he couldn't get his fill. "I got a tale."

It was halfway to full dark, the sun below the hills trailing a brilliant wash of red and purple across the western sky. Sheets of light rippled across the lake water.

Chris Kelly scraped up the last of the beans. "Build me one of those smokes, would you?" He watched Cord's fingers move. "A man your age, you'd think he'd somewhere along the line learn to roll a cigarette better than that," Kelly said. Cord used a twig from the fire to light the misshapen cigarette, then tucked it between Chris Kelly's lips.

Cord waited patiently. A hawk came out from above the trees downshore and made a few desultory passes at the water. After a while Chris Kelly took a last long drag on the butt, spit it out, exhaled a long lungful of smoke, and began his story.

William Deane Majors started life as a third-generation, middle-class American boy. His father's people were English, his mother's Alsatian. The family string of three neighborhood butcher shops would go to his older brother some day, and probably Majors was not so interested anyway in spending his life in a bloody smock cutting meat, so he got taken on as a clerk by a Baltimore attorney. "He picked up a little law," Chris Kelly said. "Enough to get some notions on how to break it and get away clean. After that he went into banking."

"That figures."

Chris Kelly laughed. "Within a couple years, he was head cashier at the First Mercantile Trust of Baltimore. This is maybe twenty years back, not long after the end of the war. He was a real ambitious boy, our Majors. He worked ten hours a day, and he went back at night. The bank officers loved his butt.

"Only thing was," Chris Kelly said, "at night he wasn't working. He was pawing through the accounts."

"What was he looking for?"

"Opportunities."

According to the story, Majors found them. One night he discovered that a client of the bank, a textile mill, was way out on a cash limb and ripe to crash. The next morning he started buying up the company's shares.

"On a bookkeeper's pay?" Cord asked.

Chris Kelly smiled broadly. "He embezzled the money from the bank."

"All right—but if this textile outfit was going belly-up, what did he want with shares?"

"I'm coming to that."

In a couple of weeks, buying through several fictitious names, Majors owned a majority of the voting stock. His next step was to spread rumors that the company's bankruptcy was imminent, supporting the rumors by circulating documents stolen from the bank that revealed the company's precarious position. Investors sold more shares, and Majors snapped them up.

"He was trying to steal the company," Cord guessed.

"It's more complicated than that. Follow along: A lot of investors figured it was a sure thing that this company would go under, and they wanted to profit on the deal. Sort of like vultures circling over a snakebit cow. So they started selling the shares short. That means they borrowed shares from someone who had them, sold the shares, and figured they would buy them back later for a lot less—there is their profit—and pay back the lender."

"Like betting against the shooter in dice," Cord said slowly.

"Pretty much," Chris Kelly agreed. "Anyway, Majors's next move is to go into cahoots with the man who owns the mill. Majors embezzles more money, passes it to the mill hombre, and he uses it to fatten the company again. Instead of dropping, the price of the shares shoots up, and Majors has himself what they call a 'short corner.'

"You can see what happens," Chris Kelly said. "All the folk who sold short are scrambling to buy shares, so they can pay back them they borrowed from. But the only one who has any shares to speak of is our friend, and he charges dearly for them. A lot of speculators got hurt bad, and at least a half-dozen got wiped out."

"Well I got no sympathy for them," Cord said. "Trading paper—what kind of nonsense is that?"

"It made a hell of a lot of money for Majors. It wasn't long before he owned that bank—which made it lots easier to cover up his tracks—and he had plenty enough shares left after he pulled off the short squeeze to take over the textile mill.

"Only trouble was, the fellow who owned the mill didn't want to give it up," Chris Kelly said. "So Majors called in that Jaeger son of a bitch. He was wearing a Baltimore cop uniform, but he was as good a crook as any of them, running lottery numbers and whores and opium, any damned thing for easy money. He did a cute trick for Majors: He killed that mill man's wife and framed him for the job. So that got Majors the mill."

"But it also got him stuck with Jaeger." The way those two cat-and-moused around each other made sense now. They were like Siamese twins, tied by a common guilt and the fear that came with it.

"How is it you understand this business?" Cord asked. Shares and stocks and the inner workings of capitalism were as exotic to him as Javanese temple dancers.

"My other life."

"Huh?"

"I never come west until I was twenty-three," Chris Kelly said. "Before that I was bookkeeper for a customs house in Detroit, Michigan." Chris Kelly looked at the fire's coals. "One day I was sitting on my high stool peering at column after column of tiny numbers in an account book, thinking how after I factored them up I would go home to my rooming house, and then out to dinner with this snaggled-toothed girl named Phyllis I was proposing to marry. I got up and sharpened about a dozen pencils, carefully and to perfect points, and then I went back to my desk and lay them down and got my hat and left. I run out on Detroit and bookkeeping and Phyllis, and I never went back."

Chris Kelly looked up from his memories. "Anyway," he said, "there is the kind of ruthless turd-sucker you got in Majors. A double-dealer and a thief and a murderer, and what do you figure he will do when you turn me over and stand there waiting for your reward?"

"I've been thinking on that," Cord said.

"That's fine," Chris Kelly said ironically. "I'd say the time is come to give it some consideration."

Cord stared at the ropes still binding Kelly's wrists. "How did you come by this fairy tale?" he demanded.

"It's no fairy tale, pard. I'm going to make you a believer." He licked at his lips. "I wish we had some whiskey."

"We don't."

"Probably just as well," Chris Kelly said. "It was nine months back," he went on. "The end of last summer. Me and Jewel hadn't hooked up yet, and she still doesn't know anything about all this. Anyway, I was crossing the high desert there in northwestern Nevada, coming north toward Gerlach from Pyramid Lake, just riding through, which is all anybody does in that country. Along about nightfall I saw an old line-camp with smoke rising from the chimney, so I rode in to holler up whoever was living there. I was tired and didn't mind the idea of a roof and a ready-made fire, and I figured whoever lived to hell-and-gone out there would be happy for company. This old man came out and right away I was half-sure he was crazy, but when he opened the flap I could smell the coffee, and I reckoned I could listen to his ranting long enough to drink a cup.

"Turned out," Chris Kelly said, "he wasn't so crazy after all. He cottoned to me when he found out about my book-keeper days, because he figured I'd be able to understand him."

"Everyone has got their tale to tell."

"You already know most of this one. The old man's name was Karp, and he was the owner of the textile mill, the man Majors and Jaeger robbed and framed for murder. Karp managed to run off one step ahead of the law, and he'd changed his name and been grubbing his living in the West ever since. He was tending windmills for sheep ranchers when I ran into him.

"To prove he is not mush-brained," Chris Kelly said, "Karp pulls out a trunk, and finds a sheaf of papers—records, newspaper clippings, contracts, stock certificates, and a half-dozen ledger books. I spent the rest of the night looking it all over under the light of his kerosene lamp, and by morning I was damned sure he had a case—not for the law, probably, but maybe for some one-time bookkeeper with the habit of packing a well-oiled Colt.

"Meanwhile," Chris Kelly said, "the old man has had this fantasy for years: He wants to bring Majors down from his peak and to his knees. Majors doesn't even know the evidence exists, he says. Well, that was all right, but the old man was just blowing smoke; anybody could see he would never use the stick he had. Anyway, he was dying, this year or the next. A lifetime of those roll-your-own cigarettes had got his wind." He paused significantly, and after a moment Cord got the idea and took out his own makings.

"I offered to buy what he had and use it on Majors," Chris Kelly said. "The old man told me to take 'em for nothing, said the idea of Majors squirming was payment enough. So that morning I rode out the way I'd come in, except now I was carrying those papers rolled in waxed paper and tucked into my sleeping blankets and tarp.

"I been sending him some money anyway," Chris Kelly, "once a month since then. I send it in care of Gerlach or the ranch at Spanish Meadows. I told some people I would pay his keep, in case he got clear down and couldn't work."

Cord licked at a clumsy cigarette, lit it, and passed it over. "So you been blackmailing Majors ever since."

"Sure enough, and Jaeger with him. I sent those two snakes a sample of what I got, and directed Majors how and where to pay five hundred every month, if he didn't want to live out his years in prison. I wasn't greedy. I didn't want to bleed him, just scratch him up a little. I figured he could live with a modest setup like that for many years. I figured he was a meal ticket, and I didn't want to run him under." Chris Kelly blew out smoke. "Guess I figured wrong."

"How come you got mixed up in that Lewiston job, then?"

"I got bored—or maybe careless. Too much money will do that sometimes."

It was full dark by now. Cord stared across the fire at Chris Kelly. "That tears it then," Cord said.

Cord stood and drew his thin-bladed stockman's knife,

went around the fire and dropped to one knee in front of Chris Kelly. Kelly gave him a long questioning look, then presented his bound wrists. "Soon as Majors has hold of you he'll kill the three of us, you and me and Chi." Cord sawed at the thick ropes. "Tell everyone we resisted arrest and bury us somewhere out in the desert so no one will see the bullet holes, or notice they were in our backs."

"That's why he wanted you running his trap line in the first place," Chris Kelly said patiently. "He could dispose of you like a torn shirt." The ropes parted and fell away.

Cord got up and kicked at the fire. "All right," he said, looking into the flames. "We got to think of something."

"Is that right?" Chris Kelly asked coldly. He was rubbing at his wrists.

Cord stared at him.

"You aren't trying, pard. How about those papers?"

"Huh?"

"I'm tired of sucking on Majors," Chris Kelly said. "Too much trouble, and no fun anymore. You take the papers, pard. You earned them."

Kelly's tone thickened with sarcasm. "Well, hell, you turned Jewel loose—I owe you for that. And now here you are, gonna turn me loose too." He held up his chafed wrists. "Ain't you gonna turn me loose, Mister Cord, old pard? You can pay off the rest some other day. You owe me drinks for life. Then again, could be I'm interested in helping out a woman I used to like. Whatever you say." His voice went sharp. "For chrissake, Cord, do I have to cipher it out for you? Can't you figure a way to swap those documents for Chi?"

Cord lifted his head and stared out to the stars. It could work.

"Where are these valuable papers?" he asked.

"In the safe upstairs at the Rosebud House in Denver, where my old friend Polly Dougall runs the whores. I'll wire her, and she can ship the packet to you by Wells, Fargo registered express. Two days from now you can pick them up in Boise and see to your business."

"Maybe . . ."

"You do trust me, don't you, pard?"

"Listen, Chris."

"No, pard," and the word twisted worse than ever. "You listen. I am doing this for her—for Chi. You bear that in mind."

Kelly got to his feet, moving a little stiffly. "I'll be riding right now," he announced. "I don't want to be around in the morning."

Cord watched Chris Kelly roll up his blankets and tie them on behind his saddle with two rawhide thongs. It was too late to say anything now.

Chris Kelly mounted and gathered in the reins. He looked down at Cord. "You were going to do it. You were going to turn me over to that fat, murdering bastard."

Cord met Kelly's gaze.

"Good as killing me," Chris Kelly said. "Good as pulling the trigger yourself."

There was no answer to that either.

"Now that I think of it," Chris Kelly said, "you can keep those damned drinks. You and I will not be raising glasses together again, not ever. Not after what you tried. The more I think—the more I got to be with you—the madder I get."

Cord watched him ride into the dark night and sat by the fire until the ashes turned gray and winked out. He gave due time to it, looking at his deep hole card, examining his misgivings, but when he rolled up in his blankets he finally put it aside. It was time to look ahead, and for goddamned sure it was time to do something right. He drifted into sleep thinking of Chi, seeing her hair over her shoulders and smelling the clean scent of her in the morning, before the coffee boiled.

Chapter Fourteen

THE INTERIOR OF THE WELLS, FARGO EXPRESS office on River Street in Boise was all dark varnished oak and stuffy clerks in tinted celluloid visors and arm garters, and clocks ticking discreetly on the wall while people talked in muffled tones. It reminded Cord of a bank and made him uneasy, because it had been years since he'd entered a bank on legitimate business. The floor was marble, polished every day from the look of it.

Cord waited in line behind a woman sending money to her daughter. The girl was going to college at Radcliffe in Cambridge—wherever that was—and setting up to be a medical doctor after that. "That's swell," the clerk said glumly and put her change on the counter without looking up. Cord was busy wondering if anyone had spotted him slipping into town. He didn't bother to try to skulk through back streets but came in like everyone else, another drifter wearing trail dust in the morning.

"Oosterbahn," he said to the clerk. "Helmut Oosterbahn. You have a package registered through to me from Denver."

Cord signed the receipt and took the package to the writing desk set against one hardwood wall. It was the size of a hatbox, tied with twine and sealed with wax. Cord leafed through a sheaf of receipts and then paged through the top ledger book. Most of the evidence was beyond his comprehension, but he could make out enough to see that Kelly was playing a straight hand with him. These papers were a rope, already knotted around the neck of Governor William Deane Majors.

The offices of the Boise *Capital Intelligencer* were four blocks down the street. It was nearing noon, and there were only three reporters in the newsroom that Cord could see, two drinking coffee and arguing, the third writing busily in a log book.

Cord stood in the doorway and looked them over. The most critical part of this business was yet to come, and he was running on instinct and the quick nerve-rush he felt when he could see the end not far ahead. Then he spotted the fourth man, seated in the back of the open newsroom behind a desk heaped with books, broadsides, magazines, and crumpled balls of paper. The man's feet were planted atop the mess and he was reading a copy of his own newspaper, occasionally shaking his head with dismay.

This fellow was in his mid-twenties, with red hair that shined bright as minted pennies. He wore a look of permanent cynicism, a white shirt with celluloid collar, britches with suspenders, no jacket, and a straw boater with a broken brim. His face was spackled with freckles.

Cord made his way across the cluttered room, weaving between close-set desks. The two reporters stopped arguing and stared at him, but the red-haired man did not look up when Cord came to stand across his desk. He wet a thumb on his tongue, turned the page of his newspaper, and without raising his eyes said, "What can I do for you, friend?"

"I want to buy you a drink."

The reporter lowered the newspaper and took his time looking Cord up and down. Finally he dropped his feet to the floor and unfolded himself from the chair. He unhooked a rumpled seersucker jacket from a coat tree and shrugged into it. "The name is McNamer," he said, "and any friend of Irish whiskey is a friend of mine."

The barroom around the corner was quiet, and dark and cool after the midday heat rising from the city streets. There were a few businessmen at a couple of tables, a bow-tied bartender browsing over a short beer, and an elaborately stocked free-lunch counter. Cord led the reporter to a booth table built into the back wall, laid the packet of papers down, then woke up the bartender for a bottle of Irish and two glasses. McNamer poured, and Cord watched him drink.

Cord put a hand on the box. "What I got here is something for you to look over."

Cord rolled and smoked two cigarettes whole McNamer pawed through the receipts and accounts books and clippings, but had only a sip of the whiskey. This was not a drinking day for him. He kept McNamer's glass full.

Finally McNamer looked up and smiled.

"Your governor is a crook," Cord said.

"Does a pig shit in the pen? So are you, Mister Cord." He watched Cord's face to see how the name registered. "We reporters are trained to be observant, friend. I keep my eye on the wanted posters, so I'll be even on the game when some desperado like you comes walking up to my desk. Not that it ever happened before."

"We're not talking about me."

"What are we talking about?" McNamer reached inside the seersucker jacket and took out a narrow notebook.

"Nothing for you to write down."

McNamer shrugged and put the notebook away. Whatever hunch had led him to this man was a good one. It was late in the game, but at least he was starting to get it right.

So Cord told him the whole story, from the time the playacting son of a bitch Jaeger came up to them in the cafe, right up to two nights earlier, when Chris Kelly cursed him and rode off into the night, and he didn't leave out anything in between. If Majors pulled a double-cross, Cord wanted someone to know—and besides, he was tired and wanted to talk, and there was a bottle of Irish whiskey between them.

"If he screws you," McNamer said, "how will I know?"

"You'll know. He'll be showing us off like big horn sheep trophy heads."

"Let me borrow that box for a day."

Cord shook his head no. "You've seen it, and you're a newspaper man. You'll figure a way."

"What are you going to do with it?"

"I told you: trade for my partner."

"You could squeeze him. You could get her back, and crucify the bastard as well, fry him in his own lard. All you have to do is..."

Cord held up a hand and McNamer shut up.

"I figured all that out," Cord said. "But someplace this

has got to stop. For the last week I've seen nothing but tricks and cheating and lying, and I've had a bellyful. I got to play it straight if I'm going to look in the shaving mirror. All these double-tongued sons—Majors and Jaeger..." Cord shut up. Every one of them—Dunraven and his man Dicker, the woman named Jewel, Chris Kelly, Lanett Sayre the soulless bounty hunter—all had been playing some kind of double game. "I've seen nothing but trickery, and I'm sick of it."

"From your story," McNamer said, "you tried to play a few tricks too."

"Yeah," Cord said. "No more. I'm going out straight." He took a shallow sip of the Irish, but it tasted too good and he put the glass down again. "That's why I picked you. If this works out and we get free, my partner and I, you forget everything."

"I'm a reporter," McNamer said.

"You are also a man. Now let's finish up." He refilled McNamer's glass. "I need your help."

McNamer drank.

"Pick one piece of paper to send Majors," Cord said, "and help me write a letter to go with it."

McNamer looked over his glass. "Shouldn't I be out on the streets, looking for lost dogs or something?"

"You got one here."

McNamer shrugged. "Won't be my first afternoon over whiskey." He gestured to the sleepy-eyed bartender, who came around the counter and to the table. "Give him ten dollars," McNamer said.

Cord unfolded a bill and laid it out. The bartender studied it curiously, then peeled it off the tabletop and tucked it in the watch pocket of his dark vest.

"Fetch Gilley," McNamer said, "but first bring me my pen and ink and a sheet of clean writing paper from the drawer there left of the cashbox." He smiled at Cord. "I keep writing materials around town in strategic places. You never know when it will take a drink to get the words flowing. We'll send the toady bastard a random page from one of the account books, so he can have fun trying to guess what comes before and after."

The bartender returned with an ink bottle, pen, blotter,

and three sheets of stiff, white paper. "Thought you might make a couple of false starts."

"Smartass," McNamer said and wrote the letter out without a single blot:

Majors:
   I have the evidence from Chris Kelly. I want Chi and the signed amnesty papers. We will exchange goods upriver in the Boise canyon, a mile and a half above where old man Peters planted the peach orchard. Go there now and wait. I'll be along.

                    Your friend,
                    Mister Cord

"Where's this peach orchard?" Cord said when he'd finished reading.

"Upriver about ten miles, on a shelf above the canyon. The rock walls fall straight away close to five hundred feet to the river. You can look down on it from the hills, and they can't surprise you with anything. You can see for miles in all directions. I would let them stew for at least a half day while you keep watch. Then go around, and there's a trail up from the river they likely won't know about. I'll draw you a map."

McNamer sketched it out, and they were into a long, slow meditation over the Irish when a compact dark man showed up beside the table. "Say good afternoon, Gilley," McNamer said. The compact man scowled. He wore a peaked hack-driver's cap and had a sharp-featured hatchet face; he looked like he would gill-net his mother for fifty dollars. "Give ten to him, too," McNamer said, and Cord laid out another bill.

McNamer folded the ledger sheet inside the letter and handed it to Gilley. "Take this to Jaeger," he said. "No one else."

"You know Jaeger," Cord said when the hackie had gone off.

"Enough to stay clear of him." McNamer finished his drink and shook his head when Cord started to pour again. The bottle was halfway down, but McNamer didn't seem any drunker than Cord was. "I do have business on the streets of the city, Mister Cord, though it has been a good forenoon." He stood and gave Cord a judicious look. "I don't suppose you would like company on your ride today."

"That's not such a good idea," Cord said.

McNamer nodded. "But then, none of this was." He offered his hand and wished Cord luck and left him alone with a half glass of Irish whiskey. It looked dark and smoky and soothing. But one drink was always too much and never enough, and there were things to attend to. Cord let go of the whiskey and went out into the glare of midday.

Chapter Fifteen

IT WAS COMING ON TO TWILIGHT, AND THE BOISE River, swollen high with runoff and at least a hundred yards straight down from where Cord stood on the narrow ridge of trail, was already shrouded in shadow. Not far above his position was the lava-rock table where Majors and Jaeger and the rest were waiting—where they had been waiting since about four that afternoon.

That much had gone according to McNamer's plan, but the newspaper man likely didn't have much firsthand knowledge of the art of ambush, because there were some things he had overlooked. Cord drew breath, winded by the long climb and close to dizzy from the height. But it was time to go on, and make the best of McNamer's oversights.

The trail he was on must have been worn into the rock long before Europeans ever saw this country, by Indians coming up from the canyon to the little spring where Majors and his crew were waiting. That was part of Cord's problem. The spring drained through a steep rock-walled gully, maybe forty feet deep and fifty yards long, which spewed a long feathery waterfall into the main canyon. The walls of the gully were lined with a growth of stunted gnarled juniper and high brush, perfect cover for gunmen waiting in ambush for Cord to ride in. His one edge was that they did not know about the old trail from the canyon bottom.

But from this point the trail followed the gully, so Cord moved off looking for a side route. Within a few yards he was climbing almost perpendicular rock in his slippery leather-soled boots, careful to keep his eyes straight ahead. He edged up a crack in the lava shelf, feeling his way hand over hand, getting each foothold secure and solid before seeking another. He could make it, long as he didn't rush. Sweat ran in his eyes, but he could not free a hand to rub it out. Once he forgot and looked down; immediately he felt nauseating, swirling vertigo and had to stop, clutching at rocks, his face pressed against the rough lichen.

After a time his stomach calmed, and he looked up and saw a way. He cleared his mind of everything but the problems of climbing and made himself go on. Then he was at the upper edge, pulling himself up and slithering over the top on his belly, moving slowly to avoid noise, controlling his breathing. He turned over on his back in the sandy loam where the sage grew right up to the edge of the great rockfall, rubbing the stinging salt from his eyes. An eagle rose and fell on the air above, close enough so Cord could see the bird's terrible cold eyes.

You'll have some meat, Cord thought.

He rolled to his feet and catfooted along the upper rim of the gully, stopping every couple of steps to scan the territory, moving again. He heard men talking in low voices down by the little spring—and then he saw Steens, crouched out of sight from the gully, a Winchester across his knees.

Got you, Cord thought. But he took long careful minutes working himself around behind the man, balancing on the balls of his feet, stepping from open ground to open ground, making no sound.

Cord slipped his Colt from its holster and put it up under the man's ear. "Aren't you looking fine this evening, Mister Steens."

Steens gasped and tried to turn his head, and Cord laid the barrel of his gun against Steens's jawbone, drawing blood. It was a debt owed and paid. Steens fell over on one knee and whimpered, and Cord hit him again. Steens stopped whimpering.

Cord edged his way to the overlook where Steens had been posted, and felt vast relief. From the distant hills where he had first staked out this encampment he could not for sure tell one figure from another.

But everyone who was supposed to be was there, gathered around the little spring like Sunday picnickers after church. Thirty feet below Cord's position, Majors sat like a lump in the shade of the sparse willows, fanning himself with his white straw planter's hat. Jaeger, the stubby, greasy little shit, stood above him. And there was Chi, standing with her back to an enormous lava boulder. Her hands were hidden under her serape, so Cord couldn't tell if she was tied. Her hair was braided down her back and looked to have been washed, and she—Cord stopped himself. Jaeger was covering her with a pistol, and that was the business at hand.

Steens whimpered again and his eyes fluttered open. Cord pulled back from the rim and put his knee on Steens's chest and the Colt in his face. "How many?"

Steens opened and closed his mouth a couple of times and said, "Three men. One more this side, two on the other."

Nothing to do but bluff it out. "You get up, Mister Steens. Nice and cautious, and not a peep out of you."

Steens got his feet under him and stood. Blood oozed out of his cheek and ran down his jawline to drip from the point of his chin. Cord grabbed Steens's right wrist and whipped him around, jamming the arm up behind him. Steens groaned softly.

"I can break it," Cord whispered in his ear. "Easy as snapping a wishbone. I'll do it too—maybe just for fun."

Cord pushed gently and guided Steens to the rimrock, right up to the edge. Only thirty feet from here to the table rock—but still the height made Cord's head swirl.

"Majors!"

The fat man looked up, and horror crossed his face.

"Tell your men to hold fire. I'll kill you first, if anything wrong happens."

Cord was shielded by Steens, and his Colt was tracked onto Majors's face. They all understood he could make the shot. Majors took off his white hat and squinted into the reflected sunlight, and Cord could see the scabbed-over burn on his forehead, where Chi had gotten him with the cigarette. Cord chanced a look at her; her hands were out in the open, and her wrists were tied.

"This is how it will happen, Majors," Cord called. "Give her the amnesties and send her out to the horses, alone. Now. You two will walk in front of me, and I'll hold on to Steens here." Steens trembled. Cord cranked up a little harder on his arm.

"Where are my . . . what you promised?"

"I've got them."

"I want to—"

"Jaeger!" Cord interrupted. "Toss your knife out on the ground, blade open." Jaeger fished in his pants and did as he was told, and Chi came forward and started cutting herself free. It was awkward business, but Cord would not have Jaeger near her with an open knife in his hand.

"All right," he called when she was done. "Start by having those men on the rim throw down their rifles.

"They will like hell," Jaeger said and went for his Colt. He dropped to a crouch and Cord had to give it to him: Jaeger could shoot, and he had guts. He shot Steens dead in the chest.

Cord let Steens go, and for a moment he tottered stiffly. Then he flopped forward in a limp dive. He hit the table rock a few feet in front of Majors, headfirst, and made a noise like someone thumping a ripe melon.

Chi was on Jaeger before he could fire again, riding his back and knocking him sideways into the dirt, the two of them rolling and catfighting. Jaeger's gun went off again and he jerked free of Chi. But then he flopped over limp on his back. His mouth gaped and his eyes rolled up, his body convulsing and gurgling as his bowels let go their cargo.

Chi had Jaeger's gun. She scrambled to where Majors sat and buried the barrel in his soft gut.

Steens's men on the rim began firing, which was about good as you'd expect from their sort of buckethead, Cord thought. But it was getting dark along the canyon now, and

they were too leery of plugging their boss to present much
of a danger.

"Majors," Chi hollered into the fat man's face, loud enough
for everyone to hear. "Shut them down, or I will pull this
trigger and spread your shit all over these rocks." She wanted
to do it—Cord could tell from her voice—and he wondered
what Majors had done to her.

"Hold your fire!" Majors bleated.

"I want to hear three rifles dropping into the canyon,"
Cord ordered. "One at a time. Then no one moves."

"Do it," Majors quavered.

The rifles came down, clattering off the rocks before making faint splashing sounds.

"Now let's do some trading," Cord called.

Majors was staring at Jaeger's corpse. He shuddered.

"There is a bonus for you," Cord said. "Don't know why
you didn't kill him yourself, years back."

"Where are those papers?" Majors looked ready to weep.

Cord pulled a sheaf from inside his shirt. "I got some
here, and I got others elsewhere. If I don't get word back,
the others go to a newspaper."

"You tricked me."

"No shit," Cord said. "And I got you. Now give us those
amnesty papers, fat man, or we'll take them off your corpse
and wipe the blood off later."

Majors eased the papers from his inside coat pocket with
a shaking hand. Chi backed off and turned them toward the
fading light, squinting at the print. "*Bueno*," she called. The
amnesties disappeared under her serape.

"Come on up," Cord said. "You can pick up the trail off
between those peak-rocks."

"You promised me," Majors whined.

Chi put a bullet between Majors's feet—and her hand
quivered too.

"Get up here," Cord called, too sharply. She stared at
him for a moment, then started for the trail. In a minute he
heard her pass behind him, and he holstered his Colt and
pulled back.

The horses were picketed back a hundred yards from the
rim, hidden among a juniper thicket, the stocking-footed

gelding and a blue roan mare. Cord had considered taking one of Majors's horses, but he'd seen how his crew cared for animals, and he wanted a mount for Chi that would eat a lot of ground in a hurry. So he'd gone back and borrowed three hundred dollars from McNamer to add to the money he had left from Majors. McNamer gave him a funny look when he came back from the bank teller's window and handed over the money. "But I guess you proved you can be trusted," he grinned.

Chi was already mounted up—and Cord could not stop himself from asking. "Are you all right?"

"Better," she said, and he still was not sure.

He fished the ledger books and the rest of the papers from his saddlebag and circled back to the rim. One of the riflemen was standing across the gap, smiling as if he were enjoying this.

Majors was cowered back against a rock, staring up at Cord through tiny frightened eyes.

"Here is what you wanted, fat man," Cord shouted. "Here is what this was all about."

He flung handfuls of papers out into the canyon, and they fluttered down like spring snow, all the way to the bottom, swirling on updrafts and into the water. Cord watching as the rapids swept them away, and then he wheeled the black gelding and followed after Chi, already trotting west into the last glow of the setting sun.

Chapter Sixteen

CORD SAT IN THE LITTLE CAFE AT FORT MCDER-
mitt and stirred his coffee. The Indian woman who ran
the place was kneading bread dough, her elbows deep in the
mass of it, huffing as she worked. Cord started to roll a
cigarette and through the window saw Chi coming from across
the street.

Their last two days together had been good as could be
hoped, as they rode south from Boise toward this place on
the Oregon-Nevada border. They would be at brother Jim's
place in the Owyhee country by suppertime the day after
tomorrow. There they could rest in and lick the sore spots.

Chi hadn't said anything about her week spent caged up,
but Cord guessed nothing too bad had happend. They were
partners, and he'd sense any real hurt. She was glad to be
free and riding again, happy to drift quietly and enjoy the
distant look of the high country desert southwest of the
Snake.

He told her the story, in bits and pieces as they rode,
finishing it up over coffee and a campfire the first night. She
seemed to accept what he had done—even what he might
have done. Only when he first mentioned Chris Kelly did
she react, her eyes softening and going distant for a moment.

So Cord watched her cross the street from the old frame
hotel where they'd bunked the night before, and thought,
such a fine-looking woman, walking the way she does. He
put the cigarette makings out in front of his plate, hoping
she would take the hint.

She came in and to the table, and flopped down a copy
of the Boise *Capital Intelligencer*. "Look here," she said and

picked up the makings. "I'll bet you are an hombre who could use a smoke."

On the front page of the newspaper there was an article by Ned Seamus McNamer noting the granting of amnesty to the two one-time outlaws known as Cord and Chi. According to the article, the amnesties had been granted by the Governor, William Deane Majors, "in the interest of justice, and for reasons of the general commonweal of the Territory of Idaho." McNamer went on to describe the general dismay with which the Governor's action was viewed and quoted the critical comments of several prominent citizens.

A front-page editorial echoed the sentiments, castigating Majors for freeing from the grasp of the law two notorious outlaws at the same time his own officers were unable to apprehend Chris Kelly, leader of the murderous Lewiston gang. "It does not encourage the march of this Territory toward order and statehood," the editorial said, "when it required the quasi-legal services of a bounty hunter to bring in the slaughtered bodies of wanted men."

An article in the corner of the page, without byline and only three paragraphs long, reported the accidental shooting deaths of United States Marshal Bruno Jaeger and Deputy State Police Officer Gaber Steens, both victims of mistaken identity during a stakeout assignment, no charges to be filed.

The Indian woman brought a pot and poured coffee for Chi, who murmured, "*Gracias.*" She handed a brown-paper cigarette to Cord and started work on one for herself.

"Well now," Cord said meaninglessly, wondering how to begin, and about what?

About them staying together, and what new forms their partnership might take, and about what would happen if he reached across the table and took her hand.

But it was too much for him, and all he could get out was, "*Qué piensas, amiga?*"

Chi scraped a lucifer on the underside of the table and held the flame to his cigarette. "We'll see, *querido.* We will see."

Afterword: A Historical Note

U P IN THE RUGGED BREAKS COUNTRY OF THE Missouri River, not far from where it flows through the Charles M. Russell National Wildlife Refuge, is the Montana town of Landusky. The Fort Belknap Indian Reservation lies just north, and if you look at a Montana map you will see that when the reservation boundary lines were drawn up, a notch was cut out of the southern border—for here is gold country, to be reserved for exploitation. Today Landusky is home to company mining, and big dredges suck gravel from the placer beds. But even now, if you take a pan up to an unclaimed stretch of one of the little creeks, you will show color. Not paying color, of course—but pure gold just the same.

It was gold that brought men to Landusky in the early days—gold and an isolation from society and law that made the town a comfortable retreat for a man on the run. The town of Lord, the fictional robbers' roost in *Cord: Hunt The Man Down*, has its inspiration in Landusky.

Jowell Landusky came to Fort Benton, at the headwaters of the navigable Missouri, in 1864, and moved on to the gold strike at Last Chance Gulch (now Helena, the state capital) in 1872. He was originally from Pike County, Missouri (from where Sweet Betsy of the song came), and Pike became his frontier nickname. In the late eighties Landusky joined the prospectors in Little Alder Gulch, just east of the Little Rocky Mountains in what was then Chouteau County; and in 1894, his trading post there was incorporated as the town of Landusky. Pike Landusky stood six one and weighed one ninety, and by all accounts was a dead shot and a mean, petty bully.

156

Landusky's town was instantly attractive to gunmen, rustlers, army deserters, and other riffraff. For one thing, the timing was right: down in Wyoming, the stockgrowers were becoming increasingly militant and organized against rustlers, so many of the stock-thiefs transferred operations to Montana. For another, Landusky was geographically convenient for rustlers, who often both stole and marketed stock over the Canadian border, a few days' drive to the north. Finally, Landusky was all the law there was, and he was no law at all. In spending his adult lifetime in Montana, he had established a universal reputation as a corrupt renegade who was interested only in how much money a man carried, not where he got it.

Primary among Landusky's many unattractive qualities was his passionate and mindless hatred for Indians. While he would readily take on any man who challenged him, he attacked Indians without provocation. Teddy Blue Abbott, who rode with Landusky for rancher Granville Stuart, claims Landusky carried a tobacco pouch fashioned from the dried-and-tanned bladder of a Sioux Indian he had killed. John Ritch, a newspaperman who lived in Landusky in 1894, reports that Landusky once gave up a chance to shoot a Sioux in the back in favor of running him down on river ice and chopping him to death with an ax. On another occasion, by Ritch's account, Landusky was surrounded in his camp by 22 Sioux. Instead of yielding, Landusky tried to rifle-whip the entire band. The Sioux, convinced Landusky was insane—and therefore touched by divinity—withdrew, returning the next day with two horses as a gift to placate the spirits that bewitched him.

In 1880, the drunken Landusky fired a shotgun into a Blackfoot encampment, killing the wife of White Calf. In retaliation White Calf shot off the lower half of the left side of Landusky's jawbone with a buffalo gun. After that, Ritch writes, "it was hard to tell just how good looking he might have been." Landusky lived on whiskey for 17 days while friends transported him to the nearest surgeon. From then on, Abbott says, "when the weather got cold he would slobber out of that side of his face." But Landusky wore the repulsive mutilation proudly, like a badge of his bigotry.

As the social center for this city of rogues, Landusky's saloon hummed nightly. His bartender was a man named Jake Harris and known as "Jew Jake," whose bona fides included having lost a leg in a gunfight with the Great Falls sheriff. Ritch, who was there, recalls: "When Jake had the shift at the bar he used only the left-hand crutch, leaving the right hand free to use a No. 8 sawed-off shotgun he always kept within reach. If it was an exceptionally lively night in the bar he used the shotgun as a crutch. . . ." Another resident claimed that on occasions of liquor-induced shoot-'em-up hijinks, you "could have swung a pint cup around and caught a quart of bullets."

The prefigurement of Pike Landusky's fall was the arrival of the four Logan brothers, also from Missouri: Harvey, Lonny, John, and Hank ("the honest Logan"). The Logan boys bought a ranch six miles south of town, and Landusky became their nearest neighbor. By some accounts they got along passably for a few years. It's possible, since they had plenty in common: with the exception of Hank, who soon moved to California, the Logans were as thoroughly worthless, vicious, and contemptible as Landusky.

In the sanitized version, the Logan-Landusky feud is set off by a dispute over a borrowed plow; or perhaps Landusky's blind prejudice was aroused by rumors that the Logans' grandmother was Cherokee. More likely, one of the Logans impregnated Landusky's buxom daughter Elfie. Only the result really matters: Oldest brother Harvey and Pike Landusky, both deadly, blustering, quick-triggered men, determined to loathe each other.

In 1894, Landusky had Harvey arrested for rustling by the sheriff of Chouteau County. The sheriff, probably in response to a bribe, promptly remanded temporary custody to Landusky. Once the sheriff lit out, Landusky chained the unarmed Harvey to a log and, in Ritch's words, "threatened him with a nameless indignity." When the rustling charge was dismissed and Harvey released, Landusky warned him that he'd shoot him on sight if he tried to return to town.

The showdown came at Christmas of the same year. Months before, someone had come up with the idea of a community celebration. The word went out, and on Christ-

mas Eve over a hundred guests had arrived from as far as
sixty miles away. Rustlers, outlaws, and thugs of every stripe
checked their guns and joined with ranchers and other gen-
tlefolk in the holiday celebration. The pièce de résistance of
the dinner was four dozen quarts of fresh oysters, shipped
upriver and fashioned into two wash-boilersful of oyster stew
by Tie-up George, reputedly the best cowboy cook in the
breaks country.

The dance was held at the Logans' newly built barn and
went on for two days and nights. Lonny played the fiddle,
accompanied by a Mason & Hamlin organ that had been
laboriously buckboarded in from an outback ranch.

No one was especially anxious to abandon the convivi-
ality and return into the heart of the flesh-freezing badlands
winter—especially those outlaws with no urgent legitimate
business—and the action continued at Jew Jake's saloon.
There, at 10:30 on the morning of December 27, Pike Landusky arrived and ordered an eye-opener.

Before Landusky could pour, Harvey Logan, brother
Lonny, and their ranching partner Jim Thornhill came in.
Harvey walked up to Landusky at the bar, slapped him on
the back, and when he turned punched him in the face.
Lonny and Thornhill drew guns and covered the crowd, so
everyone behaved and watched the fight. Pike Landusky was
over fifty, and his mobility was limited by his thick fur coat.
Harvey got atop him, pinned his arms under his knees, and
began to bang his head into the floorboards.

Logan backed off only when Landusky feebly gestured
his surrender. His face streaming blood, Landusky climbed
to his feet—and right then someone slipped him a gun. Unfortunately, its safety was set, and before Landusky could
click it off, Harvey Logan killed him with two bullets.

While Jew Jake and his customers kept their heads down,
Harvey, Lonny, and Jim Thornhill went out the back door,
where brother Johnny waited in a spring wagon. Lonny and
Thornhill later gave themselves up and were tried and ac-
quitted of conspiracy on grounds of self-defense, but Harvey
left the area with a cousin, took to calling himself Kid Curry,
and embarked on a ten-year career of crime.

As a robbers' roost, the town of Landusky died with its

tsar, but the Logan boys went on to various enterprises, mostly ill-fated. Johnny was shotgunned to death on February 1, 1896, during a feud with a neighbor. Four years and a month later, Lonny was killed and cousin Bob arrested by a posse of Pinkertons and local lawmen who traced them home to Dodson, Missouri, by following a trail of banknotes from a long-ago robbery, which they were only now spending.

But Kid Curry had outlaw luck. After a series of successful train jobs he ended up in Knoxville, Tennessee, where he settled in to a life of drinking (apricot brandy was his tipple of choice), whoring, and playing pocket billards. When asked his line, he replied solemnly, "Railroad man."

He should have given it up right then, because civilization and technology were long-established back East and bound to trip up a frontiersman like the Kid. When he fled after killing a cop come to break up a poolroom brawl, the alarm went out by telephone, and he was captured by four shopkeepers in Jefferson City. This was the autumn of 1902.

When his identity was discovered, the Kid was tried in Federal court on the most airtight case against him, involving the theft of U.S. banknotes. He was convicted and sentenced to twenty years in a Federal pen. Yet Harvey still enjoyed the sort of fortune that makes one doubt divine justice: Before he could be transferred from the Knoxville city jail, he lassoed a jailer with a broom-wire and escaped.

Kid Curry's story ends on June 7, 1904, in Parachute, Colorado—maybe. On that day three masked men held up the Adams Company express car on a Denver & Rio Grande train. A posse trailed the men, caught up, and one of the three was killed in the ensuing gun battle. He was identified as Tap Duncan, a ranch hand from the area.

At the time the Pinkerton agency had an arrangement with many local lawmen under which they received photographs of any dead outlaws. Using Bertillon charts of physical characteristics, William A. Pinkerton determined that Tap Duncan was in fact the notorious Harvey Logan, AKA Kid Curry.

The conclusion seems to contradict the facts. First, Tap Duncan was a local man and was originally and positively identified by other local men when his corpse was hours old.

The revisionist identification was made by Pinkerton Operative Lowell Spence six weeks later, and Spence admitted that the body, never embalmed, was badly decomposed and lacked several identifying scars.

Second, the Kid was a notorious villain who had eluded the Pinkertons—and the $5,000 bounty the agency placed on his head—for over five years. The convenient identification of the Parachute train robber as the wanted man erased an embarrassment.

Maybe Kid Curry did die in a penny-ante railroad job in a Colorado town with a silly name. Or maybe he lived it up for years in Miami, or Ecuador, or Paris. Maybe he spent his last days a crazed old man, telling stories in bars of his bold bandito days, so desperate for drink he did not care when they laughed in his face. There is the thing about the West: You are always free to choose between history and myth—and if you don't like the options, you can make up your own.

Landusky, Montana, lies near the northern end of what has been dubbed the Outlaw Trail. As delineated by present-day historians, the trail winds south to central Wyoming, then west to cross South Pass, south along the Green River into Utah, and on through Arizona and New Mexico to its terminus at El Paso. This conjures up visions of a vast highway of lawlessness running the breadth of the West, overrun by desperadoes of every black stripe. But this Outlaw Trail is an artificial construction, an arbitrary link-up of several of the trails that ran north-south not far from the Continental Divide.

"The Outlaw Trail" more accurately described the central section of this link-up, no more than 500 miles long. The pilgrims passing along were mostly rustlers moving stolen stock, and the real trail connects the three best-known hideouts used by stock-thieves and their herds.

Any discussion of the famous hole-ups is inextricably tied to the curious and complex crime of rustling, which we will use to refer only to stealing cattle and not to the far more serious crime of horse theft. Originally, the term "rustling" meant "gathering," as when one "rustles up some grub."

Similarly, when a group of hands went out onto the great open range of eastern Montana or western Texas to search for strays and unbranded calves, they were rustling up cattle. By usage, common sense, and an understanding that the rules of probability would evenly distribute loose stock, mavericks were considered the property of whoever found them.

Rustling became a crime through acts of nature. In the summer of 1884 a severe drought swept the Northern Plains. Rather than see their cows die, stockmen flooded the market, and prices dropped from near thirty dollars a head to as little as eight dollars. Then in the winter of 1886–87, six weeks of sub-zero cold and blinding blizzards killed hundreds of thousands of cows from Montana to New Mexico; some ranchers lost 95 percent of their herds.

In the wake of the natural disasters, many bankrupted stock operations were taken over by absentee corporate interests who understood the ways of capitalism far better than the ways of the frontier. To hamstring competition and the threat posed to the open range by nesters, the big ranchers were sometimes too quick to fling the charge of rustling. This tactic backfired when some home steaders, broke and angry, did turn to rustling, reasoning they might as well be hung for a wolf as a lamb. At the same time, some of the cowboys who had been abruptly laid off with little chance of finding other wage-work felt it was within their right to appropriate a pair or two as the basis of an independent herd.

However, there remains a clear distinction between stock-gathering and rustling. Citizens who might otherwise consider themselves upright might occasionally overlook a grand to augment their herds. Rustlers, on the other hand, were concerned with selling the beef on the hoof for instant profit. The best customers were corrupt meat sellers contracting to supply railroad construction crews or the Indian reservations.

The hole-ups along the Outlaw Trail were the province of the organized criminal gangs. These bunches operated for about fifteen years, and because herds of animals are cumbersome and need food, water, and rest on the way to the black market, the hideout holes were essential to their illegal business.

Robbers Roost was the southernmost of the three primary stations. It lies at the west end of Wayne Country in south-eastern Utah, about fifty miles due south of the town of Green River, a vast, arid, and starkly foreboding desert plateau on the summit of the San Rafael Swell. To the east, the Roost is bounded by Green River, and to the south by the five black peaks of the Henry Mountains; to the north and west the rugged country seems to go on forever.

This country remains potentially lethal to a stranger. High flat-top buttes and spire-rocks are cut by dry washes, and barren gullies erode upthrust fault-walls. Every feature seems enormous, yet distances are deceptively foreshortened. After a time, every wash looks the same, and a newcomer is lost—and good as dead.

But among the breaks were wide grassy spring-fed swales, and these were fine places to rest herds of stolen horses or beeves, if you knew where they were. The rustlers did and carefully guarded the information, leading posses into ambush or shaking them deep in some maze of canyons out of which the lawmen were sure to emerge desperately thirsty, if at all.

Brown's Hole, also known as Brown's Park, at the midpoint of the trail, straddles the Utah-Colorado line a few miles from Wyoming. Bounded by the Diamond Mountains, the Douglas Mountains, and the Owi-ya-kuts plateau, Brown's Hole is on Green River just south of what was then a roiling canyon and is now Flaming Gorge Reservoir. There the sandstone walls open out into a deep lush valley, thirty miles long and five wide, accessible only by river or a few precariously steep trails descending from the rim rocks.

But the best-known of all rustlers' nests is Hole-in-the-Wall, most famous as the base for Butch Cassidy's Wild Bunch, which began to gang up there in 1896. In the nineties, as many as five hundred outlaws were present at a time, planning jobs or hiding out from the results of jobs just pulled. Those too lazy to rustle could turn to road agentry on the Bozeman Trail, fifteen miles away, or railroad business on the Union Pacific main line to Salt Lake, two days ride south.

All was not badman teeth-baring in the Hole, however; there was renegade play as well. Days were passed in target matches, horse races, card games, and the inevitable drinking. And do not think these were thoroughly unthoughtful men. Cassidy's partner, the Sundance Kid, for example, occupied his spare moments extolling the salubrity of his favorite meal, Ralston's breakfast food. "He is always talking about its benefits," one outlaw complained.

Hole-in-the-Wall is in east-central Wyoming, in the Buffalo Creek country south of the Middle Fork of Powder River, fifty miles south of the town of Buffalo and about seventy from Casper. Of all the hidden outlaw ranges, the Hole is by far the most defensible, a natural fortress. In prehistoric times it was a broad lake, but over the millennia the waters eroded an outlet in the sandstone scarp at the east end, forming over time a V-shaped gorge. Today the Hole is a sloping thirty-five-mile-long grassy valley along Buffalo Creek. To the west, the Big Horn Mountains rise abruptly; to the south, the preciptious banks of the Buffalo Valley hem in the Hole; to the north and east are sheer cliffs. The only access remains the gap washed through the Red Wall.

Within Hole-in-the-Wall there is no wind, and an eerie unnatural silence prevails. In the summer, the air is vaguely flavored with the ozone scent of hot rock, and tule grass the color of burnished brass carpets the valley. Today Johnson County stockmen graze cattle and sheep here, and what rustling does take place is generally limited to the occasional poaching of a "slow elk."

In the last decade of the last century, though hundreds of men and tens of thousands of stolen animals sojourned at Hole-in-the-Wall, this best of all robbers' roosts was seriously breached only once. In July, 1897, R. M. "Bob" Divine (sometimes given as "Devine"), foreman of the CY Ranch, one of the largest cattle companies in Wyoming, determined to go into Hole-in-the-Wall to retrieve rustled CY stock. Divine's particular object was a family named Smith: brothers Al and George, and brother-in-law Bob. Though Divine had a legitimate beef regarding his boss's stolen cattle, he apparently also had a personal grudge against the Smiths.

The Smiths were among the first settlers of Johnson County, hardly pure outlaws in the Butch Cassidy/Harvey Logan class, but rather "ranchers who rustled on the side." Powder River country historian Helena Huntington Smith writes, "They had little sense of bovine property rights and a failing for bad company, yet they were not drifters but substantial people."

On July 22, Bob Divine led a party of twelve men through the Hole: foremen representing other area cattle companies, a few cowhands, a cook, and two livestock inspectors representing Montana interests. Among the latter was Joe Le Fors, the ubiquitous frontier detective who organized the posse that hounded the Wild Bunch, and later wrung from Tom Horn the drunken confession that condemned him to the gallows for the murder of a 14-year-old boy.

By the afternoon of the second day Divine's group had gathered 170 head bearing the CY brand, or an allegedly altered version of it. At that point they encountered Bob and Al Smith, and a partner, Bob Taylor. According to the account in the July 29, 1897 issue of the Natrona County [Wyoming] *Tribune*, Foreman Divine asked the Smiths if they had seen any CY stock.

Instead of answering, Bob Smith snapped, "You damn old son of a bitch, I am going to get you this time!" and went for his Colt.

"Don't you shoot me, Smith," Divine is supposed to have said.

"Yes I will, you old son of a bitch," Smith replied, and fired.

Divine was grazed, but Bob Smith was mortally wounded and died the next morning. Years later LeFors, never a man to shrink from public admiration, claimed he was Smith's killer. However, it was Divine who was charged with murder in Johnson County, where Bob Taylor was also arrested in the battle's aftermath. In the interests of cooling the feud, all charges were quickly dismissed.

However, Bob Divine was convinced that there were still hundreds of head of stolen CY cows in the valley and that it would take an army to get them out. So he formed one, gathering fifty-four men for another invasion.

But first he issued a challenge, in the form of a public letter to the *Tribune*. "I am going to work that country [Buffalo Creek]," he wrote. "The time has come for all honest working men to declare themselves in favor of law and justice. And if those men want to fight us when we know we are right, I say fight."

In reply, Divine received this note:

> Bob Devine you think you have played hell you have just begun you will get your dose there is men enuff up here yet to kill you. We are going to get you or lose twelve more men you must stay out of this country if you want to live we are not going to take any chances any more but will get you any way we can we want one hair apiece out of that damned old chin of yours you have give us the worst of it all the way thorugh and you must stay out or die. You had better keep your damned outfit out if you want to keep them. Don't stick your damned old gray head of yours in this country again if you don't want it shot off we are the 12 men appointed a purpose to get you if you dont stay out of here.
>
> REVENGE GANGE

But the "Gange" was never heard from again. On July 30, Divine's army rode back to the Hole. The atmosphere was tense: Divine, LeFors, and company were blatantly breaching the security of what was to this point purely rustlers' domain. But although they saw armed men at a distance several times, by some miracle no confrontation materialized. The invaders gathered five hundred head of cattle bearing Wyoming and Montana cattle-company brands, as well as fifty head with altered brands and another twenty-eight steers on which the brands had been knife-skinned from the living animal and the edges sewn together; the stockmen took these last seventy-eight on general principles. Despite the exchange of public threats, and unfortunately for romancers, no shots were fired. The silence might have been memorial, because not long after the robbers' roosts would be abandoned.

Rustlers' hole-ups could have existed only on the open western plains, where law enforcement was necessarily spread thin. The private Pinkerton Agency was the only organization approaching a national police force; sanctioned peace-keeping was locally administered, and its mandate was the protection of the citizens of communities, and the capitalist institutions such as the railroads. Outback ranchers had to protect themselves.

Yet it was neither citizen vigilance nor law which closed down the hole-ups, but encroaching civilization. Modern communication, transportation, and technology shrunk the open spaces. Two-story brick banks, grand hotels, and respectability came to the West, and outlawry is an outrage to socialized folk. Butch and Sundance became expatriates in Bolivia, more from love of a way of life they must have, than from fear of the law at home.

Ghosts still ride the Outlaw Trail. There is Black Jack Ketchum, whose hanging was bungled by a miscalculation in the counterweighting: when the trap was sprung, his head was separated from his torso. Think of Elza Lay, the Wild Bunch outlaw who after his release from prison became field guide to Professor Edward Boyle of Yale. Around the campfire Boyle conducted informal seminars in petroleum geology, and by summer's end Lay had read the professor's textbook and was confidently discussing anticlines and synclines and hydrostatic pressure with the learned academic.

The women of the trail are no less exotic in their ways. Etta Place, the Sundance Kid's common-law wife, stuck through the exodus to South America. "She was the best housekeeper on the Pampas," said Butch Cassidy cheerfully, "but she was a whore at heart." Laura Bullion, the lover of Wild Bunch member Ben Kilpatrick, lived with the gang for several years. Her letters to her mother in Fort Worth are extant, and full of plaintive and strikingly vivid descriptions of the isolation and discomfort of life in Hole-in-the-Wall.

The histories of James D. Horan remain among our most valuable sources. Horan covers in detail aspects of the Outlaw Trail and the robbers' roosts in *The Authentic Wild West: The Gunfighters*, *The Authentic Wild West: The Outlaws*, *Pictorial History of the Wild West* (with Paul Sann), and *The Wild Bunch*. *The Outlaw Trail*, by Robert Redford, is stiffly written and too often historically inaccurate, but includes spectacular photographs by Jonathan Blair of outlaw country.

The most accurate and flavorful description of the town of Landusky, and the feud between Pike and the Logans, is the firsthand account by John B. Ritch, an article entitled "True Story of Pike Landusky Better Than Beadle's Best Thriller," in *The Great Falls* [Montana] *Tribune* for January 20, 1935. In *We Pointed Them North: Recollections of a Cowpuncher*, by E. C. Abbott ("Teddy Blue") and Helena Huntington Smith, Abbott describes in detail his experiences as a hand, range-rider, and stock detective for Granville Stuart, when he was partnered up with Pike Landusky.

For somewhat differing versions of Bob Divine's 1897 invasion of Hole-in-the-Wall, see "The Hole-in-the-Wall," in *History of Natrona County, Wyoming, 1888–1922*, by Alfred James Mokler; and Helena Huntington Smith, "The Truth about the Hole-in-the-Wall Fight," in *Montana: The Magazine of Western History*, XI,3.

Several of the novels of Zane Grey are set in the neighborhoods of the best-known hole-ups. One of the better ones is *Robbers Roost*; it is later Grey, dense and psychologically complex, with vivid evocative descriptions of the desolation of the breaks country, and the beauty of the watered draws. According to Redford, the character of Herrick, the tenderfoot British rancher in the novel, is based on J. D. Buhr, an English tailor who came to the desert to cure his asthma. He settled at Granite Ranch in the foothills of the Henrys and spent a lot of time at the roost; the congenial and gentlemanly Butch Cassidy was Buhr's idol. To Buhr's infinite delight, the outlaws honored him with a "trail handle": "Wheezin' Buhr," after his affliction.

The best filmic treatment of the outlaw hole-up notion is *Rancho Notorious* (1952), the third of three American westerns directed by the Austrian-born Fritz Lang. Marlene Dietrich plays the proprietor of a breaks-country resort for crooks on the lam in one of the more quirky Western movies of the early fifties, a fertile period for quirky Westerns.

But best sources of all are the hundreds of people still living in Wyoming and Montana who were there when Kid Curry shot Pike Landusky dead in the Missouri breaks country, when Butch and Sundance and all the rest drove thundering herds down the Outlaw Trail. The other day we had dinner with a woman who grew up near Kaycee, Wyoming. Over drinks we started a debate about the merits of the murder charge against Tom Horn, in which we argued for his guilt. How could our friend be so positive that Horn was framed? we pressed. What did she know that wasn't in the books?

"For one thing," she said, "my grandfather testified for the defense."

We shut up, and wished we had not mouthed off in the first place.

William Kittredge
Steven M. Krauzer
Missoula, Montana
Summer, 1983

About the Author

Owen Rountree is the pseudonym of Steven M. Krauzer and William Kittredge, who live in Missoula, Montana. Kittredge is Professor of English at the University of Montana; his latest book is a collection of short stories, *We Are Not In This Together*, from Greywolf Press. Krauzer has published six novels in addition to the *Cord* series. Under their own names, Kittredge and Krauzer have edited four anthologies of popular American fiction.

GREAT TALES
from the
OLD WEST

OWEN ROWNTREE

'Banjo' Paterson

The Works of
'Banjo' Paterson

with an Introduction and Bibliography

Wordsworth Poetry Library

This edition published 1995 by Wordsworth Editions Ltd,
Cumberland House, Crib Street, Ware, Hertfordshire SG12 9ET.

Copyright © Wordsworth Editions Ltd 1995.

ISBN 1-85326-430-X

Typeset in the UK by Antony Gray.
Printed and bound in Denmark by Nørhaven.

INTRODUCTION

In general, ballads can be divided into those which stem from a pre-literate rural community and which tend to be tragic, romantic and heroic in content, and those which developed after the spread of the printing press and the growth of towns with their associated communities, which are more often comic, realistic and unheroic. The nineteenth- and early-twentieth-century Australian ballads stand astride these two traditions; although composed in the machine age, they hark back to the minstrelsy of the border ballads of England and Scotland as well as to the heroic songs of Ireland from which so many early Australian settlers had come. As with all ballads, they tell a story in verse, verse which is often written in simple iambic ballad metre, partly to assist the memorability of what is essentially an oral verse form, but also to make the ballads more adaptable to basic musical requirements when they are sung. However, with their development, much syllabic irregularity is introduced, together with considerable ingenuity of stress and internal rhyme.

There are several theories as to why the Australian ballad came to fruition when it did. The most likely is the most obvious; that men, away from home in harsh conditions, whether droving or mining, deprived of normal human intercourse and customary amusements, must make their own entertainment. This age-old phenomenon is to be encountered in any society living on a frontier, whether literal or metaphorical, from the earliest warriors and sailors to the pioneers and settlers of new lands. Many of the Australians contributed anonymous ballads celebrating heroic deeds, such as 'The Kelly Gang' or 'Stringybark Creek', both mildly subversive accounts of the infamous Ned Kelly gang of bushrangers; others were sentimental songs of longing for home or for the 'good old days', some described the hardships of mining in the newly discovered goldfields, while others were comic accounts of how protagonists get their come-uppance – the well-known Australian 'tall poppy' syndrome gave rise to as much hilarity in the nineteenth century as it does today – but many of the finest ballads stemmed from the drovers, their horses and the horse-racing that is so essential a part of equine culture. Horses and sporting events were popularised by the English immigrant Adam Lindsay Gordon (1833–70) in *Sea Spray and Smoke Drift* (1867) and in *Bush Ballads and Galloping Rhymes* (1870). Ten years after Gordon's suicide on a beach near Melbourne, J. F. Archibald and John Haynes founded *The Bulletin* in Sydney, and encouraged contributions about rural life and the outback.

Songs of the range, of the campfire and of shearing arrived at *The Bulletin,* many of them imitative (though this is unsurprising since they emanated from drovers and farmers cut off from normal literary contact), but even when borrowing the forms, metres and tunes of earlier songs and ballads, they often had an amazing power to evoke the rough life and values of the outback. At the end of 1889, *The Bulletin,* over the pseudonym 'The Banjo', published 'Clancy of The Overflow' by A. B. Paterson. Rolf Boldrewood described it as 'the best bush ballad since Gordon', and even today there are many expatriate Australians who, while professing to know nothing of the rich tradition of Australian poetry, can still quote, without hesitation, the first two verses of Paterson's first published poem. Paterson continued to submit similar verses to *The Bulletin,* and in 1895 his first collection, *The Man from Snowy River and Other Verses,* was published, and the identity of 'The Banjo' was revealed.

Andrew Barton Paterson (1864–1941) was born of Scottish ancestry at Narambla, near Orange, in New South Wales. Until he was ten he lived on the family station at Illalong in the Yass district, and there he acquired his love of the outback, its lore and folklore. Although his father had not enjoyed success as a grazier and had to mortgage the Illalong station, he remained there as the manager in reasonable prosperity. 'Banjo' was sent to Sydney Grammar School, staying with his maternal grandmother who was prominent in Sydney literary circles – indeed the whole family had a literary bent: 'Banjo's' father was published in *The Bulletin,* and his sister Jessie was also a contributor. 'Banjo' trained as a solicitor, and though he contributed regularly to the press, the law remained his chief livelihood until 1899, when he sailed to South Africa to report the Boer War for the *Sydney Morning Herald;* the briefness of the Boxer Rebellion in China prevented him from arriving in time to cover that as a war correspondent. After his return to Sydney, via London, he embarked on a lecture tour describing his experiences in South Africa. He married in 1903, and became, successively, editor of the *Sydney Evening News* and the *Town and Country Journal*. During the First World War he served as an ambulance driver in France and as a Remount Officer for the Australian forces in Egypt. On his return to Australia he settled in Sydney, and became a freelance writer. He was made a CBE in 1939. His three volumes of poetry were *The Man from Snowy River and Other Verses* (1895), *Rio Grande's Last Race and Other Verses* (1902) and *Saltbush Bill J.P. and Other Verses* (1917); they were combined in one volume and published as *The Collected Verse of A. B. Paterson* in 1921. He wrote two novels, *An Outback Marriage* (1906) and *The Shearer's Colt* (1936), a collection of stories, *Three Elephant Power and Other Stories* (1917), a book of reminiscences, *Happy Dispatches* (1934), and published his notable collection, *Old Bush Songs Composed and Sung During the Bushranging and Overlanding Days* in 1905.

In many ways, Paterson can be seen as the national bard of Australia. Though Adam Lindsay Gordon's bust may stand in Poets' Corner in Westminster Abbey, the man who wrote 'Waltzing Matilda' has a higher claim to immortality than the flawed Gordon. Henry Kendall, a solicitor like Paterson, has his advocates, but his poetry lacks the popular memorability of Paterson's. This memorability can best be compared with that of Kipling or Betjeman; it is technically conservative, deceptively simple and hugely popular – so popular that even the *London Literary Yearbook* considered that *The Man from Snowy River and Other Verses* gave Paterson a public wider than any other writer in English except for Rudyard Kipling. Though Paterson never had to endure the sneering patronage that came the way of Kipling and Betjeman, he was severely attacked by the poet and short-story writer Henry Lawson, who considered many of Paterson's ballads as a city-dweller's idealised view of life in the bush. Paterson, on the other hand, considered Lawson's verse gloomy and pessimistic, and 'An Answer to Various Bards' gives a good-humoured response to the attacks, though it is doubtful whether the handicapped and embittered Lawson ever accepted the invitation in the last line 'to come to Sydney, and vermilionise the bars'.

Naturally, Paterson was not a consistently successful poet. Some of his vernacular conversation grates on the ear, as did some of Kipling's barrack room verse; some, like 'Rio Grande's Last Race', are disappointing. But 'The Man from Snowy River', 'Clancy of The Overflow' and 'The Man from Ironbark' go straight to the heart of

Australian bush culture, showing it as it might have been, even if it was not all quite like that. The narrative power, the humour, the pace and the surprise endings all give Paterson his place among the great balladeers, from the anonymous composer of 'Edward' in medieval times to Paterson's near-contemporary Robert W. Service, with his poems of pioneering on the Yukon in *Songs of a Sourdough*. Not only Australia, but the world, owes A. B. ('Banjo') Paterson a great debt for chronicling through affectionate eyes the enthusiasms, the tall stories and the take-downs that played so major a part in the making of the contemporary Australian character.

FURTHER READING

V. Palmer, *The Legend of the Nineties*, 1954
D. Stewart and N. Keesing (eds), *Australian Bush Ballads*, 1955
C. Semmler, *The Banjo of the Bush*, 1966
L. Oliff, *Andrew Barton Paterson*, 1971

CONTENTS

THE MAN FROM SNOWY RIVER
AND OTHER VERSES

RIO GRANDE AND OTHER VERSES

SALTBUSH BILL, J.P., AND OTHER VERSES

THE MAN FROM SNOWY RIVER
AND OTHER VERSES

Prelude

I have gathered these stories afar
    In the wind and the rain,
In the land where the cattle-camps are,
    On the edge of the plain.
On the overland routes of the west,
    When the watches were long,
I have fashioned in earnest and jest
    These fragments of song.

They are just the rude stories one hears
    In sadness and mirth,
The records of wandering years —
    And scant is their worth.
Though their merits indeed are but slight,
    I shall not repine
If they give you one moment's delight,
    Old comrades of mine.

The Man from Snowy River

There was movement at the station, for the word had passed
  around
   That the colt from old Regret had got away,
And had joined the wild bush horses – he was worth a thousand
  pound,
   So all the cracks had gathered to the fray.
All the tried and noted riders from the stations near and far
   Had mustered at the homestead overnight,
For the bushmen love hard riding where the wild bush horses are,
   And the stock-horse snuffs the battle with delight.

There was Harrison, who made his pile when Pardon won the cup,
   The old man with his hair as white as snow;
But few could ride beside him when his blood was fairly up –
   He would go wherever horse and man could go.
And Clancy of the Overflow came down to lend a hand,
   No better horseman ever held the reins;
For never horse could throw him while the saddle-girths would
  stand –
   He learnt to ride while droving on the plains.

And one was there, a stripling on a small and weedy beast;
   He was something like a racehorse undersized,
With a touch of Timor pony – three parts thoroughbred at least –
   And such as are by mountain horsemen prized.
He was hard and tough and wiry – just the sort that won't say die –
   There was courage in his quick impatient tread;
And he bore the badge of gameness in his bright and fiery eye,
   And the proud and lofty carriage of his head.

But still so slight and weedy, one would doubt his power to stay,
   And the old man said, 'That horse will never do
For a long and tiring gallop – lad, you'd better stop away,
   Those hills are far too rough for such as you.'
So he waited, sad and wistful – only Clancy stood his friend –
   'I think we ought to let him come,' he said;
'I warrant he'll be with us when he's wanted at the end,
   For both his horse and he are mountain bred.

'He hails from Snowy River, up by Kosciusko's side,
    Where the hills are twice as steep and twice as rough;
Where a horse's hoofs strike firelight from the flint stones every
        stride,
    The man that holds his own is good enough.
And the Snowy River riders on the mountains make their home,
    Where the river runs those giant hills between;
I have seen full many horsemen since I first commenced to roam,
    But nowhere yet such horsemen have I seen.'

So he went; they found the horses by the big mimosa clump,
    They raced away towards the mountain's brow,
And the old man gave his orders, 'Boys, go at them from the jump,
    No use to try for fancy riding now.
And, Clancy, you must wheel them, try and wheel them to the
        right.
    Ride boldly, lad, and never fear the spills,
For never yet was rider that could keep the mob in sight,
    If once they gain the shelter of those hills.'

So Clancy rode to wheel them – he was racing on the wing
    Where the best and boldest riders take their place,
And he raced his stock-horse past them, and he made the ranges
        ring
    With the stockwhip, as he met them face to face.
Then they halted for a moment, while he swung the dreaded lash,
    But they saw their well-loved mountain full in view,
And they charged beneath the stockwhip with a sharp and sudden
        dash,
    And off into the mountain scrub they flew.

Then fast the horsemen followed, where the gorges deep and black
    Resounded to the thunder of their tread,
And the stockwhips woke the echoes, and they fiercely answered
        back
    From cliffs and crags that beetled overhead.
And upward, ever upward, the wild horses held their way,
    Where mountain ash and kurrajong grew wide;
And the old man muttered fiercely, 'We may bid the mob good day,
    No man can hold them down the other side.'

When they reached the mountain's summit, even Clancy took a
     pull –
  It well might make the boldest hold their breath;
The wild hop scrub grew thickly, and the hidden ground was full
  Of wombat holes, and any slip was death.
But the man from Snowy River let the pony have his head,
  And he swung his stockwhip round and gave a cheer,
And he raced him down the mountain like a torrent down its bed,
  While the others stood and watched in very fear.

He sent the flint-stones flying, but the pony kept his feet,
  He cleared the fallen timber in his stride,
And the man from Snowy River never shifted in his seat –
  It was grand to see that mountain horseman ride.
Through the stringy barks and saplings, on the rough and broken
     ground,
  Down the hillside at a racing pace he went;
And he never drew the bridle till he landed safe and sound
  At the bottom of that terrible descent.

He was right among the horses as they climbed the farther hill,
  And the watchers on the mountain, standing mute,
Saw him ply the stockwhip fiercely; he was right among them still,
  As he raced across the clearing in pursuit.
Then they lost him for a moment, where two mountain gullies met
  In the ranges – but a final glimpse reveals
On a dim and distant hillside the wild horses racing yet,
  With the man from Snowy River at their heels.

And he ran them single-handed till their sides were white with
     foam;
  He followed like a bloodhound on their track,
Till they halted, cowed and beaten; then he turned their heads for
     home,
  And alone and unassisted brought them back.
But his hardy mountain pony he could scarcely raise a trot,
  He was blood from hip to shoulder from the spur;
But his pluck was still undaunted, and his courage fiery hot,
  For never yet was mountain horse a cur.

And down by Kosciusko, where the pine-clad ridges raise
    Their torn and rugged battlements on high,
Where the air is clear as crystal, and the white stars fairly blaze
    At midnight in the cold and frosty sky,
And where around the Overflow the reed-beds sweep and sway
    To the breezes, and the rolling plains are wide,
The Man from Snowy River is a household word today,
    And the stockmen tell the story of his ride.

Old Pardon, The Son of Reprieve

You never heard tell of the story?
    Well, now, I can hardly believe!
Never heard of the honour and glory
    Of Pardon, the son of Reprieve?
But maybe you're only a Johnnie
    And don't know a horse from a hoe?
Well, well, don't get angry, my sonny,
    But, really, a young un should know.

They bred him out back on the 'Never',
    His mother was Mameluke breed.
To the front – and then stay there – was ever
    The root of the Mameluke creed.
He seemed to inherit their wiry
    Strong frames – and their pluck to receive –
As hard as a flint and as fiery
    Was Pardon, the son of Reprieve.

We ran him at many a meeting
    At crossing and gully and town,
And nothing could give him a beating –
    At least when our money was down.
For weight wouldn't stop him, nor distance,
    Nor odds, though the others were fast;
He'd race with a dogged persistence,
    And wear them all down at the last.

At the Turon the Yattendon filly
    Led by lengths at the mile-and-a-half,
And we all began to look silly,
    While her crowd were starting to laugh;
But the old horse came faster and faster,
    His pluck told its tale, and his strength,
He gained on her, caught her, and passed her,
    And won it, hands-down, by a length.

And then we swooped down on Menindie
   To run for the President's Cup;
Oh! that's a sweet township – a shindy
   To them is board, lodging, and sup.
Eye-openers they are, and their system
   Is never to suffer defeat;
It's 'win, tie, or wrangle' – to best 'em
   You must lose 'em , or else it's 'dead heat'.

We strolled down the township and found 'em
   At drinking and gaming and play;
If sorrows they had, why they drowned 'em ,
   And betting was soon under way.
Their horses were good uns and fit uns,
   There was plenty of cash in the town;
They backed their own horses like Britons,
   And, Lord! how we rattled it down!

With gladness we thought of the morrow,
   We counted our wages with glee,
A simile homely to borrow –
   'There was plenty of milk in our tea.'
You see we were green; and we never
   Had even a thought of foul play,
Though we well might have known that the clever
   Division would 'put us away'.

Experience *docet*, they tell us,
   At least so I've frequently heard
But, 'dosing' or 'stuffing', those fellows
   Were up to each move on the board:
They got to his stall – it is sinful
   To think what such villains will do –
And they gave him a regular skinful
   Of barley – green barley – to chew.

He munched it all night, and we found him
   Next morning as full as a hog –
The girths wouldn't nearly meet round him;
   He looked like an overfed frog.

We saw we were done like a dinner –
  The odds were a thousand to one
Against Pardon turning up winner,
  'Twas cruel to ask him to run.

We got to the course with our troubles,
  A crestfallen couple were we;
And we heard the 'books' calling the doubles –
  A roar like the surf of the sea;
And over the tumult and louder
  Rang 'Any price Pardon, I lay!'
Says Jimmy, 'The children of Judah
  Are out on the warpath today.'

Three miles in three heats: – Ah, my sonny,
  The horses in those days were stout,
They had to run well to win money;
  I don't see such horses about.
Your six-furlong vermin that scamper
  Half-a-mile with their feather-weight up,
They wouldn't earn much of their damper
  In a race like the President's Cup.

The first heat was soon set a-going;
  The Dancer went off to the front;
The Don on his quarters was showing,
  With Pardon right out of the hunt.
He rolled and he weltered and wallowed –
  You'd kick your hat faster, I'll bet;
They finished all bunched, and he followed
  All lathered and dripping with sweat.

But troubles came thicker upon us,
  For while we were rubbing him dry
The stewards came over to warn us:
  'We hear you are running a bye!
If Pardon don't spiel like tarnation
  And win the next heat – if he can –
He'll earn a disqualification;
  Just think over *that* now, my man!'

Our money all gone and our credit,
   Our horse couldn't gallop a yard;
And then people thought that *we* did it
   It really was terribly hard.
We were objects of mirth and derision
   To folks in the lawn and the stand,
And the yells of the clever division
   Of 'Any price Pardon!' were grand.

We still had a chance for the money,
   Two heats still remained to be run;
If both fell to us – why, my sonny,
   The clever division were done.
And Pardon was better, we reckoned,
   His sickness was passing away,
So we went to the post for the second
   And principal heat of the day.

They're off and away with a rattle,
   Like dogs from the leashes let slip,
And right at the back of the battle
   He followed them under the whip.
They gained ten good lengths on him quickly
   He dropped right away from the pack;
I tell you it made me feel sickly
   To see the blue jacket fall back.

Our very last hope had departed –
   We thought the old fellow was done,
When all of a sudden he started
   To go like a shot from a gun.
His chances seemed slight to embolden
   Our hearts; but, with teeth firmly set,
We thought, 'Now or never! The old un
   May reckon with some of 'em yet.'

Then loud rose the war-cry for Pardon;
   He swept like the wind down the dip,
And over the rise by the garden
   The jockey was done with the whip.

The field was at sixes and sevens –
    The pace at the first had been fast –
And hope seemed to drop from the heavens,
    For Pardon was coming at last.

And how he did come! It was splendid;
    He gained on them yards every bound,
Stretching out like a greyhound extended,
    His girth laid right down on the ground.
A shimmer of silk in the cedars
    As into the running they wheeled,
And out flashed the whips on the leaders,
    For Pardon had collared the field.

Then right through the ruck he was sailing –
    I knew that the battle was won –
The son of Haphazard was failing,
    The Yattendon filly was done;
He cut down The Don and The Dancer,
    He raced clean away from the mare –
He's in front! Catch him now if you can, sir!
    And up went my hat in the air!

Then loud from the lawn and the garden
    Rose offers of 'Ten to one *on*!'
'Who'll bet on the field? I back Pardon!'
    No use; all the money was gone.
He came for the third heat light-hearted,
    A-jumping and dancing about;
The others were done ere they started
    Crestfallen, and tired, and worn out.

He won it, and ran it much faster
    Than even the first, I believe;
Oh, he was the daddy, the master,
    Was Pardon, the son of Reprieve.
He showed 'em the method of travel –
    The boy sat still as a stone –
They never could see him for gravel;
    He came in hard-held, and alone.

        *   *   *   *   *

But he's old – and his eyes are grown hollow
    Like me, with my thatch of the snow;
When he dies, then I hope I may follow,
    And go where the racehorses go.
I don't want no harping nor singing –
    Such things with my style don't agree;
Where the hoofs of the horses are ringing
    There's music sufficient for me.

And surely the thoroughbred horses
    Will rise up again and begin
Fresh races on far-away courses,
    And p'raps they might let me slip in.
It would look rather well the race-card on
    'Mongst Cherubs and Seraphs and things,
'Angel Harrison's black gelding Pardon,
    Blue halo, white body and wings.'

And if they have racing hereafter,
    (And who is to say they will not?)
When the cheers and the shouting and laughter
    Proclaim that the battle grows hot;
As they come down the racecourse a-steering,
    He'll rush to the front, I believe;
And you'll hear the great multitude cheering
    For Pardon, the son of Reprieve.

Clancy of The Overflow

I had written him a letter which I had, for want of better
   Knowledge, sent to where I met him down the Lachlan years ago;
He was shearing when I knew him, so I sent the letter to him,
   Just on spec, addressed as follows, 'Clancy, of The Overflow'.

And an answer came directed in a writing unexpected
   (And I think the same was written with a thumb-nail dipped
      in tar);
'Twas his shearing mate who wrote it, and *verbatim* I will quote it:
   'Clancy's gone to Queensland droving, and we don't know where
      he are.'

      *   *   *   *   *

In my wild erratic fancy visions come to me of Clancy
   Gone a-droving 'down the Cooper' where the Western drovers
      go;
As the stock are slowly stringing, Clancy rides behind them singing,
   For the drover's life has pleasures that the townsfolk never know.

And the bush has friends to meet him, and their kindly voices greet
      him
   In the murmur of the breezes and the river on its bars,
And he sees the vision splendid of the sunlit plains extended,
   And at night the wondrous glory of the everlasting stars.

      *   *   *   *   *

I am sitting in my dingy little office, where a stingy
   Ray of sunlight struggles feebly down between the houses tall,
And the foetid air and gritty of the dusty, dirty city,
   Through the open window floating, spreads its foulness over all.

And in place of lowing cattle, I can hear the fiendish rattle
   Of the tramways and the buses making hurry down the street;
And the language uninviting of the gutter children fighting
   Comes fitfully and faintly through the ceaseless tramp of feet.

And the hurrying people daunt me, and their pallid faces haunt me
  As they shoulder one another in their rush and nervous haste,
With their eager eyes and greedy, and their stunted forms and
      weedy,
  For townsfolk have no time to grow, they have no time to waste.

And I somehow rather fancy that I'd like to change with Clancy,
  Like to take a turn at droving where the seasons come and go,
While he faced the round eternal of the cash-book and the
      journal –
  But I doubt he'd suit the office, Clancy, of The Overflow.

Conroy's Gap

This was the way of it, don't you know —
    Ryan was 'wanted' for stealing sheep,
And never a trooper, high or low,
    Could find him — catch a weasel asleep!
Till Trooper Scott, from the Stockman's Ford —
    A bushman, too, as I've heard them tell —
Chanced to find him drunk as a lord
    Round at the Shadow of Death Hotel.

D'you know the place? It's a wayside inn,
    A low grog-shanty — a bushman trap,
Hiding away in its shame and sin
    Under the shelter of Conroy's Gap —
Under the shade of that frowning range
    The roughest crowd that ever drew breath —
Thieves and rowdies, uncouth and strange,
    Were mustered round at the 'Shadow of Death'.

The trooper knew that his man would slide
    Like a dingo pup, if he saw the chance;
And with half a start on the mountain side
    Ryan would lead him a merry dance.
Drunk as he was when the trooper came,
    To him that did not matter a rap —
Drunk or sober, he was the same,
    The boldest rider in Conroy's Gap.

'I want you, Ryan,' the trooper said,
    'And listen to me, if you dare resist,
So help me heaven, I'll shoot you dead!'
    He snapped the steel on his prisoner's wrist,
And Ryan, hearing the handcuffs click,
    Recovered his wits as they turned to go,
For fright will sober a man as quick
    As all the drugs that the doctors know.

There was a girl in that shanty bar
   Went by the name of Kate Carew,
Quiet and shy as the bush girls are,
   But ready-witted and plucky, too.
She loved this Ryan, or so they say,
   And passing by, while her eyes were dim
With tears, she said in a careless way,
   'The Swagman's round in the stable, Jim.'

Spoken too low for the trooper's ear,
   Why should she care if he heard or not?
Plenty of swagmen far and near –
   And yet to Ryan it meant a lot.
That was the name of the grandest horse
   In all the district from east to west;
In every show ring, on every course,
   They always counted The Swagman best.

He was a wonder, a raking bay –
   One of the grand old Snowdon strain –
One of the sort that could race and stay
   With his mighty limbs and his length of rein.
Born and bred on the mountain side,
   He could race through scrub like a kangaroo;
The girl herself on his back might ride,
   And The Swagman would carry her safely through.

He would travel gaily from daylight's flush
   Till after the stars hung out their lamps;
There was never his like in the open bush,
   And never his match on the cattle-camps.
For faster horses might well be found
   On racing tracks, or a plain's extent,
But few, if any, on broken ground
   Could see the way that The Swagman went.

When this girl's father, old Jim Carew,
   Was droving out on the Castlereagh
With Conroy's cattle, a wire came through
   To say that his wife couldn't live the day.
And he was a hundred miles from home,
   As flies the crow, with never a track

Through plains as pathless as ocean's foam;
   He mounted straight on The Swagman's back.

He left the camp by the sundown light,
   And the settlers out on the Marthaguy
Awoke and heard, in the dead of night,
   A single horseman hurrying by.
He crossed the Bogan at Dandaloo,
   And many a mile of the silent plain
That lonely rider behind him threw
   Before they settled to sleep again.

He rode all night, and he steered his course
   By the shining stars with a bushman's skill,
And every time that he pressed his horse
   The Swagman answered him gamely still.
He neared his home as the east was bright.
   The doctor met him outside the town,
'Carew! How far did you come last night?'
   'A hundred miles since the sun went down.'

And his wife got round, and an oath he passed,
   So long as he or one of his breed
Could raise a coin, though it took their last,
   The Swagman never should want a feed.
And Kate Carew, when her father died,
   She kept the horse and she kept him well;
The pride of the district far and wide,
   He lived in style at the bush hotel.

Such was The Swagman; and Ryan knew
   Nothing about could pace the crack;
Little he'd care for the man in blue
   If once he got on The Swagman's back.
But how to do it? A word let fall
   Gave him the hint as the girl passed by;
Nothing but 'Swagman – stable wall;
   Go to the stable and mind your eye.'

He caught her meaning, and quickly turned
   To the trooper: 'Reckon you'll gain a stripe
By arresting me, and it's easily earned;
   Let's go to the stable and get my pipe,

The Swagman has it.' So off they went,
    And as soon as ever they turned their backs
The girl slipped down, on some errand bent
    Behind the stable and seized an axe.

The trooper stood at the stable door
    While Ryan went in quite cool and slow,
And then (the trick had been played before)
    The girl outside gave the wall a blow.
Three slabs fell out of the stable wall –
    'Twas done 'fore ever the trooper knew –
And Ryan, as soon as he saw them fall,
    Mounted The Swagman and rushed him through.

The trooper heard the hoof-beats ring
    In the stable yard, and he slammed the gate,
But The Swagman rose with a mighty spring
    At the fence, and the trooper fired too late
As they raced away, and his shots flew wide,
    And Ryan no longer need care a rap,
For never a horse that was lapped in hide
    Could catch The Swagman in Conroy's Gap.

And that's the story. You want to know
    If Ryan came back to his Kate Carew;
Of course he should have, as stories go,
    But the worst of it is this story's true:
And in real life it's a certain rule,
    Whatever poets and authors say
Of high-toned robbers and all their school,
    These horsethief fellows aren't built that way.

Come back! Don't hope it – the slinking hound,
    He sloped across to the Queensland side,
And sold The Swagman for fifty pound,
    And stole the money, and more beside.
And took to drink, and by some good chance
    Was killed – thrown out of a stolen trap.
And that was the end of this small romance,
    The end of the story of Conroy's Gap.

Our New Horse

The boys had come back from the races
    All silent and down on their luck;
They'd backed 'em , straight out and for places,
    But never a winner they struck.
They lost their good money on Slogan,
    And fell most uncommonly flat
When Partner, the pride of the Bogan,
    Was beaten by Aristocrat.

And one said, 'I move that instanter
    We sell out our horses and quit;
The brutes ought to win in a canter,
    Such trials they do when they're fit.
The last one they ran was a snorter –
    A gallop to gladden one's heart –
Two-twelve for a mile and a quarter,
    And finished as straight as a dart.

'And then when I think that they're ready
    To win me a nice little swag,
They are licked like the veriest neddy –
    They're licked from the fall of the flag.
The mare held her own to the stable,
    She died out to nothing at that,
And Partner he never seemed able
    To pace with the Aristocrat.

'And times have been bad, and the seasons
    Don't promise to be of the best;
In short, boys, there's plenty of reasons
    For giving the racing a rest.
The mare can be kept on the station –
    Her breeding is good as can be –
But Partner, his next destination
    Is rather a trouble to me.

'We can't sell him here, for they know him
    As well as the clerk of the course;

He's raced and won races till, blow him,
  He's done as a handicap horse.
A jady, uncertain performer,
  They weight him right out of the hunt,
And clap it on warmer and warmer
  Whenever he gets near the front.

'It's no use to paint him or dot him
  Or put any fake on his brand,
For bushmen are smart, and they'd spot him
  In any sale-yard in the land.
The folk about here could all tell him,
  Could swear to each separate hair;
Let us send him to Sydney and sell him,
  There's plenty of Jugginses there.

'We'll call him a maiden, and treat 'em
  To trials will open their eyes;
We'll run their best horses and beat 'em ,
  And then won't they think him a prize.
I pity the fellow that buys him,
  He'll find in a very short space,
No matter how highly he tries him,
  The beggar won't *race* in a race.'

      *   *   *   *   *

Next week, under 'Seller and Buyer',
  Appeared in the *Daily Gazette*:
'A racehorse for sale, and a flyer;
  Has never been started as yet;
A trial will show what his pace is;
  The buyer can get him in light,
And win all the handicap races.
  Apply before Saturday night.'

He sold for a hundred and thirty,
  Because of a gallop he had
One morning with Bluefish and Bertie,
  And donkey-licked both of 'em bad.
And when the old horse had departed,
  The life on the station grew tame;

The race-track was dull and deserted,
   The boys had gone back on the game.

  *   *   *   *   *

The winter rolled by, and the station
   Was green with the garland of Spring;
A spirit of glad exultation
   Awoke in each animate thing;
And all the old love, the old longing,
   Broke out in the breasts of the boys –
The visions of racing came thronging
   With all its delirious joys.

The rushing of floods in their courses,
   The rattle of rain on the roofs,
Recalled the fierce rush of the horses,
   The thunder of galloping hoofs.
And soon one broke out: 'I can suffer
   No longer the life of a slug;
The man that don't race is a duffer,
   Let's have one more run for the mug.

'Why, everything races, no matter
   Whatever its method may be:
The waterfowl hold a regatta;
   The possums run heats up a tree;
The emus are constantly sprinting
   A handicap out on the plain;
It seems that all nature is hinting
   'Tis time to be at it again.

'The cockatoo parrots are talking
   Of races to far-away lands;
The native companions are walking
   A go-as-you-please on the sands;
The little foals gallop for pastime;
   The wallabies race down the gap;
Let's try it once more for the last time –
   Bring out the old jacket and cap.

'And now for a horse; we might try one
   Of those that are bred on the place.

But I fancy it's better to buy one,
    A horse that has proved he can race.
Let us send down to Sydney to Skinner,
    A thorough good judge who can ride,
And ask him to buy us a spinner
    To clean out the whole country-side.'

They wrote him a letter as follows:
    'We want you to buy us a horse;
He must have the speed to catch swallows,
    And stamina with it, of course.
The price ain't a thing that'll grieve us,
    It's getting a bad un annoys
The undersigned blokes, and believe us,
    We're yours to a cinder, "the boys".'

He answered: 'I've bought you a hummer,
    A horse that has never been raced;
I saw him run over The Drummer,
    He held him outclassed and outpaced.
His breeding's not known, but they state he
    Is born of a thoroughbred strain.
I've paid them a hundred and eighty,
    And started the horse in the train.'

They met him – alas, that these verses
    Aren't up to the subject's demands,
Can't set forth their eloquent curses –
    For Partner was back on their hands.
They went in to meet him in gladness,
    They opened his box with delight –
A silent procession of sadness
    They crept to the station at night.

And life has grown dull on the station,
    The boys are all silent and slow;
Their work is a daily vexation,
    And sport is unknown to them now.
Whenever they think how they stranded,
    They squeal just as guinea-pigs squeal;
They'd bit their own hook, and were landed
    With fifty pounds loss on the deal.

An Idyll of Dandaloo

On Western plains, where shade is not,
      'Neath summer skies of cloudless blue,
Where all is dry and all is hot,
      There stands the town of Dandaloo —
A township where life's total sum
Is sleep, diversified with rum.

Its grass-grown streets with dust are deep;
      'Twere vain endeavour to express
The dreamless silence of its sleep,
      Its wide, expansive drunkenness.
The yearly races mostly drew
A lively crowd at Dandaloo.

There came a sportsman from the East,
      The eastern land where sportsmen blow,
And brought with him a speedy beast —
      A speedy beast as horses go.
He came afar in hope to 'do'
The little town of Dandaloo.

Now this was weak of him, I wot —
      Exceeding weak, it seemed to me —
For we in Dandaloo were not
      The Jugginses we seemed to be;
In fact, we rather thought we knew
Our book by heart in Dandaloo.

We held a meeting at the bar,
      And met the question fair and square —
'We've stumped the country near and far
      To raise the cash for races here;
We've got a hundred pounds or two —
Not half so bad for Dandaloo.

'And now, it seems we have to be
   Cleaned out by this here Sydney bloke,
With his imported horse; and he
   Will scoop the pool and leave us broke.
Shall we sit still, and make no fuss
While this chap climbs all over us?'

     *   *   *   *   *

The races came to Dandaloo,
   And all the cornstalks from the West
On every kind of moke and screw
   Come forth in all their glory drest.
The stranger's horse, as hard as nails,
Look'd fit to run for New South Wales.

He won the race by half a length –
   Quite half a length, it seemed to me –
But Dandaloo, with all its strength,
   Roared out 'Dead heat!' most fervently;
And, after hesitation meet,
The judge's verdict was 'Dead heat!'

And many men there were could tell
   What gave the verdict extra force.
The stewards – and the judge as well –
   They all had backed the second horse.
For things like this they sometimes do
In larger towns than Dandaloo.

They ran it off, the stranger won,
   Hands down, by near a hundred yards.
He smiled to think his troubles done;
   But Dandaloo held all the cards.
They went to scale and – cruel fate! –
His jockey turned out under weight.

Perhaps they'd tampered with the scale!
   I cannot tell. I only know
It weighed him out all right. I fail
   To paint that Sydney sportsman's woe.
He said the stewards were a crew
Of low-lived thieves in Dandaloo.

He lifted up his voice, irate,
    And swore till all the air was blue;
So then we rose to vindicate
    The dignity of Dandaloo.
'Look here,' said we, 'you must not poke
Such oaths at us poor country folk.'

We rode him softly on a rail,
    We shied at him, in careless glee,
Some large tomatoes, rank and stale,
    And eggs of great antiquity –
Their wild, unholy fragrance flew
About the town of Dandaloo.

He left the town at break of day,
    He led his racehorse through the streets,
And now he tells the tale, they say,
    To every racing man he meets.
And Sydney sportsmen all eschew
The atmosphere of Dandaloo.

The Geebung Polo Club

It was somewhere up the country, in a land of rock and scrub,
That they formed an institution called the Geebung Polo Club.
They were long and wiry natives from the rugged mountain side,
And the horse was never saddled that the Geebungs couldn't ride;
But their style of playing polo was irregular and rash —
They had mighty little science, but a mighty lot of dash:
And they played on mountain ponies that were muscular and
     strong,
Though their coats were quite unpolished, and their manes and
     tails were long.
And they used to train those ponies wheeling cattle in the scrub;
They were demons, were the members of the Geebung Polo Club.

It was somewhere down the country, in a city's smoke and steam,
That a polo club existed, called 'The Cuff and Collar Team'.
As a social institution 'twas a marvellous success,
For the members were distinguished by exclusiveness and dress.
They had natty little ponies that were nice, and smooth, and sleek,
For their cultivated owners only rode 'em once a week.
So they started up the country in pursuit of sport and fame,
For they meant to show the Geebungs how they ought to play the
     game;
And they took their valets with them — just to give their boots a rub
Ere they started operations on the Geebung Polo Club.

Now my readers can imagine how the contest ebbed and flowed,
When the Geebung boys got going it was time to clear the road;
And the game was so terrific that ere half the time was gone
A spectator's leg was broken — just from merely looking on.
For they waddied one another till the plain was strewn with dead,
While the score was kept so even that they neither got ahead.
And the Cuff and Collar Captain, when he tumbled off to die
Was the last surviving player — so the game was called a tie.

Then the Captain of the Geebungs raised him slowly from the
    ground,
Though his wounds were mostly mortal, yet he fiercely gazed
    around;
There was no one to oppose him – all the rest were in a trance,
So he scrambled on his pony for his last expiring chance,
For he meant to make an effort to get victory to his side;
So he struck at goal – and missed it – then he tumbled off and
    died.

    *   *   *   *   *

By the old Campaspe River, where the breezes shake the grass,
There's a row of little gravestones that the stockmen never pass,
For they bear a rude inscription saying, 'Stranger, drop a tear,
For the Cuff and Collar players and the Geebung boys lie here.'
And on misty moonlit evenings, while the dingoes howl around,
You can see their shadows flitting down that phantom polo ground;
You can hear the loud collisions as the flying players meet,
And the rattle of the mallets, and the rush of ponies' feet,
Till the terrified spectator rides like blazes to the pub –
He's been haunted by the spectres of the Geebung Polo Club.

The Travelling Post Office

The roving breezes come and go, the reed-beds sweep and sway,
The sleepy river murmurs low, and loiters on its way,
It is the land of lots o' time along the Castlereagh

*   *   *   *   *

The old man's son had left the farm, he found it dull and slow,
He drifted to the great North-west, where all the rovers go.
'He's gone so long,' the old man said, 'he's dropped right out of
        mind,
But if you'd write a line to him I'd take it very kind;
He's shearing here and fencing there, a kind of waif and stray –
He's droving now with Conroy's sheep along the Castlereagh.

*   *   *   *   *

'The sheep are travelling for the grass, and travelling very slow;
They may be at Mundooran now, or past the Overflow,
Or tramping down the black-soil flats across by Waddiwong
But all those little country towns would send the letter wrong.
The mailman, if he's extra tired, would pass them in his sleep;
It's safest to address the note to "Care of Conroy's sheep",
For five and twenty thousand head can scarcely go astray,
You write to "Care of Conroy's sheep along the Castlereagh".'

By rock and ridge and riverside the western mail has gone
Across the great Blue Mountain Range to take that letter on.
A moment on the topmost grade while open fire-doors glare,
She pauses like a living thing to breathe the mountain air,
Then launches down the other side across the plains away
To bear that note to 'Conroy's sheep along the Castlereagh'.

And now by coach and mailman's bag it goes from town to
        town,
And Conroy's Gap and Conroy's Creek have marked it 'Further
        down'.
Beneath a sky of deepest blue, where never cloud abides,
A speck upon the waste of plain the lonely mailman rides.
Where fierce hot winds have set the pine and myall boughs
        asweep

He hails the shearers passing by for news of Conroy's sheep.
By big lagoons where wildfowl play and crested pigeons flock,
By camp-fires where the drovers ride around their restless stock,
And past the teamster toiling down to fetch the wool away
My letter chases Conroy's sheep along the Castlereagh.

Saltbush Bill

Now this is the law of the Overland that all in the West obey –
A man must cover with travelling sheep a six-mile stage a day;
But this is the law which the drovers make, right easily understood,
They travel their stage where the grass is bad, but they camp where
        the grass is good;
They camp, and they ravage the squatter's grass till never a blade
        remains,
Then they drift away as the white clouds drift on the edge of the
        saltbush plains;
From camp to camp and from run to run they battle it hand to hand
For a blade of grass and the right to pass on the track of the
        Overland.
For this is the law of the Great Stock Routes, 'tis written in white
        and black –
The man that goes with a travelling mob must keep to a half-mile
        track;
And the drovers keep to a half-mile track on the runs where the
        grass is dead,
But they spread their sheep on a well-grassed run till they go with a
        two-mile spread.
So the squatters hurry the drovers on from dawn till the fall of night,
And the squatters' dogs and the drovers' dogs get mixed in a deadly
        fight.
Yet the squatters' men, though they hunt the mob, are willing the
        peace to keep,
For the drovers learn how to use their hands when they go with the
        travelling sheep;
But this is the tale of a Jackaroo that came from a foreign strand,
And the fight that he fought with Saltbush Bill, the King of the
        Overland.

Now Saltbush Bill was a drover tough as ever the country knew,
He had fought his way on the Great Stock Routes from the sea
      to the big Barcoo;
He could tell when he came to a friendly run that gave him a
      chance to spread,
And he knew where the hungry owners were that hurried his
      sheep ahead;
He was drifting down in the Eighty drought with a mob that
      could scarcely creep
(When the kangaroos by the thousand starve, it is rough on the
      travelling sheep),
And he camped one night at the crossing-place on the edge of
      the Wilga run;
'We must manage a feed for them here,' he said, 'or half of the
      mob are done!'
So he spread them out when they left the camp wherever they
      liked to go,
Till he grew aware of a Jackaroo with a station-hand in tow.
They set to work on the straggling sheep, and with many a
      stockwhip crack
They forced them in where the grass was dead in the space of
      the half-mile track;
And William prayed that the hand of Fate might suddenly strike
      him blue
But he'd get some grass for his starving sheep in the teeth of
      that Jackaroo.
So he turned and he cursed the Jackaroo; he cursed him, alive
      or dead
From the soles of his great unwieldly feet to the crown of his
      ugly head,
With an extra curse on the moke he rode and the cur at his
      heels that ran,
Till the Jackaroo from his horse got down and went for the
      drover-man;
With the station-hand for his picker-up, though the sheep ran
      loose the while,
They battled it out on the well-grassed plain in the regular prize-
      ring style.

Now, the new chum fought for his honour's sake and the pride
    of the English race,
But the drover fought for his daily bread with a smile on his
    bearded face;
So he shifted ground, and he sparred for wind, and he made it a
    lengthy mill,
And from time to time as his scouts came in they whispered to
    Saltbush Bill –
'We have spread the sheep with a two-mile spread, and the
    grass it is something grand;
You must stick to him, Bill, for another round for the pride of
    the Overland.'
The new chum made it a rushing fight, though never a blow got
    home,
Till the sun rode high in the cloudless sky and glared on the
    brick-red loam,
Till the sheep drew in to the shelter-trees and settled them
    down to rest;
Then the drover said he would fight no more, and gave his
    opponent best.

So the new chum rode to the homestead straight, and told them
    a story grand
Of the desperate fight that he fought that day with the King of
    the Overland;
And the tale went home to the Public Schools of the pluck of
    the English swell –
How the drover fought for his very life, but blood in the end
    must tell.
But the travelling sheep and the Wilga sheep were boxed on the
    Old Man Plain;
'Twas a full week's work ere they drafted out and hunted them
    off again;
A week's good grass in their wretched hides, with a curse and a
    stockwhip crack
They hunted them off on the road once more to starve on the
    half-mile track.
And Saltbush Bill, on the Overland, will many a time recite
How the best day's work that he ever did was the day that he
    lost the fight.

A Mountain Station

I bought a run a while ago
    On country rough and ridgy,
Where wallaroos and wombats grow –
    The Upper Murrumbidgee.
The grass is rather scant, it's true,
    But this a fair exchange is,
The sheep can see a lovely view
    By climbing up the ranges.

And She-oak Flat's the station's name,
    I'm not surprised at that, sirs:
The oaks were there before I came,
    And I supplied the flat, sirs.
A man would wonder how it's done,
    The stock so soon decreases –
They sometimes tumble off the run
    And break themselves to pieces.

I've tried to make expenses meet,
    But wasted all my labours;
The sheep the dingoes didn't eat
    Were stolen by the neighbours.
They stole my pears – my native pears –
    Those thrice-convicted felons,
And ravished from me unawares
    My crop of paddy-melons.

And sometimes under sunny skies,
    Without an explanation,
The Murrumbidgee used to rise
    And overflow the station.
But this was caused (as now I know)
    When summer sunshine glowing
Had melted all Kiandra's snow
    And set the river going.

Then in the news, perhaps, you read:
   'Stock Passings. Puckawidgee,
Fat cattle: Seven hundred head
   Swept down the Murrumbidgee;
Their destination's quite obscure,
   But, somehow, there's a notion,
Unless the river falls, they're sure
   To reach the Southern Ocean.'

So after that I'll give it best;
   No more with Fate I'll battle.
I'll let the river take the rest,
   For those were all my cattle.
And with one comprehensive curse
   I close my brief narration,
And advertise it in my verse –
   'For Sale! A Mountain Station.'

Been There Before

There came a stranger to Walgett town,
   To Walgett town when the sun was low,
And he carried a thirst that was worth a crown,
   Yet how to quench it he did not know;
But he thought he might take those yokels down,
   The guileless yokels of Walgett town.

They made him a bet in a private bar,
   In a private bar when the talk was high,
And they bet him some pounds no matter how far
   He could pelt a stone, yet he could not shy
A stone right over the river so brown,
   The Darling River at Walgett town.

He knew that the river from bank to bank
   Was fifty yards, and he smiled a smile
As he trundled down; but his hopes they sank,
   For there wasn't a stone within fifty mile;
For the saltbush plain and the open down
   Produce no quarries in Walgett town.

The yokels laughed at his hopes o'erthrown,
   And he stood awhile like a man in a dream;
Then he out of his pocket he fetched a stone,
   And pelted it over the silent stream –
He'd been there before; he had wandered down
   On a previous visit to Walgett town.

The Man Who was Away

The widow sought the lawyer's room with children three in tow,
She told the lawyer man her tale in tones of deepest woe.
She said, 'My husband took to drink for pains in his inside,
And never drew a sober breath from then until he died.

'He never drew a sober breath, he died without a will,
And I must sell the bit of land the childer's mouths to fill.
There's some is grown and gone away, but some is childer yet,
And times is very bad indeed – a livin's hard to get.

'There's Min and Sis and little Chris, they stops at home with me,
And Sal has married Greenhide Bill that breaks for Bidgeree.
And Fred is drovin' Conroy's sheep along the Castlereagh
And Charley's shearin' down the Bland, and Peter is away.'

The lawyer wrote the details down in ink of legal blue –
'There's Minnie, Susan, Christopher, they stop at home with you;
There's Sarah, Frederick, and Charles, I'll write to them today,
But what about the other son – the one who is away?

'You'll have to furnish his consent to sell the bit of land.'
The widow shuffled in her seat, 'Oh, don't you understand?
I thought a lawyer ought to know – I don't know what to say -
You'll have to do without him, boss, for Peter is away.'

But here the little boy spoke up – said he, 'We thought you knew;
He's done six months in Goulburn gaol – he's got six more to do.'
Thus in one comprehensive flash he made it clear as day,
The mystery of Peter's life – the man who was away.

The Man from Ironbark

It was the man from Ironbark who struck the Sydney town,
He wandered over street and park, he wandered up and
      down.
He loitered here, he loitered there, till he was like to drop,
Until at last in sheer despair he sought a barber's shop.
' 'Ere! shave my beard and whiskers off, I'll be a man of
      mark,
I'll go and do the Sydney toff up home in Ironbark.'

The barber man was small and flash, as barbers mostly are,
He wore a strike-your-fancy sash, he smoked a huge cigar:
He was a humorist of note and keen at repartee,
He laid the odds and kept a 'tote', whatever that may be.
And when he saw our friend arrive, he whispered 'Here's a
      lark!
Just watch me catch him all alive this man from Ironbark.'

There were some gilded youths that sat along the barber's
      wall,
Their eyes were dull, their heads were flat, they had no
      brains at all;
To them the barber passed the wink, his dexter eyelid shut,
'I'll make this bloomin' yokel think his bloomin' throat is
      cut.'
And as he soaped and rubbed it in he made a rude remark:
'I s'pose the flats is pretty green up there in Ironbark.'

A grunt was all reply he got; he shaved the bushman's chin,
Then made the water boiling hot and dipped the razor in.
He raised his hand, his brow grew black, he paused awhile
      to gloat,
Then slashed the red-hot razor-back across his victim's
      throat;
Upon the newly-shaven skin it made a livid mark –
No doubt it fairly took him in – the man from Ironbark.

He fetched a wild up-country yell might wake the dead to
       hear,
And though his throat, he knew full well, was cut from ear
       to ear,
He struggled gamely to his feet, and faced the murderous
       foe.
'You've done for me! you dog, I'm beat! one hit before I go!
I only wish I had a knife, you blessed murdering shark!
But you'll remember all your life the man from Ironbark.'

He lifted up his hairy paw, with one tremendous clout
He landed on the barber's jaw, and knocked the barber out.
He set to work with tooth and nail, he made the place a
       wreck;
He grabbed the nearest gilded youth, and tried to break his
       neck.
And all the while his throat he held to save his vital spark,
And 'Murder! Bloody Murder!' yelled the man from
       Ironbark.

A peeler man who heard the din came in to see the show;
He tried to run the bushman in, but he refused to go.
And when at last the barber spoke, and said ' 'Twas all in
       fun –
'Twas just a little harmless joke, a trifle overdone.'
'A joke!' he cried, 'By George, that's fine; a lively sort of lark;
I'd like to catch that murdering swine some night in
       Ironbark.'

And now while round the shearing-floor the listening
       shearers gape,
He tells the story o'er and o'er, and brags of his escape.
'Them barber chaps what keeps a tote, by George, I've had
       enough,
One tried to cut my bloomin' throat, but thank the Lord it's
       tough.'
And whether he's believed or no, there's one thing to
       remark,
That flowing beards are all the go way up in Ironbark.

The Open Steeplechase

I had ridden over hurdles up the country once or twice,
By the side of Snowy River with a horse they called 'The
    Ace'.
And we brought him down to Sydney, and our rider, Jimmy
    Rice,
Got a fall and broke his shoulder, so they nabbed me in a
    trice –
Me, that never wore the colours, for the Open Steeplechase.

'Make the running,' said the trainer, 'it's your only chance
    whatever,
Make it hot from start to finish, for the old black horse can
    stay,
And just think of how they'll take it, when they hear on
    Snowy River
That the country boy was plucky, and the country horse was
    clever.
You must ride for old Monaro and the mountain boys
    today.'

'Are you ready?' said the starter, as we held the horses back.
All ablazing with impatience, with excitement all aglow;
Before us like a ribbon stretched the steeplechasing track,
And the sun-rays glistened brightly on the chestnut and the
    black
As the starter's words came slowly, 'Are – you – ready? Go!'

Well I scarcely knew we'd started, I was stupid-like with
    wonder
Till the field closed up beside me and a jump appeared
    ahead.
And we flew it like a hurdle, not a baulk and not a blunder,
As we charged it all together, and it fairly whistled under,
And then some were pulled behind me and a few shot out
    and led.

So we ran for half the distance, and I'm making no pretences

When I tell you I was feeling very nervous-like and queer,
For those jockeys rode like demons; you would think they'd
      lost their senses
If you saw them rush their horses at those rasping five-foot
      fences –
And in place of making running I was falling to the rear.

Till a chap came racing past me on a horse they called 'The
      Quiver',
And said he, 'My country joker, are you going to give it best?
Are you frightened of the fences? does their stoutness make
      you shiver?
Have they come to breeding cowards by the side of Snowy
      River?
Are there riders on Monaro? ' but I never heard the rest.

For I drove The Ace and sent him just as fast as he could
      pace it
At the big black line of timber stretching fair across the track,
And he shot beside The Quiver. 'Now,' said I, 'my boy, we'll
      race it.
You can come with Snowy River if you're only game to face it,
Let us mend the pace a little and we'll see who cries a crack.'

So we raced away together, and we left the others standing,
And the people cheered and shouted as we settled down to
      ride,
And we clung beside The Quiver. At his taking off and
      landing
I could see his scarlet nostril and his mighty ribs expanding,
And The Ace stretched out in earnest, and we held him stride
      for stride.

But the pace was so terrific that they soon ran out their
      tether –
They were rolling in their gallop, they were fairly blown and
      beat –
But they both were game as pebbles – neither one would
      show the feather.
And we rushed them at the fences, and they cleared them

both together,
Nearly every time they clouted, but they somehow kept their
feet.

Then the last jump rose before us, and they faced it game as
ever –
We were both at spur and whipcord, fetching blood at every
bound –
And above the people's cheering and the cries of 'Ace' and
'Quiver',
I could hear the trainer shouting, 'One more run for Snowy
River.'
Then we struck the jump together and came smashing to the
ground.

Well, The Quiver ran to blazes, but The Ace stood still and
waited,
Stood and waited like a statue while I scrambled on his back.
There was no one next or near me for the field was fairly
slated,
So I cantered home a winner with my shoulder dislocated,
While the man who rode The Quiver followed limping down
the track.

And he shook my hand and told me that in all his days he
never
Met a man who rode more gamely, and our last set-to was
prime.
Then he wired them on Monaro how we chanced to beat The
Quiver,
And they sent us back an answer, 'Good old sort from Snowy
River:
Send us word each race you start in and we'll back you every
time.' ·

The Amateur Rider

Him going to ride for us! *Him* – with the pants and the
      eyeglass and all.
Amateur! don't he just look it – it's twenty to one on a fall.
Boss must be gone off his head to be sending our
      steeplechase crack
Out over fences like these with an object like that on his
      back.

Ride! Don't tell *me* he can ride. With his pants just as loose
      as balloons,
How can he sit on a horse? and his spurs like a pair of
      harpoons;
Ought to be under the Dog Act, he ought, and be kept off
      the course.
Fall! why, he'd fall off a cart, let alone off a steeplechase
      horse.

      *   *   *   *   *

Yessir! the 'orse is all ready – I wish you'd have rode him
      before;
Nothing like knowing your 'orse, sir, and this chap's a terror
      to bore;
Battleaxe always could pull, and he rushes his fences like
      fun –
Stands off his jump twenty feet, and then springs like a shot
      from a gun.

Oh, he can jump 'em all right, sir, you make no mistake, 'e's
      a toff --
Clouts 'em in earnest, too, sometimes; you mind that he
      don't clout you off –
Don't seem to mind how he hits 'em , his shins is as hard as
      a nail,
Sometimes you'll see the fence shake and the splinters fly up
      from the rail.

All you can do is to hold him and just let him jump as he
 likes,
Give him his head at the fences, and hang on like death if he
 strikes;
Don't let him run himself out – you can lie third or fourth in
 the race –
Until you clear the stone wall, and from that you can put on
 the pace.

Fell at that wall once, he did, and it gave him a regular
 spread,
Ever since that time he flies it – he'll stop if you pull at his
 head,
Just let him race – you can trust him – he'll take first-class
 care he don't fall,
And I think that's the lot – but remember, he must have his
 head at the wall.

*   *   *   *   *

Well, he's down safe as far as the start, and he seems to sit
 on pretty neat,
Only his baggified breeches would ruinate anyone's seat –
They're away – here they come – the first fence, and he's
 head over heels for a crown!
Good for the new chum, he's over, and two of the others are
 down!

Now for the treble, my hearty – By Jove, he can ride, after
 all;
Whoop, that's your sort – let him fly them! He hasn't much
 fear of a fall.
Who in the world would have thought it? And aren't they
 just going a pace?
Little Recruit in the lead there will make it a stoutly-run
 race.

Lord! but they're racing in earnest – and down goes Recruit
 on his head,
Rolling clean over his boy – it's a miracle if he ain't dead.
Battleaxe, Battleaxe, yet! By the Lord, he's got most of 'em
 beat –

Ho! did you see how he struck, and the swell never moved
      in his seat?

Second time round, and, by Jingo! he's holding his lead of
      'em well;
Hark to him clouting the timber! It don't seem to trouble
      the swell.
Now for the wall – let him rush it. A thirty-foot leap, I
      declare –
Never a shift in his seat, and he's racing for home like a
      hare.

What's that that's chasing him – Rataplan – regular demon
      to stay!
Sit down and ride for your life now! Oh, good, that's the
      style – come away!
Rataplan's certain to beat you, unless you can give him the
      slip;
Sit down and rub in the whalebone – now give him the
      spurs and the whip!

Battleaxe, Battleaxe, yet – and it's Battleaxe wins for a
      crown;
Look at him rushing the fences, he wants to bring t'other
      chap down.
Rataplan never will catch him if only he keeps on his pins;
Now! the last fence, and he's over it! Battleaxe, Battleaxe
      wins!

     *   *   *   *   *

Well, sir, you rode him just perfect – I knew from the fust
      you could ride.
Some of the chaps said you couldn't, an' I says just like this
      a' one side:
Mark me, I says, that's a tradesman – the saddle is where he
      was bred.
Weight! you're all right, sir, and thank you; and them was
      the words that I said.

On Kiley's Run

The roving breezes come and go
               On Kiley's Run,
The sleepy river murmurs low,
And far away one dimly sees
Beyond the stretch of forest trees –
Beyond the foothills dusk and dun –
The ranges steeping in the sun
               On Kiley's Run.

'Tis many years since first I came
               To Kiley's Run,
More years than I would care to name
Since I, a stripling, used to ride
For miles and miles at Kiley's side,
The while in stirring tones he told
The stories of the days of old
               On Kiley's Run.

I see the old bush homestead now
               On Kiley's Run,
Just nestled down beneath the brow
Of one small ridge above the sweep
Of river-flat, where willows weep
And jasmine flowers and roses bloom:
The air was laden with perfume
               On Kiley's Run.

We lived the good old station life
               On Kiley's Run,
With little thought of care or strife.
Old Kiley seldom used to roam,
He liked to make the Run his home;
The swagmen never turned away
With empty hand at close of day
               From Kiley's Run.

We kept a racehorse now and then
               On Kiley's Run.
And neighbouring stations brought their men
To meetings where the sport was free,
And dainty ladies came to see
Their champions ride; with laugh and song
The old house rang the whole night long
               On Kiley's Run.

The station-hands were friends, I wot,
               On Kiley's Run,
A reckless, merry-hearted lot –
All splendid riders, and they knew
The boss was kindness through and through.
Old Kiley always stood their friend,
And so they served him to the end
               On Kiley's Run.

But droughts and losses came apace
               To Kiley's Run,
Till ruin stared him in the face;
He toiled and toiled while lived the light,
He dreamed of overdrafts at night:
At length, because he could not pay,
His bankers took the stock away
               From Kiley's Run.

Old Kiley stood and saw them go
               From Kiley's Run.
The well-bred cattle marching slow;
His stockmen, mates for many a day,
They wrung his hand and went away.
Too old to make another start,
Old Kiley died – of broken heart,
               On Kiley's Run.

The owner lives in England now
               Of Kiley's Run.
He knows a racehorse from a cow;
But that is all he knows of stock:

His chiefest care is how to dock
Expenses, and he sends from town
To cut the shearers' wages down
           On Kiley's Run.

There are no neighbours anywhere
           Near Kiley's Run.
The hospitable homes are bare,
The gardens gone; for no pretence
Must hinder cutting down expense;
The homestead that we held so dear
Contains a half-paid overseer
           On Kiley's Run.

All life and sport and hope have died
           On Kiley's Run.
No longer there the stockmen ride;
For sour-faced boundary riders creep
On mongrel horses after sheep,
Through ranges where, at racing speed,
Old Kiley used to 'wheel the lead'
           On Kiley's Run.

There runs a lane for thirty miles
           Through Kiley's Run.
On either side the herbage smiles,
But wretched travelling sheep must pass
Without a drink or blade of grass
Through that long lane of death and shame:
The weary drovers curse the name
           Of Kiley's Run.

The name itself is changed of late
           Of Kiley's Run.
They call it 'Chandos Park Estate'.
The lonely swagman through the dark
Must hump his swag past Chandos Park –
The name is English, don't you see;
The old name sweeter sounds to me
           Of Kiley's Run.

I cannot guess what fate will bring
                To Kiley's Run –
For chances come and changes ring –
I scarcely think 'twill always be
Locked up to suit an absentee;
And if he lets it out in farms
His tenants soon will carry arms
                On Kiley's Run.

Frying Pan's Theology

SCENE: On Monaro.
   Dramatis Personae
Shock-headed blackfellow,
   Boy (on a pony).

Snowflakes are falling
   Gentle and slow,
Youngster says, 'Frying Pan
   What makes it snow?'

Frying Pan, confident,
   Makes the reply –
'Shake 'im big flour bag
   Up in the sky!'

'What! when there's miles of it?
   Surely that's brag.
Who is there strong enough
   Shake such a bag?'

'What parson tellin' you,
   Ole Mister Dodd,
Tell you in Sunday-school?
   Big pfeller God!

'Him drive 'im bullock dray,
   Then thunder go;
Him shake 'im flour bag –
   Tumble down snow!'

The Two Devines

It was shearing-time at the Myall Lake,
    And then rose the sound through the livelong day
Of the constant clash that the shear-blades make
    When the fastest shearers are making play;
But there wasn't a man in the shearers' lines
That could shear a sheep with the two Devines.

They had rung the sheds of the east and west,
    Had beaten the cracks of the Walgett side,
And the Cooma shearers had given them best –
    When they saw them shear, they were satisfied.
From the southern slopes to the western pines
They were noted men, were the two Devines.

'Twas a wether flock that had come to hand,
    Great struggling brutes, that shearers shirk,
For the fleece was filled with the grass and sand,
    And seventy sheep was a big day's work.
'At a pound a hundred it's dashed hard lines
To shear such sheep,' said the two Devines.

But the shearers knew that they'd make a cheque
    When they came to deal with the station ewes;
They were bare of belly and bare of neck
    With a fleece as light as a kangaroo's.
'We will show the boss how a shear-blade shines
When we reach those ewes,' said the two Devines.

But it chanced next day, when the stunted pines
    Were swayed and stirred by the dawn-wind's breath,
That a message came for the two Devines
    That their father lay at the point of death.
So away at speed through the whispering pines
Down the bridle-track rode the two Devines.

It was fifty miles to their father's hut,
    And the dawn was bright when they rode away;
At the fall of night, when the shed was shut
    And the men had rest from the toilsome day,
To the shed once more through the darkening pines
On their weary steeds came the two Devines.

'Well, you're back right sudden,' the super said;
    'Is the old man dead and the funeral done?'
'Well, no sir, he ain't not exactly dead,
    But as good as dead,' said the eldest son –
'And we couldn't bear such a chance to lose,
So we came straight back to tackle the ewes.'

*   *   *   *   *

They are shearing ewes at the Myall Lake,
    And the shed is merry the livelong day
With the clashing sound that the shear-blades make
    When the fastest shearers are making play;
And a couple of 'hundred and ninety-nines'
Are the tallies made by the two Devines.

In the Droving Days

'Only a pound,' said the auctioneer,
'Only a pound; and I'm standing here
Selling this animal, gain or loss –
Only a pound for the drover's horse?
One of the sort that was ne'er afraid,
One of the boys of the Old Brigade;
Thoroughly honest and game, I'll swear,
Only a little the worse for wear;
Plenty as bad to be seen in town,
Give me a bid and I'll knock him down;
Sold as he stands, and without recourse,
Give me a bid for the drover's horse.'

Loitering there in an aimless way
Somehow I noticed the poor old grey,
Weary and battered and screwed, of course;
Yet when I noticed the old grey horse,
The rough bush saddle, and single rein
Of the bridle laid on his tangled mane,
Straightway the crowd and the auctioneer
Seemed on a sudden to disappear,
Melted away in a kind of haze —
For my heart went back to the droving days.

Back to the road, and I crossed again
Over the miles of the saltbush plain —
The shining plain that is said to be
The dried-up bed of an inland sea.
Where the air so dry and so clear and bright
Refracts the sun with a wondrous light,
And out in the dim horizon makes
The deep blue gleam of the phantom lakes.

At dawn of day we could feel the breeze
That stirred the boughs of the sleeping trees,
And brought a breath of the fragrance rare
That comes and goes in that scented air;
For the trees and grass and the shrubs contain
A dry sweet scent on the saltbush plain.
For those that love it and understand
The saltbush plain is a wonderland,
A wondrous country, where Nature's ways
Were revealed to me in the droving days.

We saw the fleet wild horses pass,
And kangaroos through the Mitchell grass;
The emu ran with her frightened brood
All unmolested and unpursued.
But there rose a shout and a wild hubbub
When the dingo raced for his native scrub,
And he paid right dear for his stolen meals
With the drovers' dogs at his wretched heels.
For we ran him down at a rattling pace,

While the pack-horse joined in the stirring chase.
And a wild halloo at the kill we'd raise –
We were light of heart in the droving days.

'Twas a drover's horse, and my hand again
Made a move to close on a fancied rein.
For I felt the swing and the easy stride
Of the grand old horse that I used to ride.
In drought or plenty, in good or ill,
The same old steed was my comrade still;
The old grey horse with his honest ways
Was a mate to me in the droving days.

When we kept our watch in the cold and damp,
If the cattle broke from the sleeping camp,
Over the flats and across the plain,
With my head bent down on his waving mane,
Through the boughs above and the stumps below,
On the darkest night I could let him go
At a racing speed; he would choose his course,
And my life was safe with the old grey horse.
But man and horse had a favourite job,
When an outlaw broke from a station mob;
With a right good will was the stockwhip plied,
As the old horse raced at the straggler's side,
And the greenhide whip such a weal would raise –
We could use the whip in the droving days.

*   *   *   *   *

'Only a pound!' and was this the end –
Only a pound for the drover's friend.
The drover's friend that has seen his day,
And now was worthless and cast away
With a broken knee and a broken heart
To be flogged and starved in a hawker's cart.
Well, I made a bid for a sense of shame
And the memories dear of the good old game.

'Thank you? Guinea! and cheap at that!
Against you there in the curly hat!

Only a guinea, and one more chance,
Down he goes if there's no advance,
Third, and the last time, one! two! three!'
And the old grey horse was knocked down to me.
And now he's wandering, fat and sleek,
On the lucerne flats by the Homestead Creek;
I dare not ride him for fear he'd fall,
But he does a journey to beat them all,
For though he scarcely a trot can raise,
He can take me back to the droving days.

Lost

'He ought to be home,' said the old man, 'without there's
      something amiss.
He only went to the Two-mile – he ought to be back by this.
He *would* ride the Reckless filly, he *would* have his wilful way;
And here, he's not back at sundown – and what will his mother
      say?

'He was always his mother's idol, since ever his father died;
And there isn't a horse on the station that he isn't game to ride.
But that Reckless mare is vicious, and if once she gets away
He hasn't got strength to hold her – and what will his mother say?'

The old man walked to the sliprail, and peered up the darkening
      track,
And looked and longed for the rider that would never more come
      back;
And the mother came and clutched him, with sudden, spasmodic
      fright:
'What has become of my Willie? – why isn't he home tonight?'

Away in the gloomy ranges, at the foot of an ironbark,
The bonnie, winsome laddie was lying stiff and stark;
For the Reckless mare had smashed him against a leaning limb,
And his comely face was battered, and his merry eyes were dim.

And the thoroughbred chestnut filly, the saddle beneath her flanks,
Was away like fire through the ranges to join the wild mob's ranks;
And a broken-hearted woman and an old man worn and white
Were searching all day in the ranges till the sundown brought the
　　　　night.

And the mother kept feebly calling, with a hope that would not die,
'Willie! where are you, Willie?' But how can the dead reply?
And hope died out with the daylight, and the darkness brought
　　　　despair.
God pity the stricken mother, and answer the widow's prayer!

Though far and wide they sought him, they found not where he
　　　　fell;
For the ranges held him precious, and guarded their treasure well.
The wattle blooms above him, and the bluebells blow close by,
And the brown bees buzz the secret, and the wild birds sing reply.

But the mother pined and faded, and cried, and took no rest,
And rode each day to the ranges on her hopeless, weary quest,
Seeking her loved one ever, she faded and pined away,
But with strength of her great affection she still sought every day.

'I know that sooner or later I shall find my boy,' she said.
But she came not home one evening, and they found her lying
　　　　dead,
And stamped on the poor pale features, as the spirit homeward
　　　　passed,
Was an angel smile of gladness – she had found her boy at last.

Over the Range

Little bush maiden, wondering-eyed,
   Playing alone in the creek-bed dry,
In the small green flat on every side
   Walled in by the Moonbi ranges high;
Tell me the tale of your lonely life
   'Mid the great grey forests that know no change.
'I never have left my home,' she said,
   'I have never been over the Moonbi Range.

'Father and mother are both long dead,
   And I live with granny in yon wee place.'
'Where are your father and mother?' I said.
   She puzzled awhile with thoughtful face,
Then a light came into the shy brown eye,
   And she smiled, for she thought the question
      strange
On a thing so certain – 'When people die
   They go to the country over the range.'

'And what is this country like, my lass?'
   'There are blossoming trees and pretty flowers,
And shining creeks where the golden grass
   Is fresh and sweet from the summer showers.
They never need work, nor want, nor weep;
   No troubles can come their hearts to estrange.
Some summer night I shall fall asleep,
   And wake in the country over the range.'

Child, you are wise in your simple trust,
   For the wisest man knows no more than you.
Ashes to ashes, and dust to dust:
   Our views by a range are bounded too;
But we know that God hath this gift in store,
   That, when we come to the final change,
We shall meet with our loved ones gone before
   To the beautiful country over the range.

Only a Jockey

*Richard Bennison, a jockey, aged fourteen, while riding
William Tell in his training, was thrown and killed. The
horse is luckily uninjured.*   Melbourne Wire

Out in the grey cheerless chill of the morning light,
 Out on the track where the night shades still lurk,
Ere the first gleam of the sungod's returning light
 Round come the racehorses early at work.

Reefing and pulling and racing so readily,
 Close sit the jockey-boys holding them hard,
'Steady the stallion there – canter him steadily,
 Don't let him gallop so much as a yard.'

Fiercely he fights while the others run wide of him,
 Reefs at the bit that would hold him in thrall,
Plunges and bucks till the boy that's astride of him
 Goes to the ground with a terrible fall.

'Stop him there! Block him there! Drive him in carefully,
 Lead him about till he's quiet and cool.
Sound as a bell! though he's blown himself fearfully,
 Now let us pick up this poor little fool.

'Stunned? Oh, by Jove, I'm afraid it's a case with him:
 Ride for the doctor! keep bathing his head!
Send for a cart to go down to our place with him' –
 No use! One long sigh and the little chap's dead.

Only a jockey-boy, foul-mouthed and bad you see,
 Ignorant, heathenish, gone to his rest.
Parson or Presbyter, Pharisee, Sadducee,
 What did you do for him? – bad was the best.

Negroes and foreigners, all have a claim on you;
 Yearly you send your well-advertised hoard,

But the poor jockey-boy – shame on you, shame on you,
   'Feed ye My little ones' – what said the Lord?

Him ye held less than the outer barbarian,
   Left him to die in his ignorant sin;
Have you no principles, humanitarian?
   Have you no precept – 'Go gather them in'?

Knew he God's name? In his brutal profanity
   That name was an oath – out of many but one.
What did he get from our famed Christianity?
   Where has his soul – if he had any – gone?

Fourteen years old, and what was he taught of it?
   What did he know of God's infinite Grace?
Draw the dark curtain of shame o'er the thought of it
   Draw the shroud over the jockey-boy's face.

How M'Ginnis Went Missing

Let us cease our idle chatter,
    Let the tears bedew our cheek,
For a man from Tallangatta
    Has been missing for a week.

Where the roaring flooded Murray
    Covered all the lower land,
There he started in a hurry,
    With a bottle in his hand.

And his fate is hid for ever,
    But the public seem to think
That he slumbered by the river,
    'Neath the influence of drink.

And they scarcely seem to wonder
    That the river, wide and deep,
Never woke him with its thunder,
    Never stirred him in his sleep.

As the crashing logs came sweeping
    And their tumult filled the air,
Then M'Ginnis murmured, sleeping,
    ' 'Tis a wake in ould Kildare.'

So the river rose and found him
    Sleeping softly by the stream.
And the cruel waters drowned him
    Ere he wakened from his dream.

And the blossom-tufted wattle,
    Blooming brightly on the lea,
Saw M'Ginnis and the bottle
    Going drifting out to sea.

A Voice from Town

A sequel to Mowbray Morris's 'A Voice from the Bush'

I thought, in the days of my droving,
    Of steps I might hope to retrace,
To be done with the bush and the roving
    And settle once more in my place.
With a heart that was wellnigh to breaking,
    In the long, lonely rides on the plain,
I thought of the pleasure of taking
    The hand of a lady again.

I am back into civilization,
    Once more in the stir and the strife,
But the old joys have lost their sensation –
    The light has gone out of my life;
The men of my time they have married,
    Made fortunes or gone to the wall;
Too long from the scene I have tarried,
    And, somehow, I'm out of it all.

For I go to the balls and the races
    A lonely, companionless elf,
And the ladies bestow all their graces
    On others less grey than myself;
While the talk goes around I'm a dumb one
    'Midst youngsters that chatter and prate,
And they call me 'The Man who was Some One
    'Way back in the year Sixty-eight'.

And I look, sour and old, at the dancers
    That swing to the strains of the band,
And the ladies all give me the Lancers,
    No waltzes – I quite understand.
For matrons, intent upon matching
    Their daughters with infinite push,
Would scarce think him worthy the catching,
    The broken-down man from the bush.

New partners have come and new faces,
    And I, of the bygone brigade,
Sharply feel that oblivion my place is –
    I must lie with the rest in the shade.
And the youngsters, fresh-featured and pleasant,
    They live as we lived – fairly fast;
But I doubt if the men of the present
    Are as good as the men of the past.

Of excitement and praise they are chary,
    There is nothing much good upon earth;
Their watchword is *nil admirari,*
    They are bored from the days of their birth.
Where the life that we led was a revel
    They 'wince and relent and refrain' –
I could show them the road – to the Devil,
    Were I only a youngster again.

I could show them the road where the stumps are,
    The pleasures that end in remorse,
And the game where the Devil's three trumps are
    The woman, the card, and the horse.
Shall the blind lead the blind -- shall the sower
    Of wind reap the storm as of yore?
Though they get to their goal somewhat slower,
    They march where we hurried before.

For the world never learns – just as we did
    They gallantly go to their fate,
Unheeded all warnings, unheeded
    The maxims of elders sedate.
As the husbandman, patiently toiling,
    Draws a harvest each year from the soil,
So the fools grow afresh for the spoiling,
    And a new crop of thieves for the spoil.

But a truce to this dull moralizing,
    Let them drink while the drops are of gold.
I have tasted the dregs – 'twere surprising
    Were the new wine to me like the old;

And I weary for lack of employment
   In idleness day after day,
For the key to the door of enjoyment
   Is Youth – and I've thrown it away.

A Bunch of Roses

Roses ruddy and roses white,
   What are the joys that my heart discloses?
Sitting alone in the fading light
Memories come to me here tonight
   With the wonderful scent of the big red roses.

Memories come as the daylight fades
   Down on the hearth where the firelight dozes;
Flicker and flutter the lights and shades,
And I see the face of a queen of maids
   Whose memory comes with the scent of roses.

Visions arise of a scene of mirth,
   And a ballroom belle who superbly poses –
A queenly woman of queenly worth,
And I am the happiest man on earth
   With a single flower from a bunch of roses.

Only her memory lives tonight –
   God in His wisdom her young life closes;
Over her grave may the turf be light,
Cover her coffin with roses white –
   She was always fond of the big white roses.

    *   *   *   *   *

Such are the visions that fade away –
   Man proposes and God disposes;
Look in the glass and I see today
Only an old man, worn and grey,
   Bending his head to a bunch of roses.

Black Swans

As I lie at rest on a patch of clover
In the Western Park when the day is done,
I watch as the wild black swans fly over
With their phalanx turned to the sinking sun;
And I hear the clang of their leader crying
To a lagging mate in the rearward flying,
And they fade away in the darkness dying,
Where the stars are mustering one by one.

O ye wild black swans, 'twere a world of wonder
For a while to join in your westward flight,
With the stars above and the dim earth under,
Through the cooling air of the glorious night.
As we swept along on our pinions winging,
We should catch the chime of a church-bell ringing,
Or the distant note of a torrent singing,
Or the far-off flash of a station light.

From the northern lakes with the reeds and rushes,
Where the hills are clothed with a purple haze,
Where the bell-birds chime and the songs of thrushes
Make music sweet in the jungle maze,
They will hold their course to the westward ever,
Till they reach the banks of the old grey river,
Where the waters wash, and the reed-beds quiver
In the burning heat of the summer days.

O ye strange wild birds, will ye bear a greeting
To the folk that live in that western land?
Then for every sweep of your pinions beating
Ye shall bear a wish to the sunburnt band.
To the stalwart men who are stoutly fighting
With the heat and drought and the dust-storm smiting,
Yet whose life somehow has a strange inviting,
When once to the work they have put their hand.

Facing it yet! O my friend stout-hearted,
What does it matter for rain or shine,
For the hopes deferred and the gain departed?
Nothing could conquer that heart of thine.
And thy health and strength are beyond confessing
As the only joys that are worth possessing.
May the days to come be as rich in blessing
As the days we spent in the auld lang syne.

I would fain go back to the old grey river,
To the old bush days when our hearts were light;
But, alas! those days they have fled for ever,
They are like the swans that have swept from sight.
And I know full well that the strangers' faces
Would meet us now in our dearest places;
For our day is dead and has left no traces
But the thoughts that live in my mind tonight.

There are folk long dead, and our hearts would sicken –
We should grieve for them with a bitter pain;
If the past could live and the dead could quicken,
We then might turn to that life again.
But on lonely nights we should hear them calling,
We should hear their steps on the pathways falling,
We should loathe the life with a hate appalling
In our lonely rides by the ridge and plain.

           *   *   *   *   *

In the silent park is a scent of clover,
And the distant roar of the town is dead.
And I hear once more, as the swans fly over,
Their far-off clamour from overhead.
They are flying west, by their instinct guided,
And for man likewise is his fate decided,
And griefs apportioned and joys divided
By a mighty power with a purpose dread.

The All Right Un

He came from 'further out',
That land of heat and drought
And dust and gravel.
He got a touch of sun,
And rested at the run
Until his cure was done,
And he could travel.

When spring had decked the plain,
He flitted off again
As flit the swallows.
And from that western land,
When many months were spanned,
A letter came to hand,
Which read as follows:

'Dear Sir, I take my pen
In hopes that all your men
And you are hearty.
You think that I've forgot
Your kindness, Mr Scott;
Oh, no, dear sir, I'm not
That sort of party.

'You sometimes bet, I know.
Well, now you'll have a show
The "books" to frighten.
Up here at Wingadee
Young Billy Fife and me
We're training Strife, and he
Is a all right un.

'Just now we're running byes,
But, sir, first time he tries
I'll send you word of.
And running "on the crook"
Their measures we have took;
It is the deadest hook
You ever heard of.

'So when we lets him go,
Why then I'll let you know,
And you can have a show
To put a mite on.
Now, sir, my leave I'll take,
Yours truly, William Blake.
P.S. – Make no mistake,
He's a all right un.'

*   *   *

By next week's *Riverine*
I saw my friend had been
A bit too cunning.
I read: 'The racehorse Strife
And jockey William Fife
Disqualified for life –
Suspicious running.'

But though they spoilt his game,
I reckon all the same
I fairly ought to claim
My friend a white un.
For though he wasn't straight,
His deeds would indicate
His heart at any rate
Was 'a all right un'.

The Boss of the Admiral Lynch

Did you ever hear tell of Chili? I was readin' the other day
Of President Balmaceda and of how he was sent away.
It seems that he didn't suit 'em – they thought that they'd like a
        change,
So they started an insurrection and chased him across the range.
They seem to be restless people – and, judging by what you hear,
They raise up these revolutions 'bout two or three times a year;
And the man that goes out of office, he goes for the boundary
        quick,
For there isn't no vote by ballot – it's bullets that does the trick.
And it ain't like a real battle, where the prisoners' lives are spared,
And they fight till there's one side beaten and then there's a truce
        declared,
And the man that has got the licking goes down like a blooming
        lord
To hand in his resignation and give up his blooming sword,
And the other man bows and takes it, and everything's all polite –
This wasn't that sort of a picnic, this wasn't that sort of a fight.
For the pris'ners they took – they shot 'em , no odds were they
        small or great;
If they'd collared old Balmaceda, they reckoned to shoot him
        straight.
A lot of bloodthirsty devils they were – but there ain't a doubt
They must have been real plucked uns, the way that they fought it
        out,
And the king of 'em all, I reckon, the man that could stand a pinch,
Was the boss of a one-horse gunboat. They called her the *Admiral
        Lynch*.

Well, he was for Balmaceda, and after the war was done,
And Balmaceda was beaten and his troops had been forced to run,
The other man fetched his army and proceeded to do things brown.
He marched 'em into the fortress and took command of the town,
Cannon and guns and horses troopin' along the road,
Rumblin' over the bridges; and never a foeman showed

Till they came in sight of the harbour – and the very first thing
they see
Was this mite of a one-horse gunboat a-lying against the quay;
And there as they watched they noticed a flutter of crimson rag
And under their eyes he hoisted old Balmaceda's flag.

Well, I tell you it fairly knocked 'em – it just took away their
breath,
For he must ha' known, if they caught him, 'twas nothin' but
sudden death.
An' he'd got no fire in his furnace, no chance to put out to sea,
So he stood by his gun and waited with his vessel against the quay.
Well, they sent him a civil message to say that the war was done,
And most of his side were corpses, and all that were left had run,
And blood had been spilt sufficient; so they gave him a chance to
decide
If he'd haul down his bit of bunting and come on the winning
side.
He listened and heard their message, and answered them all polite
That he was a Spanish hidalgo, and the men of his race *must* fight!
A gunboat against an army, and with never a chance to run,
And them with their hundred cannon and him with a single gun:
The odds were a trifle heavy – but he wasn't the sort to flinch.
So he opened fire on the army, did the boss of the *Admiral Lynch*.

They pounded his boat to pieces, they silenced his single gun,
And captured the whole consignment, for none of 'em cared to
run;
And it don't say whether they shot him – it don't even give his
name –
But whatever they did I'll wager that he went to his graveyard
game.
I tell you those old hidalgos, so stately and so polite,
They turn out the real Maginnis when it comes to an uphill fight.
There was General Alcantara, who died in the heaviest brunt,
And General Alzereca was killed in the battle's front;
But the king of 'em all, I reckon – the man that could stand a
pinch –
Was the man who attacked the army with the gunboat *Admiral
Lynch*.

A Bushman's Song

I'm travelling down the Castlereagh, and I'm a station-hand,
I'm handy with the ropin' pole, I'm handy with the brand,
And I can ride a rowdy colt, or swing the axe all day,
But there's no demand for a station-hand along the Castlereagh.

So it's shift, boys, shift, for there isn't the slightest doubt
That we've got to make a shift to the stations further out,
With the pack-horse runnin' after, for he follows like a dog,
We must strike across the country at the old jig-jog.

This old black horse I'm riding – if you'll notice what's his brand,
He wears the crooked R, you see – none better in the land.
He takes a lot of beatin', and the other day we tried,
For a bit of a joke, with a racing bloke, for twenty pound a side.

It was shift, boys, shift, for there wasn't the slightest doubt
That I had to make him shift, for the money was nearly out,
But he cantered home a winner, with the other one at the flog –
He's a red-hot sort to pick up with his old jig-jog.

I asked a cove for shearin' once along the Marthaguy:
'We shear non-union here,' says he. 'I call it scab,' says I.
I looked along the shearin' floor before I turned to go –
There were eight or ten dashed Chinamen a-shearin' in a row.

It was shift, boys, shift, for there wasn't the slightest doubt
It was time to make a shift with the leprosy about.
So I saddled up my horses, and I whistled to my dog,
And I left his scabby station at the old jig-jog.

I went to Illawarra, where my brother's got a farm;
He has to ask his landlord's leave before he lifts his arm:
The landlord owns the country-side – man, woman, dog, and cat,
They haven't the cheek to dare to speak without they touch their
      hat.

It was shift, boys, shift, for there wasn't the slightest doubt
Their little landlord god and I would soon have fallen out;
Was I to touch my hat to him? – was I his bloomin' dog?
So I makes for up the country at the old jig-jog.

But it's time that I was movin', I've a mighty way to go
Till I drink artesian water from a thousand feet below;
Till I meet the overlanders with the cattle comin' down –
And I'll work a while till I make a pile, then have a spree in
    town.

So it's shift, boys, shift, for there isn't the slightest doubt
We've got to make a shift to the stations further out:
The pack-horse runs behind us, for he follows like a dog,
And we cross a lot of country at the old jig-jog.

How Gilbert Died

There's never a stone at the sleeper's head,
    There's never a fence beside,
And the wandering stock on the grave may tread
    Unnoticed and undenied;
But the smallest child on the Watershed
    Can tell you how Gilbert died.

For he rode at dusk with his comrade Dunn
    To the hut at the Stockman's Ford;
In the waning light of the sinking sun
    They peered with a fierce accord.
They were outlaws both – and on each man's head
    Was a thousand pounds reward.

They had taken toll of the country round,
    And the troopers came behind
With a black who tracked like a human hound
    In the scrub and the ranges blind:
He could run the trail where a white man's eye
    No sign of track could find.

He had hunted them out of the One Tree Hill
    And over the Old Man Plain,
But they wheeled their tracks with a wild beast's skill,
    And they made for the range again;
Then away to the hut where their grandsire dwelt
    They rode with a loosened rein.

And their grandsire gave them a greeting bold:
    'Come in and rest in peace,
No safer place does the country hold –
    With the night pursuit must cease,
And we'll drink success to the roving boys,
    And to hell with the black police.'

But they went to death when they entered there
    In the hut at the Stockman's Ford,
For their grandsire's words were as false as fair –
    They were doomed to the hangman's cord.
He had sold them both to the black police
    For the sake of the big reward.

In the depth of night there are forms that glide
    As stealthily as serpents creep,
And around the hut where the outlaws hide
    They plant in the shadows deep,
And they wait till the first faint flush of dawn
    Shall waken their prey from sleep.

But Gilbert wakes while the night is dark –
    A restless sleeper aye.
He has heard the sound of a sheep-dog's bark,
    And his horse's warning neigh,
And he says to his mate, 'There are hawks abroad,
    And it's time that we went away.'

Their rifles stood at the stretcher head,
    Their bridles lay to hand;
They wakened the old man out of his bed,
    When they heard the sharp command:
'In the name of the Queen lay down your arms,
    Now, Dunn and Gilbert, stand!'

Then Gilbert reached for his rifle true
    That close at hand he kept;
He pointed straight at the voice, and drew,
    But never a flash outleapt,
For the water ran from the rifle breech –
    It was drenched while the outlaws slept.

Then he dropped the piece with a bitter oath,
    And he turned to his comrade Dunn:
'We are sold,' he said, 'we are dead men both! –
    Still, there may be a chance for one;
I'll stop and I'll fight with the pistol here,
    You take to your heels and run.'

So Dunn crept out on his hands and knees
    In the dim, half-dawning light,
And he made his way to a patch of trees,
    And was lost in the black of night;
And the trackers hunted his tracks all day,
    But they never could trace his flight.

But Gilbert walked from the open door
    In a confident style and rash;
He heard at his side the rifles roar,
    And he heard the bullets crash.
But he laughed as he lifted his pistol-hand,
    And he fired at the rifle flash.

Then out of the shadows the troopers aimed
    At his voice and the pistol sound.
With rifle flashes the darkness flamed –
    He staggered and spun around,
And they riddled his body with rifle balls
    As it lay on the blood-soaked ground.

There's never a stone at the sleeper's head,
    There's never a fence beside,
And the wandering stock on the grave may tread
    Unnoticed and undenied;
But the smallest child on the Watershed
    Can tell you how Gilbert died.

The Flying Gang

I served my time, in the days gone by,
    In the railway's clash and clang,
And I worked my way to the end, and I
    Was the head of the 'Flying Gang'.
'Twas a chosen band that was kept at hand
    In case of an urgent need;
Was it south or north, we were started forth
    And away at our utmost speed.
If word reached town that a bridge was down,
    The imperious summons rang –
'Come out with the pilot engine sharp,
    And away with the flying gang.'

Then a piercing scream and a rush of steam
    As the engine moved ahead;
With measured beat by the slum and street
    Of the busy town we fled,
By the uplands bright and the homesteads white,
    With the rush of the western gale –
And the pilot swayed with the pace we made
    As she rocked on the ringing rail.
And the country children clapped their hands
    As the engine's echoes rang,
But their elders said: 'There is work ahead
    When they send for the flying gang.'

Then across the miles of the saltbush plain
    That gleamed with the morning dew,
Where the grasses waved like the ripening grain
    The pilot engine flew –
A fiery rush in the open bush
    Where the grade marks seemed to fly,
And the order sped on the wires ahead,
    The pilot *must* go by.
The Governor's special must stand aside,
    And the fast express go hang;
Let your orders be that the line is free
    For the boys of the flying gang.

Shearing at Castlereagh

The bell is set a-ringing, and the engine gives a toot,
There's five-and-thirty shearers here a-shearing for the loot,
So stir yourselves, you penners-up, and shove the sheep along –
The musterers are fetching them a hundred thousand strong –
And make your collie dogs speak up; what would the buyers say
In London if the wool was late this year from Castlereagh?

The man that 'rung' the Tubbo shed is not the ringer here,
That stripling from the Cooma-side can teach him how to shear.
They trim away the ragged locks, and rip the cutter goes,
And leaves a track of snowy fleece from brisket to the nose;
It's lovely how they peel it off with never stop nor stay,
They're racing for the ringer's place this year at Castlereagh.

The man that keeps the cutters sharp is growling in his cage,
He's always in a hurry; and he's always in a rage –
'You clumsy-fisted mutton-heads, you'd turn a fellow sick,
You pass yourselves as shearers, you were born to swing a pick.
Another broken cutter here, that's two you've broke today.'
It's lovely how they peel it off with never stop nor stay.

The youngsters picking up the fleece enjoy the merry din,
They throw the classer up the fleece, he throws it to the bin;
The pressers standing by the rack are waiting for the wool,
There's room for just a couple more, the press is nearly full;
Now jump upon the lever, lads, and heave and heave away,
Another bale of golden fleece is branded 'Castlereagh'.

The Wind's Message

There came a whisper down the Bland between the dawn and dark,
Above the tossing of the pines, above the river's flow;
It stirred the boughs of giant gums and stalwart ironbark;
It drifted where the wild ducks played amid the swamps below;
It brought a breath of mountain air from off the hills of pine,
A scent of eucalyptus trees in honey-laden bloom;
And drifting, drifting far away along the southern line
It caught from leaf and grass and fern a subtle strange perfume.

It reached the toiling city folk, but few there were that heard –
The rattle of their busy life had choked the whisper down;
And some but caught a fresh-blown breeze with scent of pine that
        stirred
A thought of blue hills far away beyond the smoky town;
And others heard the whisper pass, but could not understand
The magic of the breeze's breath that set their hearts aglow,
Nor how the roving wind could bring across the Overland
A sound of voices silent now and songs of long ago.

But some that heard the whisper clear were filled with vague unrest;
The breeze had brought its message home, they could not fixed
        abide;
Their fancies wandered all the day towards the blue hills' breast,
Towards the sunny slopes that lie along the riverside.
The mighty rolling western plains are very fair to see,
Where waving to the passing breeze the silver myalls stand,
But fairer are the giant hills, all rugged though they be,
From which the two great rivers rise that run along the Bland.

Oh, rocky range, and rugged spur, and river running clear
That swings around the sudden bends with swirl of snow-white
        foam,
Though we, your sons, are far away, we sometimes seem to hear
The message that the breezes bring to call the wanderers home.
The mountain peaks are white with snow that feeds a thousand rills,
Along the river-banks the maize grows tall on virgin land,
And we shall live to see once more those sunny southern hills,
And strike once more the bridle-track that leads along the Bland.

Johnson's Antidote

Down along the Snakebite River where the overlanders camp,
Where the serpents are in millions, all of the most deadly stamp;
Where the station-cook in terror, nearly every time he bakes,
Mixes up among the doughboys half a dozen poison-snakes;
Where the wily free-selector walks in armour-plated pants,
And defies the stings of scorpions, and the bites of bull-dog ants:
Where the adder and the viper tear each other by the throat –
There it was that William Johnson sought his snake-bite antidote.

Johnson was a free-selector, and his brain went rather queer,
For the constant sight of serpents filled him with a deadly fear;
So he tramped his free-selection, morning, afternoon, and night,
Seeking for some great specific that would cure the serpent's bite
Till King Billy, of the Mooki, chieftain of the flour-bag head,
Told him, 'Spos'n snake bite pfeller, pfeller mostly drop down dead;
Spos'n snake bite old goanna, then you watch a while you see
Old goanna cure himself with eating little pfeller tree.'
'That's the cure,' said William Johnson, 'point me out this plant
        sublime,'
But King Billy, feeling lazy, said he'd go another time.
Thus it came to pass that Johnson, having got the tale by rote,
Followed every stray goanna seeking for the antidote.

          *   *   *   *   *

Loafing once beside the river, while he thought his heart would
        break,
There he saw a big goanna fight with a tiger-snake.
In and out they rolled and wriggled, bit each other, heart and soul,
Till the valiant old goanna swallowed his opponent whole.
Breathless, Johnson sat and watched him, saw him struggle up the
        bank,
Saw him nibbling at the branches of some bushes, green and rank;
Saw him, happy and contented, lick his lips, as off he crept,
While the bulging of his stomach showed where his opponent slept.
Then a cheer of exultation burst aloud from Johnson's throat;
'Luck at last,' said he, 'I've struck it! 'tis the famous antidote.

'Here it is, the Grand Elixir, greatest blessing ever known –
Twenty thousand men in India die each year of snakes alone;
Think of all the foreign nations, negro, chow, and blackamoor,
Saved from sudden expiration by my wondrous snakebite cure.
It will bring me fame and fortune! In the happy days to be
Men of every clime and nation will be round to gaze on me –
Scientific men in thousands, men of mark and men of note,
Rushing down the Mooki River, after Johnson's antidote.
It will cure *delirium tremens* when the patient's eyeballs stare
At imaginary spiders, snakes which really are not there.
When he thinks he sees them wriggle, when he thinks he sees them
    bloat,
It will cure him just to think of Johnson's Snakebite Antidote.'

Then he rushed to the museum, found a scientific man –
'Trot me out a deadly serpent, just the deadliest you can;
I intend to let him bite me, all the risk I will endure.
Just to prove the sterling value of my wondrous snakebite cure.
Even though an adder bit me, back to life again I'd float;
Snakes are out of date, I tell you, since I've found the antidote.'
Said the scientific person, 'If you really want to die,
Go ahead – but, if you're doubtful, let your sheep-dog have a try.
Get a pair of dogs and try it, let the snake give both a nip;
Give your dog the snakebite mixture, let the other fellow rip;
If he dies and yours survives him then it proves the thing is good.
Will you fetch your dog and try it?' Johnson rather thought he
    would.
So he went and fetched his canine, hauled him forward by the
    throat.
'Stump, old man,' says he, 'we'll show them we've the genwine
    antidote.'

Both the dogs were duly loaded with the poison-gland's contents;
Johnson gave his dog the mixture, then sat down to wait events.
'Mark,' he said, 'in twenty minutes Stump'll be a-rushing round,
While the other wretched creature lies a corpse upon the ground.'
But, alas for William Johnson! ere they'd watched a half-hour's
    spell
Stumpy was as dead as mutton, t'other dog was live and well.
And the scientific person hurried off with utmost speed,

Tested Johnson's drug and found it was a deadly poison-weed;
Half a tumbler killed an emu, half a spoonful killed a goat –
All the snakes on earth were harmless to that awful antidote.

*   *   *   *   *

Down along the Mooki River, on the overlanders' camp,
Where the serpents are in millions, all of the most deadly stamp,
Wanders, daily, William Johnson, down among those poisonous
        hordes,
Shooting every stray goanna calls them 'black and yaller frauds'.
And King Billy, of the Mooki, cadging for the cast-off coat,
Somehow seems to dodge the subject of the snakebite antidote.

Ambition and Art

AMBITION

I am the maid of the lustrous eyes
    Of great fruition,
Whom the sons of men that are over-wise
    Have called Ambition.

And the world's success is the only goal
    I have within me;
The meanest man with the smallest soul
    May woo and win me.

For the lust of power and the pride of place
    To all I proffer.
Wilt thou take thy part in the crowded race
    For what I offer?

The choice is thine, and the world is wide –
    Thy path is lonely.
I may not lead and I may not guide –
    I urge thee only.

I am just a whip and a spur that smites
    To fierce endeavour.
In the restless days and the sleepless nights
    I urge thee ever.

Thou shalt wake from sleep with a startled cry,
    In fright unleaping
At a rival's step as it passes by
    Whilst thou art sleeping.

Honour and truth shall be overthrown
    In fierce desire;
Thou shalt use thy friend as a stepping-stone
    To mount thee higher.

When the curtain falls on the sordid strife
    That seemed so splendid,
Thou shalt look with pain on the wasted life
    That thou hast ended.

Thou hast sold thy life for a guerdon small
    In fitful flashes;
There has been reward – but the end of all
    Is dust and ashes.

For the night has come and it brings to naught
    Thy projects cherished,
And thine epitaph shall in brass be wrought –
    'He lived, and perished.'

ART

I wait for thee at the outer gate,
    My love, mine only;
Wherefore tarriest thou so late
    While I am lonely?

Thou shalt seek my side with a footstep swift;
   In thee implanted
Is the love of Art and the greatest gift
   That God has granted.

And the world's concerns with its rights and wrongs
   Shall seem but small things –
Poet or painter, or singer of songs,
   Thine art is all things.

For the wine of life is a woman's love
   To keep beside thee;
But the love of Art is a thing above –
   A star to guide thee.

As the years go by with the love of Art
   All undiminished,
Thou shalt end thy days with a quiet heart –
   Thy work is finished.

So the painter fashions a picture strong
   That fadeth never,
And the singer singeth a wondrous song
   That lives for ever.

In Defence of the Bush

So you're back from up the country, Mister Lawson, where
   you went,
And you're cursing all the business in a bitter discontent;
Well, we grieve to disappoint you, and it makes us sad to
   hear
That it wasn't cool and shady – and there wasn't whips of
   beer,
And the looney bullock snorted when you first came into
   view –
Well, you know it's not so often that he sees a swell like you;
And the roads were hot and dusty, and the plains were burnt
   and brown,
And no doubt you're better suited drinking lemon-squash in
   town.
Yet, perchance, if you should journey down the very track
   you went
In a month or two at furthest, you would wonder what it
   meant;
Where the sunbaked earth was gasping like a creature in its
   pain
You would find the grasses waving like a field of summer
   grain,
And the miles of thirsty gutters, blocked with sand and
   choked with mud,
You would find them mighty rivers with a turbid, sweeping
   flood.
For the rain and drought and sunshine make no changes in
   the street,
In the sullen line of buildings and the ceaseless tramp of feet;
But the bush has moods and changes, as the seasons rise and
   fall,
And the men who know the bushland – they are loyal
   through it all.

* * * * *

But you found the bush was dismal and a land of no delight –
Did you chance to hear a chorus in the shearers' huts at
      night?
Did they 'rise up William Riley' by the camp-fire's cheery
      blaze?
Did they rise him as we rose him in the good old droving
      days?
And the women of the homesteads and the men you chanced
      to meet –
Were their faces sour and saddened like the 'faces in the
      street'?
And the 'shy selector children' – were they better now or
      worse
Than the little city urchins who would greet you with a curse?
Is not such a life much better than the squalid street and
      square
Where the fallen women flaunt it in the fierce electric glare,
Where the sempstress plies her needle till her eyes are sore
      and red
In a filthy, dirty attic toiling on for daily bread?

Did you hear no sweeter voices in the music of the bush
Than the roar of trams and buses, and the war-whoop of 'the
      push'?
Did the magpies rouse your slumbers with their carol sweet
      and strange?
Did you hear the silver chiming of the bell-birds on the range?
But, perchance, the wild birds' music by your senses was
      despised,
For you say you'll stay in townships till the bush is civilized.
Would you make it a tea-garden, and on Sundays have a band
Where the 'blokes' might take their 'donahs', with a 'public'
      close at hand?
You had better stick to Sydney and make merry with the
      'push',
For the bush will never suit you, and you'll never suit the
      bush.

Last Week

Oh, the new-chum went to the backblock run,
But he should have gone there last week.
He tramped ten miles with a loaded gun,
But of turkey or duck saw never a one,
For he should have been there last week,
    They said,
There were flocks of 'em there last week.

He wended his way to a waterfall,
And he should have gone there last week.
He carried a camera, legs and all,
But the day was hot and the stream was small,
For he should have gone there last week,
    They said,
They drowned a man there last week.

He went for a drive, and he made a start,
Which should have been made last week,
For the old horse died of a broken heart;
So he footed it home and he dragged the cart –
But the horse was all right last week,
    They said,
He trotted a match last week.

So he asked the bushies who came from afar
To visit the town last week
If they'd dine with him, and they said 'Hurrah!'
But there wasn't a drop in the whisky jar –
You should have been here last week,
    He said,
I drank it all up last week!

Those Names

The shearers sat in the firelight, hearty and hale and strong,
After the hard day's shearing, passing the joke along:
The 'ringer' that shore a hundred, as they never were shorn
before,
And the novice who, toiling bravely, had tommy-hawked half a
score,
The tarboy, the cook and the slushy, the sweeper that swept the
board,
The picker-up, and the penner, with the rest of the shearing
horde.
There were men from the inland stations where the skies like a
furnace glow,
And men from the Snowy River, the land of the frozen snow;
There were swarthy Queensland drovers who reckoned all land
by miles,
And farmers' sons from the Murray, where many a vineyard
smiles.
They started at telling stories when they wearied of cards and
games,
And to give these stories flavour they threw in some local names,
Then a man from the bleak Monaro, away on the tableland,
He fixed his eyes on the ceiling, and he started to play his hand.
He told them of Adjintoothbong, where the pine-clad mountains
freeze,
And the weight of the snow in summer breaks branches off the
trees,
And, as he warmed to the business, he let them have it strong –
Nimitybelle, Conargo, Wheeo, Bongongolong;
He lingered over them fondly, because they recalled to mind
A thought of the old bush homestead, and the girl that he left
behind.
Then the shearers all sat silent till a man in the corner rose;
Said he 'I've travelled a-plenty but never heard names like those.
Out in the western districts, out on the Castlereagh
Most of the names are easy – short for a man to say.
You've heard of Mungrybambone and the Gundabluey pine,

Quobbotha, Girilambone, and Terrramungamine,
Quambone, Eunonyhareenyha, Wee Waa, and Buntijo – '
But the rest of the shearers stopped him: 'For the sake of your
      jaw, go slow,
If you reckon those names are short ones out where such names
      prevail,
Just try and remember some long ones before you begin the tale.'
And the man from the western district, though never a word he
      said,
Just winked with his dexter eyelid, and then he retired to bed.

A Bush Christening

On the outer Barcoo where the churches are few,
    And men of religion are scanty,
On a road never cross'd 'cept by folk that are lost
    One Michael Magee had a shanty.

Now this Mike was the dad of a ten-year-old lad,
    Plump, healthy, and stoutly conditioned;
He was strong as the best, but poor Mike had no rest
    For the youngster had never been christened.

And his wife used to cry, 'If the darlin' should die
    Saint Peter would not recognize him.'
But by luck he survived till a preacher arrived,
    Who agreed straightaway to baptize him.

Now the artful young rogue, while they held their collogue,
    With his ear to the keyhole was listenin';
And he muttered in fright, while his features turned white,
    'What the divil and all is this christenin'?'

He was none of your dolts – he had seen them brand colts,
    And it seemed to his small understanding,
If the man in the frock made him one of the flock,
    It must mean something very like branding.

So away with a rush he set off for the bush,
　　While the tears in his eyelids they glistened –
' 'Tis outrageous,' says he, 'to brand youngsters like me;
　　I'll be dashed if I'll stop to be christened!'

Like a young native dog he ran into a log,
　　And his father with language uncivil,
Never heeding the 'praste', cried aloud in his haste
　　'Come out and be christened, you divil!'

But he lay there as snug as a bug in a rug,
　　And his parents in vain might reprove him,
Till his reverence spoke (he was fond of a joke)
　　'I've a notion,' says he, 'that'll move him.

'Poke a stick up the log, give the spalpeen a prog;
　　Poke him aisy – don't hurt him or maim him;
'Tis not long that he'll stand, I've the water at hand,
　　As he rushes out this end I'll name him.

'Here he comes, and for shame! ye've forgotten the name –
　　Is it Patsy or Michael or Dinnis?'
Here the youngster ran out, and the priest gave a shout –
　　'Take your chance, anyhow, wid "Maginnis!" '

As the howling young cub ran away to the scrub
　　Where he knew that pursuit would be risky,
The priest, as he fled, flung a flask at his head
　　That was labelled 'Maginnis's Whisky'!

Now Maginnis Magee has been made a J.P.,
　　And the one thing he hates more than sin is
To be asked by the folk, who have heard of the joke,
　　How he came to be christened Maginnis!

How the Favourite Beat Us

'Ay,' said the boozer, 'I tell you, it's true, sir,
I once was a punter with plenty of pelf,
But gone is my glory; I'll tell you the story
How I stiffened my horse and got stiffened myself.

''Twas a mare called The Cracker, I came down to back her,
But found she was favourite all of a rush;
The folk just did pour on to lay six to four on,
And several bookies were killed in the crush.

'It seems old Tomato was stiff, though a starter;
They reckoned him fit for the Caulfield to keep.
The Bloke and The Donah were scratched by their owner –
He only was offered three-fourths of the sweep.

'We knew Salamander was slow as a gander,
The mare could have beat him the length of the straight,
And old Manumission was out of condition,
And most of the others were running off weight.

'No doubt someone "blew it", for everyone knew it;
The bets were all gone, and I muttered in spite
"If I can't get a copper, by Jingo, I'll stop her!
Let the public fall in, it will serve the brutes right."

'I said to the jockey, "Now listen, my cocky,
You watch as you're cantering down by the stand;
I'll wait where that toff is and give you the office,
You're only to win if I lift up my hand."

'I then tried to back her – What price is The Cracker?
"Our books are at full, sir," each bookie did swear;
My mind, then, I made up, my fortune I played up,
I bet every shilling against my own mare.

'I strolled to the gateway; the mare in the straightway
Was shifting and dancing, and pawing the ground;
The boy saw me enter and wheeled for his canter,
When a darned great mosquito came buzzing around.

'They breed 'em at Hexham, it's risky to vex 'em ,
They suck a man dry at a sitting, no doubt;
But just as the mare passed, he fluttered my hair past –
I lifted my hand, and I flattened him out.

'I was stunned when they started; the mare simply darted
Away to the front when the flag was let fall,
For none there could match her, and none tried to catch
          her –
She finished a furlong in front of them all.

'You bet that I went for the boy, whom I sent for
The moment he weighed and came out of the stand –
"Who paid you to win it? Come, own up this minute."
"Lord love yer," said he "why you lifted your hand."

' 'Twas true, by St Peter; that cursed "muskeeter"
Had broke me so broke that I hadn't a brown;
And you'll find the best course is when dealing with
          horses
To win when you're able, and *keep your hands down*.'

The Great Calamity

MacFierce'un came to Whiskeyhurst
   When summer days were hot,
And bided there wi' Jock MacThirst,
   A brawny brother Scot.
Good faith! They made the whisky fly
   Like Highland chieftains true,
And when they'd drunk the beaker dry
   They sang 'We are nae fou!
There's nae folk like oor ain folk,
   Sae gallant and sae true.'
They sang the only Scottish joke
   Which is 'We are nae fou'.
Said bold MacThirst, 'Let Saxons jaw
   Aboot their great concerns,
But Bonnie Scotland beats them a',
   The Land o' Cakes and Burns,
The land of pairtridge, deer, and grouse;
   Fill up your glass, I beg,
There's muckle whuskey i' the house,
   Forbye what's in the keg.'
And here a hearty laugh he laughed,
   'Just come wi' me, I beg.'
MacFierce'un saw with pleasure daft
   A fifty-gallon keg.

'Losh, man, that's graund,' MacFierce'un cried,
   'Saw ever man the like,
Noo, wi' the daylicht, I maun ride
   To meet a Southron tyke,
But I'll be back ere summer's gone,
   So bide for me, I beg;
We'll mak' a graund assault upon
   Yon deevil of a keg.'

*   *   *   *   *

MacFierce'un rode to Whiskeyhurst
    When summer days were gone,
And there he met with Jock MacThirst
    Was greetin' all alone.
'MacThirst, what gars ye look sae blank?
    Hae all your wuts gane daft?
Has that accursed Southron bank
    Called up your overdraft?
Is all your grass burnt up wi' drouth?
    Is wool and hides gane flat?'
MacThirst replied, 'Guid friend, in truth,
    'Tis muckle waur than that.'

'Has sair misfortune cursed your life
    That you should weep sae free?
Is harm upon your bonnie wife,
    The children at your knee?
Is scaith upon your house and hame?'
    MacThirst upraised his head:
'My bairns hae done the deed of shame —
    'Twere better they were dead.
To think my bonnie infant son
    Should do the deed o' guilt —
He let the whuskey spigot run,
    And a' the whuskey's spilt!'

*   *   *   *   *

Upon them both these words did bring
    A solemn silence deep;
Good faith, it is a fearsome thing
    To see two strong men weep.

Come-by-Chance

As I pondered very weary o'er a volume long and dreary –
For the plot was void of interest; 'twas the Postal Guide, in
    fact –
There I learnt the true location, distance, size, and
    population
Of each township, town, and village in the radius of the Act.

And I learnt that Puckawidgee stands beside the
    Murrumbidgee,
And the Booleroi and Bumble get their letters twice a year,
Also that the post inspector, when he visited Collector,
Closed the office up instanter, and re-opened Dungalear.

But my languid mood forsook me, when I found a name that
    took me;
Quite by chance I came across it – 'Come-by-Chance' was
    what I read;
No location was assigned it, not a thing to help one find it,
Just an N which stood for northward, and the rest was all
    unsaid.

I shall leave my home, and forthward wander stoutly to the
    northward
Till I come by chance across it, and I'll straightway settle
    down;
For there can't be any hurry, nor the slightest cause for
    worry
Where the telegraph don't reach you nor the railways run to
    town.

And one's letters and exchanges come by chance across the
    ranges,
Where a wiry young Australian leads a pack-horse once a
    week,
And the good news grows by keeping, and you're spared the
    pain of weeping
Over bad news when the mailman drops the letters in the
    creek.

But I fear, and more's the pity, that there's really no such
      city,
For there's not a man can find it of the shrewdest folk I
      know;
'Come-by-Chance', be sure it never means a land of fierce
      endeavour –
It is just the careless country where the dreamers only go.

    *   *   *   *   *

Though we work and toil and hustle in our life of haste and
      bustle,
All that makes our life worth living comes unstriven for and
      free;
Man may weary and importune, but the fickle goddess
      Fortune
Deals him out his pain or pleasure, careless what his worth
      may be.

All the happy times entrancing, days of sport and nights of
      dancing,
Moonlit rides and stolen kisses, pouting lips and loving
      glance:
When you think of these be certain you have looked behind
      the curtain,
You have had the luck to linger just a while in 'Come-by-
      Chance'

Under the Shadow of Kiley's Hill

This is the place where they all were bred;
   Some of the rafters are standing still;
Now they are scattered and lost and dead,
Every one from the old nest fled,
   Out of the shadow of Kiley's Hill.

Better it is that they ne'er came back –
   Changes and chances are quickly rung;
Now the old homestead is gone to rack,
Green is the grass on the well-worn track
   Down by the gate where the roses clung.

Gone is the garden they kept with care;
   Left to decay at its own sweet will,
Fruit-trees and flower-beds eaten bare,
Cattle and sheep where the roses were,
   Under the shadow of Kiley's Hill.

Where are the children that strove and grew
   In the old homestead in days gone by?
One is away on the far Barcoo
Watching his cattle the long year through,
   Watching them starve in the droughts and die.

One, in the town where all cares are rife,
   Weary with troubles that cramp and kill,
Fain would be done with the restless strife,
Fain would go back to the old bush life,
   Back to the shadow of Kiley's Hill.

One is away on the roving quest,
   Seeking his share of the golden spoil;
Out in the wastes of the trackless west,
Wandering ever he gives the best
   Of his years and strength to the hopeless toil

What of the parents? That unkept mound
   Shows where they slumber united still;
Rough is their grave, but they sleep as sound
Out on the range as in holy ground,
   Under the shadow of Kiley's Hill.

Jim Carew

Born of a thoroughbred English race,
   Well proportioned and closely knit,
Neat, slim figure and handsome face,
   Always ready and always fit,
Hardy and wiry of limb and thew,
That was the ne'er-do-well Jim Carew.

One of the sons of the good old land --
   Many a year since his like was known;
Never a game but he took command,
   Never a sport but he held his own;
Gained at his college a triple blue --
Good as they make them was Jim Carew.

Came to grief -- was it card or horse?
   Nobody asked and nobody cared;
Ship him away to the bush of course,
   Ne'er-do-well fellows are easily spared;
Only of women a sorrowing few
Wept at parting from Jim Carew.

Gentleman Jim on the cattle-camp,
   Sitting his horse with an easy grace;
But the reckless living has left its stamp
   In the deep drawn lines of that handsome face,
And the harder look in those eyes of blue:
Prompt at a quarrel is Jim Carew.

Billy the Lasher was out for gore –
   Twelve-stone navvy with chest of hair –
When he opened out with a hungry roar
   On a ten-stone man, it was hardly fair;
But his wife was wise if his face she knew
By the time you were done with him, Jim Carew.

Gentleman Jim in the stockmen's hut
   Works with them, toils with them, side by side;
As to his past – well, his lips are shut.
   'Gentleman once,' say his mates with pride,
And the wildest Cornstalk can ne'er outdo
In feats of recklessness Jim Carew.

What should he live for? A dull despair!
   Drink is his master and drags him down,
Water of Lethe that drowns all care.
   Gentleman Jim has a lot to drown,
And he reigns as king with a drunken crew,
Sinking to misery, Jim Carew.

Such is the end of the ne'er-do-well –
   Jimmy the Boozer, all down at heel;
But he straightens up when he's asked to tell
   His name and race, and a flash of steel
Still lightens up in those eyes of blue –
'I am, or – no, I *was* – Jim Carew.'

The Swagman's Rest

We buried old Bob where the bloodwoods wave
   At the foot of the Eaglehawk;
We fashioned a cross on the old man's grave
   For fear that his ghost might walk;
We carved his name on a bloodwood tree
   With the date of his sad decease
And in place of 'Died from effects of spree'
   We wrote 'May he rest in peace'.

For Bob was known on the Overland,
   A regular old bush wag,
Tramping along in the dust and sand,
   Humping his well-worn swag.
He would camp for days in the river-bed,
   And loiter and 'fish for whales'.
'I'm into the swagman's yard,' he said,
   'And I never shall find the rails.'

But he found the rails on that summer night
   For a better place – or worse,
As we watched by turns in the flickering light
   With an old black gin for nurse.
The breeze came in with the scent of pine,
   The river sounded clear,
When a change came on, and we saw the sign
   That told us the end was near.

He spoke in a cultured voice and low –
   'I fancy they've "sent the route";
I once was an army man, you know,
   Though now I'm a drunken brute;
But bury me out where the bloodwoods wave,
   And, if ever you're fairly stuck,
Just take and shovel me out of the grave
   And, maybe, I'll bring you luck.

'For I've always heard – ' here his voice grew weak,
   His strength was wellnigh sped.
He gasped and struggled and tried to speak,
   Then fell in a moment – dead.
Thus ended a wasted life and hard,
   Of energies misapplied –
Old Bob was out of the 'swagman's yard'
   And over the Great Divide.

    *   *   *   *   *

The drought came down on the field and flock,
    And never a raindrop fell,
Though the tortured moans of the starving stock
    Might soften a fiend from hell.
And we thought of the hint that the swagman gave
    When he went to the Great Unseen —
We shovelled the skeleton out of the grave
    To see what his hint might mean.

We dug where the cross and the grave posts were,
    We shovelled away the mould,
When sudden a vein of quartz lay bare
    All gleaming with yellow gold.
'Twas a reef with never a fault nor baulk
    That ran from the range's crest,
And the richest mine on the Eaglehawk
    Is known as 'The Swagman's Rest'.

Daylight is Dying

The daylight is dying
    Away in the west,
The wild birds are flying
    In silence to rest;
In leafage and frondage
    Where shadows are deep,
They pass to its bondage —
    The kingdom of sleep.

And watched in their sleeping
    By stars in the height,
They rest in your keeping,
    O wonderful night.
When night doth her glories
    Of starshine unfold,
'Tis then that the stories
    Of bush-land are told.

Unnumbered I hold them
　　In memories bright,
But who could unfold them,
　　Or read them aright?
Beyond all denials
　　The stars in their glories,
The breeze in the myalls,
　　Are part of these stories.

The waving of grasses,
　　The song of the river
That sings as it passes
　　For ever and ever,
The hobble-chains' rattle,
　　The calling of birds,
The lowing of cattle
　　Must blend with the words.

Without these, indeed, you
　　Would find it ere long,
As though I should read you
　　The words of a song
That lamely would linger
　　When lacking the rune,
The voice of a singer,
　　The lilt of the tune.

But, as one half-hearing
　　An old-time refrain,
With memory clearing,
　　Recalls it again,
These tales roughly wrought of
　　The Bush and its ways,
May call back a thought of
　　The wandering days;

And, blending with each
　　In the memories that throng
There haply shall reach
　　You some echo of song.

RIO GRANDE AND OTHER VERSES

Rio Grande

Now this was what Macpherson told
    While waiting in the stand;
A reckless rider, over-bold,
The only man with hands to hold
    The rushing Rio Grande.

He said, 'This day I bid goodbye
    To bit and bridle rein,
To ditches deep and fences high,
For I have dreamed a dream, and I
    Shall never ride again.

'I dreamt last night I rode this race
    That I today must ride,
And cantering down to take my place
I saw full many an old friend's face
    Come stealing to my side.

'Dead men on horses long since dead,
    They clustered on the track;
The champions of the days long fled,
They moved around with noiseless tread –
    Bay, chestnut, brown, and black.

'And one man on a big grey steed
    Rode up and waved his hand;
Said he, "We help a friend in need,
And we have come to give a lead
    To you and Rio Grande.

' "For you must give the field the slip;
    So never draw the rein,
But keep him moving with the whip,
And, if he falter, set your lip
    And rouse him up again.

' "But when you reach the big stone wall
   Put down your bridle-hand
And let him sail – he cannot fall,
But don't you interfere at all;
   You trust old Rio Grande."

'We started, and in front we showed,
   The big horse running free:
Right fearlessly and game he strode,
And by my side those dead men rode
   Whom no one else could see.

'As silently as flies a bird,
   They rode on either hand;
At every fence I plainly heard
The phantom leader give the word,
   "Make room for Rio Grande!"

'I spurred him on to get the lead,
   I chanced full many a fall;
But swifter still each phantom steed
Kept with me, and at racing speed
   We reached the big stone wall.

'And there the phantoms on each side
   Drew in and blocked his leap;
"Make room! make room!" I loudly cried,
But right in front they seemed to ride –
   I cursed them in my sleep.

'He never flinched, he faced it game,
   He struck it with his chest,
And every stone burst out in flame –
And Rio Grande and I became
   Phantoms among the rest.

'And then I woke, and for a space
   All nerveless did I seem;
For I have ridden many a race
But never one at such a pace
   As in that fearful dream.

'And I am sure as man can be
    That out upon the track
Those phantoms that men cannot see
Are waiting now to ride with me;
    And I shall not come back.

'For I must ride the dead men's race,
    And follow their command;
'Twere worse than death, the foul disgrace
If I should fear to take my place
    Today on Rio Grande.'

He mounted, and a jest he threw,
    With never sign of gloom;
But all who heard the story knew
That Jack Macpherson, brave and true,
    Was going to his doom.

They started, and the big black steed
    Came flashing past the stand;
All single-handed in the lead
He strode along at racing speed,
    The mighty Rio Grande.

But on his ribs the whalebone stung –
    A madness, sure, it seemed –
And soon it rose on every tongue
That Jack Macpherson rode among
    The creatures he had dreamed.

He looked to left, and looked to right,
    As though men rode beside;
And Rio Grande, with foam-flecks white,
Raced at his jumps in headlong flight
    And cleared them in his stride.

But when they reached the big stone wall,
    Down went the bridle-hand,
And loud we heard Macpherson call
'Make room, or half the field will fall!
    Make room for Rio Grande!'

'He's down! he's down!' And horse and man
    Lay quiet side by side!
No need the pallid face to scan,
We knew with Rio Grande he ran
    The race the dead men ride.

With French to Kimberley

The Boers were down on Kimberley with siege and Maxim gun;
The Boers were down on Kimberley, their numbers ten to one!
Faint were the hopes the British had to make the struggle good –
Defenceless in an open plain the Diamond City stood.
They built them forts with bags of sand, they fought from roof and
    wall,
They flashed a message to the south, 'Help! or the town must fall!'
Then down our ranks the order ran to march at dawn of day,
And French was off to Kimberley to drive the Boers away.

He made no march along the line; he made no front attack
Upon those Magersfontein heights that held the Seaforths back;
But eastward over pathless plains, by open veldt and vley.
Across the front of Cronje's force his troopers held their way.
The springbuck, feeding on the flats where Modder River runs,
Were startled by his horses' hoofs, the rumble of his guns.
The Dutchman's spies that watched his march from every rocky wall
Rode back in haste: 'He marches East! He threatens Jacobsdal!'
Then north he wheeled as wheels the hawk, and showed to their
    dismay
That French was off to Kimberley to drive the Boers away.

His column was five thousand strong – all mounted men – and guns:
There met, beneath the world-wide flag, the world-wide Empire's
    sons;
They came to prove to all the earth that kinship conquers space,
And those who fight the British Isles must fight the British race!
From far New Zealand's flax and fern, from cold Canadian snows,
From Queensland plains, where hot as fire the summer sunshine
    glows –

And in the front the Lancers rode that New South Wales had sent:
With easy stride across the plain their long, lean Walers went.
Unknown, untried, those squadrons were, but proudly out they drew
Beside the English regiments that fought at Waterloo.
From every coast, from every clime, they met in proud array
To go with French to Kimberley to drive the Boers away.

He crossed the Reit and fought his way towards the Modder bank.
The foemen closed behind his march, and hung upon the flank.
The long, dry grass was all ablaze (and fierce the veldt fire runs);
He fought them through a wall of flame that blazed around the guns!
Then limbered up and drove at speed, though horses fell and died;
We might not halt for man nor beast on that wild, daring ride.
Black with the smoke and parched with thirst, we pressed the
          livelong day
Our headlong march to Kimberley to drive the Boers away.

We reached the drift at fall of night, and camped across the ford.
Next day from all the hills around the Dutchman's cannon roared.
A narrow pass ran through the hills, with guns on either side;
The boldest man might well turn pale before that pass he tried,
For, if the first attack should fail, then every hope was gone:
But French looked once, and only once, and then he said, 'Push on!'
The gunners plied their guns amain; the hail of shrapnel flew;
With rifle fire and lancer charge their squadrons back we threw;
And through the pass between the hills we swept in furious fray,
And French was through to Kimberley to drive the Boers away.

Ay, French was through to Kimberley! And ere the day was done
We saw the Diamond City stand, lit by the evening sun:
Above the town the heliograph hung like an eye of flame:
Around the town the foemen camped – they knew not that we came;
But soon they saw us, rank on rank; they heard our squadrons' tread;
In panic fear they left their tents, in hopeless rout they fled –
And French rode into Kimberley; the people cheered amain,
The women came with tear-stained eyes to touch his bridle rein,
The starving children lined the streets to raise a feeble cheer,
The bells rang out a joyous peal to say 'Relief is here!'
Ay! we that saw that stirring march are proud that we can say
We went with French to Kimberley to drive the Boers away.

By the Grey Gulf-water

Far to the Northward there lies a land,
    A wonderful land that the winds blow over,
And none may fathom or understand
    The charm it holds for the restless rover;
A great grey chaos – a land half made,
    Where endless space is and no life stirreth;
There the soul of a man will recoil afraid
    From the sphinx-like visage that Nature weareth.
But old Dame Nature, though scornful, craves
    Her dole of death and her share of slaughter;
Many indeed are the nameless graves
    Where her victims sleep by the Grey Gulf-water.

Slowly and slowly those grey streams glide,
    Drifting along with a languid motion,
Lapping the reed-beds on either side,
    Wending their way to the North Ocean.
Grey are the plains where the emus pass
    Silent and slow, with their staid demeanour;
Over the dead men's graves the grass
    Maybe is waving a trifle greener.
Down in the world where men toil and spin
    Dame Nature smiles as man's hand has taught her;
Only the dead men her smiles can win
    In the great lone land by the Grey Gulf-water.

For the strength of man is an insect's strength
    In the face of that mighty plain and river,
And the life of a man is a moment's length
    To the life of the stream that will run for ever.
And so it comes that they take no part
    In small world worries; each hardy rover
Rides like a paladin, light of heart,
    With the plains around and the blue sky over.
And up in the heavens the brown lark sings
    The songs that the strange wild land has taught her;
Full of thanksgiving her sweet song rings –
    And I wish I were back by the Grey Gulf-water.

With the Cattle

The drought is down on field and flock,
    The river-bed is dry;
And we must shift the starving stock
    Before the cattle die.
We muster up with weary hearts
    At breaking of the day,
And turn our heads to foreign parts,
    To take the stock away.
      And it's hunt 'em up and dog 'em ,
      And it's get the whip and flog 'em ,
For it's weary work, is droving, when they're dying
      every day;
      By stock routes bare and eaten,
      On dusty roads and beaten,
With half a chance to save their lives we take the stock
      away.

We cannot use the whip for shame
    On beasts that crawl along;
We have to drop the weak and lame,
    And try to save the strong;
The wrath of God is on the track,
    The drought fiend holds his sway;
With blows and cries and stockwhip crack
    We take the stock away.
      As they fall we leave them lying,
      With the crows to watch them dying,
Grim sextons of the Overland that fasten on their
      prey;
      By the fiery dust-storm drifting,
      And the mocking mirage shifting,
In heat and drought and hopeless pain we take the
      stock away.

In dull despair the days go by
  With never hope of change,
But every stage we feel more nigh
  The distant mountain range;
And some may live to climb the pass,
  And reach the great plateau,
And revel in the mountain grass
  By streamlets fed with snow.
    As the mountain wind is blowing
    It starts the cattle lowing
And calling to each other down the dusty long array;
    And there speaks a grizzled drover:
    'Well, thank God, the worst is over,
The creatures smell the mountain grass that's twenty
    miles away.'

They press towards the mountain grass,
  They look with eager eyes
Along the rugged stony pass
  That slopes towards the skies;
Their feet may bleed from rocks and stones,
  But, though the blood-drop starts,
They struggle on with stifled groans,
  For hope is in their hearts.
    And the cattle that are leading,
    Though their feet are worn and bleeding,
Are breaking to a kind of run – pull up, and let them
    go!
    For the mountain wind is blowing,
    And the mountain grass is growing,
They'll settle down by running streams ice-cold with
    melted snow.

        *   *   *   *   *

The days are gone of heat and drought
   Upon the stricken plain;
The wind has shifted right about,
   And brought the welcome rain;
The river runs with sullen roar,
   All flecked with yellow foam,
And we must take the road once more
   To bring the cattle home.
      And it's 'Lads! we'll raise a chorus,
      There's a pleasant trip before us.'
And the horses bound beneath us as we start them
      down the track;
      And the drovers canter, singing,
      Through the sweet green grasses springing,
Towards the far-off mountain-land, to bring the cattle
      back.

Are these the beasts we brought away
   That move so lively now?
They scatter off like flying spray
   Across the mountain's brow;
And dashing down the rugged range
   We hear the stockwhips crack –
Good faith, it is a welcome change
   To bring such cattle back.
      And it's 'Steady down the lead there!'
      And it's 'Let 'em stop and feed there!'
For they're wild as mountain eagles, and their sides
      are all afoam;
      But they're settling down already,
      And they'll travel nice and steady;
With cheery call and jest and song we fetch the cattle
      home.

We have to watch them close at night
   For fear they'll make a rush,
And break away in headlong flight
   Across the open bush;
And by the camp-fire's cheery blaze,
   With mellow voice and strong,
We hear the lonely watchman raise
   The Overlander's song:
      'Oh! it's when we're done with roving,
      With the camping and the droving,
It's homeward down the Bland we'll go, and never
      more we'll roam';
      While the stars shine out above us,
      Like the eyes of those who love us –
The eyes of those who watch and wait to greet the
      cattle home.

The plains are all awave with grass,
   The skies are deepest blue;
And leisurely the cattle pass
   And feed the long day through;
But when we sight the station gate
   We make the stockwhips crack,
A welcome sound to those who wait
   To greet the cattle back:
      And through the twilight falling
      We hear their voices calling,
As the cattle splash across the ford and churn it into
      foam;
      And the children run to meet us,
      And our wives and sweethearts greet us,
Their heroes from the Overland who brought the
      cattle home.

The First Surveyor

'The opening of the railway line! – the Governor and all!
With flags and banners down the street, a banquet and a ball.
Hark to 'em at the station now! They're raising cheer on cheer!
The man who brought the railway through – our friend the
          engineer.

'They cheer *his* pluck and enterprise and engineering skill!
'Twas my old husband found the pass behind that big red hill.
Before the engineer was born we'd settled with our stock
Behind that great big mountain chain, a line of range and
          rock –
A line that kept us starving there in weary weeks of drought,
With ne'er a track across the range to let the cattle out.

' 'Twas then, with horses starved and weak and scarcely fit to
          crawl,
My husband went to find a way across the rocky wall.
He vanished in the wilderness – God knows where he was
          gone --
He hunted till his food gave out, but still he battled on.
His horses strayed ('twas well they did), they made towards
          the grass,
And down behind that big red hill they found an easy pass.

'He followed up and blazed the trees, to show the safest track,
Then drew his belt another hole and turned and started back.
His horses died – just one pulled through with nothing much
          to spare;
God bless the beast that brought him home, the old white
          Arab mare!
We drove the cattle through the hills, along the new-found
          way,
And this was our first camping-ground – just where I live
          today.

'Then others came across the range and built the township
       here,
And then there came the railway line and this young engineer;
He drove about with tents and traps, a cook to cook his meals,
A bath to wash himself at night, a chain-man at his heels.
And that was all the pluck and skill for which he's cheered
       and praised,
For after all he took the track, the same my husband blazed!

'My poor old husband, dead and gone with never feast nor
       cheer;
He's buried by the railway line! I wonder can he hear
When by the very track he marked, and close to where he's
       laid,
The cattle trains go roaring down the one-in-thirty grade.
I wonder does he hear them pass, and can he see the sight
When, whistling shrill, the fast express goes flaming by at
       night.

'I think 'twould comfort him to know there's someone left to
       care;
I'll take some things this very night and hold a banquet there –
The hard old fare we've often shared together, him and me,
Some damper and a bite of beef, a pannikin of tea:
We'll do without the bands and flags, the speeches and the
       fuss,
We know who *ought* to get the cheers – and that's enough for
       us.

'What's that? They wish that I'd come down – the oldest
       settler here!
Present me to the Governor and that young engineer!
Well, just you tell his Excellency, and put the thing polite,
I'm sorry, but I can't come down – I'm dining out tonight!'

Mulga Bill's Bicycle

'Twas Mulga Bill, from Eaglehawk, that caught the cycling
     craze;
He turned away the good old horse that served him many days;
He dressed himself in cycling clothes, resplendent to be seen;
He hurried off to town and bought a shining new machine;
And as he wheeled it through the door, with air of lordly pride,
The grinning shop assistant said, 'Excuse me, can you ride?'

'See here, young man,' said Mulga Bill, 'from Walgett to the
     sea,
From Conroy's Gap to Castlereagh, there's none can ride like
     me.
I'm good all round at everything, as everybody knows,
Although I'm not the one to talk – I hate a man that blows.

'But riding is my special gift, my chiefest, sole delight;
Just ask a wild duck can it swim, a wild cat can it fight.
There's nothing clothed in hair or hide, or built of flesh or
     steel,
There's nothing walks or jumps, or runs, on axle, hoof, or
     wheel,
But what I'll sit, while hide will hold and girths and straps are
     tight;
I'll ride this here two-wheeled concern right straight away at
     sight.'

'Twas Mulga Bill, from Eaglehawk, that sought his own abode,
That perched above the Dead Man's Creek, beside the
     mountain road.
He turned the cycle down the hill and mounted for the fray,
But ere he'd gone a dozen yards it bolted clean away.
It left the track, and through the trees, just like a silver streak,
It whistled down the awful slope towards the Dead Man's
     Creek.

It shaved a stump by half an inch, it dodged a big white-box:
The very wallaroos in fright went scrambling up the rocks,
The wombats hiding in their caves dug deeper underground,
But Mulga Bill, as white as chalk, sat tight to every bound.
It struck a stone and gave a spring that cleared a fallen tree,
It raced beside a precipice as close as close could be;
And then, as Mulga Bill let out one last despairing shriek,
It made a leap of twenty feet into the Dead Man's Creek.

'Twas Mulga Bill, from Eaglehawk, that slowly swam ashore:
He said, 'I've had some narrer shaves and lively rides before;
I've rode a wild bull round a yard to win a five-pound bet,
But this was sure the derndest ride that I've encountered
          yet.
I'll give that two-wheeled outlaw best; it's shaken all my
          nerve
To feel it whistle through the air and plunge and buck and
          swerve.
It's safe at rest in Dead Man's Creek – we'll leave it lying
          still;
A horse's back is good enough henceforth for Mulga Bill.'

The Pearl Diver

Kanzo Makame, the diver, sturdy and small Japanee,
Seeker of pearls and of pearl-shell down in the depths of the
          sea,
Trudged o'er the bed of the ocean, searching industriously.

Over the pearl-grounds the lugger drifted – a little white speck:
Joe Nagasaki, the 'tender', holding the life-line on deck,
Talked through the rope to the diver, knew when to drift or to
          check.

Kanzo was king of his lugger, master and diver in one,
Diving wherever it pleased him, taking instructions from none;
Hither and thither he wandered, steering by stars and by sun.

Fearless he was beyond credence, looking at death eye to eye:
This was his formula always, 'All man go dead by and by –
S'posing time come no can help it – s'pose time no come, then
      no die.'

Dived in the depths of the Darnleys, down twenty fathom and
      five;
Down where by law, and by reason, men are forbidden to dive;
Down in a pressure so awful that only the strongest survive:

Sweated four men at the air pumps, fast as the handles could go,
Forcing the air down that reached him heated and tainted, and
      slow –
Kanzo Makame the diver stayed seven minutes below;

Came up on deck like a dead man, paralysed body and brain;
Suffered, while blood was returning, infinite tortures of pain:
Sailed once again to the Darnleys – laughed and descended
      again!

      *   *   *   *   *

Scarce grew the shell in the shallows, rarely a patch could they
      touch;
Always the take was so little, always the labour so much;
Always they thought of the Islands held by the lumbering
      Dutch –

Islands where shell was in plenty lying in passage and bay,
Islands where divers could gather hundreds of shell in a day.
But the lumbering Dutch in their gunboats they hunted the
      divers away.

Joe Nagasaki, the 'tender', finding the profits grow small,
Said, 'Let us go to the Islands, try for a number one haul!
If we get caught, go to prison – let them take lugger and all!'

Kanzo Makame, the diver – knowing full well what it meant –
Fatalist, gambler, and stoic, smiled a broad smile of content,
Flattened in mainsail and foresail, and off to the Islands they
      went.

Close to the headlands they drifted, picking up shell by the ton,
Piled up on deck were the oysters, opening wide in the sun,
When, from the lee of the headland, boomed the report of a gun.

Then if the diver was sighted, pearl-shell and lugger must go –
Joe Nagasaki decided (quick was the word and the blow),
Cut both the pipe and the life-line, leaving the diver below!

Kanzo Makame, the diver, failing to quite understand,
Pulled the 'haul up' on the life-line, found it was slack in his
        hand;
Then, like a little brown stoic, lay down and died on the sand.

Joe Nagasaki, the 'tender', smiling a sanctified smile,
Headed her straight for the gunboat – throwing out shells all
        while –
Then went aboard and reported, 'No makee dive in three mile!

'Dress no have got and no helmet – diver go shore on the spree;
Plenty wind come and break rudder – lugger get blown out to
        sea:
Take me to Japanee Consul, he help a poor Japanee!'

                *   *   *   *   *

So the Dutch let him go; but they watched him, as off from the
        Islands he ran,
Doubting him much – but what would you? You have to be sure
        of your man
Ere you wake up that nest-ful of hornets – the little brown men
        of Japan.

Down in the ooze and the coral, down where earth's wonders
        are spread,
Helmeted, ghastly, and swollen, Kanzo Makame lies dead.
Joe Nagasaki, his 'tender', is owner and diver instead.

Wearer of pearls in your necklace, comfort yourself if you can.
These are the risks of the pearling – these are the ways of Japan;
'Plenty more Japanee diver, plenty more little brown man!'

City of Dreadful Thirsts

The stranger came from Narromine and made his little joke;
'They say we folks in Narromine are narrow-minded folk;
But all the smartest men down here are puzzled to define
A kind of new phenomenon that came to Narromine.

'Last summer up in Narromine 'twas gettin' rather warm –
Two hundred in the water-bag, and lookin' like a storm –
We all were in the private bar, the coolest place in town,
When out across the stretch of plain a cloud came rollin'
    down.

'We don't respect the clouds up there, they fill us with
    disgust,
They mostly bring a Bogan shower – three raindrops and
    some dust;
But each man, simultaneous-like, to each man said, "I think
That cloud suggests it's up to us to have another drink!"

'There's clouds of rain and clouds of dust – we'd heard of
    them before,
And sometimes in the daily press we read of "clouds of war".
But – if this ain't the Gospel truth I hope that I may burst –
That cloud that came to Narromine was just a cloud of thirst.

'It wasn't like a common cloud, 'twas more a sort of haze;
It settled down about the street, and stopped for days and
    days;
And not a drop of dew could fall, and not a sunbeam shine
To pierce that dismal sort of mist that hung on Narromine.

'Oh, Lord! we had a dreadful time beneath that cloud of
    thirst!
We all chucked-up our daily work and went upon the burst.
The very blacks about the town, that used to cadge for grub,
They made an organized attack and tried to loot the pub.

'We couldn't leave the private bar no matter how we tried;
Shearers and squatters, union-men and blacklegs side by side
Were drinkin' there and dursn't move, for each was sure, he
   said,
Before he'd get a half-a-mile the thirst would strike him dead!

'We drank until the drink gave out; we searched from room to
   room,
And round the pub, like drunken ghosts, went howling
   through the gloom.
The shearers found some kerosene and settled down again,
But all the squatter chaps and I, we staggered to the train.

'And once outside the cloud of thirst we felt as right as pie,
But while we stopped about the town we had to drink or die.
I hear today it's safe enough; I'm going back to work
Because they say the cloud of thirst has shifted on to Bourke.

'But when you see those clouds about – like this one over
   here –
All white and frothy at the top, just like a pint of beer,
It's time to go and have a drink, for if that cloud should burst
You'd find the drink would all be gone, for that's a cloud of
   thirst!'

   *   *   *   *   *

We stood the man from Narromine a pint of half-and-half;
He drank it off without a gasp in one tremendous quaff;
'I joined some friends last night,' he said, 'in what *they* called
   a spree;
But after Narromine 'twas just a holiday to me.'

And now beyond the Western Range, where sunset skies are
   red,
And clouds of dust, and clouds of thirst, go drifting overhead,
The railway-train is taking back, along the Western Line,
That narrow-minded person on his road to Narromine.

Saltbush Bill's Gamecock

'Twas Saltbush Bill, with his travelling sheep, was making his way
    to town;
He crossed them over the Hard Times Run, and he came to the
    Take 'Em Down;
He counted through at the boundary gate, and camped at the
    drafting yard:
For Stingy Smith, of the Hard Times Run, had hunted him rather
    hard.
He bore no malice to Stingy Smith – 'twas simply the hand of Fate
That caused his waggon to swerve aside and shatter old Stingy's
    gate;
And being only the hand of Fate, it follows, without a doubt,
It wasn't the fault of Saltbush Bill that Stingy's sheep got out.
So Saltbush Bill, with an easy heart, prepared for what might
    befall,
Commenced his stages on Take 'Em Down, the station of Rooster
    Hall.

'Tis strange how often the men out back will take to some curious
    craft,
Some ruling passion to keep their thoughts away from the
    overdraft;
And Rooster Hall, of the Take 'Em Down, was widely known to
    fame
As breeder of champion fighting cocks – his *forte* was the British
    Game.

The passing stranger within his gates that camped with old
    Rooster Hall
Was forced to talk about fowls all night, or else not talk at all.
Though droughts should come, and though sheep should die, his
    fowls were his sole delight;
He left his shed in the flood of work to watch two game-cocks
    fight.
He held in scorn the Australian Game, that long-legged child of
    sin;

In a desperate fight, with the steel-tipped spurs, the British game
        must win!
The Australian bird was a mongrel bird, with a touch of the
        jungle cock;
The want of breeding must find him out, when facing the English
        stock;
For British breeding, and British pluck, must triumph it over all –
And that was the root of the simple creed that governed old
        Rooster Hall.

       *   *   *   *   *

’Twas Saltbush Bill to the station rode ahead of his travelling
        sheep,
And sent a message to Rooster Hall that wakened him out of his
        sleep –
A crafty message that fetched him out, and hurried him as he
        came –
‘A drover has an Australian bird to match with your British
        Game.’
’Twas done, and done in half a trice; a five-pound note a side;
Old Rooster Hall, with his champion bird, and the drover’s bird
        untried.

‘Steel spurs, of course?’ said old Rooster Hall; ‘you’ll need ’em ,
        without a doubt!’
‘You stick the spurs on your bird!’ said Bill, ‘but mine fights best
        without.’
‘Fights best without?’ said old Rooster Hall; ‘he can’t fight best
        unspurred!
You must be crazy!’ But Saltbush Bill said, ‘Wait till you see my
        bird!’
So Rooster Hall to his fowl-yard went, and quickly back he came,
Bearing a clipt and a shaven cock, the pride of his English Game;
With an eye as fierce as an eaglehawk, and a crow like a trumpet
        call,
He strutted about on the garden walk, and cackled at Rooster
        Hall.
Then Rooster Hall sent off a boy with a word to his cronies two,
McCrae (the boss of the Black Police) and Father Donahoo.

Full many a cockfight old McCrae had held in his empty Court,
With Father D. as the picker-up – a regular all-round Sport!
They got the message of Rooster Hall, and down to his run they came,
Prepared to scoff at the drover's bird, and to bet on the English Game;
They hied them off to the drover's camp, while Saltbush rode before –
Old Rooster Hall was a blithsome man, when he thought of the treat
      in store.
They reached the camp, where the drover's cook, with countenance all
      serene,
Was boiling beef in an iron pot, but never a fowl was seen.

'Take off the beef from the fire,' said Bill, 'and wait till you see the
      fight;
There's something fresh for the bill-of-fare – there's game-fowl stew
      tonight!
For Mister Hall has a fighting cock, all feathered and clipped and
      spurred;
And he's fetched him here, for a bit of sport, to fight our Australian
      bird.
I've made a match that our pet will win, though he's hardly a fighting
      cock,
But he's game enough, and it's many a mile that he's tramped with
      the travelling stock.'
The cook he banged on a saucepan lid; and, soon as the sound was
      heard,
Under the dray, in the shallow hid, a something moved and stirred:
A great tame emu strutted out. Said Saltbush, 'Here's our bird!'
But Rooster Hall, and his cronies two, drove home without a word.

The passing stranger within his gates that camps with old Rooster Hall
Must talk about something else than fowls, if he wishes to talk at all.
For the record lies in the local Court, and filed in its deepest vault,
That Peter Hall, of the Take 'Em Down, was tried for a fierce assault
On a stranger man, who, in all good faith, and prompted by what he
      heard,
Had asked old Hall if a British Game could beat an Australian bird;
And Old McCrae, who was on the Bench, as soon as the case was
      tried,
Remarked, 'Discharged with a clean discharge – the assault was
      justified!'

Hay and Hell Booligal

'You come and see me, boys,' he said;
'You'll find a welcome and a bed
    And whisky any time you call;
Although our township hasn't got
The name of quite a lively spot –
    You see, I live in Booligal.

'And people have an awful down
Upon the district and the town –
    Which worse than hell itself the call;
In fact, the saying far and wide
Along the Riverina side
    Is "Hay and Hell and Booligal".

'No doubt it suits 'em very well
To say its worse than Hay or Hell,
    But don't you heed their talk at all;
Of course, there's heat – no one denies –
And sand and dust and stacks of flies,
    And rabbits, too, at Booligal.

'But such a pleasant, quiet place –
You never see a stranger's face;
    They hardly ever care to call;
The drovers mostly pass it by –
They reckon that they'd rather die
    Than spend the night in Booligal.

'The big mosquitoes frighten some –
You'll lie awake to hear 'em hum –
    And snakes about the township crawl;
But shearers, when they get their cheque,
They never come along and wreck
    The blessed town of Booligal.

But down to Hay the shearers come
And fill themselves with fighting-rum,
   And chase blue devils up the wall,
And fight the snaggers every day,
Until there is the deuce to pay –
   There's none of that in Booligal.

'Of course, there isn't much to see –
The billiard-table used to be
   The great attraction for us all,
Until some careless, drunken curs
Got sleeping on it in their spurs,
   And ruined it, in Booligal.

'Just now there is a howling drought
That pretty near has starved us out –
   It never seems to rain at all;
But, if there *should* come any rain,
You couldn't cross the black-soil plain –
   You'd have to stop in Booligal.'

    *   *   *   *   *

'*We'd have to stop!*' With bated breath
We prayed that both in life and death
   Our fate in other lines might fall:
'Oh, send us to our just reward
In Hay or Hell, but, gracious Lord,
   Deliver us from Booligal!'

A Walgett Episode

The sun strikes down with a blinding glare;
    The skies are blue and the plains are wide,
The saltbush plains that are burnt and bare
    By Walgett out on the Barwon side –
The Barwon River that wanders down
In a leisurely manner by Walgett Town.

There came a stranger – a 'Cockatoo' –
    The word means farmer, as all men know,
Who dwell in the land where the kangaroo
    Barks loud at dawn, and the white-eyed crow
Uplifts his song on the stock-yard fence
As he watches the lambkins passing hence.

The sunburnt stranger was gaunt and brown,
    But it soon appeared that he meant to flout
The iron law of the country town,
    Which is – that the stranger has got to shout:
'If he will not shout we must take him down,'
Remarked the yokels of Walgett Town.

They baited a trap with a crafty bait,
    With a crafty bait, for they held discourse
Concerning a new chum who there of late
    Had bought such a thoroughly lazy horse;
They would wager that no one could ride him down
The length of the city of Walgett Town.

The stranger was born on a horse's hide;
    So he took the wagers, and made them good
With his hard-earned cash – but his hopes they died,
    For the horse was a clothes-horse, made of wood! –
'Twas a well-known horse that had taken down
Full many a stranger in Walgett Town.

The stranger smiled with a sickly smile –
   'Tis a sickly smile that the loser grins –
And he said he had travelled for quite a while
   A-trying to sell some marsupial skins.
'And I thought that perhaps, as you've took me down,
You would buy them from me, in Walgett Town!'

He said that his home was at Wingadee,
   At Wingadee, where he had for sale
Some fifty skins and would guarantee
   They were full-sized skins, with the ears and tail
Complete; and he sold them for money down
To a venturesome buyer in Walgett Town.

Then he smiled a smile as he pouched the pelf,
   'I'm glad that I'm quit of them, win or lose:
You can fetch them in when it suits yourself,
   And you'll find the skins – on the kangaroos!'
Then he left – and the silence settled down
Like a tangible thing upon Walgett Town.

Father Riley's Horse

'Twas the horse thief, Andy Regan, that was hunted like a
    dog
  By the troopers of the Upper Murray side;
They had searched in every gully, they had looked in every
    log
  But never sight or track of him they spied,
Till the priest at Kiley's Crossing heard a knocking very late
  And a whisper 'Father Riley – come across!'
So his Reverence, in pyjamas, trotted softly to the gate
  And admitted Andy Regan – and a horse!

'Now, it's listen, Father Riley, to the words I've got to say,
  For it's close upon my death I am tonight.
With the troopers hard behind me I've been hiding all the
    day
  In the gullies keeping close and out of sight.
But they're watching all the ranges till there's not a bird
      could fly,
  And I'm fairly worn to pieces with the strife,
So I'm taking no more trouble, but I'm going home to die,
  'Tis the only way I see to save my life.

'Yes, I'm making home to mother's, and I'll die o' Tuesday
    next
  An' buried on the Thursday – and, of course,
I'm prepared to do my penance; but with one thing I'm
      perplexed
  And it's – Father, it's this jewel of a horse!
He was never bought nor paid for, and there's not a man can
    swear
  To his owner or his breeder, but I know
That his sire was by Pedantic from the Old Pretender mare,
  And his dam was close related to The Roe.

'And there's nothing in the district that can race him for a
    step –
  He could canter while they're going at their top:
He's the king of all the leppers that was ever seen to lep;
  A five-foot fence – he'd clear it in a hop!
So I'll leave him with you, Father, till the dead shall rise
    again,
  'Tis yourself that knows a good un; and, of course,
You can say he's got by Moonlight out of Paddy Murphy's
    plain
  If you're ever asked the breeding of the horse!

'But it's getting on to daylight, and it's time to say goodbye,
  For the stars above the East are growing pale.
And I'm making home to mother – and it's hard for me to
    die!
  But it's harder still, is keeping out of gaol!
You can ride the old horse over to my grave across the dip,
  Where the wattle-bloom is waving overhead.
Sure he'll jump them fences easy – you must never raise the
    whip
  Or he'll rush 'em! – now, goodbye!' and he had fled!

So they buried Andy Regan, and they buried him to rights,
  In the graveyard at the back of Kiley's Hill;
There were five-and-twenty mourners who had five-and-
    twenty fights
  Till the very boldest fighters had their fill.
There were fifty horses racing from the graveyard to the pub,
  And the riders flogged each other all the while –
And the lashins of the liquor! And the lavins of the grub!
  Oh, poor Andy went to rest in proper style.

Then the races came to Kiley's – with a steeplechase and all,
  For the folk were mostly Irish round about,
And it takes an Irish rider to be fearless of a fall;
  They were training morning in and morning out.
But they never started training till the sun was on the course,
  For a superstitious story kept 'em back.
That the ghost of Andy Regan on a slashing chestnut horse
  Had been training by the starlight on the track.

And they read the nominations for the races with surprise
    And amusement at the Father's little joke,
For a novice had been entered for the steeplechasing prize,
    And they found that it was Father Riley's moke!
He was neat enough to gallop, he was strong enough to stay!
    But his owner's views of training were immense,
For the Reverend Father Riley used to ride him every day,
    And he never saw a hurdle nor a fence.

And the priest would join the laughter; 'Oh,' said he, 'I put
      him in,
    For there's five-and-twenty sovereigns to be won;
And the poor would find it useful if the chestnut chanced to
      win,
    As he'll maybe do when all is said and done!'
He had called him Faugh-a-ballagh (which is French for
      "Clear the course"),
    And his colours were a vivid shade of green:
All the Dooleys and O'Donnells were on Father Riley's horse,
    While the Orangeman were backing Mandarin!

It was Hogan, the dog-poisoner – aged man and very wise,
    Who was camping in the racecourse with his swag,
And who ventured the opinion, to the township's great
      surprise,
    That the race would go to Father Riley's nag.
'You can talk about your riders – and the horse has not been
      schooled,
    And the fences is terrific, and the rest!
When the field is fairly going, then ye'll see ye've all been
      fooled.
    And the chestnut horse will battle with the best.

'For there's some has got condition, and they think the race
      is sure,
    And the chestnut horse will fall beneath the weight;
But the hopes of all the helpless, and the prayers of all the
      poor,
    Will be running by his side to keep him straight.

And it's what the need of schoolin' or of workin' on the
    track,
  Whin the Saints are there to guide him round the course!
I've prayed him over every fence – I've prayed him out and
    back!
  And I'll bet my cash on Father Riley's horse!'

       *   *   *   *   *

Oh, the steeple was a caution! They went tearin' round and
    round,
  And the fences rang and rattled where they struck.
There was some that cleared the water – there was more fell
    in and drowned –
  Some blamed the men and others blamed the luck!
But the whips were flying freely when the field came into
    view
  For the finish down the long green stretch of course,
And in front of all the flyers, jumpin' like a kangaroo,
  Came the rank outsider – Father Riley's horse!

Oh, the shouting and the cheering as he rattled past the post!
  For he left the others standing, in the straight;
And the rider – well, they reckoned it was Andy Regan's
    ghost,
  And it beat 'em how a ghost would draw the weight!
But he weighed in, nine stone seven; then he laughed and
    disappeared,
  Like a Banshee (which is Spanish for an elf),
And old Hogan muttered sagely, 'If it wasn't for the beard
  They'd be thinking it was Andy Regan's self!'

And the poor at Kiley's Crossing drank the health at
    Christmastide
  Of the chestnut and his rider dressed in green.
There was never such a rider, not since Andy Regan died,
  And they wondered who on earth he could have been,
But they settled it among 'em , for the story got about,
  'Mongst the bushmen and the people on the course,
That the Devil had been ordered to let Andy Regan out
  For the steeplechase on Father Riley's horse!

The Scottish Engine

With eyes that searched in the dark,
Peering along the line,
Stood the grim Scotsman, Hector Clark,
Driver of 'Forty-nine'.
And the veldt-fire flamed on the hills ahead,
Like a blood-red beacon sign.

There was word of a fight to the north,
And a column too hardly pressed,
So they started the Highlanders forth,
Heedless of food or rest.

But the pipers gaily played,
Chanting their fierce delight,
And the armoured carriages rocked and swayed,
Laden with men of the Scots Brigade,
Hurrying up to the fight,
And the grim, grey Highland engineer
Driving them into the night.

Then a signal light glowed red,
And a picket came to the track.
'Enemy holding the line ahead;
Three of our mates we have left for dead,
Only we two got back.'
And far to the north through the still night air
They heard the rifles crack.

And the boom of a gun rang out,
Like the sound of a deep appeal,
And the picket stood in doubt
By the side of the driving-wheel.

But the engineer looked down,
With his hand on the starting-bar,
'Ride ye back to the town,

Ye know what my orders are,
Maybe they're wanting the Scots Brigade
Up on those hills afar.

'I am no soldier at all,
Only an engineer;
But I could not bear that the folk should say
Over in Scotland – Glasgow way –
That Hector Clark stayed here
With the Scots Brigade till the foe was gone,
With ever a rail to run her on.
Ready behind! Stand clear!

'Fireman, get you gone
Into the armoured train –
I will drive her alone;
One more trip – and perhaps the last –
With a well-raked fire and an open blast;
Hark to the rifles again!'

*   *   *   *   *

On through the choking dark,
Never a lamp nor a light,
Never an engine spark
Showing her hurried flight,
Over the lonely plain
Rushed the great armoured train,
Hurrying up to the fight.

Then with her living freight
On to the foe she came,
And the rifles snapped their hate,
And the darkness spouted flame.

Over the roar of the fray
The hungry bullets whined,
As she dashed through the foe that lay
Loading and firing blind,
Till the glare of the furnace, burning clear,
Showed them the form of the engineer
Sharply and well defined.

Through! They are safely through!
Hark to the column's cheer!
Surely the driver knew
He was to halt her here;
But he took no heed of the signals red,
And the fireman found, when he climbed ahead,
There on the floor of his engine – dead –
The Scottish Engineer!

Song of the Future

'Tis strange that in a land so strong,
So strong and bold in mighty youth,
We have no poet's voice of truth
To sing for us a wondrous song.

Our chiefest singer yet has sung
In wild, sweet notes a passing strain,
All carelessly and sadly flung
To that dull world he thought so vain.

'I care for nothing, good nor bad,
My hopes are gone, my pleasures fled
I am but sifting sand,' he said:
What wonder Gordon's songs were sad!

And yet, not always sad and hard;
In cheerful mood and light of heart
He told the tale of Britomarte,
And wrote the Rhyme of Joyous Garde.

And some have said that Nature's face
To us is always sad; but these
Have never felt the smiling grace
Of waving grass and forest trees
On sunlit plains as wide as seas.

'A land where dull Despair is king
O'er scentless flower and songless bird!'
But we have heard the bell-birds ring
Their silver bells at eventide,
Like fairies on the mountain side,
The sweetest note man ever heard.

The wild thrush lifts a note of mirth;
The bronzewing pigeons call and coo
Beside their nests the long day through;
The magpie warbles clear and strong
A joyous, glad, thanksgiving song,

For all God's mercies upon earth.
And many voices such as these
Are joyful sounds for those to tell,
Who know the Bush and love it well,
With all its hidden mysteries.

We cannot love the restless sea,
That rolls and tosses to and fro
Like some fierce creature in its glee;
For human weal or human woe
It has no touch of sympathy.

For us the bush is never sad:
Its myriad voices whisper low,
In tones the bushmen only know,
Its sympathy and welcome glad.
For us the roving breezes bring
From many a blossom-tufted tree –
Where wild bees murmur dreamily –
The honey-laden breath of Spring.

*   *   *   *   *

We have our tales of other days,
Good tales the northern wanderers tell
When bushmen meet and camp-fires blaze
And round the ring of dancing light
The great, dark bush with arms of night
Folds every hearer in its spell.

We have our songs – not songs of strife
And hot blood spilt on sea and land;
But lilts that link achievement grand
To honest toil and valiant life.

Lift ye your faces to the sky
Ye barrier mountains in the west
Who lie so peacefully at rest
Enshrouded in a haze of blue;
'Tis hard to feel that years went by
Before the pioneers broke through
Your rocky heights and walls of stone,
And made your secrets all their own.

For years the fertile Western plains
Were hid behind your sullen walls,
Your cliffs and crags and waterfalls
All weatherworn with tropic rains.

Between the mountains and the sea,
Like Israelites with staff in hand,
The people waited restlessly:
They looked towards the mountains old
And saw the sunsets come and go
With gorgeous golden afterglow,
That made the West a fairyland,
And marvelled what that West might be
Of which such wondrous tales were told.

For tales were told of inland seas
Like sullen oceans, salt and dead,
And sandy deserts, white and wan,
Where never trod the foot of man,
Nor bird went winging overhead,
Nor ever stirred a gracious breeze
To wake the silence with its breath –
A land of loneliness and death.

At length the hardy pioneers
By rock and crag found out the way,
And woke with voices of today
A silence kept for years and years.

Upon the Western slope they stood
And saw – a wide expanse of plain
As far as eye could stretch or see
Go rolling westward endlessly.
The native grasses, tall as grain,
Bowed, waved and rippled in the breeze;
From boughs of blossom-laden trees
The parrots answered back again.
They saw the land that it was good,
A land of fatness all untrod,
And gave their silent thanks to God.

The way is won! The way is won!
And straightway from the barren coast
There came a westward-marching host,
That aye and ever onward prest
With eager faces to the West,
Along the pathway of the sun.

The mountains saw them marching by:
They faced the all-consuming drought,
They would not rest in settled land:
But, taking each his life in hand,
Their faces ever westward bent
Beyond the farthest settlement,
Responding to the challenge cry
Of 'better country farther out'.

And lo, a miracle! the land
But yesterday was all unknown,
The wild man's boomerang was thrown
Where now great busy cities stand.
It was not much, you say, that these
Should win their way where none withstood;
In sooth there was not much of blood –
No war was fought between the seas.

It was not much! but we who know
The strange capricious land they trod –
At times a stricken, parching sod,
At times with raging floods beset –
Through which they found their lonely way,
Are quite content that you should say
It was not much, while we can feel
That nothing in the ages old,
In song or story written yet
On Grecian urn or Roman arch,
Though it should ring with clash of steel,
Could braver histories unfold
Than this bush story, yet untold –
The story of their westward march.

        *   *   *   *   *

But times are changed, and changes rung
From old to new – the olden days,
The old bush life and all its ways,
Are passing from us all unsung.
The freedom, and the hopeful sense
Of toil that brought due recompense,
Of room for all, has passed away,
And lies forgotten with the dead.
Within our streets men cry for bread

In cities built but yesterday.
About us stretches wealth of land,
A boundless wealth of virgin soil
As yet unfruitful and untilled!
Our willing workmen, strong and skilled,
Within our cities idle stand,
And cry aloud for leave to toil.

The stunted children come and go
In squalid lanes and alleys black;
We follow but the beaten track
Of other nations, and we grow
In wealth for some – for many, woe.

And it may be that we who live
In this new land apart, beyond
The hard old world grown fierce and fond
And bound by precedent and bond,
May read the riddle right, and give
New hope to those who dimly see
That all things yet shall be for good,
And teach the world at length to be
One vast united brotherhood.

*   *   *   *   *

So may it be! and he who sings
In accents hopeful, clear, and strong,
The glories which that future brings
Shall sing, indeed, a wondrous song.

Anthony Considine

Out in the wastes of the West countrie,
　　Out where the white stars shine,
Grim and silent as such men be,
Rideth a man with a history –
　　Anthony Considine.

For the ways of men they are manifold
　　As their differing views in life;
Some sell themselves for the lust of gold,
　　And some for the lust of strife:
But this man counted the world well lost
　　For the love of his neighbour's wife.

They fled together, as those must flee
　　Whom all men hold in blame;
Each to the other must all things be
Who cross the gulf of iniquity
　　And live in the land of shame.

But a light-o'-love, if she sins with one,
　　She sinneth with ninety-nine:
The rule holds good since the world begun -
　　Since ever the streams began to run
And the stars began to shine.
　　The rule holds still, and he found it true –
Anthony Considine.

A nobler spirit had turned in scorn
　　From a love that was stained with mire;
A weaker being might mourn and mourn
　　For the loss of his Heart's Desire:
But the anger of Anthony Considine
　　Blazed up like a flaming fire.

And she, with her new love, presently
    Came past with her eyes ashine;
And God so willed it, and God knows why,
She turned and laughed as they passed him by —
    Anthony Considine.

Her laughter stung as a whip might sting;
    And mad with his wounded pride
He turned and sprang with a panther's spring,
    And struck at his rival's side:
And only the woman, shuddering,
    Could tell how the dead man died!

She dared not speak — and the mystery
    Is buried in auld lang syne,
But out on the wastes of the West countrie,
Grim and silent as such men be,
Rideth a man with a history —
    Anthony Considine.

Song of the Artesian Water

Now the stock have started dying, for the Lord has sent a
        drought;
But we're sick of prayers and Providence – we're going to do
        without;
With the derricks up above us and the solid earth below,
We are waiting at the lever for the word to let her go.
                Sinking down, deeper down,
                Oh, we'll sink it deeper down:
As the drill is plugging downward at a thousand feet of level,
If the Lord won't send us water, oh, we'll get it from the devil;
Yes, we'll get it from the devil deeper down.

Now, our engine's built in Glasgow by a very canny Scot,
And he marked it twenty horse-power, but he don't know
        what is what:
When Canadian Bill is firing with the sun-dried gidgee logs,
She can equal thirty horses and a score or so of dogs.
                Sinking down, deeper down,
                Oh, we're going deeper down:
If we fail to get the water, then it's ruin to the squatter,
For the drought is on the station and the weather's growing
        hotter,
But we're bound to get the water deeper down.

But the shaft has started caving and the sinking's very slow,
And the yellow rods are bending in the water down below,
And the tubes are always jamming, and they can't be made to
        shift
Till we nearly burst the engine with a forty horse-power lift.
                Sinking down, deeper down,
                Oh, we're going deeper down:
Though the shaft is always caving, and the tubes are always
        jamming,
Yet we'll fight our way to water while the stubborn drill is
        ramming –
While the stubborn drill is ramming deeper down.

But there's no artesian water, though we've passed three
      thousand feet,
And the contract price is growing, and the boss is nearly beat.
But it must be down beneath us, and it's down we've got to go,
Though she's bumping on the solid rock four thousand feet
      below
              Sinking down, deeper down,
              Oh, we're going deeper down:
And it's time they heard us knocking on the roof of Satan's
      dwellin';
But we'll get artesian water if we cave the roof of hell in —
Oh! we'll get artesian water deeper down.

But it's hark! the whistle's blowing with a wild, exultant blast,
And the boys are madly cheering, for they've struck the flow
      at last;
And it's rushing up the tubing from four thousand feet below,
Till it spouts above the casing in a million-gallon flow.
              And it's down, deeper down —
              Oh, it comes from deeper down;
It is flowing, ever flowing, in a free, unstinted measure
From the silent hidden places where the old earth hides her
      treasure —
Where the old earth hides her treasures deeper down.

And it's clear away the timber, and it's let the water run:
How it glimmers in the shadow, how it flashes in the sun!
By the silent belts of timber, by the miles of blazing plain
It is bringing hope and comfort to the thirsty land again.
              Flowing down, further down;
              It is flowing further down
To the tortured thirsty cattle, bringing gladness in its going;
Through the droughty days of summer it is flowing, ever
      flowing —
It is flowing, ever flowing, further down.

A Disqualified Jockey's Story

You see, the thing was this way – there was me,
That rode Panoppoly, the Splendor mare,
And Ikey Chambers on the Iron Dook,
And Smith, the half-caste rider on Regret,
And that long bloke from Wagga – him that rode
Veronikew, the Snowy River horse.
Well, none of them had chances – not a chance
Among the lot, unless the rest fell dead
Or wasn't trying – for a blind man's dog
Could see Enchantress was a certain cop,
And all the books was layin' six to four.

They brought her out to show our lot the road,
Or so they said: but, then Gord's truth! you know,
You can't believe 'em , though they took an oath
On forty Bibies that they'd tell the truth.
But anyhow, an amateur was up
On this Enchantress; and so Ike and me,
We thought that we might frighten him a bit
By asking if he minded riding rough –
'Oh, not at all,' says he, 'oh, not at all!
I learnt at Robbo Park, and if it comes
To bumping I'm your Moses! Strike me blue!'

Says he, 'I'll bump you over either rail,
The inside rail or outside – which you choose
Is good enough for me' – which settled Ike.
For he was shaky since he near got killed
From being sent a buster on the rail,
When some chap bumped his horse and fetched him down
At Stony Bridge; so Ikey thought it best
To leave this bloke alone, and I agreed.

So all the books was layin' six to four
Against the favourite, and the amateur
Was walking this Enchantress up and down,

And me and Smithy backed him; for we thought
We might as well get something for ourselves,
Because we knew our horses couldn't win.
But Ikey wouldn't back him for a bob;
Because he said he reckoned he was stiff,
And all the books was layin' six to four.

Well, anyhow, before the start the news
Got around that this here amateur was stiff,
And our good stuff was blued, and all the books
Was in it, and the prices lengthened out,
And every book was bustin' of his throat,
And layin' five to one the favourite.
So there was we that couldn't win ourselves,
And this here amateur that wouldn't try,
And all the books was layin' five to one.

So Smithy says to me, 'You take a hold
Of that there moke of yours, and round the turn
Come up behind Enchantress with the whip
And let her have it; that long bloke and me
Will wait ahead, and when she comes to us
We'll pass her on and belt her down the straight,
And Ikey'll flog her home – because his boss
Is judge and steward and the Lord knows what,
And so he won't be touched; and, as for us,
We'll swear we only hit her by mistake!'
And all the books was layin' five to one.

Well, off we went, and comin' to the turn
I saw the amateur was holding back
And poking into every hole he could
To get her blocked; and so I pulled behind
And drew the whip and dropped it on the mare.
I let her have it twice, and then she shot
Ahead of me, and Smithy opened out
And let her up beside him on the rails,
And kept her there a-beltin' her like smoke
Until she struggled past him, pullin' hard,
And came to Ike; but Ikey drew his whip

And hit her on the nose, and sent her back
And won the race himself – for, after all,
It seems he had a fiver on The Dook
And never told us – so our stuff was lost.
And then they had us up for ridin' foul,
And warned us off the track for twelve months each
To get our livin' any way we could;
But Ikey wasn't touched, because his boss
Was judge and steward and the Lord knows what.

But Mister – if you'll lend us half-a-crown,
I know three certain winners at the Park –
Three certain cops as no one knows but me;
And – thank you, Mister, come an' have a beer
(I always like a beer about this time) . . .
Well so long, Mister, till we meet again.

The Road to Gundagai

The mountain road goes up and down
From Gundagai to Tumut Town.

And, branching off, there runs a track
Across the foothills grim and black,

Across the plains and ranges grey
To Sydney city far away.

*   *   *   *   *

It came by chance one day that I
From Tumut rode to Gundagai,

And reached about the evening tide
The crossing where the roads divide;

And, waiting at the crossing place,
I saw a maiden fair of face,

With eyes of deepest violet blue,
And cheeks to match the rose in hue –

The fairest maids Australia knows
Are bred among the mountain snows.

Then, fearing I might go astray,
I asked if she could show the way.

Her voice might well a man bewitch –
Its tones so supple, deep, and rich.

'The tracks are clear,' she made reply,
'And this goes down to Sydney town,
And that one goes to Gundagai.'

Then slowly, looking coyly back,
She went along the Sydney track

And I for one was well content
To go the road the lady went;

But round the turn a swain she met –
The kiss she gave him haunts me yet!

*   *   *   *   *

I turned and travelled with a sigh
The lonely road to Gundagai.

Saltbush Bill's Second Fight

The news came down on the Castlereagh, and went to the world at
    large,
That twenty thousand travelling sheep, with Saltbush Bill in charge,
Were drifting down from a dried-out run to ravage the Castlereagh;
And the squatters swore when they heard the news, and wished
        they were well away:
For the name and the fame of Saltbush Bill were over the country-side
For the wonderful way that he fed his sheep, and the dodges and
        tricks he tried.
He would lose his way on a Main Stock Route, and stray to the
        squatters' grass;
He would come to a run with the boss away, and swear he had leave
        to pass;
And back of all and behind it all, as well the squatters knew,
If he had to fight, he would fight all day, so long as his sheep got
        through:
But this is the story of Stingy Smith, the owner of Hard Times Hill,
And the way that he chanced on a fighting man to reckon with
        Saltbush Bill.

          *   *   *   *   *

'Twas Stingy Smith on his stockyard sat, and prayed for an early
        Spring,
When he started at sight of a clean-shaved tramp, who walked with a
        jaunty swing;
For a clean-shaved tramp with a jaunty walk a-swinging along the track
Is as rare a thing as a feathered frog on the desolate roads out back.
So the tramp he made for the travellers' hut, to ask could he camp the
        night;
But Stingy Smith had a bright idea, and called to him, 'Can you fight?'

'Why, what's the game?' said the clean-shaved tramp, as he looked at
        him up and down;
'If you want a battle, get off that fence, and I'll kill you for half-a-
        crown!
But, Boss, you'd better not fight with me – it wouldn't be fair nor right;
I'm Stiffener Joe, from the Rocks Brigade, and I killed a man in a fight:

I served two years for it, fair and square, and now I'm a-trampin' back,
To look for a peaceful quiet life away on the outside track.'

'Oh, it's not myself, but a drover chap,' said Stingy Smith with glee.
'A bullying fellow called Saltbush Bill, and you are the man for me.
He's on the road with his hungry sheep, and he's certain to raise a row,
For he's bullied the whole of the Castlereagh till he's got them
          under cow –
Just pick a quarrel and raise a fight, and leather him good and hard,
And I'll take good care that his wretched sheep don't wander a half a
          yard.
It's a five-pound job if you belt him well – do anything short of kill,
For there isn't a beak on the Castlereagh will fine you for Saltbush Bill.'

'I'll take the job,' said the fighting man; 'and, hot as this cove appears,
He'll stand no chance with a bloke like me, what's lived on the game
          for years;
For he's maybe learnt in a boxing school, and sparred for a round or
          so,
But I've fought all hands in a ten-foot ring each night in a travelling
          show;
They earned a pound if they stayed three rounds, and they tried for it
          every night
In a ten-foot ring! Oh, that's the game that teaches a bloke to fight,
For they'd rush and clinch – it was Dublin Rules, and we drew no
          colour line;
And they all tried hard for to earn the pound, but they got no pound of
          mine.
If I saw no chance in the opening round I'd slog at their wind, and wait
Till an opening came – and it *always* came – and I settled 'em , sure as
          fate;
Left on the ribs and right on the jaw – and, when the chance comes,
          make sure!
And it's there a professional bloke like me gets home on an amateur:
For it's my experience every day, and I make no doubt it's yours,
That a third-class pro is an over-match for the best of the amateurs – '
'Oh, take your swag to the travellers' hut,' said Smith, 'for you waste
          your breath;
You've a first-class chance, if you lose the fight, of talking your man to
          death.

I'll tell the cook you're to have your grub, and see that you eat your fill,
And come to the scratch all fit and well to leather this Saltbush Bill.'

   *   *   *   *   *

'Twas Saltbush Bill, and his travelling sheep were wending their weary way
On the Main Stock Route, through the Hard Times Run, on their six-
  mile stage a day;
And he strayed a mile from the Main Stock Route, and started to feed
  along,
And when Stingy Smith came up Bill said that the Route was surveyed
  wrong;
And he tried to prove that the sheep had rushed and strayed from their
  camp at night,
But the fighting man he kicked Bill's dog, and of course that meant a
  fight.

So they sparred and fought, and they shifted ground, and never a
  sound was heard
But the thudding fists on their brawny ribs, and the seconds' muttered
  word,
Till the fighting man shot home his left on the ribs with a mighty clout,
And his right flashed up with a half-arm blow – and Saltbush Bill 'went
  out'.
He fell face down, and towards the blow; and their hearts with fear
  were filled,
For he lay as still as a fallen tree, and they thought that he must be
  killed.

So Stingy Smith and the fighting man, they lifted him from the ground,
And sent back home for a brandy-flask, and they slowly fetched him
  round;
But his head was bad, and his jaw was hurt – in fact, he could scarcely
  speak –
So they let him spell till he got his wits; and he camped on the run a
  week,
While the travelling sheep went here and there, wherever they liked to
  stray,
Till Saltbush Bill was fit once more for the track to the Castlereagh.

   *   *   *   *   *

Then Stingy Smith he wrote a note, and gave to the fighting man:
'Twas writ to the boss of the neighbouring run, and thus the missive ran:

'The man with this is a fighting man, one Stiffener Joe by name;
He came near murdering Saltbush Bill, and I found it a costly game:
But it's worth your while to employ the chap, for there isn't the
    slightest doubt
You'll have no trouble from Saltbush Bill while this man hangs
    about.'
But an answer came by the next week's mail, with news that might
    well appal:
'The man you sent with a note is not a fighting man at all!
He has shaved his beard, and has cut his hair, but I spotted him at a
    look;
He is Tom Devine, who has worked for years for Saltbush Bill as
    cook.
Bill coached him up in the fighting yard, and taught him the tale by
    rote,
And they shammed to fight, and they got your grass, and divided
    your five-pound note.
'Twas a clean take-in; and you'll find it wise – 'twill save you a lot of
    pelf –
When next you're hiring a fighting man, just fight him a round
    yourself.

       *   *   *   *   *

And the teamsters out on the Castlereagh, when they meet with a
    week of rain,
And the waggon sinks to its axle-tree, deep down in the black-soil
    plain,
When the bullocks wade in a sea of mud, and strain at the load of
    wool,
And the cattle-dogs at the bullocks' heels are biting to make them
    pull,
When the off-side driver flays the team, and curses them while he
    flogs,
And the air is thick with the language used, and the clamour of men
    and dogs –
The teamsters say, as they pause to rest and moisten each hairy
    throat,
They wish they could swear like Stingy Smith when he read that
    neighbour's note.

Hard Luck

I left the course, and by my side
    There walked a ruined tout –
A hungry creature, evil-eyed,
    Who poured this story out.

'You see,' he said, 'there came a swell
    To Kensington today,
And, if I picked the winners well,
    A crown at least he'd pay.

'I picked three winners straight, I did;
    I filled his purse with pelf,
And then he gave me half-a-quid
    To back one for myself.

'A half-a-quid to me he cast –
    I wanted it indeed;
So help me Bob, for two days past
    I haven't had a feed.

'But still I thought my luck was in,
    I couldn't go astray –
I put it all on Little Min,
    And lost it straightaway.

'I haven't got a bite or bed,
    I'm absolutely stuck;
So keep this lesson in your head:
    Don't over-trust your luck!'

The folks went homeward, near and far,
    The tout, oh! where was he?
Ask where the empty boilers are
    Beside the Circular Quay.

Song of the Federation

As the nations sat together, grimly waiting –
    The fierce and ancient nations battle-scarred –
Grown grey in their lusting and their hating,
    Ever armed and ever ready keeping guard,
Through the tumult of their warlike preparation
    And the half-stilled clamour of the drums
Came a voice crying, 'Lo, a new-made Nation,
    To her place in the sisterhood she comes!'

And she came. She was beautiful as morning,
    With the bloom of the roses on her mouth,
Like a young queen lavishly adorning
    Her charms with the splendours of the South.
And the fierce old nations, looking on her,
    Said, 'Nay, surely she were quickly overthrown;
Hath she strength for the burden laid upon her,
    Hath she power to protect and guard her own?'

Then she spoke, and her voice was clear and ringing
    In the ears of the nations old and grey,
Saying, 'Hark, and ye shall hear my children sing
    Their war-song in countries far away.
They are strangers to the tumult of the battle,
    They are few, but their hearts are very strong,
'Twas but yesterday they called unto the cattle,
    But they now sing Australia's marching song.'

SONG OF THE AUSTRALIANS IN ACTION

For the honour of Australia, our Mother,
    Side by side with our kin from over sea,
We have fought and we have tested one another,
    And enrolled among the brotherhood are we.

There was never post of danger but we sought it
    In the fighting, through the fire, and through the flood.
There was never prize so costly but we bought it,
    Though we paid for its purchase with our blood.

Was there any road too rough for us to travel?
    Was there any path too far for us to tread?
You can track us by the blood drops on the gravel
    On the roads that we milestoned with our dead!

And for you. O our young and anxious mother,
    O'er your great gains keeping watch and ward,
Neither fearing nor despising any other,
    We will hold your possessions with the sword.

        *   *   *   *   *

Then they passed to the place of world-long sleeping,
    The grey-clad figures with their dead,
To the sound of their women softly weeping
    And the Dead March moaning at their head:

And the Nations, as the grim procession ended,
    Whispered, 'Child, thou has seen the price we pay;
From War may we ever be defended,
    Kneel thee down, new-made Sister -- Let us Pray!'

Old Australian Ways

The London lights are far abeam
   Behind a bank of cloud,
Along the shore the gaslights gleam
   The gale is piping loud;
And down the Channel, groping blind,
   We drive her through the haze
Towards the land we left behind –
The good old land of 'never mind',
   And old Australian ways.

The narrow ways of English folk
   Are not for such as we;
They bear the long-accustomed yoke
   Of staid conservancy:
But all our roads are new and strange,
   And through our blood there runs
The vagabonding love of change
That drove us westward of the range
   And westward of the suns.

The city folk go to and fro
   Behind a prison's bars,
They never feel the breezes blow
   And never see the stars;
They never hear in blossomed trees
   The music low and sweet
Of wild birds making melodies,
Nor catch the little laughing breeze
   That whispers in the wheat.

Our fathers came of roving stock
   That could not fixed abide:
And we have followed field and flock
   Since e'er we learnt to ride;
By miner's camp and shearing shed,
   In land of heat and drought,
We followed where our fortunes led,

With fortune always on ahead
   And always farther out.

The wind is in the barley-grass,
   The wattles are in bloom;
The breezes greet us as they pass
   With honey-sweet perfume;
The parakeets go screaming by
   With flash of golden wing,
And from the swamp the wild-ducks cry
Their long-drawn note of revelry,
   Rejoicing at the Spring.

So throw the weary pen aside
   And let the papers rest,
For we must saddle up and ride
   Towards the blue hill's breast:
And we must travel far and fast
   Across their rugged maze,
To find the Spring of Youth at last,
And call back from the buried past
   The old Australian ways.

When Clancy took the drover's track
   In years of long ago,
He drifted to the outer back
   Beyond the Overflow;
By rolling plain and rocky shelf,
   With stockwhip in his hand,
He reached at last (oh, lucky elf!)
The Town of Come-and-Help-Yourself
   In Rough-and-Ready Land.

And if it be that you would know
   The tracks he used to ride,
Then you must saddle up and go
   Beyond the Queensland side,
Beyond the reach of rule or law,
   To ride the long day through,
In Nature's homestead – filled with awe,
You then might see what Clancy saw
   And know what Clancy knew.

Ballad of the Calliope

By the far Samoan shore,
Where the league-long rollers pour
All the wash of the Pacific on the coral-guarded bay,
Riding lightly at their ease,
In the calm of tropic seas,
The three great nations' warships at their anchors proudly lay.

Riding lightly, head to wind,
With the coral reefs behind,
Three German and three Yankee ships were mirrored in the blue;
And on one ship unfurled
Was the flag that rules the world –
For on the old *Calliope* the flag of England flew.

When the gentle off-shore breeze,
That had scarcely stirred the trees,
Dropped down to utter stillness, and the glass began to fall,
Away across the main
Lowered the coming hurricane,
And far away to seaward hung the cloud-wrack like a pall.

If the word had passed around,
'Let us move to safer ground;
Let us steam away to seaward' – then this tale were not to tell!
But each Captain seemed to say
'If the others stay, I stay!'
And they lingered at their moorings till the shades of evening fell.

Then the cloud-wrack neared them fast,
And there came a sudden blast,
And the hurricane came leaping down a thousand miles of main!
Like a lion on its prey,
Leapt the storm fiend on the bay,
And the vessels shook and shivered as their cables felt the strain.

As the surging seas came by,
That were running mountains high,
The vessels started dragging, drifting slowly to the lee;
And the darkness of the night
Hid the coral reefs from sight,
And the Captains dared not risk the chance to grope their way to sea.

In the dark they dared not shift!
They were forced to wait and drift;
All hands stood by uncertain would the anchors hold or no.
But the men on deck could see,
If a chance for them might be,
There was little chance of safety for the men who were below.

Through that long, long night of dread,
While the storm raged overhead,
They were waiting by their engines, with the furnace fires aroar;
So they waited, staunch and true,
Though they knew, and well they knew,
They must drown like rats imprisoned if the vessel touched the shore.

When the grey dawn broke at last,
And the long, long night was past,
While the hurricane redoubled, lest its prey should steal away,
On the rocks, all smashed and strown,
Were the German vessels thrown,
While the Yankees, swamped and helpless, drifted shorewards down
the bay.

Then at last spoke Captain Kane,
'All our anchors are in vain,
And the Germans and the Yankees they have drifted to the lee!
Cut the cables at the bow!
We must trust the engines now!
Give her steam, and let her have it, lads! we'll fight her out to sea!'

And the answer came with cheers
From the stalwart engineers,
From the grim and grimy firemen at the furnaces below;
And above the sullen roar
Of the breakers on the shore
Came the throbbing of the engines as they laboured to and fro.

If the strain should find a flaw,
Should a bolt or rivet draw,
Then – God help them! for the vessel were a plaything in the tide!
With a face of honest cheer
Quoth an English engineer,
'I will answer for the engines that were built on old Thames-side!

'For the stays and stanchions taut,
For the rivets truly wrought,
For the valves that fit their faces as a glove should fit the hand.
Give her every ounce of power;
If we make a knot an hour
Then it's way enough to steer her, and we'll drive her from the land.'

Like a foam-flake tossed and thrown,
She could barely hold her own,
While the other ships all helplessly were drifting to the lee.
Through the smother and the rout
The *Calliope* steamed out –
And they cheered her from the *Trenton* that was foundering in the sea.

Ay! drifting shoreward there,
All helpless as they were,
Their vessel hurled upon the reefs as weed ashore is hurled,
Without a thought of fear
The Yankees raised a cheer –
A cheer that English-speaking folk should echo round the world.

Do They Know?

Do they know? At the turn to the straight
  Where the favourites fail,
And every last atom of weight
  Is telling its tale;
As some grim old stayer hard-pressed
  Runs true to his breed,
And with head just in front of the rest
  Fights on in the lead;
When the jockeys are out with the whips,
  With a furlong to go,
And the backers grow white to the lips –
  Do you think *they* don't know?

Do they know? As they come back to weigh
  In a whirlwind of cheers,
Though the spurs have left marks of the fray,
  Though the sweat on the ears
Gathers cold, and they sob with distress
  As they roll up the track,
They know just as well their success
  As the man on their back.
As they walk through a dense human lane
  That sways to and fro,
And cheers them again and again,
  Do you think *they* don't know?

Passing of Gundagai

'I'll introdooce a friend!' he said,
  'And if you've got a vacant pen
You'd better take him in the shed
And start him shearing straight ahead;
  He's one of these here quiet men.

'He never strikes – that ain't his game;
  No matter what the others try
He goes on shearing just the same.
I never rightly knew his name –
  We always call him "Gundagai!" '

Our flashest shearer then had gone
  To train a racehorse for a race;
And, while his sporting fit was on
He couldn't be relied upon,
  So Gundagai shore in his place.

Alas for man's veracity!
  For reputations false and true!
This Gundagai turned out to be
For strife and all-round villainy
  The very worst I ever knew!

He started racing Jack Devine,
  And grumbled when I made him stop.
The pace he showed was extra fine,
But all those pure-bred ewes of mine
  Were bleeding like a butcher's shop.

He cursed the sheep, he cursed the shed,
  From roof to rafter, floor to shelf:
As for my mongrel ewes, he said,
I ought to get a razor-blade
  And shave the blooming things myself.

On Sundays he controlled a 'school',
   And played 'two-up' the livelong day;
And many a young confiding fool
He shore of his financial wool;
   And when he lost he would not pay.

He organised a shearers' race,
   And 'touched' me to provide the prize.
His pack-horse showed surprising pace
And won hands down – he was The Ace,
   A well-known racehorse in disguise.

Next day the bruiser of the shed
   Displayed an opal-tinted eye,
With large contusions on his head,
He smiled a sickly smile, and said
   He'd 'had a cut at Gundagai!'

But, just as we were getting full
   Of Gundagai and all his ways,
A telegram for 'Henry Bull'
Arrived. Said he, 'That's me – all wool!
   Let's see what this here message says.'

He opened it; his face grew white,
   He dropped the shears and turned away.
It ran, 'Your wife took bad last night;
Come home at once – no time to write,
   We fear she may not last the day.'

He got his cheque – I didn't care
   To dock him for my mangled ewes;
His store account, we called it square,
Poor wretch! he had enough to bear,
   Confronted by such dreadful news.

The shearers raised a little purse
   To help a mate, as shearers will,
'To pay the doctor and the nurse.

And, if there should be something worse,
　To pay the undertaker's bill.'

They wrung his hand in sympathy,
　He rode away without a word,
His head hung down in misery . . .
A wandering hawker passing by
　Was told of what had just occurred.

'Well! that's a curious thing,' he said,
　'I've known that feller all his life –
He's had the loan of this here shed!
I know his wife ain't nearly dead,
　Because he *hasn't got a wife!*'

*　　*　　*　　*　　*

You should have heard the whipcord crack
　As angry shearers galloped by;
In vain they tried to fetch him back –
A little dust along the track
　Was all they saw of 'Gundagai'.

The Wargeilah Handicap

Wargeilah town is very small,
    There's no cathedral nor a club,
In fact the township, all in all,
    Is just one unpretentious pub;
And there, from all the stations round,
The local sportsmen can be found.

The sportsmen of Wargeilah-side
    Are very few but very fit:
There's scarcely any sport been tried
    But they can hold their own at it;
In fact, to search their records o'er,
They hold their own and something more.

The precincts of Wargeilah town
    An English new-chum did infest:
He used to wander up and down
    In baggy English breeches drest;
His mental aspect seemed to be
Just stolid self-sufficiency.

The local sportsmen vainly sought
    His tranquil calm to counteract
By urging that he should be brought
    Within the Noxious Creatures Act.
'Nay, harm him not,' said one more wise,
'He is a blessing in disguise!

'You see, he wants to buy a horse,
    To ride, and hunt, and steeplechase,
And carry ladies, too, of course,
    And pull a cart, and win a race.
Good gracious! he must be a flat
To think he'll get a horse like that!'

'But, since he has so little sense
    And such a lot of cash to burn,
We'll sell him some experience
    By which alone a fool can learn.
Suppose we let him have The Trap
To win Wargeilah Handicap!'

And here, I must explain to you
    That round about Wargeilah run
There lived a very aged screw
    Whose days of brilliancy were done:
A grand old warrior in his prime –
But age will beat us all in time.

A trooper's horse in seasons past
    He did his share to keep the peace,
But took to falling, and at last
    Was cast for age from the Police.
A publican at Conroy's Gap
Bought him and christened him The Trap.

When grass was good and horses dear,
    He changed his owner now and then
At prices ranging somewhere near
    The neighbourhood of two-pound-ten:
And manfully he earned his keep
By yarding cows and ration sheep.

They brought him in from off the grass
    And fed and groomed the old horse up;
His coat began to shine like glass –
    You'd think he'd win the Melbourne Cup.
And when they'd got him fat and flash
They asked the new-chum – fifty – cash!

And when he said the price was high,
    Their indignation knew no bounds.
They said, 'It's seldom you can buy
    A horse like that for fifty pounds!
We'll refund twenty if The Trap
Should fail to win the handicap!'

The deed was done, the price was paid,
   The new-chum put the horse in train.
The local sports were much afraid
   That he would sad experience gain
By racing with some shearer's hack,
Who'd beat him half-way round the track

So, on this guileless English spark
   They did most fervently impress
That he must keep the matter dark,
   And not let any person guess
That he was purchasing The Trap
To win Wargeilah Handicap.

They spoke of 'spielers from the Bland',
   And 'champions from the Castlereagh',
And gave the youth to understand
   That all of these would stop away,
And spoil the race, if they should hear
That they had got The Trap to fear.

'Keep dark! They'll muster thick as flies
   When once the news gets sent around
We're giving such a splendid prize –
   A Snowdon horse worth fifty pound!
They'll come right in from Dandaloo,
And find – that it's a gift to you!'

*   *   *   *   *

The race came on – with no display,
   Nor any calling of the card,
But round about the pub all day
   A crowd of shearers, drinking hard,
And using language in a strain
'Twere flattery to call profane.

Our hero, dressed in silk attire –
   Blue jacket and scarlet cap –
With boots that shone like flames of fire,
   Now did his canter on The Trap,
And walked him up and round about,
Until the other steeds came out.

He eyed them with a haughty look,
    But saw a sight that caught his breath!
It was Ah John! the Chinee cook!
    In boots and breeches! pale as death!
Tied with a rope, like any sack,
Upon a piebald pony's back!

The next, a colt – all mud and burrs,
    Half-broken, with a black boy up,
Who said, 'You gim'me pair o' spurs,
    I win the bloomin' Melbourne Cup!'
These two were to oppose The Trap
For the Wargeilah Handicap!

They're off! The colt whipped down his head,
    And humped his back, and gave a squeal,
And bucked into the drinking shed,
    Revolving like a Catherine wheel!
Men ran like rats! The atmosphere
Was filled with oaths and pints of beer!

But up the course the bold Ah John
    Beside The Trap raced neck and neck:
The boys had tied him firmly on,
    Which ultimately proved his wreck;
The saddle turned, and, like a clown,
He rode some distance upside-down.

His legs around the horse were tied,
    His feet towards the heavens were spread,
He swung and bumped at every stride
    And ploughed the ground up with his head!
And when they rescued him, The Trap
Had won Wargeilah Handicap!

And no enquiries we could make
    Could tell by what false statements swayed
Ah John was led to undertake
    A task so foreign to his trade!
He only smiled and said, 'Hoo Ki!
I stop topside, I win all li'!'

But never in Wargeilah Town
   Was heard so eloquent a cheer
As when the President came down,
   And toasted, in Colonial beer,
'The finest rider on the course!
The winner of the Snowdon Horse!

'You go and get your prize,' he said;
   'He's with a wild mob, somewhere round
The mountains near the Watershed;
   He's honestly worth fifty pound –
A noble horse, indeed, to win,
But none of *us* can run him in!

'We've chased him poor, we've chased him fat
   We've run him till our horses dropped;
But by such obstacles as that
   A man like you will not be stopped;
You'll go and yard him any day,
So here's your health! Hooray! Hooray!'

   *   *   *   *   *

The day wound up with booze and blow
   And fights till all were well content.
But of the new-chum all I know
   Is shown by this advertisement –
'For Sale, the well-known racehorse Trap.
He won Wargeilah Handicap!'

Any Other Time

All of us play our very best game –
    Any other time.
Golf or billiards, it's all the same –
    Any other time.
Lose a match and you always say,
'Just my luck! I was "off" today!
I could have beaten him quite half-way –
    Any other time!'

After a fiver you ought to go –
    Any other time.
Every man that you ask says 'Oh,
    Any *other* time.
Lend you a fiver? I'd lend you two,
But I'm overdrawn and my bills are due,
Wish you'd ask me – now, mind you do –
    Any other time!'

Fellows will ask you out to dine –
    Any other time.
'Not tonight for we're twenty-nine –
    Any other time.
Not tomorrow, for cook's on strike;
Not next day, I'll be out on the bike;
Just drop in whenever you like
    Any other time!'

Seasick passengers like the sea –
    Any other time.
'Something . . . I ate . . . disagreed . . . with . . . me!
    Any other time.
Ocean-travelling is . . . simply bliss,
Must be my . . . liver . . . has gone amiss . . .
Why, I would . . . laugh . . . at a sea . . . like this –
    Any other time!'

Most of us mean to be better men —
    Any other time:
Regular upright characters then —
    Any other time.
Yet somehow as the years go by
Still we gamble and drink and lie,
When it comes to the last we'll want to die —
    Any other time!

The Last Trump

'You led the trump,' the old man said
    With fury in his eye,
'And yet you hope my girl to wed!
Young man! your hopes of love are fled,
    'Twere better she should die!

'My sweet young daughter sitting there,
    So innocent and plump!
You don't suppose that she would care
To wed an outlawed man who'd dare
    To lead the thirteenth trump!

'If you had drawn their leading spade
    It meant a certain win!
But no! By Pembroke's mighty shade
The thirteenth trump you went and played
    And let their diamonds in!

'My girl, return at my command
    His presents in a lump!
Return his ring! For, understand,
No man is fit to hold your hand
    Who leads a thirteenth trump!

'But hold! Give every man his due
  And every dog his day.
Speak up and say what made you do
This dreadful thing – that is, if you
  Have anything to say!'

He spoke. 'I meant at first,' said he
  'To give their spades a bump,
Or lead the hearts; but then you see
I thought against us there might be
  Perhaps, a fourteenth trump!'

*   *   *   *   *

They buried him at dawn of day
  Beside a ruined stump:
And there he sleeps the hours away
And waits for Gabriel to play
  The last – the fourteenth trump.

Tar and Feathers

Oh! the circus swooped down
  On the Narrabri town,
For the Narrabri populace moneyed are;
    And the showman he smiled
    At the folk he beguiled
To come all the distance from Gunnedah.

But a juvenile smart,
  Who objected to 'part',
Went in on the nod, and to do it he
    Crawled in through a crack
    In the tent at the back,
For the boy had no slight ingenuity.

And says he with a grin,
    'That's the way to get in;
But I reckon I'd better be quiet or
    They'll spiflicate me,'
    And he chuckled, for he
Had the loan of the circus proprietor.

    But the showman astute
    On that wily galoot
Soon dropped – you'll be thinking he leathered him –
    Not he; with a grim
    Sort of humorous whim,
He took him and tarred him and feathered him.

    Says he, 'You can go
    Round the world with a show,
And knock every Injun and Arab wry;
    With your name and your trade
    On the posters displayed,
The feathered what-is-it from Narrabri.'

    Next day for his freak
    By a Narrabri Beak,
He was jawed with a deal of verbosity;
    For his only appeal
    Was 'professional zeal' –
He wanted another monstrosity.

    Said his Worship, 'Begob!
    You are fined forty bob,
And six shillin's costs to the clurk!' he says.
    And the Narrabri joy,
    Half bird and half boy,
Has a 'down' on himself and on circuses.

It's Grand

It's grand to be a squatter
    And sit upon a post,
And watch your little ewes and lambs
    A-giving up the ghost.

It's grand to be a 'cockie'
    With wife and kids to keep,
And find an all-wise Providence
    Has mustered all your sheep.

It's grand to be a Western man,
    With a shovel in your hand,
To dig your little homestead out
    From underneath the sand.

It's grand to be a shearer
    Along the Darling-side,
And pluck the wool from stinking sheep
    That some days since have died.

It's grand to be a rabbit
    And breed till all is blue,
And then to die in heaps because
    There's nothing left to chew.

It's grand to be a Minister
    And travel like a swell,
And tell the Central District folk
    To go to – Inverell.

It's grand to be a socialist
    And lead the bold array
That marches to prosperity
    At seven bob a day.

It's grand to be an unemployed
    And lie in the Domain,
And wake up every second day --
    And go to sleep again.

It's grand to borrow English tin
    To pay for wharves and docks,
And then to find it isn't in
    The little money-box.

It's grand to be a democrat
    And toady to the mob,
For fear that if you told the truth
    They'd hunt you from your job.

It's grand to be a lot of things
    In this fair Southern land,
But if the Lord would send us rain,
    That would, indeed, be grand!

Out of Sight

They held a polo meeting at a little country town,
And all the local sportsmen came to win themselves renown.
There came two strangers with a horse, and I am much afraid
They both belonged to what is called 'the take-you-down brigade'.

They said their horse could jump like fun, and asked an amateur
To ride him in the steeplechase, and told him they were sure
The last time round he'd sail away with such a swallow's flight
The rest would never see him go – he'd finish out of sight.

So out he went; and, when folk saw the amateur was up,
Some local genius called the race 'the Dude-in-Danger Cup'.
The horse was known as 'Who's Afraid', by 'Panic' from 'The
       Fright' –
But still his owners told the jock he'd finish out of sight.

And so he did; for Who's Afraid, without the least pretence,
Disposed of him by rushing through the very second fence;
And when they ran the last time round the prophecy was right –
For he was in the ambulance, and safely 'out of sight'.

The Road to Old Man's Town

The fields of youth are filled with flowers,
The wine of youth is strong:
What need have we to count the hours?
The summer days are long.

But soon we find to our dismay
That we are drifting down
The barren slopes that fall away
Towards the foothills grim and grey
That lead to Old Man's Town.

And marching with us on the track
Full many friends we find:
We see them looking sadly back
For those who've dropped behind.

But God forfend a fate so dread –
Alone to travel down
The dreary road we all must tread,
With faltering steps and whitening head,
The road to Old Man's Town!

The Old Timer's Steeplechase

The sheep were shorn and the wool went down
    At the time of our local racing;
And I'd earned a spell – I was burnt and brown –
So I rolled my swag for a trip to town
    And a look at the steeplechasing.

'Twas rough and ready – an uncleared course
    As rough as the blacks had found it;
With barbed-wire fences, topped with gorse,
And a water-jump that would drown a horse,
    And the steeple three times round it.

There was never a fence the tracks to guard, –
    Some straggling posts defined 'em :
And the day was hot, and the drinking hard,
Till none of the stewards could see a yard
    Before nor yet behind 'em!

But the bell was rung and the nags were out,
    Excepting an old outsider
Whose trainer started an awful rout,
For his boy had gone on a drinking bout
    And left him without a rider.

'Is there not a man in the crowd,' he cried,
    'In the whole of the crowd so clever,
Is there not one man that will take a ride
On the old white horse from the Northern side
    That was bred on the Mooki River?'

'Twas an old white horse that they called The Cow,
    And a cow would look well beside him;
But I was pluckier then than now
(And I wanted excitement anyhow),
    So at last I agreed to ride him.

And the trainer said, 'Well, he's dreadful slow,
    And he hasn't a chance whatever;
But I'm stony broke, so it's time to show
A trick or two that the trainers know
    Who train by the Mooki River.

'The first time round at the further side,
    With the trees and the scrub about you,
Just pull behind them and run out wide
And then dodge into the scrub and hide,
    And let them go round without you.

'At the third time round, for the final spin
    With the pace and the dust to blind 'em ,
They'll never notice if you chip in
For the last half-mile – you'll be sure to win,
    And they'll think you raced behind 'em .

'At the water-jump you may have to swim –
    He hasn't a hope to clear it,
Unless he skims like the swallows skim
At full speed over – but not for him!
    He'll never go next or near it.

'But don't you worry – just plunge across,
    For he swims like a well-trained setter.
Then hide away in the scrub and gorse
The rest will be far ahead, of course –
    The further ahead the better.

'You must rush the jumps in the last half-round
    For fear that he might refuse 'em ;
He'll try to baulk with you, I'll be bound;
Take whip and spurs to the mean old hound,
    And don't be afraid to use 'em .

'At the final round, when the field are slow
    And you are quite fresh to meet 'em ,
Sit down, and hustle him all you know
With the whip and spurs, and he'll have to go –
    Remember, you've *got* to beat 'em!'

            *   *   *   *   *

The flag went down, and we seemed to fly,
   And we made the timbers shiver
Of the first big fence, as the stand flashed by,
And I caught the ring of the trainer's cry:
   'Go on, for the Mooki River!'

I jammed him in with a well-packed crush,
   And recklessly – out for slaughter –
Like a living wave over fence and brush
We swept and swung with a flying rush,
   Till we came to the dreaded water.

Ha, ha! I laugh at it now to think
   Of the way I contrived to work it.
Shut in amongst them, before you'd wink,
He found himself on the water's brink,
   With never a chance to shirk it!

The thought of the horror he felt beguiles
   The heart of this grizzled rover!
He gave a snort you could hear for miles,
And a spring would have cleared the Channel Isles,
   And carried me safely over!

Then we neared the scrub, and I pulled him back
   In the shade where the gum-leaves quiver:
And I waited there in the shadows black
While the rest of the horses, round the track,
   Went on like a rushing river!

At the second round, as the field swept by,
   I saw that the pace was telling;
But on they thundered, and by-and-by
As they passed the stand I could hear the cry
   Of the folk in the distance, yelling!

Then the last time round! And the hoofbeats rang
   And I said, 'Well, it's now or never!'
And out on the heels of the throng I sprang,
And the spurs bit deep and the whipcord sang
   As I rode. For the Mooki River!

We raced for home in a cloud of dust
    And the curses rose in chorus.
'Twas flog, and hustle, and jump you must!
And The Cow ran well – but to my disgust
    There was one got home before us.

'Twas a big black horse, that I had not seen
    In the part of the race I'd ridden;
And his coat was cool and his rider clean –
And I thought that perhaps I had not been
    The only one that had hidden.

And the trainer came with a visage blue
    With rage, when the race concluded:
Said he, 'I thought you'd have pulled us through,
But the man on the black horse planted too,
    And nearer to home than you did!'

      *   *   *   *   *

Alas to think that those times so gay
    Have vanished and passed for ever!
You don't believe in the yarn, you say?
Why, man, 'twas a matter of every day
    When we raced on the Mooki River!

In the Stable

What! You don't like him; well, maybe – we all have our fancies,
    of course:
Brumby to look at, you reckon? Well, no; he's a thoroughbred
    horse;
Sired by a son of old Panic – look at his ears and his head –
Lop-eared and Roman-nosed, ain't he? – well, that's how the
    Panics are bred.
Gluttonous, ugly and lazy, rough as a tip-cart to ride,
Yet if you offered a sovereign apiece for the hairs on his hide
That wouldn't buy him, nor twice that; while I've a pound to the
    good,
This here old stager stays by me and lives like a thoroughbred
    should;
Hunt him away from his bedding, and sit yourself down by the wall,
Till you hear how the old fellow saved me from Gilbert, O'Meally
    and Hall.

          *   *   *   *   *

Gilbert and Hall and O'Meally, back in the bushranging days,
Made themselves kings of the district – ruled it in old-fashioned
    ways –
Robbing the coach and the escort, stealing our horses at night,
Calling sometimes at the homesteads and giving the women a
    fright:
Came to the station one morning (and why they did this no one
    knows),
Took a brood mare from the paddock – wanting some fun, I
    suppose –
Fastened a bucket beneath her, hung by a strap around her flank,
Then turned her loose in the timber back of the seven-mile tank.

Go? She went mad! She went tearing and screaming with fear
    through the trees,
While the curst bucket beneath her was banging her flanks and
    her knees.
Bucking and racing and screaming she ran to the back of the run,
Killed herself there in a gully; by God, but they paid for their fun!

Paid for it dear, for the black-boys found tracks, and the bucket, and all,
And I swore that I'd live to get even with Gilbert, O'Meally and Hall.

Day after day then I chased them – 'course they had friends on the sly,
Friends who were willing to sell them to those who were willing to buy.
Early one morning we found them in camp at the Cockatoo Farm;
One of us shot at O'Meally and wounded him under the arm:
Ran them for miles in the ranges, till Hall, with his horse fairly beat,
Took to the rocks and we lost him – the others made good their retreat.

It was war to the knife then, I tell you, and once, on the door of my shed,
They nailed up a notice that offered a hundred reward for my head!
Then we heard they were gone from the district; they stuck up a coach in the West,
And I rode by myself in the paddocks, just taking a bit of a rest,
Riding this colt as a youngster – awkward, half-broken and shy,
He wheeled round one day on a sudden; I looked, but I couldn't see why –
But I soon found out why, for before me the hillside rose up like a wall,
And there on the top with their rifles were Gilbert, O'Meally and Hall!

'Twas a good three-mile run to the homestead – bad going, with plenty of trees –
So I gathered the youngster together, and gripped at his ribs with my knees.
'Twas a mighty poor chance to escape them! It puts a man's nerve to the test
On a half-broken colt to be hunted by the best mounted men in the West.
But the half-broken colt was a racehorse! He lay down to work with a will.
Flashed through the scrub like a clean-skin – by heavens, we *flew* down the hill!

Over a twenty-foot gully he swept with the spring of a deer,
And they fired as we jumped, but they missed me – a bullet sang
    close to my ear –
And the jump gained us ground, for they shirked it: but I saw as we
    raced through the gap
That the rails at the homestead were fastened – I was caught like a
    rat in a trap.
Fenced with barbed wire was the paddock – barbed wire that
    would cut like a knife –
How was a youngster to clear it that never had jumped in his life?

Bang went a rifle behind me – the colt gave a spring, he was hit;
Straight at the sliprails I rode him – I felt him take hold of the bit;
Never a foot to the right or the left did he swerve in his stride,
Awkward and frightened, but honest, the sort it's a pleasure to ride!
Straight at the rails, where they'd fastened barbed wire on the top
    of the post,
Rose like a stag and went over, with hardly a scratch at the most;
Into the homestead I darted, and snatched down my gun from the
    wall,
And I tell you I made them step lively, Gilbert, O'Meally and Hall.

Yes! There's the mark of the bullet – he's got it inside of him yet,
Mixed up somehow with his victuals; but, bless you, he don't seem
    to fret!
Gluttonous, ugly, and lazy – eats anything he can bite;
Now, let us shut up the stable, and bid the old fellow good night.
Ah! we can't breed 'em , the sort that were bred when we old uns
    were young . . .
Yes, as I said, these bushrangers, none of 'em lived to be hung.
Gilbert was shot by the troopers, Hall was betrayed by his friend,
Campbell disposed of O'Meally, bringing the lot to an end.
But you can talk about riding – I've ridden a lot in the past –
Wait till there's rifles behind you, you'll know what it means to go
    fast!
I've steeplechased, raced, and 'run horses', but I think the most
    dashing of all
Was the ride when that old fellow saved me from Gilbert, O'Meally
    and Hall!

'He Giveth His Beloved Sleep'

The long day passes with its load of sorrow:
  In slumber deep
I lay me down to rest until tomorrow –
  Thank God for sleep.

Thank God for all respite from weary toiling,
  From cares that creep
Across our lives like evil shadows, spoiling
  God's kindly sleep.

We plough and sow, and, as the hours grow later,
  We strive to reap,
And build our barns, and hope to build them greater
  Before we sleep.

We toil and strain and strive with one another
  In hopes to heap
Some greater share of profit than our brother
  Before we sleep.

What will it profit that with tears or laughter
  Our watch we keep?
Beyond it all there lies the Great Hereafter!
  Thank God for sleep!

For, at the last, beseeching Christ to save us,
  We turn with deep
Heart-felt thanksgiving unto God, who gave us
  The Gift of Sleep.

Driver Smith

'Twas Driver Smith of Battery A was anxious to see a fight;
He thought of the Transvaal all the day, he thought of it all the
           night –
'Well, if the battery's left behind, I'll go to the war,' says he,
'I'll go a-driving an ambulance in the ranks of the A.M.C.

'I'm fairly sick of these here parades – it's want of a change that
           kills –
A-charging the Randwick Rifle Range and aiming at Surry Hills.
And I think if I go with the ambulance I'm certain to find a show,
For they have to send the Medical men wherever the troops can
           go.

'Wherever the rifle bullets flash and the Maxims raise a din,
It's here you'll find the Medical men a-raking the wounded
           in –
A-raking 'em in like human flies – and a driver smart like me
Will find some scope for his extra skill in the ranks of the A.M.C.'

So Driver Smith he went to the war a-cracking his driver's whip,
From ambulance to collecting base they showed him his regular
           trip.
And he said to the boys that were marching past, as he gave his
           whip a crack,
'You'll walk yourselves to the fight,' says he – 'Lord spare me, I'll
           drive you back.'

Now, the fight went on in the Transvaal hills for the half of a day
           or more,
And Driver Smith he worked his trip – all aboard for the seat of
           war!
He took his load from the stretcher men and hurried 'em
           homeward fast
  Till he heard a sound that he knew full well – a battery rolling
           past.

He heard the clink of the leading chains and the roll of the guns
     behind –
He heard the crack of the drivers' whips, and he says to 'em ,
     'Strike me blind,
I'll miss me trip with this ambulance, although I don't care to
     shirk,
But I'll take the car off the line today and follow the guns at
     work.'
Then up the Battery Colonel came a-cursing 'em black in the
     face.
'Sit down and shift 'em , you drivers there, and gallop 'em into
     place.'
So off the Battery rolled and swung, a-going a merry dance,
And holding his own with the leading gun goes Smith with his
     ambulance.

They opened fire on the mountain side, a-peppering by and
     large,
When over the hill above their flank the Boers came down at the
     charge;
They rushed the guns with a daring rush, a-volleying left and
     right,
And Driver Smith and his ambulance moved up to the edge of
     the fight.

The gunners stuck to their guns like men, and fought as the
     wild cats fight,
For a Battery man don't leave his gun with ever a hope in sight;
But the bullets sang and the Mausers cracked and the Battery
     men gave way,
Till Driver Smith with his ambulance drove into the thick of the
     fray.

He saw the head of the Transvaal troop a-thundering to and fro,
A hard old face with a monkey beard – a face that he seemed to
     know;
'Now, who's that leader?' said Driver Smith. 'I've seen him
     before today.
Why, bless my heart, but it's Kruger's self,' and he jumped for
     him straight away.

He collared old Kruger round the waist and hustled him into
the van.
It wasn't according to stretcher drill for raising a wounded
man;
But he forced him in and said, 'All aboard, we're off for a little
ride,
And you'll have the car to yourself,' says he, 'I reckon we're
full inside.'

He wheeled his team on the mountain side and set 'em a
merry pace,
A-galloping over the rocks and stones, and a lot of the Boers
gave chase;
But Driver Smith had a fairish start, and he said to the Boers,
'Good-day,
You have Buckley's chance for to catch a man that was trained
in Battery A.'

He drove his team to the hospital and said to the P.M.O.,
'Beg pardon, sir, but I missed a trip, mistaking the way to go;
And Kruger came to the ambulance and asked could we spare
a bed,
So I fetched him here, and we'll take him home to show for a
bob a head.'

So the word went round to the English troops to say they need
fight no more,
For Driver Smith with his ambulance had ended the blooming
war.
And in London now at the music halls he's starring it every
night,
And drawing a hundred pounds a week to tell how he won the
fight.

There's Another Blessed Horse Fell Down

When you're lying in your hammock, sleeping soft and
          sleeping sound,
    Without a care or trouble on your mind,
And there's nothing to disturb you but the engines going
          round,
    And you're dreaming of the girl you left behind;
In the middle of your joys you'll be wakened by a noise
    And a clatter on the deck above your crown,
And you'll hear the corporal shout as he turns the picket
          out,
    'There's another blessed horse fell down.'

You can see 'em in the morning, when you're cleaning
          out the stall,
    A-leaning on the railings nearly dead,
And you reckon by the evening they'll be pretty sure to
          fall,
    And you curse them as you tumble into bed.
Oh, you'll hear it pretty soon, 'Pass the word for Denny
          Moon,
    There's a horse here throwing handsprings like a
          clown;'
And it's shove the others back, or he'll cripple half the
          pack;
    'There's another blessed horse fell down.'

And when the war is over and the fighting all is done,
    And you're all at home with medals on your chest,
And you've learnt to sleep so soundly that the firing of a
          gun
    At your bedside wouldn't rob you of your rest;
As you lay in slumber deep, if your wife walks in her
          sleep,
    And tumbles down the stairs and breaks her crown,
Oh, it won't awaken you, for you'll say, 'It's nothing new,
    It's another blessed horse fell down.'

On the Trek

Oh, the weary, weary journey on the trek, day after day,
  With sun above and silent veldt below;
And our hearts keep turning homeward to the youngsters far
      away
  And the homestead where the climbing roses grow.
Shall we see the flats grow golden with the ripening of the
      grain?
  Shall we hear the parrots calling on the bough?
Ah! the weary months of marching ere we hear them call
      again
  For we're going on a long job now.

In the drowsy days on escort, riding slowly half asleep,
  With the endless line of waggons stretching back,
While the khaki soldiers travel like a mob of travelling
      sheep,
  Plodding silent on the never-ending track,
While the constant snap and sniping of the foe you never
      see
  Makes you wonder will your turn come – when and how?
As the Mauser ball hums past you like a vicious kind of bee –
  Oh! we're going on a long job now.

When the dash and the excitement and the novelty are dead,
  And you've seen a load of wounded once or twice,
Or you've watched your old mate dying, with the vultures
      over-head –
  Well, you wonder if the war is worth the price.
And down along the Monaro now they're starting out to
      shear,
  I can picture the excitement and the row;
But they'll miss me on the Lachlan when they call the roll
      this year,
  For we're going on a long job now.

The Last Parade

With never a sound of trumpet,
   With never a flag displayed,
The last of the old campaigners
   Lined up for the last parade.

Weary they were and battered,
   Shoeless, and knocked about;
From under their ragged forelocks
   Their hungry eyes looked out.

And they watched as the old commander
   Read out to the cheering men
The Nation's thanks, and the orders
   To carry them home again.

And the last of the old campaigners,
   Sinewy, lean, and spare –
He spoke for his hungry comrades:
   'Have we not done our share?

'Starving and tired and thirsty
   We limped on the blazing plain;
And after a long night's picket
   You saddled us up again.

'We froze on the wind-swept kopjes
   When the frost lay snowy-white,
Never a halt in the daytime,
   Never a rest at night!

'We knew when the rifles rattled
   From the hillside bare and brown,
And over our weary shoulders
   We felt warm blood run down,

'As we turned for the stretching gallop,
  Crushed to the earth with weight;
But we carried our riders through it –
  Sometimes, perhaps, too late.

'Steel! We were steel to stand it –
  We that have lasted through,
We that are old campaigners
  Pitiful, poor, and few.

'Over the sea you brought us,
  Over the leagues of foam:
Now we have served you fairly
  Will you not take us home?

'Home to the Hunter River,
  To the flats where the lucerne grows;
Home where the Murrumbidgee
  Runs white with the melted snows.

'This is a small thing, surely!
  Will not you give command
That the last of the old campaigners
  Go back to their native land?'

        *   *   *   *   *

They looked at the grim commander.
  But never a sign he made.
'Dismiss!' and the old campaigners
  Moved off from their last parade.

Johnny Boer

Men fight all shapes and sizes as the racing horses run,
And no man knows his courage till he stands before a gun.
At mixed-up fighting, hand to hand, and clawing men about
They reckon Fuzzy-Wuzzy is the hottest fighter out.
But Fuzzy gives himself away – his style is out of date,
He charges like a driven grouse that rushes on its fate;
You've nothing in the world to do but pump him full of
      lead:
But when you're fighting Johnny Boer you have to use your
      head;
He don't believe in front attacks or charging at the run,
He fights you from a kopje with his little Maxim gun.

For when the Lord He made the earth, it seems uncommon
      clear,
He gave the job of Africa to some good engineer,
Who started building fortresses on fashions of his own –
Lunettes, redoubts, and counterscarps all made of rock and
      stone.
The Boer need only bring a gun, for ready to his hand
He finds these heaven-built fortresses all scattered through
      the land;
And there he sits and winks his eye and wheels his gun
      about,
And we must charge across the plain to hunt the beggar out.
It ain't a game that grows on us – there's lots of better fun
Than charging at old Johnny with his little Maxim gun.

On rocks a goat could scarcely climb, steep as the walls of
      Troy,
He wheels a four-point-seven about as easy as a toy;
With bullocks yoked and drag-ropes manned, he lifts her up
      the rocks
And shifts her every now and then, as cunning as a fox.
At night you mark her right ahead, you see her clean and
      clear,

Next day at dawn – 'What, ho! she bumps' – from
    somewhere in the rear.
Or else the keenest-eyed patrol will miss him with the
    glass –
He's lying hidden in the rocks to let the leaders pass;
But when the mainguard comes along he opens up the fun;
There's lots of ammunition for the little Maxim gun.

But after all the job is sure, although the job is slow.
We have to see the business through, the Boer has got to go.
With Nordenfeldt and lyddite shell it's certain, soon or late,
We'll hunt him from his kopjes and across the Orange State;
And then across those open flats you'll see the beggar run,
And we'll be running after him with *our* little Maxim gun.

Right in Front of the Army

'Where 'ave you been this week or more,
'Aven't seen you about the war?
Thought perhaps you was at the rear
Guarding the waggons.' 'What, us? No fear!
Where have we been? Why, bless my heart,
Where have we been since the bloomin' start?
    Right in the front of the army,
        Battling day and night!
    Right in the front of the army,
        Teaching 'em how to fight!'
    Every separate man you see,
    Sapper, gunner, and C.I.V.,
    Every one of 'em seems to be
    Right in the front of the army!

Most of the troops to the camp had gone,
When we met with a cow-gun toiling on;
And we said to the boys, as they walked her past,
'Well, thank goodness, you're here at last!'
'Here at last! Why, what d'yer mean?

Ain't we just where we've always been?
　　　Right in the front of the army,
　　　　Battling day and night!
　　　Right in the front of the army,
　　　　Teaching 'em how to fight!'
　　　Correspondents and Vets in force,
　　　Mounted foot and dismounted horse,
　　　All of them were, as a matter of course,
　　　Right in the front of the army.

Old Lord Roberts will have to mind
If ever the enemy get behind;
For they'll smash him up with a rear attack,
Because his army has got no back!
Think of the horrors that might befall
An army without any rear at all!
　　　Right in the front of the army,
　　　　Battling day and night!
　　　Right in the front of the army,
　　　　Teaching 'em how to fight!
　　　Swede attaches and German counts,
　　　Yeomen (known as De Wet's Remounts),
　　　All of them were, by their own accounts,
　　　Right in the front of the army!

That V.C.

'Twas in the days of front attack;
　　This glorious truth we'd yet to learn it –
That every 'front' has got a back.
　　And French was just the man to turn it.

A wounded soldier on the ground
　　Was lying hid behind a hummock;
He proved the good old proverb sound –
　　An army travels on its stomach.

He lay as flat as any fish;
   His nose had worn a little furrow;
He only had one frantic wish,
   That like an ant-bear he could burrow.

The bullets whistled into space,
   The pom-pom gun kept up its braying,
The four-point-seven supplied the bass –
   You'd think the devil's band was playing.

A valiant comrade crawling near
   Observed his most supine behaviour,
And crept towards him; 'Hey! what cheer?
   Buck up,' said he, 'I've come to save yer.

'You get up on my shoulders, mate,
   And, if we live beyond the firing,
I'll get the V.C. sure as fate,
   Because our blokes is all retiring.

'It's fifty pound a year,' says he,
   'I'll stand you lots of beer and whisky.'
'No,' says the wounded man, 'not me,
   I'll not be saved – it's far too risky.

'I'm fairly safe behind this mound,
   I've worn a hole that seems to fit me;
But if you lift me off the ground
   It's fifty pounds to one they'll hit me.'

So back towards the firing-line
   Our friend crept slowly to the rear-oh!
Remarking 'What a selfish swine!
   He might have let me be a hero.'

Jock

There's a soldier that's been doing of his share
   In the fighting up and down and round about.
He's continually marching here and there,
   And he's fighting, morning in and morning out.
The Boer, you see, he generally runs;
   But sometimes, when he hides behind a rock,
And we can't make no impression with the guns,
   Oh, then you'll hear the order, 'Send for Jock!'

   Yes – it's Jock – Scotch Jock.
   He's the fellow that can give or take a knock.
   For he's hairy and he's hard,
   And his feet are by the yard,
   And his face is like the face what's on a clock.
   But when the bullets fly you will mostly hear the cry –
   'Send for Jock!'

The Cavalry have gun and sword and lance;
   Before they choose their weapon, why, they're dead.
The Mounted Foot are hampered in advance
   By holding of their helmets on their head.
And, when the Boer has dug himself a trench
   And placed his Maxim gun behind a rock,
These mounted heroes – pets of Johnny French –
   They have to sit and wait and send for Jock!

   Yes, the Jocks – Scotch Jocks,
   With their music that'd terrify an ox!
   When the bullets kick the sand
   You can hear the sharp command –
   'Forty-Second! At the double! Charge the rocks!'
   And the charge is like a flood
   When they warmed the Highland blood
   Of the Jocks!

Santa Claus

Halt! Who goes there?' The sentry's call
Rose on the midnight air
Above the noises of the camp,
The roll of wheels, the horses' tramp.
The challenge echoed over all –
'Halt! Who goes there?'

A quaint old figure clothed in white,
He bore a staff of pine,
An ivy-wreath was on his head.
'Advance, O friend,' the sentry said,
'Advance, for this is Christmas Night,
And give the countersign.'

'No sign nor countersign have I.
Through many lands I roam
The whole world over far and wide.
To exiles all at Christmastide
From those who love them tenderly
I bring a thought of home.

'From English brook and Scottish burn.
From cold Canadian snows,
From those far lands ye hold most dear
I bring you all a greeting here,
A frond of a New Zealand fern,
A bloom of English rose.

'From faithful wife and loving lass
I bring a wish divine,
For Christmas blessings on your head.
'I wish you well,' the sentry said,
'But here, alas! you may not pass
Without the countersign.'

He vanished – and the sentry's tramp
Re-echoed down the line.
It was not till the morning light
The soldiers knew that in the night
Old Santa Claus had come to camp
Without the countersign.

SALTBUSH BILL, J.P. AND OTHER VERSES

Song of the Wheat

We have sung the song of the droving days,
    Of the march of the travelling sheep –
How by silent stages and lonely ways
    Thin, white battalions creep.
But the man who now by the land would thrive
    Must his spurs to a ploughshare beat;
And the bush bard, changing his tune, may strive
    To sing the song of the Wheat!

It's west by south of the Great Divide
    The grim grey plains run out,
Where the old flock-masters lived and died
    In a ceaseless fight with drought.
Weary with waiting and hope deferred
    They were ready to own defeat,
Till at last they heard the master-word –
    And the master-word was Wheat.

Yarran and Myall and Box and Pine –
    'Twas axe and fire for all;
They scarce could tarry to blaze the line
    Or wait for the trees to fall
Ere the team was yoked, and the gates flung wide,
    And the dust of the horses' feet
Rose up like a pillar of smoke to guide
    The wonderful march of Wheat.

Furrow by furrow, and fold by fold,
    The soil is turned on the plain;
Better than silver and better than gold
    Is the surface-mine of the grain.
Better than cattle and better than sheep
    In the fight with drought and heat;
For a streak of stubbornness, wide and deep,
    Lies hid in a grain of Wheat.

When the stock is swept by the hand of fate,
    Deep down on his bed of clay
The brave brown Wheat will die and wait
    For the resurrection day –
Lie hid while the whole world thinks him dead;
    But the Spring-rain, soft and sweet,
Will over the steaming paddocks spread
    The first green flush of the Wheat.

Green and amber and gold it grows
    When the sun sinks late in the West;
And the breeze sweeps over the rippling rows
    Where the quail and the skylark nest.
Mountain or river or shining star,
    There's never a sight can beat –
Away to the sky-line stretching far –
    A sea of the ripening Wheat.

When the burning harvest sun sinks low,
    And shadows stretch on the plain,
The roaring strippers come and go
    Like ships on a sea of grain.
Till the lurching, groaning waggons bear
    Their tale of the load complete.
Of the world's great work he has done his share
    Who has garnered a crop of wheat.

Princes, Potentates, Kings and Czars,
    They travel in regal state,
But old King Wheat has a thousand cars
    For his trip to the water-gate;
And his thousand steamships breast the tide
    And plough through the wind and sleet
To the lands where the teeming millions bide
    That say: 'Thank God for Wheat!'

Brumby's Run

Brumby is the Aboriginal word for a wild horse. At a recent trial a New South Wales Supreme Court Judge, hearing of Brumby horses, asked: 'Who is Brumby, and where is his Run?'

It lies beyond the Western Pines
    Beneath the sinking sun,
And not a survey mark defines
    The bounds of 'Brumby's Run'.

On odds and ends of mountain land,
    On tracks of range and rock
Where no one else can make a stand
    Old Brumby rears his stock.

A wild, unhandled lot they are
    Of every shape and breed.
They venture out 'neath moon and star
    Along the flats to feed;

But, when the dawn makes pink the sky
    And steals along the plain,
The Brumby horses turn and fly
    Back to the hills again.

The traveller by the mountain-track
    May hear their hoof-beats pass,
And catch a glimpse of brown and black
    Dim shadows on the grass.

The eager stock-horse pricks his ears,
    And lifts his head on high
In wild excitement, when he hears
    The Brumby mob go by.

Old Brumby asks no price or fee
   O'er all his wide domains:
The man who yards his stock is free
   To keep them for his pains.

So, off to scour the mountain side
   With eager eyes aglow,
To strongholds where the wild mobs hide
   The gully-rakers go.

A rush of horses through the trees,
   A red shirt making play;
A sound of stockwhips on the breeze,
   They vanish far away!

     *   *   *   *   *

Ah, me! before our day is done
   We long with bitter pain
To ride once more on Brumby's Run
   And yard his mob again.

Saltbush Bill on the Patriarchs

Come all you little rouseabouts and climb upon my knee;
Today, you see, is Christmas Day, and so it's up to me
To give you some instruction like – a kind of Christmas tale –
So name your yarn, and off she goes. What, 'Jonah and the
      Whale?'

Well, whales is sheep I've never shore; I've never been to sea,
So all them great Leviathans is mysteries to me;
But there's a tale the Bible tells I fully understand,
About the time the Patriarchs were settling on the land.

Those Patriarchs of olden time, when all is said and done,
They lived the same as far-out men on many a Queensland run –
A lot of roving, droving men who drifted to and fro,
The same we did out Queensland way a score of years ago.

Now Isaac was a squatter man, and Jacob was his son,
And when the boy grew up, you see, he wearied of the run.
You know the way that boys grow up – there's some that stick at
      home;
But any boy that's worth his salt will roll his swag and roam.

So Jacob caught the roving fit and took the drovers' track
To where his uncle had a run, beyond the outer back;
You see they made for out-back runs for room to stretch and
      grow,
The same we did out Queensland way a score of years ago.

Now, Jacob knew the ways of stock – that's most uncommon
      clear –
For, when he got to Laban's Run, they made him overseer;
He didn't ask a pound a week, but bargained for his pay
To take the roan and strawberry calves – the same we'd take
      today.

The duns and blacks and 'Goulburn roans' (that's brindles),
      coarse and hard,
He branded them with Laban's brand, in Old Man Laban's yard;
So, when he'd done the station work for close on seven year,
Why, all the choicest stock belonged to Laban's overseer.

It's often so with overseers – I've seen the same thing done
By many a Queensland overseer on many a Queensland run.
But when the mustering time came on old Laban acted straight,
And gave him country of his own outside the boundary gate.

He gave him stock, and offered him his daughter's hand in troth;
And Jacob first he married one, and then he married both;
You see, they weren't particular about a wife or so –
No more were we up Queensland way a score of years ago.

But when the stock were strong and fat with grass and lots of rain,
Then Jacob felt the call to take the homeward track again.
It's strange in every creed and clime, no matter where you roam,
There comes a day when every man would like to make for
      home.

So off he set with sheep and goats, a mighty moving band,
To battle down the dusty road along the Overland –
It's droving mixed-up mobs like that that makes men cut their
      throats,
I've travelled rams, which Lord forget, but never travelled goats.

But Jacob knew the ways of stock, for (so the story goes)
When battling through the Philistines – selectors, I suppose –
He thought he'd have to fight his way, an awkward sort of job;
So what did Old Man Jacob do? Of course, he split the mob.

He sent the strong stock on ahead to battle out the way;
He couldn't hurry lambing ewes – no more you could today –
And down the road from run to run, his hand 'gainst every
      hand,
He moved that mighty mob of stock across the Overland.

The thing is made so clear and plain, so solid in and out,
There isn't any room at all for any kind of doubt.
It's just a plain straightforward tale – a tale that lets you know
The way they lived in Palestine three thousand years ago.

It's strange to read it all today, the shifting of the stock;
You'd think you see the caravans that loaf behind the flock,
The little donkeys and the mules, the sheep that slowly spread,
And maybe Dan or Naphthali a-ridin' on ahead.

The long, dry, dusty summer days, the smouldering fires at
      night;
The stir and bustle of the camp at break of morning light;
The little kids that skipped about, the camels' dead-slow
      tramp –
I wish I'd done a week or two in Old Man Jacob's camp!

But if I keep the narrer path some day, perhaps, I'll know
How Jacob bred them strawberry calves three thousand years ago.

The Reverend Mullineux

I'd reckon his weight at eight-stun-eight,
    And his height at five-foot-two,
With a face as plain as an eight-day clock
And a walk as brisk as a bantam-cock –
    Game as a bantam, too,
Hard and wiry and full of steam,
That's the boss of the English Team,
    Reverend Mullineux!

Makes no row when the game gets rough –
    None of your 'Strike me blue!'
'Yous wants smacking across the snout!'
Plays like a gentleman out-and-out –
    Same as he ought to do.
'Kindly remove from off my face!'
That's the way that he states his case,
    Reverend Mullineux.

Kick! He can kick like an army mule –
    Run like a kangaroo!
Hard to get by as a lawyer-plant,
Tackles his man like a bull-dog ant –
    Fetches him over too!
Didn't the public cheer and shout
Watchin' him chuckin' big blokes about,
    Reverend Mullineux!

Scrimmage was packed on his prostrate form,
    Somehow the ball got through –
Who was it tackled our big half-back,
Flinging him down like an empty sack,
    Right on our goal-line too?
Who but the man that we thought was dead,
Down with a score of 'em on his head,
    Reverend Mullineux.

Wisdom of Hafiz

My son, if you go to the races to battle with Ikey and Mo,
Remember, it's seldom the pigeon can pick out the eye of the crow;
Remember, they live by the business; remember, my son, and go slow.

If ever an owner should tell you, 'Back mine' – don't you be such a
      flat.
He knows his own cunning, no doubt – does he know what the
      others are at?
Find out what he's frightened of most, and invest a few dollars on
      that.

Walk not in the track of the trainer, nor hang round the rails at his
      stall.
His wisdom belongs to his patron – shall he give it to one and to all?
When the stable is served he may tell you – and his words are like
      jewels let fall.

Run wide of the tipster who whispers that Borak is sure to be first,
He tells the next mug that he corners a tale with the placings
      reversed;
And, remember, of judges of racing, the jockey's the absolute worst.

When they lay three to one on the field, and the runners are twenty-
      and-two,
Take a pull on yourself; take a pull – it's a mighty big field to get
      through.
Is the club handicapper a fool? If a fool is about, p'raps it's you!

Beware of the critic who tells you the handicap's absolute rot,
For this is chucked in, and that's hopeless, and somebody ought to
      be shot.
How is it he can't make a fortune himself when he knows such a lot?

From tipsters, and jockeys, and trials, and gallops, the glory has gone,
For this is the wisdom of Hafiz that sages have pondered upon,
'The very best tip in the world is to see the commission go on!'

Saltbush Bill, J.P.

Beyond the land where Leichhardt went,
    Beyond Sturt's Western track,
The rolling tide of change has sent
    Some strange J.P.'s out back.

And Saltbush Bill, grown old and grey,
    And worn for want of sleep,
Received the news in camp one day
    Behind the travelling sheep.

That Edward Rex, confiding in
    His known integrity,
By hand and seal on parchment skin
    Had made him a J.P.

He read the news with eager face
    But found no word of pay.
'I'd like to see my sister's place
    And kids on Christmas Day.

'I'd like to see green grass again,
    And watch clear water run,
Away from this unholy plain,
    And flies, and dust, and sun.'

At last one little clause he found
    That might some hope inspire,
'A magistrate may charge a pound
    For inquest on a fire.'

A big blacks' camp was built close by,
    And Saltbush Bill, says he,
'I think that camp might well supply
    A job for a J.P.'

That night, by strange coincidence,
   A most disastrous fire
Destroyed the country residence
   Of Jacky Jack, Esquire.

'Twas mostly leaves, and bark, and dirt;
   The party most concerned
Appeared to think it wouldn't hurt
   If forty such were burned.

Quite otherwise thought Saltbush Bill,
   Who watched the leaping flame.
'The home is small,' said he, 'but still
   The principle's the same.

' 'Midst palaces though you should roam,
   Or follow pleasure's tracks,
You'll find,' he said, 'no place like home –
   At least like Jacky Jack's.

'Tell every man in camp, "Come quick",
   Tell every black Maria
I give tobacco, half a stick –
   Hold inquest long-a fire.'

Each juryman received a name
   Well suited to a Court.
'Long Jack' and 'Stumpy Bill' became
   'John Long' and 'William Short'.

While such as 'Tarpot', 'Bullock Dray',
   And 'Tommy Wait-a-While',
Became, for ever and a day,
   'Scot', 'Dickens', and 'Carlyle'.

And twelve good sable men and true
   Were soon engaged upon
The conflagration that o'erthrew
   The home of John A. John.

Their verdict, 'Burnt by act of Fate',
   They scarcely had returned
When, just behind the magistrate,
   Another humpy burned!

The jury sat again and drew
   Another stick of plug.
Said Saltbush Bill, 'It's up to you
   Put some one long-a Jug.'

'I'll camp the sheep,' he said, 'and sift
   The evidence about.'
For quite a week he couldn't shift,
   The way the fires broke out.

The jury thought the whole concern
   As good as any play.
They used to 'take him oath' and earn
   Three sticks of plug a day.

At last the tribe lay down to sleep
   Homeless, beneath a tree;
And onward with his travelling sheep
   Went Saltbush Bill, J.P.

The sheep delivered, safe and sound,
   His horse to town he turned,
And drew some five-and-twenty pound
   For fees that he had earned.

And where Monaro's ranges hide
   Their little farms away –
His sister's children by his side –
   He spent his Christmas Day.

The next J.P. that went out back
   Was shocked, or pained, or both,
At hearing every pagan black
   Repeat the juror's oath.

No matter though he turned and fled
   They followed faster still;
'You make it inkwich, boss,' they said,
   'All same like Saltbush Bill.'

They even said that they'd let him see
   The fires originate.
When he refused they said that he
   Was 'No good magistrate'.

And out beyond Sturt's Western track,
   And Leichhardt's farthest tree,
They wait till fate shall send them back
   Their Saltbush Bill, J.P.

Riders in the Stand

There's some that ride the Robbo style, and bump at every stride;
While others sit a long way back, to get a longer ride.
There's some that ride as sailors do, with legs, and arms, and teeth;
And some ride on the horse's neck, and some ride underneath.

But all the finest horsemen out – the men to Beat the Band –
You'll find amongst the crowd that ride their races in the Stand.
They'll say 'He had the race in hand, and lost it in the straight.'
They'll show how Godby came too soon. and Barden came too late.

They'll say Chevalley lost his nerve, and Regan lost his head;
They'll tell how one was 'livened up' and something else was 'dead' –
In fact, the race was never run on sea, or sky, or land,
But what you'd get it better done by riders in the Stand.

The rule holds good in everything in life's uncertain fight;
You'll find the winner can't go wrong, the loser can't go right.
You ride a slashing race, and lose – by one and all you're banned!
Ride like a bag of flour, and win – they'll cheer you in the Stand.

Waltzing Matilda

(Carrying a Swag)

Oh! there once was a swagman camped in a Billabong,
   Under the shade of a Coolabah tree;
And he sang as he looked at his old billy boiling,
   'Who'll come a-waltzing Matilda with me?'

      Who'll come a-waltzing Matilda, my darling,
       Who'll come a-waltzing Matilda with me?
      Waltzing Matilda and leading a water-bag –
       Who'll come a-waltzing Matilda with me?

Down came a jumbuck to drink at the water-hole,
   Up jumped the swagman and grabbed him in glee;
And he sang as he stowed him away in his tucker-bag,
   You'll come a-waltzing Matilda with me.'

Down came the Squatter a-riding his thoroughbred;
   Down came Policemen – one, two and three.
'Whose is the jumbuck you've got in the tucker-bag?
   You'll come a-waltzing Matilda with me.'

But the swagman, he up and he jumped in the water-hole,
   Drowning himself by the Coolabah tree;
And his ghost may be heard as it sings in the Billabong
   'Who'll come a-waltzing Matilda with me?'

An Answer to Various Bards

Well, I've waited mighty patient while they all came rolling in,
Mister Lawson, Mister Dyson, and the others of their kin,
With their dreadful, dismal stories of the Overlander's camp,
How his fire is always smoky, and his boots are always damp;
And they paint it so terrific it would fill one's soul with gloom –
But you know they're fond of writing about 'corpses' and 'the tomb'.
So, before they curse the bushland, they should let their fancy range,
And take something for their livers, and be cheerful for a change.

Now, for instance, Mr Lawson – well, of course, we almost cried
At the sorrowful description how his 'little 'Arvie' died,
And we lachrymosed in silence when 'His Father's Mate' was slain;
Then he went and killed the father, and we had to weep again.
Ben Duggan and Jack Denver, too, he caused them to expire,
After which he cooked the gander of Jack Dunn, of Nevertire;
And, no doubt, the bush is wretched if you judge it by the groan
Of the sad and soulful poet with a graveyard of his own.

And he spoke in terms prophetic of a revolution's heat,
When the world should hear the clamour of those people in the
          street;
But the shearer chaps who start it – why, he rounds on them the
          blame,
And he calls 'em 'agitators who are living on the game'.
But I 'over-write' the bushmen! Well, I own without a doubt
That I always see a hero in the 'man from furthest out'.
I could never contemplate him through an atmosphere of gloom,
And a bushman never struck me as a subject for 'the tomb'.

If it ain't all 'golden sunshine' where the 'wattle branches wave',
Well, it ain't all damp and dismal, and it ain't all 'lonely grave'.
And, of course, there's no denying that the bushman's life is rough,
But a man can easy stand it if he's built of sterling stuff;
Though it's seldom that the drover gets a bed of eiderdown,
Yet the man who's born a bushman, he gets mighty sick of town,
For he's jotting down the figures, and he's adding up the bills

While his heart is simply aching for a sight of Southern hills.

Then he hears a wool-team passing with a rumble and a lurch,
And, although, the work is pressing, yet it brings him off his perch,
For it stirs him like a message from his station friends afar
And he seems to sniff the ranges in the scent of wool and tar;
And it takes him back in fancy, half in laughter, half in tears,
To a sound of other voices and a thought of other years,
When the woolshed rang with bustle from the dawning of the day,
And the shear-blades were a-clicking to the cry of 'Wool away!'

Then his face was somewhat browner, and his frame was firmer set –
And he feels his flabby muscles with a feeling of regret.
But the wool-team slowly passes, and his eyes go sadly back
To the dusty little table and the papers in the rack,
And his thoughts go to the terrace where his sickly children squall,
And he thinks there's something healthy in the bush-life after all.
But we'll go no more a-droving in the wind or in the sun,
For our fathers' hearts have failed us, and the droving days are done.

There's a nasty dash of danger where the long-horned bullock
          wheels,
And we like to live in comfort and to get our reg'lar meals.
For to hang around the townships suits us better, you'll agree,
And a job at washing bottles is the job for such as we.
Let us herd into the cities, let us crush and crowd and push
Till we lose the love of roving, and we learn to hate the bush;
And we'll turn our aspirations to a city life and beer,
And we'll slip across to England – it's a nicer place than here;

For there's not much risk of hardship where all comforts are in store,
And the theatres are in plenty, and the pubs are more and more.
But that ends it, Mr Lawson, and it's time to say goodbye,
So we must agree to differ in all friendship, you and I.
Yes, we'll work our own salvation with the stoutest hearts we may,
And if fortune only favours we will take the road some day,
And go droving down the river 'neath the sunshine and the stars,
And then return to Sydney and vermilionize the bars.

T.Y.S.O.N.

Across the Queensland border line
   The mobs of cattle go;
They travel down in sun and shine
   On dusty stage, and slow.
The drovers, riding slowly on
   To let the cattle spread,
Will say: 'Here's one old landmark gone,
   For old man Tyson's dead.'

What tales there'll be in every camp
   By men that Tyson knew!
The swagmen, meeting on the tramp,
   Will yarn the long day through,
And tell of how he passed as 'Brown',
   And fooled the local men:
'But not for me – I struck the town,
   And passed the message further down;
That's T.Y.S.O.N.!'

There stands a little country town
   Beyond the border line,
Where dusty roads go up and down,
   And banks with pubs combine.
A stranger came to cash a cheque –
   Few were the words he said –
A handkerchief about his neck,
   An old hat on his head.

A long grey stranger, eagle-eyed –
   'Know me? Of course you do?'
'It's not my work,' the boss replied,
   'To know such tramps as you.'
'Well, look here, Mister, don't be flash.'
   Replied the stranger then,
'I never care to make a splash,
I'm simple, but I've got the cash;
   I'm T.Y.S.O.N.'

But in that last great drafting-yard,
   Where Peter keeps the gate,
And souls of sinners find it barred,
   And go to meet their fate,
There's one who ought to enter in
   For good deeds done on earth,
One who from Peter's self must win
   That meed of sterling worth.

Not to the strait and narrow gate
   Reserved for wealthy men,
But to the big gate, opened wide,
The grizzled figure, eagle-eyed,
   Will saunter up – and then
Old Peter'll say: 'Let's pass him through;
There's many a thing he used to do,
Good-hearted things that no one knew;
   That's T.Y.S.O.N.'

As Long as Your Eyes are Blue

'Will you love me, sweet, when my hair is grey
    And my cheeks shall have lost their hue?
When the charms of youth shall have passed away
    Will your love as of old prove true?

'For the looks may change, and the heart may range
    And the love be no longer fond;
Will you love with truth in the years of youth
    And away to the years beyond?'

Oh, I love you, sweet, for your locks of brown
    And the blush on your cheek that lies –
But I love you most for the kindly heart
    That I see in your sweet blue eyes.

For the eyes are signs of the soul within,
    Of the heart that is leal and true,
And, my own sweetheart, I shall love you still,
    Just as long as your eyes are blue.

For the locks may bleach, and the cheeks of peach
    May be reft of their golden hue;
But, my own sweetheart, I shall love you still,
    Just as long as your eyes are blue.

Bottle-O!

I ain't the kind of bloke as takes to any steady job;
   I drives me bottle cart around the town;
A bloke what keeps 'is eyes about can always make a bob –
   I couldn't bear to graft for every brown.
There's lots of handy things about in everybody's yard,
   There's cocks and hens a-runnin' to an' fro,
And little dogs what comes and barks – we take 'em off their
      guard
   And we puts 'em with the Empty Bottle-O!

     Chorus:
     So it's any 'Empty bottles! Any empty bottle-O!'
     You can hear us round for half a mile or so.
       And you'll see the women rushing
       To take in the Monday's washing
     When they 'ear us crying, 'Empty Bottle-O!'

I'm driving down by Wexford-street and up a winder goes,
   A girl sticks out 'er 'ead and looks at me,
An all-right tart with ginger 'air, and freckles on 'er nose;
   I stops the cart and walks across to see.
'There ain't no bottles 'ere,' says she, 'since father took the
      pledge,'
   'No bottles 'ere,' says I, 'I'd like to know
What right 'ave you to stick your 'ead outside the winder ledge,
   If you 'aven't got no Empty Bottle-O!'

I sometimes gives the 'orse a spell, and then the push and me
   We takes a little trip to Chowder Bay.
Oh! ain't it nice the 'ole day long a-gazin' at the sea
   And a-hidin' of the tanglefoot away.
But when the booze gits 'old of us, and fellows starts to 'scrap',
   There's some what likes blue-metal for to throw:
But as for me, I always says for layin' out a 'trap'
   There's nothing like an Empty Bottle-O!

Story of Mongrel Grey

This is the story the stockman told
  On the cattle-camp, when the stars were bright;
The moon rose up like a globe of gold
  And flooded the plain with her mellow light.
    We watched the cattle till dawn of day
    And he told me the story of Mongrel Grey.

He was a knock-about station hack,
  Spurred and walloped, and banged and beat;
Ridden all day with a sore on his back,
  Left all night with nothing to eat.
    That was a matter of everyday
    Normal occurrence with Mongrel Grey.

We might have sold him, but someone heard
  He was bred out back on a flooded run,
Where he learnt to swim like a waterbird;
  Midnight or midday were all as one –
    In the flooded ground he would find his way;
    Nothing could puzzle old Mongrel Grey.

'Tis a trick, no doubt, that some horses learn;
  When the floods are out they will splash along
In girth-deep water, and twist and turn
  From hidden channel and billabong,
    Never mistaking the road to go;
    For a man may guess – but the horses *know*.

I was camping out with my youngest son –
  Bit of a nipper, just learnt to speak –
In an empty hut on the lower run,
  Shooting and fishing in Conroy's Creek.
    The youngster toddled about all day
    And there with our horses was Mongrel Grey.

All of a sudden a flood came down,
　　At first a freshet of mountain rain,
Roaring and eddying, rank and brown,
　　　Over the flats and across the plain.
　　　　Rising and rising – at fall of night
　　　　Nothing but water appeared in sight!

'Tis a nasty place when the floods are out,
　　Even in daylight; for all around
Channels and billabongs twist about,
　　　Stretching for miles in the flooded ground.
　　　　And to move seemed a hopeless thing to try
　　　　In the dark with the storm-water racing by.

I had to risk it. I heard a roar
　　As the wind swept down and the driving rain;
And the water rose till it reached the floor
　　　Of our highest room; and 'twas very plain –
　　　　The way the torrent was sweeping down –
　　　　We must make for the highlands at once, or drown.

Off to the stable I splashed, and found
　　The horses shaking with cold and fright;
I led them down to the lower ground,
　　　But never a yard would they swim that night!
　　　　They reared and snorted and turned away,
　　　　And none would face it but Mongrel Grey.

I bound the child on the horse's back,
　　And we started off, with a prayer to heaven,
Through the rain and the wind and the pitchy black
　　　For I knew that the instinct God has given
　　　　To prompt His creatures by night and day
　　　　Would guide the footsteps of Mongrel Grey.

He struck deep water at once and swam –
　　I swam beside him and held his mane –
Till we touched the bank of the broken dam
　　　In shallow water; then off again,
　　　　Swimming in darkness across the flood,
　　　　Rank with the smell of the drifting mud.

He turned and twisted across and back,
   Choosing the places to wade or swim,
Picking the safest and shortest track –
    The blackest darkness was clear to him.
      Did he strike the crossing by sight or smell?
      The Lord that held him alone could tell!

He dodged the timber whene'er he could,
   But timber brought us to grief at last;
I was partly stunned by a log of wood
    That struck my head as it drifted past;
      Then lost my grip of the brave old grey,
      And in half a second he swept away.

I reached a tree, where I had to stay,
   And did a perish for two days' hard;
And lived on water – but Mongrel Grey,
    He walked right into the homestead yard
      At dawn next morning, and grazed around,
      With the child strapped on to him safe and sound.

We keep him now for the wife to ride,
   Nothing too good for him now, of course;
Never a whip on his fat old hide,
    For she owes the child to that brave grey horse.
      And not Old Tyson himself could pay
      The purchase money of Mongrel Grey.

Gilhooley's Estate

*(A ballad concerning the amalgamation
of the legal profession.)*

Oh, Mr Gilhooley he turned up his toes,
    As most of us do, soon or late;
And Jones was a lawyer, as everyone knows,
    So they took him Gilhooley's Estate.

Gilhooley in life had been living so free
    'Twas thought his possessions were great,
So Jones, with a smile, says, 'There's many a fee
    For me in Gilhooley's Estate.'

They made out a list of his property fine,
    It totalled a thousand-and-eight;
But the debts were nine hundred and ninety nine –
    The debts of Gilhooley's Estate.

So Mrs Gilhooley says, 'Jones, my dear
    My childer have little to ait:
Just keep the expinses as low as you can
    Against poor Gilhooley's Estate.'

But Jones says, 'The will isn't clear in its terms,
    I fear it will need some debate,
And the law won't allow me (attorneys are worms)
    To appear in Gilhooley's Estate.'

So a barrister-man, with a wig on his head
    And a brief in his hand, quite elate,
Went up to the Court where they bury the dead,
    Just to move in Gilhooley's Estate.

But his Honour the Judge said, 'I think that the joint
    Legatees must be called to *probate* –

Ex parte Pokehorney is clear on the point –
    The point of Gilhooley's Estate.'

'I order a suit to be brought just to try
    If this is correct that I state –
A nice friendly suit – and the costs by and by,
    Must be borne by Gilhooley's Estate.'

So Mrs Gilhooley says, 'Jones, you'll appear!
    Thim barristers' fees is too great;
The suit is but friendly,' 'Attorneys, my dear,
    Can't be heard in Gilhooley's Estate.'

From the barristers' quarter a mighty hurrah
    Arises both early and late:
It's only the whoop of the Junior Bar
    Dividing Gilhooley's Estate.

The Road to Hogan's Gap

Now look, you see, it's this way like –
    You cross the broken bridge
And run the crick down, till you strike
    The second right-hand ridge.

The track is hard to see in parts,
    But still it's pretty clear;
There's been two Injun hawkers' carts
    Along that road this year.

Well, run that right-hand ridge along –
    It ain't, to say, too steep –
There's two fresh tracks might put you wrong
    Where blokes went out with sheep.

But keep the crick upon your right,
   And follow pretty straight
Along the spur, until you sight
   A wire and sapling gate.

Well, that's where Hogan's old grey mare
   Fell off and broke her back;
You'll see her carcass layin' there,
   Jist down below the track.

And then you drop two mile, or three,
   It's pretty steep and blind;
You want to go and fall a tree
   And tie it on behind.

And then you pass a broken cart
   Below a granite bluff;
And that is where you strike the part
   They reckon pretty rough.

But by the time you've got that far
   It's either cure or kill,
So turn your horses round the spur
   And face 'em up the hill.

For look, if you should miss the slope
   And get below the track,
You haven't got the slightest hope
   Of ever gettin' back.

An' half way up you'll see the hide
   Of Hogan's brindled bull;
Well, mind and keep the right-hand side.
   The left's too steep a pull.

And both the banks is full of cracks;
   An' just about at dark
You'll see the last year's bullock tracks
   Where Hogan drew the bark.

The marks is old and pretty faint –
    O'ergrown with scrub and such;
Of course the track to Hogan's ain't
    A road that's travelled much.

But turn and run the tracks along
    For half a mile or more,
And then, of course, you can't go wrong –
    You're right at Hogan's door.

When first you come to Hogan's gate
    He mightn't show perhaps;
He's pretty sure to plant, and wait
    To see it ain't the traps.

I wouldn't call it good enough
    To let your horses out;
There's some that's pretty extra rough
    Is livin' round about.

It's likely, if your horses did
    Get feedin' near the track,
It's going to cost at least a quid
    Or more to get them back.

So, if you find they're off the place,
    It's up to you to go
And flash a quid in Hogan's face –
    He'll know the blokes that know.

But listen – if you're feelin' dry,
    Just see there's no one near,
And go and wink the other eye
    And ask for ginger beer.

The blokes come in from near and far
    To sample Hogan's pop;
They reckon once they breast the bar
    They stay there till they drop.

On Sundays you can see them spread
  Like flies around the tap.
It's like that song 'The Livin' Dead'
  Up there at Hogan's Gap.

They like to make it pretty strong
  Whenever there's a chance;
So when a stranger comes along
  They always hold a dance.

There's recitations, songs, and fights –
  A willin' lot you'll meet.
There's one long bloke up there recites;
  I tell you he's a treat.

They're lively blokes all right up there,
  It's never dull a day.
I'd go meself if I could spare
  The time to get away.

   *   *   *   *   *

The stranger turned his horses
  He didn't cross the bridge;
He didn't go along the crick
  To strike the second ridge;

He didn't make the trip, because
  He wasn't feeling fit.
His business up at Hogan's was
  To serve him with a writ.

He reckoned, if he faced the pull
  And climbed the rocky stair,
The next to come might find his hide
A landmark on the mountain side,
Along with Hogan's brindled bull
  And Hogan's old grey mare!

A Singer of the Bush

There is waving of grass in the breeze
    And a song in the air,
And a murmur of myriad bees
    That toil everywhere.
There is scent in the blossom and bough,
    And the breath of the Spring
Is as soft as a kiss on a brow –
    And Springtime I sing.

There is drought on the land, and the stock
    Tumble down in their tracks
Or follow – a tottering flock –
    The scrub-cutter's axe.
While ever a creature survives
    The axes shall swing;
We are fighting with fate for their lives –
    And the combat I sing.

'Shouting' for a Camel

It was over at Coolgardie that a mining speculator,
    Who was going down the township just to make a bit o' chink,
Went off to hire a camel from a camel propagator,
    And the Afghan said he'd lend it if he'd stand the beast a drink.
Yes, the only price he asked him was to stand the beast a drink.
He was cheap, very cheap, as the dromedaries go.

So the mining speculator made the bargain, proudly thinking
    He had bested old Mahomet, he had done him in the eye.
Then he clambered on the camel, and the while the beast was
        drinking
    He explained with satisfaction to the miners standing by
That 'twas cheap, very cheap, as the dromedaries go.

But the camel kept on drinking and he filled his hold with water,
    And the more he had inside him yet the more he seemed to
        need;
For he drank it by the gallon, and his girths grew taut and tauter,
    And the miners muttered softly, 'Yes he's very dry indeed!
But he's cheap, very cheap, as the dromedaries go.'

So he drank up twenty buckets – it was weird to watch him suck it,
    (And the market price for water was per bucket half-a-crown)
Till the speculator stopped him, saying, 'Not another bucket –
    If I give him any more there'll be a famine in the town.
Take him back to old Mahomet, and I'll tramp it through the
        town.'
He was cheap, very cheap, as the speculators go.

There's a moral to this story – in your hat you ought to paste it –
    Be careful whom you shout for when a camel is about,
And there's plenty human camels who, before they'll see you waste
        it,
    Will drink up all you pay for if you're fool enough to shout;
If you chance to strike a camel when you're fool enough to shout,
You'll be cheap, very cheap, as the speculators go.

Mulligan's Mare

Oh, Mulligan's bar was the deuce of a place
To drink, and to fight, and to gamble and race;
The height of choice spirits from near and from far
Were all concentrated on Mulligan's bar.

There was 'Jerry the Swell', and the jockey-boy Ned,
'Dog-bite-me' – so called from the shape of his head –
And a man whom the boys, in their musical slang,
Designated the 'Gaffer of Mulligan's Gang'.

Now Mulligan's Gang had a racer to show,
A bad un to look at, a good un to go;
Whenever they backed her you safely might swear
She'd walk in a winner, would Mulligan's mare.

But Mulligan, having some radical views,
Neglected his business and got on the booze;
He took up with runners – a treacherous troop –
Who gave him away, and he 'fell in the soup'.

And so it turned out on a fine summer day,
A bailiff turned up with a writ of '*fi. fa.*';
He walked to the bar with a manner serene,
'I levy,' said he, 'in the name of the Queen.'

Then Mulligan wanted, in spite of the law,
To pay out the bailiff with '*one* on the jaw';
He drew out to hit him; but ere you could wink,
He changed his intention and stood him a drink.

A great consultation there straightway befell
'Twixt jockey-boy Neddy and Jerry the Swell,
And the man with the head, who remarked 'Why, you
    bet!
Dog-bite-me!' said he, 'but we'll diddle 'em yet.

'We'll slip out the mare from her stall in a crack,
And put in her place the old broken-down hack;
The hack is so like her, I'm ready to swear
The bailiff will think he has Mulligan's mare.

'So out with the racer and in with the screw,
We'll show him what Mulligan's talent can do;
And if he gets nasty and dares to say much,
I'll knock him as stiff as my grandmother's crutch.'

Then off to the town went the mare and the lad;
The bailiff came out, never dreamt he was 'had';
But marched to the stall with a confident air –
'I levy,' said he, 'upon Mulligan's mare.'

He watched her by day and he watched her by night,
She was never an instant let out of his sight,
For races were coming away in the West
And Mulligan's mare had a chance with the best.

'Here's a slant,' thought the bailiff, 'to serve my own
            ends,
I'll send off a wire to my bookmaking friends:
'Get all you can borrow, beg, snavel or snare
And lay the whole lot against Mulligan's mare.' '

The races came round, and the crowd on the course
Were laying the mare till they made themselves hoarse,
And Mulligan's party, with ardour intense,
They backed her for pounds and for shillings and pence.

But think of the grief of the bookmaking host
At the sound of the summons to go to the post –
For down to the start with her thoroughbred air
As fit as a fiddle pranced Mulligan's mare!

They started, and off went the boy to the front,
He cleared out at once, and he made it a hunt;
He steadied as rounding the corner they wheeled,
Then gave her her head – and she smothered the field.

The race put her owner right clear of his debts;
He landed a fortune in stakes and in bets,
He paid the old bailiff the whole of his pelf,
And gave him a hiding to keep for himself.

So all you bold sportsmen take warning, I pray,
Keep clear of the running, you'll find it don't pay;
For the very best rule that you'll hear in a week
Is never to bet on a thing that can speak.

And, whether you're lucky or whether you lose,
Keep clear of the cards and keep clear of the booze,
And fortune in season will answer your prayer
And send you a flyer like Mulligan's mare.

The Mountain Squatter

Herein my mountain home,
   On rugged hills and steep,
I sit and watch you come,
   O Riverina Sheep!

You come from fertile plains
   Where saltbush (sometimes) grows,
And flats that (when it rains)
   Will blossom like the rose.

But when the summer sun
   Gleams down like burnished brass,
You have to leave your run
   And hustle off for grass.

'Tis then that – forced to roam –
   You come to where I keep,
Here in my mountain home,
   A boarding-house for sheep.

Around me where I sit
   The wary wombat goes –
A beast of little wit,
   But what he knows, he *knows*.

The very same remark
   Applies to me also;
I don't give out a spark,
   But what I know, I *know*.

My brain perhaps would show
   No convolutions deep,
But anyhow I know
   The way to handle sheep.

These Riverina cracks,
   They do not care to ride
The half-inch hanging tracks
   Along the mountain side.

Their horses shake with fear
   When loosened boulders go
With leaps, like startled deer,
   Down to the gulfs below.

Their very dogs will shirk,
   And drop their tails in fright
When asked to go and work
   A mob that's out of sight.

My little collie pup
   Works silently and wide;
You'll see her climbing up
   Along the mountain side.

As silent as a fox
   You'll see her come and go,
A shadow through the rocks
   Where ash and messmate grow.

Then, lost to sight and sound
    Behind some rugged steep
She works her way around
    And gathers up the sheep;

And, working wide and shy,
    She holds them rounded up.
The cash ain't coined to buy
    That little collie pup.

And so I draw a screw
    For self and dog and keep
To boundary-ride for you,
    O Riverina Sheep!

And, when the autumn rain
    Has made the herbage grow,
You travel off again,
    And glad – no doubt – to go.

But some are left behind
    Around the mountain's spread,
For those we cannot find
    We put them down as dead.

So, when we say adieu
    And close the boarding job,
I always find a few
    Fresh ear-marks in my mob.

And, what with those I sell,
    And what with those I keep,
You pay me pretty well,
    O Riverina Sheep!

It's up to me to shout
    Before we say goodbye –
'Here's to a howlin' drought
    All west of Gundagai!'

Pioneers

They came of bold and roving stock that would not fixed
      abide;
They were the sons of field and flock since e'er they learnt
      to ride,
We may not hope to see such men in these degenerate years
As those explorers of the bush – the brave old pioneers.

'Twas they who rode the trackless bush in heat and storm
      and drought;
'Twas they who heard the master-word that called them
      farther out;
'Twas they who followed up the trail the mountain cattle
      made,
And pressed across the mighty range where now their bones
      are laid.

But now the times are dull and slow, the brave old days are
      dead
When hardy bushmen started out, and forced their way
      ahead
By tangled scrub and forests grim towards the unknown
      west,
And spied at last the promised land from off the range's
      crest.

O ye that sleep in lonely graves by distant ridge and plain,
We drink to you in silence now as Christmas comes again,
To you who fought the wilderness through rough unsettled
      years –
The founders of our nation's life, the brave old pioneers.

Santa Claus in the Bush

It chanced out back at the Christmas time,
    When the wheat was ripe and tall,
A stranger rode to the farmer's gate –
    A sturdy man and a small.

'Rin doon, rin doon, my little son Jack,
    And bid the stranger stay;
And we'll hae a crack for Auld Lang Syne,
    For the morn is Christmas Day.'

'Nay noo, nay noo,' said the dour guidwife,
    'But ye should let him be;
He's maybe only a drover chap
    Frae the land o' the Darling Pea.

'Wi' a drover's tales, and a drover's thirst
    To swiggle the hail nicht through;
Or he's maybe a life assurance carle
    To talk ye black and blue.'

'Guidwife, he's never a drover chap,
    For their swags are neat and thin;
And he's never a life assurance carle,
    Wi' the brick-dust burnt in his skin.

'Guidwife, guidwife, be nae sae dour,
    For the wheat stands ripe and tall,
And we shore a seven-pound fleece this year,
    Ewes and weaners and all.

'There is grass tae spare, and the stock are fat
    Where they whiles are gaunt and thin,
And we owe a tithe to the travelling poor,
    So we maun ask him in.

'Ye can set him a chair tae the table side,
    And gi' him a bite tae eat;
An omelette made of a new-laid egg,
    Or a tasty bit of meat.

'But the native cats have taen the fowls,
    They havena left a leg;
And he'll get nae omelette at a'
    Till the emu lays an egg!'

'Rin doon, rin doon, my little son Jack,
    To whaur the emus bide,
Ye shall find the auld hen on the nest,
    While the auld cock sits beside.

'But speak them fair, and speak them saft,
    Lest they kick ye a fearsome jolt.
Ye can gi' them a feed of thae half-inch nails
    Or a rusty carriage bolt.'

So little son Jack ran blithely down
    With the rusty nails in hand,
Till he came where the emus fluffed and scratched
    By their nest in the open sand.

And there he has gathered the new-laid egg –
    'Twould feed three men or four –
And the emus came for the half-inch nails
    Right up to the settler's door.

'A waste o' food,' said the dour guidwife,
    As she took the egg, with a frown,
'But he gets nae meat, unless ye rin
    A paddy-melon down.'

'Gang oot, gang oot, my little son Jack,
    Wi' your twa-three doggies sma';
Gin ye come nae back wi' a paddy-melon,
    Then come nae back at a'.'

So little son Jack he raced and he ran,
    And he was bare o' the feet,
And soon he captured a paddy-melon,
    Was gorged with the stolen wheat.

'Sit doon, sit doon, my bonny wee man,
    To the best that the hoose can do –
An omelette made of the emu egg
    And a paddy-melon stew.'

''Tis well, 'tis well,' said the bonny wee man;
    'I have eaten the wide world's meat,
And the food that is given with right good-will
    Is the sweetest food to eat.

'But the night draws on to the Christmas Day
    And I must rise and go,
For I have a mighty way to ride
    To the land of the Esquimaux.

'And it's there I must load my sledges up,
    With the reindeers four-in-hand,
That go to the North, South, East, and West,
    To every Christian land.'

'Tae the Esquimaux,' said the dour guidwife,
    'Ye suit my husband well!
For when he gets up on his journey horse
    He's a bit of a liar himsel'.'

Then out with a laugh went the bonny wee man
    To his old horse grazing nigh,
And away like a meteor flash they went
Far off to the Northern sky.

    *   *   *   *   *

When the children woke on the Christmas morn
    They chattered with might and main –
For a sword and gun had little son Jack,
    And a braw new doll had Jane,
And a packet o' screws had the twa emus;
    But the dour guidwife gat nane.

'In Re a Gentleman, One'

When an attorney is called before the Full Court to answer for any alleged misconduct it is not usual to publish his name until he is found guilty; until then the matter appears in the papers as 'In Re a Gentleman, One of the Attorneys of the Supreme Court,' or, more shortly, 'In re a Gent., One.'

We see it each day in the paper,
    And know that there's mischief in store;
That some unprofessional caper
    Has landed a shark on the shore.
We know there'll be plenty of trouble
    Before they get through with the fun,
Because he's been coming the double
    On clients, has 'Gentleman, One'.

Alas for the gallant attorney,
    Intent upon cutting a dash!
He starts on life's perilous journey
    With rather more cunning than cash.
And fortune at first is inviting –
    He struts his brief hour in the sun --
But, lo! on the wall is the writing
    Of Nemesis, 'Gentleman, One'.

For soon he runs short of the dollars,
    He fears he must go to the wall;
So Peters' trust-money he collars
    To pay off his creditor, Paul;
Then robs right and left – for he goes it
    In earnest when once he's begun.
Descensus Averni – he knows it;
    It's easy for 'Gentleman, One'.

The crash comes as sure as the seasons;
    He loses his coin in a mine,

Or booming in land, or for reasons
    Connected with women and wine
Or maybe the cards or the horses
    A share of the damage have done –
No matter; the end of the course is
    The same: '*Re* a Gentleman, One.'

He struggles awhile to keep going,
    To stave off detection and shame;
But creditors, clamorous growing,
    Ere long put an end to the game.
At length the poor soldier of Satan
    His course to a finish has run –
    And just think of Windeyer waiting
To deal with 'A Gentleman, One'!

And some face it boldly, and brazen
    The shame and the utter disgrace;
While others, more sensitive, hasten
    Their names and their deeds to efface.
They snap the frail thread which the Furies
    And Fates have so cruelly spun.
May the great Final Judge and His juries
    Have mercy on 'Gentleman, One'!

At the Melting of the Snow

There's a sunny Southern land,
    And it's there that I would be
Where the big hills stand,
    In the South Countrie!
When the wattles bloom again,
    Then it's time for us to go
To the old Monaro country
    At the melting of the snow.

To the East or to the West,
　　Or wherever you may be,
You will find no place
　　Like the South Countrie.
For the skies are blue above,
　　And the grass is green below,
In the old Monaro country
　　At the melting of the snow.

Now the team is in the plough,
　　And the thrushes start to sing,
And the pigeons on the bough
　　Sit a-welcoming the Spring.
So come, my comrades all,
　　Let us saddle up and go
To the old Monaro country
　　At the melting of the snow.

A Dream of the Melbourne Cup

(1886)

Bring me a quart of colonial beer
And some doughy damper to make good cheer.
    I must make a heavy dinner;
Heavily dine and heavily sup,
Of indigestible things fill up,
Next month they run the Melbourne Cup,
    And I have to dream the winner.

Stoke it in, boys! the half-cooked ham,
The rich ragout and the charming cham.,
    I've got to mix my liquor;
Give me a gander's gaunt hind leg,
Hard and tough as a wooden peg,
And I'll keep it down with a hard-boiled egg,
    'Twill make me dream the quicker.

Now that I'm full of fearful feed,
Oh, but I'll dream of a winner indeed
    In my restless, troubled slumber;
While the night-mares race through my heated brain
And their devil-riders spur amain,
The trip for the Cup will reward my pain,
    And I'll spot the winning number.

Thousands and thousands and thousands more,
Like sands on the white Pacific shore,
    The crowding people cluster;
For evermore is the story old,
While races are bought and backers are sold,
Drawn by the greed of the gain of gold,
    In their thousands still they muster.

*   *   *   *   *

And the bookies' cries grow fierce and hot,
'I'll lay the Cup! The double, if not!'
   'Five monkeys, Little John, sir!'
'Here's fives bar one, I lay, I lay!'
And so they shout through the livelong day,
And stick to the game that is sure to pay,
   While fools put money on, sir!

And now in my dream I seem to go
And bet with a 'book' that I seem know
   A Hebrew money-lender;
A million to five is the price I get –
Not bad! but before I book the bet
The horse's name I clean forget,
   Its number and even gender.

Now for the start, and here they come,
And the hoof-strokes roar like a mighty drum
   Beat by a hand unsteady;
They come like a rushing, roaring flood,
Hurrah for the speed of the Chester blood;
For Acme is making the pace so good
   They are some of 'em done already.

But round the back she begins to tire,
And a mighty shout goes up 'Crossfire!'
   The magpie jacket's leading;
And Crossfire challenges, fierce and bold,
And the lead she'll have and the lead she'll hold,
But at length gives way to the black and gold,
   Which right to the front is speeding.

Carry them on and keep it up –
A flying race is the Melbourne Cup,
   You must race and stay to win it;
And old Commotion, Victoria's pride,
Now takes the lead with his raking stride,
And a mighty roar goes far and wide –
   'There's only Commotion in it!'

But one draws out from the beaten ruck
And up on the rails by a piece of luck
   He comes in a style that's clever;
'It's Trident! Trident! Hurrah for Hales!'
'Go at 'em now while their courage fails;'
'Trident! Trident! for New South Wales!'
   'The blue and white for ever!'

Under the whip! with the ears flat back,
Under the whip! though the sinews crack,
   No sign of the base white feather:
Stick to it now for your breeding's sake,
Stick to it now though your hearts should break,
While the yells and roars make the grand-stand shake,
   They come down the straight together.

Trident slowly forges ahead,
The fierce whips cut and the spurs are red,
   The pace is undiminished
Now for the Panics that never fail!
But many a backer's face grows pale
As old Commotion swings his tail
   And swerves – and the Cup is finished.

     *   *   *   *   *

And now in my dream it all comes back:
I bet my coin on the Sydney crack,
   A million I've won, no question!
'Give me my money, you hook-nosed hog!
Give me my money, bookmaking dog!'
But he disappeared in a kind of fog,
   And I woke with 'the indigestion'.

The Gundaroo Bullock

Oh, there's some that breeds the Devon that's as solid as a
    stone,
And there's some that breeds the brindle which they call the
    'Goulburn Roan';
But amongst the breeds of cattle there are very, very few
Like the hairy-whiskered bullock that they bred at Gundaroo.

Far away by Grabben Gullen, where the Murrumbidgee flows,
There's a block of broken country-side where no one ever goes;
For the banks have gripped the squatters, and the free selectors
    too,
And their stock are always stolen by the men of Gundaroo.

There came a low informer to the Grabben Gullen side,
And he said to Smith the squatter, 'You must saddle up and
    ride,
For your bullock's in the harness-cask of Morgan Donahoo –
He's the greatest cattle-stealer in the whole of Gundaroo.'

'Oh, ho!' said Smith, the owner of the Grabben Gullen run,
'I'll go and get the troopers by the sinking of the sun,
And down into his homestead tonight we'll take a ride,
With warrants to identify the carcass and the hide.'

That night rode down the troopers, the squatter at their head,
They rode into the homestead, and pulled Morgan out of bed.
'Now, show to us the carcass of the bullock that you slew –
The hairy-whiskered bullock that you killed in Gundaroo.'

They peered into the harness-cask, and found it wasn't full,
But down among the brine they saw some flesh and bits of
    wool.
'What's this?' exclaimed the trooper; 'an infant, I declare;'
Said Morgan. ''Tis the carcass of an old man native bear.
I heard that ye were coming, so an old man bear I slew,
Just to give you kindly welcome to my home in Gundaroo.

'The times are something awful, as you can plainly see,
The banks have broke the squatters, and they've broke the likes
    of me;
We can't afford a bullock – such expense would never do –
So an old man bear for breakfast is a treat in Gundaroo.'
And along by Grabben Gullen, where the rushing river flows,
In the block of broken country where there's no one ever goes,
On the Upper Murrumbidgee, they're a hospitable crew –
But you mustn't ask for 'bullock' when you go to Gundaroo.

Lay of the Motor-Car

We're away! and the wind whistles shrewd
    In our whiskers and teeth;
And the granite-like grey of the road
    Seems to slide underneath.
As an eagle might sweep through the sky,
    So we sweep through the land;
And the pallid pedestrians fly
    When they hear us at hand.

We outpace, we outlast, we outstrip!
    Not the fast-fleeing hare,
Nor the racehorses under the whip,
    Nor the birds of the air
Can compete with our swiftness sublime,
    Our ease and our grace.
We annihilate chickens and time
    And policemen and space.

Do you mind that fat grocer who crossed?
    How he dropped down to pray
In the road when he saw he was lost;
    How he melted away
Underneath, and there rang through the fog
    His earsplitting squeal
As he went – Is that he or a dog,
    That stuff on the wheel?

The Corner-Man

I dreamt a dream at the midnight deep,
    When fancies come and go
To vex a man in his soothing sleep
    With thoughts of awful woe –
I dreamt that I was a corner-man
    Of a nigger minstrel show.

I cracked my jokes, and the building rang
    With laughter loud and long;
I hushed the house as I softly sang
    An old plantation song –
A tale of the wicked slavery days
    Of cruelty and wrong.

A small boy sat on the foremost seat –
    A mirthful youngster he;
He beat the time with his restless feet
    To each new melody,
And he picked me out as the brightest star
    Of the black fraternity.

'Oh father,' he said, 'what *would* we do
    If the corner-man should die?
I never saw such a man – did you?
    He makes the people cry,
And then, when he likes, he makes them laugh.'
    The old man made reply –

'We each of us fill a very small space
    In the great creation's plan,
If a man don't keep his lead in the race
    There's plenty more that can;
The world can very soon fill the place
    Of even a corner-man.'

*   *   *   *   *

I woke with a jump, rejoiced to find
  Myself at home in bed,
And I framed a moral in my mind
  From the words the old man said.
The world will jog along just the same
  When its corner-men are dead.

When Dacey Rode the Mule

'Twas to a small, up-country town,
  When we were boys at school,
There came a circus with a clown,
  Likewise a bucking mule.
The clown announced a scheme they had
  Spectators for to bring –
They'd give a crown to any lad
  Who'd ride him round the ring.

    And, gentle reader, do not scoff
      Nor think a man a fool –
    To buck a porous-plaster off
      Was pastime to that mule.

The boys got on he bucked like sin;
  He threw them in the dirt.
What time the clown would raise a grin
  By asking, 'Are you hurt?'
But Johnny Dacey came one night,
  The crack of all the school;
Said he, 'I'll win the crown all right;
  Bring in your bucking mule.

    The elephant went off his trunk,
      The monkey played the fool,
    And all the band got blazing drunk
      When Dacey rode the mule.

But soon there rose a galling shout
    Of laughter, for the clown
From somewhere in his pants drew out
    A little paper crown.
He placed the crown on Dacey's head
    While Dacey looked a fool;
'Now, there's your crown, my lad,' he said,
    'For riding of the mule!'

      The band struck up with 'Killaloe',
        And 'Rule Britannia, Rule',
      And 'Young Man from the Country', too
        When Dacey rode the mule.

Then Dacey, in a furious rage,
    For vengeance on the show
Ascended to the monkeys' cage
    And let the monkeys go;
The blue-tailed ape and the chimpanzee
    He turned abroad to roam;
Good faith! It was a sight to see
    The people step for home.

      For big baboons with canine snout,
        Are spiteful, as a rule –
      The people didn't sit it out,
        When Dacey rode the mule.

And from the beasts he let escape,
    The bushmen all declare,
Were born some creatures partly ape
    And partly native-bear.
They're rather few and far between,
    The race is nearly spent;
But some of them may still be seen
    In Sydney Parliament.

      And when those legislators fight,
        And drink, and act the fool,
      Just blame it on that torrid night
        When Dacey rode the mule.

The Mylora Elopement

By the winding Wollondilly where the weeping willows weep,
And the shepherd, with his billy, half awake and half asleep,
Folds his fleecy flocks that linger homewards in the setting sun
Lived my hero, Jim the Ringer, 'cocky' on Mylora Run.

Jimmy loved the super's daughter, Miss Amelia Jane McGrath.
Long and earnestly he sought her, but he feared her stern papa;
And Amelia loved him truly – but the course of love, if true,
Never yet ran smooth or duly, as I think it ought to do.

Pondering o'er his predilection, Jimmy watched McGrath, the
        boss,
Riding past his lone selection, looking for a station 'oss
That was running in the ranges with a mob of outlaws wild.
Mac the time of day exchanges – off goes Jim to see his child;

Says, 'The old man's after Stager, which he'll find is no light job,
And tomorrow I will wager he will try and yard the mob.
Will you come with me tomorrow? I will let the parson know,
And for ever, joy or sorrow, he will join us here below.

'I will bring my nags so speedy, Crazy Jane and Tambourine,
One more kiss – don't think I'm greedy – goodbye, lass, before
        I'm seen –
Just one more – God bless you, dearie! Don't forget to meet me
        here,
Life without you is but weary; now, once more, goodbye, my
        dear.'

            *   *   *   *   *

            The daylight shines on figures twain
            That ride across Mylora plain,
            Laughing and talking – Jim arid Jane.
            'Steadily, darling. There's lots of time,
            Didn't we slip the old man prime!
            I knew he'd tackle that Bowneck mob,
            I reckon he'll find it too big a job.

They've beaten us all. I had a try,
But the warrigal devils seem to fly.
That Sambo's a real good bit of stuff
No doubt, but not quite good enough.
He'll have to gallop the livelong day,
To cut and come, to race and stay.
I hope he yards 'em , 'twill do him good;
To see us going I don't think would.'
A turn in the road and, fair and square,
They meet the old man standing there.
'What's up?' 'Why, running away, of course,'
Says Jim, emboldened. The old man turned,
His eye with wild excitement burned.
'I've raced all day through the scorching heat
After old Bowneck: and now I'm beat.
But over that range I think you'll find
The Bowneck mob all run stone-blind.
Will you go, and leave the mob behind?
Which will you do? Take the girl away,
Or ride like a white man should today,
And yard old Bowneck? Go or stay?'
Says Jim, 'I can't throw this away,
We can bolt some other day, of course —
Amelia Jane, get off that horse!
Up you get, Old Man. Whoop, halloo!
Here goes to put old Bowneck through!'
Two distant specks on the mountain side,
Two stockwhips echoing far and wide . . .
Amelia Jane sat down and cried.

          *   *   *   *   *

'Sakes, Amelia, what's up now?
Leading old Sambo, too, I vow,
And him deadbeat. Where have you been?
"Bolted with Jim!" What *do* you mean?
"Met the old man with Sambo, licked
From running old Bowneck." Well, I'm kicked —
"Ran 'em till Sambo nearly dropped?"
What did Jim do when you were stopped?
Did you bolt from father across the plain?

"Jim made you get off Crazy Jane!
And father got on, and away again
The two of 'em went to the ranges grim."
Good boy, Jimmy! Oh, well done, Jim!
They're sure to get them now, of course,
That Tambourine is a spanking horse.
And Crazy Jane is good as gold.
And Jim, they say, rides pretty bold –
Not like your father, but very fair.
Jim will have to follow the mare.'
'It never was yet in father's hide
To best my Jim on the mountain side.
Jim can rally, and Jim can ride.'
But here again Amelia cried.

     *   *   *   *   *

The sound of a whip comes faint and far,
A rattle of hoofs, and here they are,
In all their tameless pride.
The fleet wild horses snort with fear,
And wheel and break as the yard draws near.
Now, Jim the Ringer, ride!
Wheel 'em! wheel 'em! Whoa back there, whoa!
And the foam-flakes fly like the driven snow,
As under the whip the horses go
Adown the mountain side.
And Jim, hands down, and teeth firm set,
On a horse that never has failed him yet,
Is after them down the range.
Well ridden! well ridden! they wheel – whoa back!
And long and loud the stockwhips crack,
Their flying course they change;
'Steadily does it – let Sambo go!
Open those sliprails down below.
Smart! or you'll be too late.

     *   *   *   *   *

'They'll follow old Sambo up – look out!
Wheel that black horse – give Sam a clout.
They're in! Make fast the gate.'

     *   *   *   *   *

The mob is safely in the yard!
The old man mounts delighted guard.
No thought has he but for his prize.

    *   *   *   *   *

Jim catches poor Amelia's eyes.
'Will you come after all? The job is done,
And Crazy Jane is fit to run
For a prince's life – now don't say no;
Slip on while the old man's down below
At the inner yard, and away we'll go.
Will you come, my girl?' 'I will, you bet;
We'll manage this here elopement yet.'

        *   *   *   *   *

By the winding Wollondilly stands the hut of Ringer Jim.
And his loving little Meely makes a perfect god of him.
He has stalwart sons and daughters, and, I think, before he's
        done,
There'll be numerous 'Six-fortys' taken on Mylora run.

The Pannikin Poet

There's nothing here sublime,
But just a roving rhyme,
Run off to pass the time,
    With nought titanic in.
The theme that it supports,
And, though it treats of quarts,
It's bare of golden thoughts –
It's just a pannikin.

I think it's rather hard
That each Australian bard –
Each wan, poetic card –
    With thoughts galvanic in
His fiery soul alight,
In wild aerial flight,
Will sit him down and write
    About a pannikin.

He makes some new-chum fare
From out his English lair
To hunt the native bear,
    That curious mannikin;
And then when times get bad
That wandering English lad
Writes out a message sad
    Upon his pannikin:

'O mother, think of me
Beneath the wattle tree'
(For you may bet that he
    Will drag the wattle in)
'O mother, here I think
That I shall have to sink,
There ain't a single drink
    The water-bottle in.'

The dingo homeward hies,
The sooty crows uprise
And caw their fierce surprise
    A tone Satanic in;
And bearded bushmen tread
Around the sleeper's head –
'See here – the bloke is dead!
    Now where's his pannikin?'

They read his words and weep,
And lay him down to sleep
Where wattle-branches sweep,
    A style mechanic in;
And, reader, that's the way
The poets of today
Spin out their little lay
    About a pannikin.

The Protest

I say 'e *isn't* Remorse!
   'Ow do I know?
Saw 'im on Riccarton course
   Two year ago!
Think I'd forget any 'orse?
   Course 'e's The Crow!

Bumper Maginnis and I
   After a 'go',
Walkin' our 'orses to dry,
   I says 'Hello!
What's that old black goin' by?'
   Bumper says 'Oh!
That's an old cuddy of Flanagan's –
   Runs as The Crow!'

Now they make out 'e's Remorse.
    Well, but I *know*.
Soon as I came on the course
    I says ' 'Ello!
    'Ere's the old Crow.'
Once a man's seen any 'orse,
    Course 'e must know.
Sure as there's wood in this table,
    I say 'e's The Crow.

(*Cross-examined by the Committee.*)
'Ow do I know the moke
    After one sight?
S'posin' you meet a bloke
    Down town at night,
Wouldn't you know 'im again when you met 'im?
    That's *'im* all right!

What was the brand on 'is 'ide?
    I couldn't say,
Brands can be transmogrified.
    That ain't the way –
It's the *look* of a 'orse and the way that 'e moves
    That I'd know any day

What was the boy on 'is back?
    Why, 'e went past
All of a minute, and off down the track.
    – 'The 'orse went as fast?'
True, so 'e did! But, my eyes, what a treat!
'Ow can I notice the 'ands and the seat
Of each bumble-faced kid of a boy that I meet?
    Lor'! What a question to ast!
        (*Protest Dismissed.*)

An Evening in Dandaloo

It was while we held our races –
Hurdles, sprints and steeplechases –
    Up in Dandaloo,
That a crowd of Sydney stealers,
Jockeys, pugilists and spielers
Brought some horses, real heelers,
    Came and put us through.

Beat our nags and won our money,
Made the game by no means funny,
    Made us rather blue;
When the racing was concluded,
Of our hard-earned coin denuded
Dandaloonies sat and brooded
    There in Dandaloo.

*   *   *   *   *

Night came down on Johnson's shanty
Where the grog was no way scanty,
    And a tumult grew
Till some wild, excited person
Galloped down the township cursing,
'Sydney push have mobbed Macpherson,
    Roll up, Dandaloo!'

Great St Denis! what commotion!
Like the rush of stormy ocean
    Fiery horsemen flew.
Dust and smoke and din and rattle,
Down the street they spurred their cattle
To the war-cry of the battle,
    'Wade in, Dandaloo!'

So the boys might have their fight out,
Johnson blew the bar-room light out,
    Then, in haste, withdrew.

And in darkness and in doubting
Raged the conflict and the shouting,
'Give the Sydney push a clouting,
    Go it, Dandaloo!'

Jack Macpherson seized a bucket,
Every head he saw he struck it —
    Struck in earnest, too;
And a man from Lower Wattle,
Whom a shearer tried to throttle,
Hit out freely with a bottle
    There in Dandaloo.

Skin and hair were flying thickly,
When a light was fetched, and quickly
    Brought a fact to view —
On the scene of the diversion
Every single, solid person
Come along to help Macpherson —
    All were Dandaloo!

When the list of slain was tabled —
Some were drunk and some disabled —
    Still we found it true.
In the darkness and the smother
We'd been belting one another;
Jack Macpherson bashed his brother
    There in Dandaloo.

So we drank, and all departed —
How the 'mobbing' yarn was started
    No one ever knew —
And the stockmen tell the story
Of that conflict fierce and gory,
How he fought for love and glory
    Up in Dandaloo.

It's a proverb now, or near it —
At the races you can hear it,
    At the dog-fights, too!

Every shrieking, dancing drover
As the canines topple over
Yells applause to Grip or Rover,
  'Give him "Dandaloo"!'

And the teamster slowly toiling
Through the deep black country, soiling
    Wheels and axles, too,
Lays the whip on Spot and Banker,
Rouses Tarboy with a flanker –
'Redman! Ginger! Heave there! Yank her!
    Wade in, Dandaloo!'

A Ballad of Ducks

The railway rattled and roared and swung
With jolting carriage and bumping trucks.
The sun, like a billiard red ball, hung
In the Western sky: and the tireless tongue
Of the wild-eyed man in the corner told
This terrible tale of the days of old,
And the party that ought to have kept the ducks.

'Well, it ain't all joy bein' on the land
With an overdraft that'd knock you flat;
And the rabbits have pretty well took command;
But the hardest thing for a man to stand
Is the feller who says "Well, I told you so!
You should ha' done this way, don't you know!" –
I could lay a bait for a man like that.

'The grasshoppers struck us in ninety-one
And what they leave – well, it ain't *de luxe*.
But a growlin' fault-findin' son of a gun
Who'd lent some money to stock our run –
I said they'd eaten what grass we had –
Says he, "Your management's very bad;
You had a right to have kept some ducks!"

'To have kept some ducks! And the place was white!
Wherever you went you had to tread
On grasshoppers guzzlin' day and night;
And then with a swoosh they rose in flight,
If you didn't look out for yourself they'd fly
Like bullets into your open eye
And knock it out of the back of your head.

'There isn't a turkey or goose or swan,
Or a duck that quacks, or a hen that clucks,
Can make a difference on a run
When a grasshopper plague has once begun;
"If you'd finance us," I says, "I'd buy
Ten thousand emus and have a try;
The job," I says, "is too big for ducks!"

' "You must fetch a duck when you come to stay;
A great big duck – a Muscovy toff –
Ready and fit," I says, "for the fray;
And if the grasshoppers come our way
You turn your duck into the lucerne patch,
And I'd be ready to make a match
That the grasshoppers eat his feathers off!"

'He came to visit us by and by,
And it just so happened one day in spring
A kind of a cloud came over the sky –
A wall of grasshoppers nine miles high,
And nine miles thick, and nine hundred wide,
Flyin' in regiments, side by side,
And eatin' up every living thing.

'All day long, like a shower of rain,
You'd hear 'em smackin' against the wall,
Tap, tap, tap, on the window pane,
And they'd rise and jump at the house again
Till their crippled carcasses piled outside.
But what did it matter if thousands died –
A million wouldn't be missed at all.

'We were drinkin' grasshoppers – so to speak –
Till we skimmed their carcasses off the spring;
And they fell so thick in the station creek
They choked the waterholes all the week.
There was scarcely room for a trout to rise,
And they'd only take artificial flies –
They got so sick of the real thing.

'An Arctic snowstorm was beat to rags
When the hoppers rose for their morning flight
With the flipping noise like a million flags:
And the kitchen chimney was stuffed with bags
For they'd fall right into the fire, and fry
Till the cook sat down and began to cry –
And never a duck or fowl in sight!

'We strolled across to the railroad track –
Under a cover beneath some trucks,
I sees a feather and hears a quack;
I stoops and I pulls the tarpaulin back –
Every duck in the place was there,
No good to them was the open air.
"Mister," I says, "There's your blanky ducks!" '

Tommy Corrigan

(KILLED, STEEPLECHASING AT FLEMINGTON)

You talk of riders on the flat, of nerve and pluck and pace –
Not one in fifty has the nerve to ride a steeplechase.
It's right enough, while horses pull and take their fences
    strong,
To rush a flier to the front and bring the field along;
But what about the last half-mile, with horses blown and
    beat –
When every jump means all you know to keep him on his
    feet.

When any slip means sudden death – with wife and child to
    keep –
It needs some nerve to draw the whip and flog him at the
    leap –
But Corrigan would ride them out, by danger undismayed,
He never flinched at fence or wall, he never was afraid;
With easy seat and nerve of steel, light hand and smiling
    face,
He held the rushing horses back, and made the sluggards
    race.

He gave the shirkers extra heart, he steadied down the rash,
He rode great clumsy boring brutes, and chanced a fatal
    smash;
He got the rushing Wymlet home that never jumped at all –
But clambered over every fence and clouted every wall.
You should have heard the cheers, my boys, that shook the
    members' stand
Whenever Tommy Corrigan weighed out to ride Lone Hand.

They were, indeed, a glorious pair – the great upstanding
    horse,
The gamest jockey on his back that ever faced a course.
Though weight was big and pace was hot and fences stiff
    and tall,
'You follow Tommy Corrigan' was passed to one and all.
And every man on Ballarat raised all he could command
To put on Tommy Corrigan when riding old Lone Hand.

But now we'll keep his memory green while horsemen come
    and go;
We may not see his like again where silks and satins glow.
We'll drink to him in silence, boys – he's followed down the
    track
Where many a good man went before, but never one came
    back.
And, let us hope, in that far land where the shades of brave
    men reign,
The gallant Tommy Corrigan will ride Lone Hand again.

The Maori's Wool

Now, this is just a simple tale to tell the reader how
They civilized the Maori tribe at Rooti-iti-au.

> *   *   *   *   *

The Maoris are a mighty race – the finest ever known;
Before the missionaries came they worshipped wood and
      stone;
They went to war and fought like fiends, and when the war
      was done
They pacified their conquered foes by eating every one.
But now-a-days about the pahs in idleness they lurk,
Prepared to smoke or drink or talk – or anything but work.
The richest tribe in all the North in sheep and horse and cow,
Were those who led their simple lives at Rooti-iti-au.

'Twas down to town at Wellington a noble Maori came,
A Rangatira of the best, Rerenga was his name –
(The word Rerenga means a 'snag' – but until he was gone
This didn't strike the folk he met – it struck them later on).
He stalked into the Bank they call the 'Great Financial Hell',
And told the Chief Financial Fiend the tribe had wool to sell.
The Bold Bank Manager looked grave – the price of wool was
      high.
He said, 'We'll lend you what you need -- we're not disposed
      to buy.

'You ship the wool to England, Chief! – You'll find it's good
      advice,
And meanwhile you can draw from us the local market price.'
The Chief he thanked him courteously and said he wished to
      state
In all the Rooti-iti tribe his mana would be great,
But still the tribe were simple folk, and did not understand
This strange finance that gave them cash without the wool in
      hand.
So off he started home again, with trouble on his brow,
To lay the case before the tribe at Rooti-iti-au.

They held a great korero in the Rooti-iti clan,
With speeches lasting half a day from every leading man.
They called themselves poetic names – 'lost children in a
          wood';
They said the Great Bank Manager was Kapai – extra good!
And so they sent Rerenga down, full-powered and well-
          equipped,
To draw as much as he could get, and let the wool be
          shipped;
And wedged into a 'Cargo Tank', full up from stern to bow,
A mighty clip of wool went Home from Rooti-iti-au.

It was the Bold Bank Manager who drew a heavy cheque;
Rerenga cashed it thoughtfully, then clasped him round the
          neck;
A hug from him was not at all a thing you'd call a lark –
You see he lived on mutton-birds and dried remains of
          shark –
But still it showed his gratitude; and, as he pouched the pelf,
'I'll haka for you, sir,' he said, 'in honour of yourself!'
The haka is a striking dance – the sort they don't allow
In any place more civilized than Rooti-iti-au.

He 'haka'd' most effectively – then, with an airy grace,
Rubbed noses with the Manager, and vanished into space.
But when the wool return came back, ah me, what sighs and
          groans!
For every bale of Maori wool was loaded up with stones!
Yes – thumping great New Zealand rocks among the wool
          they found;
On every rock the Bank had lent just eighteen-pence a pound.
And now the Bold Bank Manager, with trouble on his brow,
Is searching vainly for the chief from Rooti-iti-au.

Sunrise on the Coast

Grey dawn on the sand-hills – the night wind has drifted
   All night from the rollers a scent of the sea;
With the dawn the grey fog his battalions has lifted,
   At the call of the morning they scatter and flee.

Like mariners calling the roll of their number
   The sea-fowl put out to the infinite deep.
And far overhead – sinking softly to slumber –
   Worn out by their watching the stars fall asleep.

To eastward, where rests the broad dome of the skies on
   The sea-line, stirs softly the curtain of night;
And far from behind the enshrouded horizon
   Comes the voice of a God saying 'Let there be light.'

And lo, there is light! Evanescent and tender,
   It glows ruby-red where 'twas now ashen-grey;
And purple and scarlet and gold in its splendour –
   Behold, 'tis that marvel, the birth of a day!

Song of the Pen

Not for the love of women toil we, we of the craft,
 Not for the people's praise;
Only because our goddess made us her own and laughed,
 Claiming us all our days,

Claiming our best endeavour – body and heart and brain
 Given with no reserve –
Niggard is she towards us, granting us little gain:
 Still, we are proud to serve.

Not unto us is given choice of the tasks we try,
 Gathering grain or chaff;
One of her favoured servants toils at an epic high,
 One, that a child may laugh.

Yet if we serve her truly in our appointed place,
 Freely she doth accord
Unto her faithful servants always this saving grace,
 Work is its own reward!

INDEX OF POEM TITLES

INDEX OF FIRST LINES

DISTRIBUTORS
for the Wordsworth Poetry Library

AUSTRALIA, BRUNEI,
MALAYSIA & SINGAPORE

Reed Editions
22 Salmon Street
Port Melbourne
Vic 3207
Australia

Tel: (03) 646 6716
Fax: (03) 646 6925

GREAT BRITAIN & IRELAND

Wordsworth Editions Ltd
Cumberland House
Crib Street
Ware
Hertfordshire SG12 9ET

HOLLAND & BELGIUM

Uitgeverij en Boekhandel
Van Gennup BV, Spuistraat 283
1012 VR Amsterdam, Holland

INDIA

Om Book Service
1690 First Floor
Nai Sarak, Delhi - 110006

Tel: 3279823/3265303
Fax: 3278091

ITALY

Magis Books
Piazza della Vittoria 1/C
42100 Reggio Emilia

Tel: 0522-452303
Fax: 0522-452845

NEW ZEALAND

Whitcoulls Limited
Private Bag 92098, Auckland

SOUTHERN AFRICA

Struik Book Distributors (Pty) Ltd
Graph Avenue
Montague Gardens
7441
P O Box 193
Maitland
7405
South Africa

Tel: (021) 551-5900
Fax: (021) 551-1124

USA, CANADA & MEXICO

Universal Sales & Marketing
230 Fifth Avenue
Suite 1212
New York, NY 10001 USA

Tel: 212-481-3500
Fax: 212-481-3534